Truth & Temptation

A Summer Love Novel

RILEY EDGEWOOD

Also by Riley Edgewood

Rock & Release
Surf & Surrender

Copyright © 2015 Riley Edgewood

All rights reserved. No part of this book may be reproduced or transmitted in any form or by any means without permission in writing from the publisher except for the use of brief quotations in a book review.

This is a work of fiction. Any resemblance it bears to reality is entirely coincidental.

Cover designed by Sarah Hansen at Okay Creations

ISBN-10: 1515066479
ISBN-13: 978-1515066477
ISBN (ebook) 9780986213052

*To Nelson again,
I will be forever grateful*

CHAPTER ONE

"ANYWAY, I BANGED him like a screen door all winter. Had to stay warm somehow, you know what I mean?" I line up my shot, aim for the ten-ball, and miss wildly. "Whatever. I blow imaginary dust off my pool stick before turning to my best friend, Cassidy, and to the amusement across her face. "But now it's summer and we all know how cruel Virginia summers can be. I let him go."

"You kill me," she says, cracking up and grabbing her own cue. "But he lasted longer than your usual boys, right?"

My usual boys. I consider her words and slide a strand of auburn hair out of my eyes, tucking it behind my ear. Against the wall a few pool tables over, someone changes the jukebox song to some twangy country piece that I instantly hate. "You could say that."

"*You* could say," she bends over the table, taking aim, "that this twelve-ball's about to hit that corner pocket."

Half the pool hall is staring at her ass right now. Not that I blame them—she's got an awesome ass. Wish mine wasn't so flat, but *blah, blah,* self-deprecation's lame and I'm over it. Nobody looks away when Cassidy shoots up with a little victory dance after her ball goes exactly where she says it will. Because of course it does.

But it's my turn to laugh. "Too bad I'm stripes and you totally just sank that for me."

She pauses mid-wiggle. "I'm stripes."

"Nope," I say, grinning. "I sank the nine-ball first. Numbers over eight are striped, under are solid." I've been repeating it to myself all night. "So. Thank you for my point...or whatever it's called in pool."

"Teag. You hit the six-ball in." She walks around the table to the place where balls return and pulls out a...nine-ball. *Ha!*

Nope. Wait. Looking at it the wrong way.

It's the six-ball. Green, *solid.*

Damn it.

"Why didn't you say anything when I was aiming for the ten-ball?" I ask, keeping my tone as light as I can. Because there's no need to get pissed off about this.

"You were shooting for the ten-ball?" she asks, pulling her blonde hair into a messy ponytail that's instantly, effortlessly, annoyingly stylish. "I couldn't tell."

"Oh, fuck you." I smile, forcing it to show in my eyes. *See? Look, I'm not getting heated over something so stupid.*

Even though I am.

Even though *knowing* how stupid it is makes me even more irritated.

Great. And now she's studying my face, trying to tell if I'm actually mad. Because she knows I have...issues, and she wants to help me.

Even though she can't.

And knowing she knows how fucked up I am and can read me the way she does? It makes me furious.

Which is stupid.

And—*here we go again*—knowing how stupid it is, that I'm angry because she cares about me? Yeah. It makes it worse.

God.

My jokes about my sex life might kill Cassidy, but this? This cycle of meaningless anger I can't find my way out of is what's killing me.

Thank the fucking lord, our friend Vera returns from the bar with our drinks.

"Finally." I accept mine and guzzle until the frostiness of the hard cider reaches the pit of my belly, quelling some of the fire there.

"You're welcome," she says, her words short. Pointed. But her dark eyes sparkle in the dim lighting. "If I took too long, maybe next time *you* go wait at the bar."

"Listen. You're on the new side of this friendship, but you should know by now," I say. "You have to accept me for who I am."

"It's true." Cassidy rests her hip against the pool table, taking a sip of her beer.

Vera slides a hand through her short black hair, lifting a brow at me. "Do *you* accept you for who you are?"

Ugh. Why are my friends such *friends?* "I don't know, but your dad did last night."

"My dad is dead." She blinks, and the music over the pool hall's speakers is suddenly sharper in my ears. I hate myself.

"I'm sorry, Ver. I didn't mean it. I didn't know." I'm such an asshole. She stares at me, her eyes all wide and sad, and I want to crawl into a hole in the ground and stay there for the rest of my life.

And then... She laughs. "He's not dead. But screw you for joking about banging him."

My breath shudders out, relief taking its place in my lungs. "Screw *you* for the heart attack."

"You're on the new side of this friendship, but...how the hell did you not know my father was alive?"

"I don't even know who my own father is, so why on earth would I keep track of yours?" I retort. It comes out with more of a bite than I mean it to—*shocker*—and when her face falls, I wave it off. I don't feel sorry for myself about it, so she sure as shit shouldn't either. "Anyway. I'm about to kick Cassidy's ass in this game—you want to take me on next?"

Cassidy blows out an exaggerated sigh, a gesture that reminds me so much of her dead brother it nearly takes my breath away. "Big words for someone who didn't even know if she was stripes or solids."

She's only teasing.

I slice my stick toward her, stopping short of her face. She doesn't even flinch; she knows I'd never hit her.

What she doesn't know is how hard it is to remind myself that she's only teasing, that I don't need to get pissed off at her reminder of what an idiot I am.

She kicks my ass the rest of the game, and I end up on the sidelines, watching Vera give Cassidy a run for her money. It's fine by me because I need another drink anyway. In fact, I'll buy the next round. Only I cringe when the bartender brings me the total. And then I pull out some crumpled bills from my purse and pay it anyway. Soon, it won't matter. I start a new job on Monday.

It's why we're here tonight. There was some snazzy Friday happy hour thing across the street, and I dragged Cassidy with me because it's the company her dad works for, and he said I should come meet some people. *Some people* was an understatement. I met a lot. It was overwhelming and we hightailed it out as soon as it was acceptable.

So yeah. I fight a second cringe and I leave a nice tip when the bartender brings me all our drinks, because I'm salaried as of Monday. Granted, it's an itty-bitty salary with no starting benefits, but it'll still be steadier than what I made at the salon.

Screw that place.

I grab my cider, Cassidy's beer, and Vera's ridiculous and super girlie peaches-and-cream concoction (that I secretly wish I wasn't too cheap to buy for myself, too) and turn—and nearly face-plant into the guy sliding onto the stool beside me.

"Whoa there." His voice is smooth, and he steadies me with his hands on my shoulders, and I can tell before I've even looked up at him he's going to be hot—and cocky. Because his fingers are resting against my skin with that perfect sort of pressure, the kind that says *I touch tons of girls and I know how to make them respond with nothing more than a quick squeeze from my fingertips.* Then I lift my face and… Wow.

He's more than hot. Pretty, but in a rugged way. An angular chin, covered with stubble. Straight nose. Sharp cheeks. Hooded eyes that are somewhere between deep brown and midnight with lashes for freaking miles. And his hair? It's basically fine black silk—a little too long, but in that carelessly messy sort of way that actually makes it the perfect length. There's enough…I don't know? *Practiced casual poise*…in his expression to make me think he's a couple years older than I am.

Plus, he's tall. I'm arching my neck to look up at him and his chest is in front of my face and…his button-up shirt's not so tight that I'd make fun of it—but it sits well enough across his chest that I can tell he works out. And he smells good. Like a woodsy sort of aftershave or something.

I mean, really. Get the fuck out of here with all that.

"*Whoa there?* I'm not a horse." Not my best choice of words, probably, but sarcasm is the best shield against guys who look like this. Plus, the only thing happening in my brain right now is the assessment of how intensely he's staring at me. It's making my neck tingle. Other places, too.

"No," he says, releasing me with one hand to drag it across his sexy mouth. "Horse isn't the animal that'd come to mind... Perhaps a fox. Or maybe a kitten. Though you look like you might bite. Are you feral, little kitten?"

"You don't take your hand off of me, you'll find out real quick."

He waits a second longer than appropriate and, instead of letting go all at once, he slides his fingers over my shoulder and across my collarbone, letting them fall away at their own slow pace.

My skin straight up goose bumps at his touch. So I do what any smart girl would do. I walk away from him without another glance.

Because he's the kind of guy I avoid at all costs. Pretty face, sexy attitude, smelling all masculine and honeyed enough to make my mouth water? Nope. No, no, no. Those guys are to be avoided.

Those guys cost me my mother.

Those guys are assholes.

"That guy's watching you with so much intensity, I'm not sure how you aren't in flames right now," Cassidy says, taking her beer.

I knew it. I knew I could feel that stupid gaze across the backs of my shoulders. "Whatever. Who cares? This is a girls' night, right?"

I definitely am not going to look over my shoulder.

Oh my God, it's difficult not to look over my shoulder.

"Shots," I say, instead. "Somebody go get us shots. Stat." When Cassidy turns toward the bar, I grab her arm. "And steer clear of that dude, okay? He's too slick to be bothered with. And don't bring us whiskey, you weirdo."

She rolls her eyes. "I'm aware I'm hanging out with the girliest drinkers ever. Don't worry."

So we have a round of lemon drops. And then another.

He doesn't do it often enough to be stalkerish, but I feel the guy's eyes on me more than what I'd consider coincidence.

I find my eyes on him almost as much.

The worst is when he catches me and I look away immediately, because I freaking hate looking away, hate giving him that power.

But he's got something in his stare that startles my system. Makes my skin flush and my chin go up, even though I can't maintain eye contact.

I borrowed a blazer from Cassidy for the thing tonight, but it's hanging over a stool now. I'm tempted to put it on though, because I'm too aware of how much skin my tank top flaunts. But the jacket's constricting and it's hot in here. And he's looking at me and I'm *glad* my skin is showing.

Wait. Not that last thing.

"I'd win a game if I could fucking concentrate," I mutter, after Vera schools me yet again.

Whatever. Pool isn't my strong suit. Who cares?

Plus, if the two of them duke it out all night, I don't have to worry whether or not I look dumb leaning on the table with his eyes on me. I may be in professional-looking black pants, but they're a little too small for me—and they get much tighter around my ass when I bend over. And not in a sexy way. I position myself on a stool with my back to the guy I wish I wasn't so aware of.

But after Vera gets us another round of shots, it doesn't even matter that my back's to him, because he comes to us. With drinks. The same ones we've all been drinking. Vera's concoction. My hard cider—which I take without comment. And Cassidy's beer, which he holds out with a smile a bit too wide for my liking.

"She has a boyfriend," I tell him, my tone edgier than I intend.

"Retract the claws, kitten." His voice is silkier when it's not competing with the noises closer to the bar. So silky, in fact, it pairs perfectly with his hair.

"I'm making sure you're aware." I squeeze my fingers tighter around the cider to keep from reaching up and running them through his locks. "Don't try to hit on her."

Cassidy slams me with her elbow. "Dude, chill."

"She's not the one I'm hitting on," he says, his eyes on mine for so long my face heats, and Vera and Cassidy giggle.

I'm inclined to make a snarky response, but nothing comes to me when I open my lips—except the thought of how his might feel against them.

Oh. Hmm.

I could be in a little bit of trouble here.

CHAPTER TWO

"HOW DO I know you didn't drug these?" I ask, holding out the cider he handed me.
   He takes it, his fingers brushing over mine, and puts it to his lips, drinking it long and slow. Like I'd be able to concentrate on anything other than his throat as he swallows. Like he knows the path the liquid travels, down past his Adam's apple, would appear nearly mesmerizing. So annoying.
   "What about theirs?" I ask, my tone coming out completely unaffected when he hands it back to me.
   "May I?" he asks, holding out a hand toward Cassidy.
   She lifts a shoulder, glancing at me, and gives him her beer.
   He drinks, again.
   I watch, again.
   "Your boyfriend going to have a problem with me drinking on your beer?" he asks her, returning it.
   "Considering you've made it clear you're not hitting on me," she says, dryly, "he'll be fine with it."
   I open my mouth.
   Shut it.
   He reaches for Vera's drink, but she's already halfway done with it. "Sorry," she says, giggling. "I guess I trust you."

She's way too trusting. Has been since I've known her.

The guy looks at me.

Oh. Right. "Thanks for the drinks," I say.

"My name's—"

"Nobody asked for your name," I say.

Cassidy sighs. "Don't mind my friend. She hasn't gotten laid in a while and all that pent-up frustration makes it hard for her to remember her manners."

"Are you *kidding* me?" I glare at her because no way can I meet *his* eyes anymore. I want to die. I seriously want to fucking die. "That's none of his business!" Then, I hastily remember to add: "And it's not even true."

"*Anyway*." Vera, always the mediator, sticks out her hand, and it sways a bit in the air before he takes it. "I'm Vera. And this is Cassidy. And this is—"

"Cindy," I finish for her. Because I don't want him to know my real name. Because as a rule I don't get involved with guys like him, but he's so freaking hot and I'm exactly the right amount of tipsy to make an exception tonight. And I'll need an easy way to escape without a trace. Especially if he keeps looking at me like he wants to take a bite of me.

"Cindy," he purrs over the two syllables. "I've always liked that name."

"Funny enough, so have I." At least this part isn't a lie. "Thanks for the drinks, but we're in the middle of a girls' night."

"I figured," he says, smiling. God, even his teeth are beautiful. "I'll leave you alone, then."

"Actually," Vera slurs *this* word into about seven syllables. She holds up a finger to keep him from walking away. "I have to go home—and clean."

I lift a brow. Or…maybe I do. I might be a little drunker than I thought. "You're leaving girls' night to clean?"

"My mom's coming to town tomorrow. She… I can't even try to explain her right now." She doesn't need to, though. I've known Vera almost a year and practically all she ever talks about is her mom and how annoying she is. She sounds like a nightmare. Sometimes I'm thankful I don't have a mother nagging me the way Vera's does.

Most of the time I wish I did. But whatever.

"Fine. It'll be the original two, then," I say, turning to Cassidy. But her expression's way too apologetic for my words to be true. Ugh. "You too?"

"Um... Gage is waiting outside. He's going to drive us home." Her boyfriend. Her sexy, annoyingly perfect boyfriend who would of course wait outside so he wouldn't interrupt our night until Cassidy wants to leave. Which means she called him at some point without me noticing.

What the hell? "I don't want to go."

She glances at Mr. Sex-on-an-Extra-Thick-Stick and then at me, a knowing expression across her stupid face. "So don't."

"I'll stay and play," he says, nodding toward the pool table. And, really, who could say no to his freaking dimples when he grins, all deep and dazzling?

"One more drink," I tell him. "And if someone better comes along, I'm out of here."

"Tea—Cindy." Vera gives me an exasperated look. "Lighten *up*."

I know. I know.

I'm a bitch.

I can't help it. Sometimes, I don't even want to.

But he doesn't seem to mind—especially when he smirks and asks, "If another screen door comes along, you mean?"

"What?" At first I don't understand, even though Cassidy bursts out laughing beside me.

"Someone to bang all summer?" he asks, his smirk widening. "I get it. You find him—or her—and I'll leave you alone."

Who knew cheeks were made of kindling? Because his words spark mine and they erupt into flames.

"I don't get it," Vera says. "What am I missing?"

"Were you *spying* on me? On us, I mean," I demand, aiming for an indignant tone regardless of how neon my face must be. Damn red-haired complexion...

"I was walking past your pool table," he says.

"Right." I don't believe him. I would've seen him.

"He was," Cassidy says. "He walked behind you. I...noticed." Her cheeks go a pretty light pink color that is so unfair.

"You sell screen doors?" Vera asks, still confused.

I'd laugh as hard as *he* does at her question, but a different thought suddenly turns my stomach sour. "So what? You thought I'd make an easy mark? Because, trust me, I'm not going to—"

"Nothing about you seems easy to me," he says—and it wins him some points, to be honest. "But you're pretty, and you're feisty—and I'm into the combination."

"And that's our cue," Cassidy says, her tone full of approval. She glances at her phone and links her arm through Vera's. "Let's go, V." She looks at me. "You cool?"

"As ice," I say and sip my cider, even if my blood's heating more and more every second this dude's standing beside me. "Tell Gage I say he sucks. And also hi. I'll call you tomorrow."

"I have a feeling you've never been cool as ice," the guy says to me while my friends walk away. "You're too fiery for that."

"You're smooth." I roll my eyes to keep from looking at his face for at least one second longer, wondering if he actually *sees me* already or if this is his game. Then I study his hand when he holds it out toward me.

Trim, even fingernails. Long fingers. Big palm. He clears his throat. "Guess I should tell you my name now, if I'll be keeping you company until someone better comes along."

I wrap both hands around my cider. "I don't want to know your name. In fact, I'll choose one for you. How about…Frank?" Because I don't like the name Frank. Because maybe if I call him Frank, I'll find him less attractive.

This is what I tell myself as I drag my eyes to his face, and…

Ha.

Ha ha.

Eyes as dark as his should appear soulless. But nope. Staring into them is like peering into an endless night sky. Filled with stars you can't see but know are there, waiting to be unveiled if you focus long enough.

"…game of pool?" Frank's question comes through a second too late. I didn't even catch his reaction to my name for him, damn it.

"No. I suck at pool. Let's drink." Which is probably a stupid decision, but everything in me seems to be click-click-clicking into doing something even more stupid (stupider?) (ugh, who cares?) with this guy. With *Frank*. And I need a little more liquid courage to grease the gears that will wind me into being confident enough to do it.

"You're at a pool hall and you don't enjoy pool?" he asks. "Odd choice. Or did your friends drag you here?"

"I had a work thing nearby," I say, loving the way the words glide through my mouth. *A work thing.* Like I have a real job. Even if I had to beg for it from my best friend's father. Still. I'm working a real nine-to-fiver.

I'm tempted to brag about the company, Chambers & Britt. But I don't know enough about the equity firm—or about mergers and acquisitions—to answer any questions if he asks. And even if I'm proud of the company's name, I'm still only starting as a second assistant. Not super impressive to someone like this guy.

"Apparently this is the area happy hour hotspot strip," he says. "This row of bars and restaurants is always slammed right at five."

"You just get off?" I ask, then my cheeks heat all over again. Damn, this guy makes me jittery. "Of work, I mean?"

He nods. "Figured a drink or six might wash the day away."

"Want to talk about it?" Wait. I don't want to get to know him. What the hell am I asking for?

Thankfully, he says, "Not really. My boss turned down a proposal I've been working on."

"That sucks." But on the inside, I'm all *cry me a freaking river, dude. You're too hot to have real problems.*

"Sucks even more that the boss also happens to be my father. But the less I talk about it, the better."

"Good," I say. "Less talking, more drinking."

"Well, Cindy," he says, purring my fake name again. Now I kind of wish I'd given him the real one, to hear him stroke it like that with his tongue. "If drinking's what you're after, there are two seats at the bar."

I step toward where he motions, and he places his hand flat against the small of my back, and for a moment everything slows down. My heart pumps my blood in heavy glugs, like the fluid in my veins is actually molasses. My ears go a little fuzzy. The sudden excess of saliva pooling in my mouth takes eons to travel down my throat.

The warmth from his palm is seeping through my top and into my skin and igniting an entirely different sort of heat everywhere else.

Shit, shit, shit.

Or maybe...

Finally, finally, *finally*.

That's probably the alcohol talking, though. Which means I should have some more.

I let him lead me to the bar, which I lean against instead of grabbing a stool so he'll keep his hand on me a little longer. And while we stand there, waiting for the bartender, he traces little paths back and forth with his thumb, and even though I don't look at him, his presence is everywhere, all tall and muscular. His scent—aftershave or rainy pine tree forest or whatever it is—keeps wafting over to me and my entire body is completely *aware* of his and every time I inhale I get tingles in my lower belly and by the time we order drinks, I kind of want to jump him.

But with a guy like this? I don't even know where to begin.

Not that it's going to keep me from trying.

CHAPTER THREE

FRANK DOESN'T DRINK nearly as much as he should, which I continue to tell him every time I order another round for myself. He laughs and sips on his stupid Jack and Coke.

"Oh, I get it," I say (or maybe slur). "You're worried about getting it up later?"

Yep. Liquid courage is in full effect.

But this guy, this *Frank*... He's too much. Too hot. Too smooth. Too...just...*standing here* already making my entire body flush.

He laughs again, but this time he wipes a hand across his face, like he's embarrassed. His words say otherwise, though. "Believe me, that wouldn't be an issue. But I don't know if I want to be an addition to your screen door collection."

Maybe it's from the fuzziness that comes with alcohol, or maybe it's because it sometimes takes me a split second longer than other people to get things, but his remark sits between us for a moment before it sinks in. And then it burns.

"One," I say, holding up a finger, "fuck you. And two, why?" I can't believe I asked. I don't want to hear that I'm not pretty enough or funny enough or smart enough. Not that he knows me well enough to know the last two yet. Which means—oh, *great*—he isn't attracted to me. Story of my life.

I think of Vera and Cassidy and my stomach twists. Vera's stick-straight, jet-black satin-otherwise-known-as-hair, her slender build, her beautiful, flawless skin. Cassidy's annoyingly perfect blonde hair, her level-headed intelligence, and her sexy-as-sin curves... Next to them I'm a lump. Bland. Next to them, I'm—

"Hey, where'd you go?" Frank nudges me.

"Nothing. Never mind." I sip on my cider and watch a couple of guys taking shots at the end of the bar. I can't bring myself to look at Frank. Instead, I say, "I'm going home."

"Oh, no, you're not getting out of this one." He puts his hand over mine on the bar, grabbing it when I try to slide my fingers away. "You are the first reason I've had to smile this entire shitty day."

Now I look at him. It's easier when I'm pissed. "You're gonna keep me from leaving? I'd like to see you try."

Yeah, I actually would like to see him try. But guys like Frank don't beg girls like me to stick around.

Then he says, "You can leave if you want to. But I want my chance to answer your question first."

Again, I try to slide my hand from the bar. He tightens his grip, but not so much that I couldn't break free if I truly wanted to. Which is annoying because if I let him keep my hand in place, it tells him that I want this.

I do want this. I'm just not partial to being so open in my admission.

His palm is rough against my skin, scratchy. Hmm. How would it feel against other parts of my body?

I keep my hand where it is.

"I'm not interested in being someone's disposable screen door, Cindy." He watches my face. I temper my expression, glad he doesn't know my real name—but also full of regret over my lie. "You're sexy enough to be tempting, but that's not the kind of guy I am."

"So you're saying it's not me, it's you?" I lift a brow again, pretty sure I make it happen this time. And then, I realize he called me sexy. And there's this glow that slides softly through me, making my bones all melty... "Are you reverse psychology-ing me?"

He studies me over the rim of his glass, taking a sip before answering. "So we're clear, what exactly are you talking about?"

"Telling me you don't want to sleep with me while mentioning in the same breath that you think I'm sexy. Like you're trying to get me to bang you to beg me." Or...that didn't come out right... "Wait. No. Like you're trying to get me to beg you to bang me. Which I won't be doing," I add with a smug tilt to my mouth.

Which slides away when he leans in until his lips are at my ear and says, "I never said I didn't want to sleep with you. But I don't enjoy being used and tossed aside. Trust me, kitten, sleeping with you? My imagination roars just thinking about it."

"Oh." Needing to steady myself, I grab a stool, finally, and slide into it, though his face stays close to mine. In fact, I'm pretty sure if I were to angle my head to the side, his lips would find their way to my neck.

I tuck my hair over my opposite shoulder to free up some skin, and I...chicken out. I lean away from him, turning my face toward his but with a safe distance between us. "I'm pretty choosy about my screen door selection, anyway. I'm not sure you'd make the cut."

"Maybe we should find out." A smile plays around his mouth, and I can't help admiring his very soft-looking, very kissable lips. There's a perfect little dip on the upper one and I kind of want to lick it.

"And how would we do that?" I ask instead, keeping my tongue from doing anything embarrassing. I grab a few napkins from a stack on the bar and wipe up a leftover spill in front of where I'm sitting.

"We'll play a game." He moves smoothly into his own seat and motions the bartender over for another drink.

The bartender looks at me, expecting me to order another shot probably, but I ask for water. Because any more liquid courage right now risks souring into liquid puke...

"What sort of game?" I'm tempted to run a finger along the line of his jaw, over his stubble. I'm drunk enough to do it, but I pop the finger in my mouth instead. He watches, his gaze following my finger, lingering on my mouth...and I start to think maybe he meant what he said about finding me sexy. And I'm not exactly sure what to do with the feeling.

"Two truths," he says, raising his voice when someone turns up the music, "and one lie." And when I stare at him, puzzled, he says,

"Oh, come on. You've never played this before? It's the standard corporate icebreaker."

"I must've missed that day," I say. "And if it's so *standard*, it's probably boring anyway."

"Not the way we're going to play." He tilts his head toward me. "Tell me three—no, actually let's make it harder—four secrets. Two truths, two lies. If I guess something true, you take a shot. If I don't, I take one."

"Why do they have to be secrets?"

"To keep it from being boring."

Hmm. Yeah, okay. This sounds kind of fun. And like something I'll kick his ass at. Whether or not the room's spinning a little bit around me.

"Ready?" I scoot further into my stool and wait for him to nod, truths and lies filtering easily through my mind. "My mother's famous. My father's a baker. I can tie a cherry stem in a knot with my tongue in less than five seconds. And," I bite back a laugh, "I'm a virgin."

Frank doesn't hold in his laugh; his eyes dance, all delighted. His dimples flash all deep and lickable. "That makes things a little easier..."

"I thought you said nothing about me seemed easy?"

"That's still true. But you made the game easier. I'm going with option B as one of the true statements. Your father's a baker—even though that doesn't count as a secret."

"Maybe he's a *secret* baker." I run my fingers up his sleeve, my stomach jumping at the hard muscle they encounter underneath it, and flick his shoulder. "But no. Drink up, bitch."

"Really? He isn't a baker?"

When I shake my head, he slides his face along mine, toward my hair, and takes a long inhale that sends goose bumps running down my body. "Then why do you smell so sweet? I had your whole story in my head, picturing your dad as a baker with the big white hat and everything. You as a little girl with flour on your nose. Growing into something this red-hot... It made sense for baking to be in your bones."

His tone is teasing, but his words push a wave of longing through me. I shake it off and motion the bartender over again. "Tequila," I say, pointing at Frank. "For this guy."

"You're looking for some trouble if you want me drinking tequila tonight."

"You made the rules," I remind him. "Plus, it's your turn."

"Oh, I don't think so. If your father's not a baker, that means your mom's famous *and* you can tie a cherry stem into a knot with your tongue in less than five seconds. I can't decide which I want to focus on more at the moment." His eyes fall to my lips. "You think our bartender will give you a cherry if you ask?"

"Maybe," I say. "But I won't ask."

"You're going to leave me to my imagination? Picturing you tying knots in stems, over and over again?"

"Just because I say I can do something doesn't mean I will. Sorry, my friend."

"Are we friends then?"

"I don't know. Tell me your truths and we'll see."

"Fine, but if we're friends, I expect the full story about your mother."

I laugh, because yeah freaking right.

"I'm serious," he says, straight-faced. "And...I want an example of your knot-tying talents."

"I don't need a cherry stem to show the talents of my tongue." The words slip out, and my face bursts into flames *again*. Here's yet another reason I avoid guys like Frank. He's too pretty, too smooth. The second I open my mouth around him I feel like an idiot.

However, there's a sweet sort of power in the way he takes a deep breath, and the look in his eyes grows hungry. He opens his mouth to respond, but the bartender brings over the shot and he takes it instead, shaking his head when the tequila hits his mouth and sucking the lime immediately after.

Lucky, lucky lime.

There's a drop of lime juice left over in the corner of his mouth, and this time I don't stop myself from touching him, from wiping it off with my finger.

"Your turn." I slide my finger over my own lips, letting the sweet and tart aftertaste sink in. But he's staring at my mouth again, and I don't think he hears me. Pretty sure I've upped the stakes of our game... I let one corner of my mouth rise. "Frank?"

"Right." His eyes shoot to mine. "Let's make this more interesting. If you guess wrong—you take a shot, as promised. If you guess a truth, though, you come home with me."

"This...feels slanted in your favor," I say.

"It's slanted in both our favors," he counters.

I pretend to consider, even though I know exactly what I'm going to say. "I'm in."

"Good." He weaves a rather intense promise through the one word that I can't quite define—but it makes me really, *really* hope I can guess a truth. He taps the sharp line of his jaw. "Let me think..."

I sip my water while I wait and, sneaking peeks out of the corner of my eye that he continually catches, I wonder what his secrets are. Plastic surgery to have a face like that? Or maybe he's a model, but secretly a lumberjack on the side, chopping trees down for extra money and that warm woodsy scent?

Perhaps a teeny tiny penis to compensate for the rest of his perfection?

"I have a brother who's getting married in a month—"

"That is not a secret," I say, shaking my head.

"Yeah, but I was about to say he's marrying the wrong girl. Better?" He lifts his brows, pleased with himself.

"Definitely." And I can tell it's true by his tone. Usually, I'd dig for the story, but tonight's not about getting to know Frank's mind. It's about getting my hands on his body—and being able to walk away after—so I keep my mouth closed.

"Okay, that's one. Two: I love comic books. Three: I grew up with a bad stutter—it still resurfaces once in a while. And...four: Every bone in my body, and not only the obvious one, is dying for you to come home with me tonight."

If that last one isn't true, this guy's a total asshole, because my body is *revving* at his words. I should probably run. Right now. Out the door.

But really, who am I kidding? This is where the night's been heading since I first saw him. There's not a person alive who's attracted to guys who wouldn't say exactly what I'm about to.

I slide my stool back and hook Cassidy's blazer over my elbow. "I'm picking your brother marrying the wrong girl as a truth—and if the one about your bones is truth too, let's get out of here. Like, five minutes ago."

Frank stands, throwing up a hand to catch the bartender's attention, again. "We need our check. Now."

CHAPTER FOUR

FRANK PAYS THE tab, over my protests. We both stick out money—me cash, him a card—but when the bartender pauses, Frank gives him some stupid intimidating stare and my bills are ignored. Annoying.

I roll my eyes. "This isn't a date. I can buy my own drinks."

"So you're automatically assuming I'd pay if we were on a date? That's rude."

"No, I mean..." I can't bite back a small smile. He's winning with sarcasm, beating me at my own game. "Fine."

"Don't smile at me that way," he says, his tone full of warning.

"Why?" For some reason his words make me grin even wider. I shove my money in the pocket of Cassidy's blazer so I won't forget it. The blazer, that is. I never forget where I have cash.

"Because I'll never be able to say no to you if you do."

"What if I ask you to be a screen door?" Another set of words that fall from my mouth, like I'm this brazen thing who will bang anyone anytime. From what he knows, I am.

Oh, well. Clearly it doesn't bother him.

Plus, he isn't *anyone anytime*. Not that I plan to see him after tonight, but I have a feeling he'll be memorable.

His expression falters. "I asked you to come home with me, didn't

I?"

"So you're automatically assuming because I'm coming home with you we'll be...banging like screen doors? That's rude."

He laughs and scribbles his signature on the receipt when the bartender drops it off. "I don't expect anything. But I find myself hoping."

"I make no promises, but what sort of person would I be if I stomped all over your hope?" My tone says I'm sure of myself, but as we make our way toward the exit, nerves shoot through me so fast and so sharp they create a hole for my stomach to fall out of. It hits the floor, splattering everywhere, the stupid-ass nerves hopping and dancing around down there to the beat of the music in the bar.

Can I do this? Am I really going to do this?

"Why the change of heart?" I ask, stalling near an empty pool table, running my fingers along its edge. "Twenty minutes ago you were *so* against becoming a screen door."

"I don't want to be a screen door," he says. "But I do want you." He trails his fingers down my arm and runs them against the small of my back again, and my heart freaking *seizes*. From his touch—but even more from his words, which keep coming. "And maybe I can convince you in the meantime that I'm more than"—another short laugh slips through his lickable lips—"a piece of wood."

Don't look down. Do not *look at the space below his belt.* My eyes sting from all the effort to remain pointed toward his face.

His thumb moves in an arc over my lower back, and I almost jump. I need him to remove his hand. I need him to put his other one on me. I need to take another shot.

I need to get a damn grip. "Maybe you're a collection of smooth words with no substance."

"Maybe I want the chance to show you you're wrong."

"Maybe I can't figure out why." Oh shit. Too much. Didn't mean to admit that. "Or, you know, maybe I don't want to find out. Maybe I only want your hot body."

"Maybe I want yours, too."

Okay, this is definitely too much. "Whatever, this game's getting old. You got the drinks, so I'll pick up the cab."

"I have a driver." He says it casually, like an afterthought, like *everyone's* got a driver.

"Oh, right. It's a good thing, too, because my pilot's home with a cold." I pull off the sarcasm, but on the inside doubts are forming stronger than ever. This guy has a driver? God. The closest I've ever come to having a driver is when my freaking car breaks down *again* and I have to ride with a tow-truck driver to the repair shop.

Actually, that's not true. I won VIP tickets to a concert last summer, and the experience included a chauffeur. I took Cassidy with me—and spent the night giving her shit for taking an internship at her father's company, like a complete asshole.

Because it was supposed to be her brother's internship, but he died. And his death soured me.

Well. It made me more sour, anyway.

But the tables have changed this summer and now I'm the one working for Cassidy's father's company. Thank God she's a better person than I am, because she hasn't said "I told you so" even once. If I were in her shoes? I'd be merciless.

"I drive a ten-year-old Toyota with a broken taillight." I don't know why I have to make sure he knows this, that he gets we come from different worlds, but I do.

"Cool." He doesn't flinch, doesn't stutter—so that one was obviously a lie.

"It's so old you can't even tell what color it used to be." My guess has always been red, but that's probably because of all the rust.

"Do you think telling me you drive a beater is going to change my mind about wanting to take you home with me?"

Am I that transparent, or is he that good at reading people? I nibble at a fingernail, my expression as composed as I can make it. "Do you have alcohol at your place?"

Now he pauses, and then slowly nods. "But we can go to yours if you'd prefer."

That's laughable. I can imagine Gran's reaction to this guy setting foot in our place. I can hear her now, telling me I'm no better than my mother, leaving with someone like Frank. Spreading my legs for a pretty face and a bank account.

"Hey, where'd you go again?" He lets go of me, waiting for me to turn my face toward him. "I can have my driver take you home—by yourself—if you're having doubts. All you have to do is tell me."

Sometimes in cartoons a character finds herself with a devil on one shoulder and an angel on the other, battling it out over a questionable decision. For me, on one shoulder my Gran's calling me a whore, and on the other my empty shot glasses from tonight are telling me I shouldn't even wait till we get to his place to wrap my legs around him.

I cross my arms over my stomach, my hands in fists, because I'm starting to get annoyed. Not at him, but at myself. At life in general.

Ugh. Why can't I ever get out of my own head?

Okay, Teagan. Get your shit together. Let's not scare off the guy who's going to be The Guy tonight.

Deep breath.

Another.

Nope. Not working.

"Give me a second," I say, pretending to check my purse for something. Blindly, I grab my cell phone—there's a text from Cassidy. *You okay? I feel bad for leaving you with a random. He's hot and seemed nice, but still. #friendfail*

She has a point, but I can't even count the amount of times I've failed her in ways much worse. If I'm honest with myself, I'm a pretty shitty friend.

Oh, good. There's more irritation. Yep, and now it's slithering right into red-hot anger.

God.

Stop.

This has to stop.

I close my eyes and take another breath. I smell the bar, a little sour like old alcohol—because, duh—but I also inhale Frank's scent again. It's kind of calming this time.

Mentally, I shove everything away from my shoulders, and then there's only me. Standing next to a guy who's smoking hot and wants to take me home. One who's not commenting on my standoffish behavior, who's letting me have a moment to myself even though the heat of his arm is sinking into my own. The heat of his stare is searing the side of my face.

I'm starting a new job on Monday, and I want a better life to come with it. I need to learn to loosen up—and maybe the best way to do it is with a bang.

With Frank.

Who, when I turn my face toward him, is looking at me with these *come play with me* puppy-dog eyes and a charming little grin—like he knows his expression is exactly what I need to make up my mind. The last drop of irritation rolls away. I wonder how many girls he's used it on.

I don't care.

"I want your place," I say, starting toward the exit again, pulling him with me. "And liquor. And you."

CHAPTER FIVE

FRANK'S DRIVER IS a guy named Miles. He's ancient and bone-thin and smells like cigars. I like him immediately, and when he tells me to be sure to *buckle up back there* with a smarmy double eyebrow raise—as though he's maybe talking about using a condom instead of a seat belt—it's clear he and Frank have a relationship outside the realm of just driver to passenger. And also that maybe Frank gets around...

Then Miles closes the door behind me, and I'm alone in the back of a town car with Frank, with one tiny seat between us, and there goes all the ease, right out the closed car window. In its place is something cutting, something spicy. Nerves on top of nerves on top of the sizzle of attraction.

Frank, however, seems calm, leaning against his seat and glancing at me with a grin as the car starts to move. "I'm glad you decided to come."

"Yeah," is what I attempt to say, but it comes out strangled and unintelligible and I'm forced to clear my throat and repeat myself.

"Water?" He slides toward me and reaches across my seat—*across me*—to grab one of the (chilled, sparkling, and, of course, *glass* bottled) waters Miles set out for us on this little platform near the door. He pulls back, and this time he moves a little slower in the space that should be mine and, for a moment, the top of his shirt, unbuttoned, is eye-level and his scent sweeps across me like a breeze and my blood rushes through my veins like it's revived with a second wind.

I stare at his throat, at his Adam's apple, because if I lift my gaze to his face... I might be tempted to run my nose along the scruff lining his chin. Which is a weird thing to want to do, but knowing that doesn't keep away the impulse. But, also... I think if I look up, he'll kiss me. And the thought makes me panic.

And then the moment's over and he's in his seat, unscrewing the top of the water and pouring it into a thick-stemmed glass, while I sit still as a statue and try to slow my breathing.

He holds the water toward me and I take a second too long to grab it. My fingers accidentally slide over his in the exchange, and he maneuvers until mine are trapped beneath his. I can *feel* his smile widening, but I can't take my eyes off of the water. Off of his fingers—they're big, covering mine.

But I break the moment and take the water from him because damn if I don't need a sip of it with the way my mouth goes dry.

I'm so out of my element. I want to take back control of the situation.

"Tell me, honestly," I say, wrapping both hands around my glass. "Why did you want to leave with me? Why me, when you look...the way you do?"

He studies me, half a frown tugging at his mouth. "I don't know how to take that. Is it a compliment to me, or an insult to you—which would make it an insult to me too, actually?"

"Just tell me." I stare at him, unblinking, trying to keep my expression serious, even if my cheeks and my eyelids are a little heavy, like gravity's pushing harder on them than usual. He's slightly blurry in my vision, but that only means the water I drank at the bar didn't kill the swing of my buzz.

"I overheard you talking about your screen door—"

"And thought I'd be easy to bang your way into?"

He shakes his head and leans toward me until his face is tantalizingly close to mine, and even though my tone makes me an asshole, his eyes are dancing, like his own mood won't be deterred.

"Didn't we already have this conversation? I'm not in the business of sex with no emotions, remember?"

He takes away the cutesy screen door metaphor and lays the truth of it bare and I wonder how I've managed to find someone—a guy—who's so sincere. It feels...weird. And it turns me on so much I have to cross my legs. He watches my movement and amusement highlights his features. "I approached you because you sounded sure of yourself—"

"And you're using this as a way to somehow knock me down a peg?" I'm being a jerk. He's not trying to knock me down; I can spot that shit from a mile away after growing up with my grandparents. Basically, what we have here is another example of me being a bitch for no reason without the ability to stop myself.

Before I can blink, he's in his own seat and the charming twinkle in his eyes is gone. "Do you want me to have Miles take you home? Because I'm getting a hell of a mixed bag of signals from you, Cindy." I cringe. Both because of the name and that I've already managed to push him past his tipping point. "I don't want to do that, but if you're this uncomfortable with me, or this certain you have me pegged as whatever type of guy you think I am, I have some pretty strong doubts you'll be happy to wake up next to me tomorrow."

He's wrong, though.

I do want to wake up next to him tomorrow.

I want to wake up with a fresh perspective and a new me.

I want it every morning, to be honest, but...tonight could be the exact jumpstart I need.

"Will you answer my question?" I place the glass of water in a cup holder and grab Cassidy's blazer, draping the fabric over my pants, spreading it out with my hands. But Frank doesn't say anything and I think he's waiting for me to meet his eyes again. So I look up.

"You're pretty," he says. "Maybe I'm shallow, but I like the way you look. And when I walked past your conversation, you sounded sexy and confident—and I liked that even more. It made me want to know you."

"Oh." Heat pulses under the skin of my face, and yet again I wish I was a pretty blusher, all tawny pinks instead of balloon reds. But he's given me one of the best compliments I've received in a long time. Maybe ever.

Then it hits me. He heard me boasting and acting like I didn't have a care in the world. He's attracted to my fake personality, the one I wear for everyone else. Guess it goes well with the fake name. Tonight I'll be Cindy. I like her better, anyway. "I don't want Miles to take me home."

"Thank God." His tone is back to light and the mood between us shifts again, less intense now. He glances down into his lap and then at me with a huge grin. "Because there are two of us in this seat who would've been really fucking disappointed. You didn't think I was unaffected when I slid across you for the water, did you?"

I follow his gaze, because of course I do. And his pressed gray slacks are extremely tented. Because of course they are.

Of all the reactions I could possibly have in the moment, I put my face in my hands, and I giggle like a fucking schoolgirl.

CHAPTER SIX

"ARE YOU GIGGLING at my boner?" Frank asks, and when I uncover my face, his eyes widen. "You are."

The urge to keep giggling fills my stomach like a balloon. I glance toward Miles in the rearview mirror, but he's focused on the road, giving no indication that he heard Frank. *Don't giggle. Don't giggle.*

"I'm not... I mean..."

"Come on, kitten. You're kinda killing my ego."

"I didn't even touch you," I say. "You...surprised me, that's all. I don't think you're...small, or anything." The opposite actually, if the rise in his khakis is any indication. *Not* that I'd tell him that.

He winces. "Well, now his pride's pretty much nonexistent."

"Well, now *you're* speaking about your..." I clear my throat and another giggle slips out. "...*thing* like it's an actual person with actual feelings."

"*You* couldn't even use the word dick."

I'm hit with the blush of the fucking century. He's right. *What am I? Thirteen?*

Oh, but that thought pushes my mind into a better comeback. "*You're* the one who's rock hard when we haven't even kissed yet. What are you? *Thirteen?*" There. Point, me.

"I like that word...*yet*," he says. He's still smiling, but his focus is on my mouth now, and all of a sudden we aren't in a game anymore.

Or we are. But it's not the kind with silly insults and childish blushing.

This is more like…a dare situation.

I just don't know how to go about stepping up to the challenge.

Or I do, but it turns out I'm a coward. I look away first, out the window at the trees that line the parkway and streetlights that flash by. Then the trees are gone and we're passing Springs Corner—an outdoor shopping center, all lit up with restaurants, local boutiques, a huge movie theater, and even bigger pavilion in the center of it all. I pretend to be fascinated by the place, staring so hard out my window, it's a wonder the glass doesn't crack.

I tap my fingers on the seat beside me, trying to drum up the nerve to turn and kiss him. He already thinks I'm forward, so why am I feeling shy?

Because I really want him.

Because I *super* want him.

Because sitting in the back of a town car with him feels too good to be true. These things don't happen to me.

But then he covers my hand with his own, and I drop my gaze to watch, and I realize they do happen to me. Right now. This is happening. Finally. And it's perfect. One night of a fairy tale.

Granted, a fairy tale where the prince doesn't know the princess's real name, but maybe that makes it better.

He rubs his thumb over the back of my hand, trailing heat across my skin, and finally I lift my heavy eyes toward his.

"Hi," he says.

"Hi." I breathe.

"You don't need to be nervous." Another stroke of his thumb. Thank God it's over the top of my hand, because my palms are getting damp. "I won't bite."

I wipe my free hand across my lap. "Just wondering where you live."

"Oh. I thought you might be thinking about whether or not I'd bite. But you have my word I won't."

"What if I want you to?" Seriously, I'm getting whiplash. Ballsy Cindy or gun-shy Teagan. I can't keep track of myself.

"Then that's a different story." He flashes those damn dimples again. "Here we are."

Miles pulls into the circular drive-thru of a sky-high condominium complex, a sign naming it *The Grands*, to drop us off. He opens the door and I step out, craning my neck to scan up the length of the building. Floor-to-ceiling windows in every unit make the whole tower look as though it's made of glass. "Whoa."

"Wait till you see the inside," Miles says, a smile in his voice.

I turn toward him as Frank unfolds himself from the car, all long legs, long torso, long body in general. Wide shoulders. Muscular neck—this dude definitely works out. Face like...well, I've given his face more than enough attention tonight. It takes me a moment to remember what I was going to say. "Miles, thank you." I dig through the pockets of Cassidy's blazer and pull out the rest of my crumpled wad of cash. A whopping fifteen dollars. I hold it out to him.

He grins and—adorably—blushes in the bright light of the overhead archway, gently pushing my hand to the side. "I couldn't take that, but thank you."

The thought of ever brushing off a tip is foreign to me. I push the money toward him again. "But you gave such nice service."

"That's why I'm paid a salary," he says, ignoring the money. "But again, thank you."

I guess he doesn't work on commission, but still. Who turns down free money?

Then again, he works for Frank, who I'm beginning to think might be kind of loaded. This condominium building is fancy. Like, there's a doorman waiting for us. In a polished black suit. And there's a row of chandeliers hanging above us—outside—that look like they're made of diamonds. I mean, probably not though, right? Because that'd be ridiculous.

"You're sweet, you know that?" Frank chuckles as Miles drives away.

"You're probably the first person in my life to accuse me of it," I tell him, honestly.

"Accuse you? I meant it as a compliment."

When we're close enough, the doorman opens the door for us, saying, "Good evening, sir, miss."

"Good evening." Frank motions for me to go ahead. "Where's Matthew tonight?"

"Family emergency, sir."

"His daughter?" Frank sounds so genuinely concerned that I turn to him—and his expression matches his tone. "Is she back in the hospital? I thought she was feeling a little better?"

"I wouldn't know, sir." The doorman's stiff as a board and staring straight ahead. Clearly, he takes his job as seriously as the Queen's guard in England; all he needs is a red outfit instead of his all-black, and one of those tall fluffy hats. The thought has me stifling a giggle.

Frank takes the man's hint and wishes him a goodnight, and then puts his hand against my lower back to guide me into the foyer. Like last time, his touch sends sparks shooting up my spine, and I resist the urge to arch like a cat against his palm.

"Is Matthew your regular doorman?" I ask.

He nods, his eyes far away for a moment. "His daughter's been sick a lot the past year."

"I'm sorry."

"So am I."

There's a *huge* bronze light structure attached to the high-rise ceiling above us; my eyes follow it to the end of the foyer, where it slides down into an extravagant marbled water fountain. The walls are painted in vertical stripes of mint and white, and the entire space feels polished—and so spacious I bet my voice will echo when I speak. Which I do as casually as possible, like this is nothing new. "Nice place."

He glances around, his expression impassive. "My father picked it."

"You live with your parents?" The thought hadn't even occurred to me.

"God, no." He mock-shudders. "They foot the bill."

"Oh." How one single word can come out as judgmentally as mine does, I have no clue. I clear my throat. "I mean, must be nice." Nope. Not any better. What is *wrong* with me? "Are you close with your parents?"

"We participate in each other's lives." For the first time, he seems uncomfortable, so I let him lead me toward the glass elevators against the wall without asking him any of the follow-up questions I'm dying to ask. Instead, I focus on the way the palm of his hand keeps the spot on my back warm against the chilly air conditioner of the lobby.

I focus on the way that heat's keeping me warm everywhere else, too.

"You could get very naughty in these," I say—or, rather, evocative *Cindy* says—with half a smile, gesturing to the elevators, making the tension in his eyes drain away.

"If you're into letting people watch." His hand slips a little lower, right above my ass and my skin's starting to burn, hoping he'll slide it all the way down. "Let's see... So far, you're into biting and public shows of affection..."

"Maybe with you I will be." I'm not sure if I'm teasing or serious, but there's a wild energy rushing through me because every step we take gets us closer to the moment he's inside of me, and I'm starting to imagine how it might feel. How he might feel, his body over mine, the grunts he'll make, the bend of my knees when I wrap my legs around him...

Movie sex. That's what tonight will be like. Sheets wrapped around us. Sexy sweat raised on our skin. Perfect, sexy lovemaking. Someone like this guy? I bet it's how he does everything.

Oh, God. Why didn't I bring that water in from the car? My mouth is parched now. And as the elevator slides down the glass shaft, Frank studies me in the reflection. Even in dimly lit glass, he's gorgeous. His eyes appear darker than the night and just as intense.

When the door opens, I step in and try to look casual, leaning against the back glass wall.

He follows me, but stands directly in front of me instead of to my side, like I figured he would. Like, *directly* in front of me. I doubt there's room for even a ruler between us.

I can either stare at his chest, or look up at him. I choose the latter, even if it takes a few seconds to make it happen.

No turning back now.

Not that I'd want to.

Not that *any* girl would want to.

"You have very nice hair," he says, his breath washing over my face. It smells like mint, somehow, and citrus, like the faintest hint of the lime he bit into at the bar. I have roughly 0.06 seconds to process it though, because then he's twirling a strand of my hair through his fingers and the sensation of his skin brushing against my neck is dizzying. "Makes me think of summer strawberry fields, and it's so soft, I can't stop playing with it."

"I have good conditioner." *So* smooth. But somewhere on the inside, I'm beginning to shake. Little vibrations that promise to turn into epic earthquakes.

Okay.

Okay. I can do this.

I trail a hand up his stomach—*holy shit his abs are freaking tight*—and over his chest—*and yep, equally muscular pecs*—and wrap it around his neck. I run my thumb over his stubble. His breath catches, which makes mine speed up. Cassidy's brother was the last guy who affected me this way. I've waited almost two years to meet someone who excites me as much as Frank has in just a few hours. Finally, I don't have to fake it. Something tells me I won't have to fake anything with this guy.

Well, except my name.

Frank lowers his head, slowly, his eyes on mine the whole time. The air is so tense around us, it's like snapping elastics *everywhere*. So I open my mouth to whisper against his.

"You didn't press the button."

CHAPTER SEVEN

"Y-YOU'RE RIGHT." FRANK blinks after I break the spell of our almost-kiss. "Damn it."
Yes. Damn it. Why did I have to say anything?
Nerves are so *unbelievably* annoying. I need to figure out how to slice away the ones making me jittery while protecting the ones making me as aroused as I am.
There are so many areas of my life where my body has trouble differentiating between good and bad emotions. So many areas of my life in which I wish I could get the fuck out of my head for a little bit.
Frank turns to press the button for his floor—followed by a code on a keypad beside the regular numbers.
"Fancy security," I say.
He shrugs, returning to me, sliding one hand up my side and around my back, placing his other palm against the wall beside my face. "Now. Where were we?"
But this time we're interrupted when someone slams a hand in to stop the door. Behind Frank's shoulder stands a tall, thin, leggy blonde. She ignores me, but speaks to the back of Frank's head.
"Alex." The word—*his real name*—cuts through the air and he turns around like a shotgun's gone off.

"Kelly." For the first time, there's zero warmth in his tone. In fact, as the door closes behind her, all the air in the elevator suddenly feels frosty—from the chill between them, not the air-conditioning.

The ground falls away and Kelly slices her eyes over me and back to Fr—Alex. "New one tonight, huh? Not your usual fare."

"Back off," he says, warily. "Don't be so—"

"Um, excuse me?" I cut in, using what many might call my typical Teagan tone. God, it feels good to slip into me without feeling awkward. Bitch is easy. "Not his usual fare?"

"I wasn't speaking to you, sweetie." She doesn't bother looking at me, just drills holes into Alex.

"But you were speaking about me, *sweetie*. And I'm standing right here." I wait until her focus is on me. "I don't know if you're some scorned ex or whatever, but I do know your loss is going to be my gain tonight—probably multiple times. So maybe you should keep your snotty little mouth shut and get the fuck over yourself."

"Well, well," Alex murmurs, sliding closer to me. "You do have claws. And some very high—and, I promise you, very attainable—expectations for our evening. And you," he says to Kelly, "should probably do exactly as my friend says."

With perfect timing, the doors open onto her floor and she shoots us a scathing look before turning to walk—or glide, rather, with her annoyingly long, slim legs—away.

"Yeah. That's a story I'm going to have to hear...*Alex*," I say.

"About my name—"

"Nope." I put a finger to his mouth. I only wanted to say it once, to let it travel along my tongue like an indulgence. "Tonight you're Frank."

I can tell he wants to say more, but the moment passes and he nods, smiling against my finger—then he wraps his tongue around it and takes it into his mouth. And he uses his tongue to do things to my finger that make my panties wet, and the trembles from earlier are starting to echo outwards from the center of my belly, in rings of vibrations running through my arms and down my legs. Up my neck... Heat following their path.

He pushes me until the glass is at my back and his body's pressed against mine and holy hell *he's so hard*. I moan, imagining more than my mind can handle.

And I get a little nervous, too.

Okay. A lot nervous.

I slide my finger out of his mouth.

"You taste salty," he whispers in my ear, with a low hum. "Delicious." He runs his hands up the sides of my legs, over my hips, wrapping around my waist. "But I bet I can discover where you taste the sweetest."

Oh.

My.

God.

How should I respond? Why won't my brain work? Why am I turning to mush everywhere?

The elevator dings, opening, and I sigh.

"Damn we've had bad timing so far," he says, right as I think, *saved by the bell.*

"S'okay." I clear my throat, trying to hide how relieved I am. "I'm thirsty anyway."

Then I step off the elevator and discover why he needed the security code to get here. Because I've stepped into a foyer—*his* foyer. Right off of the elevator.

"Wait. Is this the penthouse?"

He walks past me—*breezes past me*—and simply says, "Yeah." Like it's no big deal. "What can I get you to drink?"

The ceilings are so high in his entryway, Frank couldn't even touch them if he jumped, and he's *tall.* Hell, not even with a ladder could he jump high enough. There's a staircase spiraling up to a second level and, I'm assuming, his bedroom. He probably has a fluffy king-sized bed, tucked in every day by personal maids. I bet the entire room is ostentatious.

Fucking awesome, probably, my mother's voice flows through my mind, and, after the shock of hearing her wears off, I shiver. On TV she always speaks with a bland sort of forced-casual manner, and in my mind, her tone stays the same. I imagine she'd look at this place and start drooling. So I refuse to.

There's space for miles past his foyer, and all the way across from me, past sets of dining and living room furniture that probably cost more than…well, more than anything I've ever owned (and let's not even mention the TV the size of a damn planet), there are walls made of glass between us and the outside. I stare out one of the panes, watching the lights from Springs Corner—and places farther out—twinkle in the night like multicolored stars.

He's waiting for me to answer him, having made his way to the open kitchen around the corner. But maybe I should walk backwards, right onto the elevator and out into the night. Back to my grandparents' rundown place. Back to real life. Because this? No matter how fun a one-night fairy tale sounds... This is almost too much.

But just *almost*.

Instead of walking backwards, I step toward him. "What's the strongest thing you have?"

"The strongest thing that you might actually like, you mean, Miss Sweet Hard Cider?" His teasing unfurls some of the unease in my chest.

"Yes." I smile to show him I appreciate the humor.

He makes us vodka tonics with a dash of sugar and a twist of orange. It's not quite sweet enough for me to love it, but it's not so bitter that I can't drink it either.

In fact, I lean against his tall kitchen island and I down it and I ask for another.

We move into his living room, which is half the size of a football field and contains a TV with corresponding proportions. And of course the furniture is fitted to him. I practically have to climb onto his couch—though it's actually comfortable once I'm settled. I could fall asleep easily with everything I've had to drink. Except for the adrenaline spiking through my veins over what's about to happen, like a both bitter and delicious drug... But maybe one more drink first.

"You keep this up," he says, when I ask for another, "and I won't feel right about taking you upstairs."

"I'm a big girl," I slur. "I can handle my liquor." He looks unsure, so I study the shape of my next words before they exit my mouth, making sure they're not as messy: "I tell you what... Make it a fresh glass and a *smaller* one, if it'll make you feel better. And anyway, I wanted to come home with you the moment I first saw you. I'd only had two drinks then."

Thank God, he turns away from me for the kitchen and misses the way I hold in a hiccup—and the way I bend over and drink the rest of my current cocktail upside down to get rid of the rest of them.

But it *works*. And the fluid path my hair takes through the air when I flip myself upright again makes me feel like surely it's all sex kitten-ish now. I glance around for a mirror, but he doesn't have any out. Not even in the foyer.

I sigh. I'm sure it was wishful thinking anyway. Pretty sure my hair's never had a sex kitten moment in all its life. The wave of confidence passes as quickly as they ever do, and I'm more than ready for the new drink when he brings it to me.

"So." I gulp half the vodka down. Huh, it doesn't even burn anymore. "Should we do this?"

"Are you flirting with me?" he asks, his expression serious. "Because if you are, I'm not getting it."

Shit. My words ring between us still, sounding like I want to get it over with. Which isn't true. Not all the way, anyway. "What do you mean?"

"You've seemed on the fence all night. I'm trying not to be blinded by the way my body reacts to you and walk you upstairs into something you'll regret in the morning."

"Are you sure *you* want to do this?" I slide toward him and rise on my tiptoes to whisper as close to his ear as I can get, which is basically his sexy, delicious-smelling neck. "Because you keep giving me ways out, when I'm very clearly not taking them."

"Cindy," he says, still serious. "Tell me the truth."

Why the fuck did I give him that name?

"I'm nervous, okay? *God*." Great, and now I'm prickly and giving him some of the truth I'm doing everything I can to keep buried tonight.

"Why?" he sounds genuinely confused.

"Um, look at you. Look at your place."

"So?"

"So you're a fucking GQ advertisement, and it makes me anxious." Maybe my *poor* is showing, but I'm too jittery to keep it so bottled up. I *want* him. So much I can barely breathe. Or maybe part of that is my nerves. And this much alcohol makes it harder to keep my Cindy mask on straight.

"Come here, little kitten," he says, demand in his tone. Usually, I'd balk at his bossiness. At the moment, though, I let it make my decision for me and I go to him. He grips my shoulders, firmly enough to hold me in place. Sensually enough to make me shiver. Especially when he leans in and breathes against my neck with his whispered words. "My place is amazing; I'm not a liar, and I won't try to pretend it's not the truth. But as amazing as it is? You're the only thing in it I can't take my eyes off of. So what does that say about *you*?"

Okay. *Swallow, Teagan.*

"I'm not a thing." My words are automatic, and they make me cringe.

Thankfully, he leans back, nodding. "You're right. But you are gorgeous. And I think you might need someone to show you that you deserve whatever you want. And I want to take you upstairs to get a head start on it."

It feels like a culminating moment. Will I, or won't I?

I've been wavering all night, but only because I'm nervous. The one thing that hasn't wavered is how attracted I am to him. It's time to be Cindy for real. It's time to do what I want.

I take a deep breath to steady my nerves, inhaling him, letting his scent wash over me before I answer. "It's about freaking time."

His bedroom is…perfect. Huge, yes, but far from ostentatious. Yes, his bed's king-sized, but it's otherwise simple and it looks really comfortable. The rest of the room is clean, but there's a misplaced sock in the corner and a crumpled shirt on the floor by his bed. And the entire space smells faintly like him, a lingering reminder of whose room it is while he's gone.

"What is that?" I turn to him and have to catch myself when the room tilts a little beneath me.

"What is what?"

"That scent. *Your* scent. It's enough to drive a girl mad."

He glances down and sniffs himself, making me giggle, and puzzles his brows when he looks at me again. "I don't smell anything."

"Oh come on. It must be a cologne if I can still smell it in here." I trail across his room, using the excuse to check out some of the things on his desk, on his dressers. Also, holding on to the furniture helps keep the ground steady.

"I'm not wearing cologne."

"Uh-huh. Sure." There isn't much to run my fingers over. A pair of cufflinks and a watch. A signed baseball. A black and white photo of a younger Frank surrounded by a group of people, friends. And that's pretty much it.

"I get it now." I spin to face him, smiling. "You're hot and you're rich—but you're *boring*. What a *relief*."

Now his brows shoot up, along with the corners of his mouth, making those dimples pop out. "Boring? I've been accused of many things in my life, but not that."

"Yeah, maybe not to your *face*."

"Oh, you think?" He's in full grin-mode now and takes a few stalking steps toward me. I back up until the foot of his bed hits my ass. I swear to God there's a look in his eye that says he wants to tickle me, and I can't keep yet another giggle from slipping up from my belly. He pauses, considering something.

"What?" I can't keep from asking. "What are you waiting for?"

"I want to get my hands on you—all over you…but I also want to show you something." He reaches his hand out, palm up. "Come here."

I hesitate. "Are you gonna get your hands all over me, or show me something?"

I'm not sure what I want his answer to be.

Both, maybe.

"Both, maybe." He says the words directly from my mind, and I'm so shocked I put my hand in his. I let him pull me out of the room and halfway down a hardwood hall before I'm ready to speak again.

"Tell me you've got a foot fetish and a hidden closet full of Jimmy Choos and I'll be yours forever." Truly, I don't care about shoes. But maybe Cindy does. And the brand is something rich people are aware of—Cassidy's mom has more pairs than I can count. So maybe he'll think Cindy's a bit closer to the level of his world than I actually am.

"Not quite," he says, laughing. "Though I do think you have pretty toes." He glances down as we walk and my feet suddenly feel very naked in my open-toed heels. Thank God I let Cassidy talk me into pedicures this afternoon.

We come to a stop in front of a closed door.

"Okay, but I have to tell you... If this is some room full of tied-up ex-girlfriends, I'm a master of jujitsu. I know enough to take you down like that." I snap my fingers.

"That might be fun." He laughs again, shaking his head, and opens the door. "But this'll be better."

CHAPTER EIGHT

THE ROOM IS completely dark, but before my eyes can adjust to make out more than a few structural shapes, Frank reaches in and flips a switch.

There's a whirring noise and then the room is filled with lights. Lots and lots of lights.

Regular ones, to brighten the room—but game lights, too, spinning around arcade games and scoreboards. Little *beeps* and *boops* and other game-type noises softly fill the air while I take it all in.

"Whoa."

And, also, thank God, because I actually don't know jujitsu.

There's a plush poker table in one corner, surrounded by leather seats and a white-cabineted wet bar behind it. A shuffleboard along one wall, which, if I wasn't in so much shock, would make me grimace because Gran loves the game. One of the only things in the world she loves. That and Gramps, for some reason. And making sure to point out every single thing wrong with me, which is basically everything. But my eyes are too busy darting all around for those thoughts to take over. An ancient-looking row of arcade games—Pac-Man's the only one I recognize. A red pool table toward the back of the room and two huge flat TVs in the upper back corners.

"This room is every teenage boy's wet dream." I step inside.

"Most grown men's, too," Frank says, following me. "And a ton of women's."

"This is…just… You're a nerd!" I spin toward him to see if he'll admit it, but my attention's drawn to the long rows of built-in shelves spreading out from the doorway behind us—and filled to the brim with comic books. Half in plastic casing, half well loved. And a few face out in glass boxes, also in plastic casing. "Like, nerd with a capital N."

He turns too, grabbing one at random and flipping through it, peeking at me over the cover with laughing eyes. "But I'm not boring."

"Definitely not." I wish he'd drop the stupid thing and put his hands back on me.

He's an undercover comic book geek. It makes me like him even more. He's not some perfectly suave GQ sort of guy.

Shit. It might be harder than I thought to leave in the morning…

"Do you like comics?" he asks, hope in his voice.

"You mean the things people need with pictures when they can't handle real books?" God, I'm such a dick sometimes. Most of the time. "That was rude. Someone said that to me once, in high school, when I thought maybe I could get into comics. Turns out I've been waiting years to use the line on someone else. So what does that say about me?"

He shrugs, carefully placing the comic book on the shelf. "It says I need to reintroduce you to comics."

"Reading's not really my thing in any form, to be honest." This is part of the fairy tale. I can tell Frank anything I want because I won't see him again.

"That's too bad," he says, honesty in his tone making me regret my words. "But I guess that means we'll have to find another way to pass the time."

Now I grin, sliding further into the room, feeling his eyes on me like feathers trailing my body. I shiver. Because every minute we're getting closer and closer, the circle's closing in. And sex is at the center. "Whatever did you have in mind?" I head to the wet bar behind the poker table, grabbing a glass. "Wanna take some shots?"

One shot of chilled vodka later—all he would agree to, the jerk—I turn toward the poker table, opening the metal case holding poker chips. The clicks of its snaps fill the room, sharp. And a moment later he's right behind me, his hands at my hips, his body pressed against mine.

His erection at my butt.

Oh, boy.

Oh, big-penised *man*.

Go big, or go home, right?

A soft laugh escapes from my stomach, up my throat, out my lips.

"Do you like this?" he asks, laying a soft kiss against the side of my neck.

I can't find my voice to speak, so I nod.

"And this?" He slides his hands up my sides, making my breath constrict in my lungs, and over my breasts.

I nod again, my nipples tightening under his touch, and he presses his mouth to the side of my neck a second time.

And oh, God, I want his lips on mine. He's moving them along my skin in sweet, tender trails, and... I start to tremble again.

He lifts his hands to fiddle with the straps of my camisole, sliding them down, whispering against my skin, "We could play cards for clothes, make it interesting."

"I suck at cards." I take a deep breath—*this is it*—and I turn, sliding my body against his, to face him. "And there's no need for strip poker if you want to get me naked."

He lifts his head and his hands slip around my neck and a rumble comes up from his throat. "I've wanted to do that since I first saw you." His gaze drops to my mouth and slowly, slowly rises to mine again. "This, too."

He's going to kiss me now. I know it.

I wet my lips, and I slide my hands up his stomach and over his chest, wrapping one around his neck. I stand on my tiptoes.

And I kiss him.

I wanted to make the first move my own, I wanted to make sure he knows—and that I know—I want this. I want him.

But it doesn't matter that I moved first because within a breath, he's dominating the kiss. His lips are smooth against mine and he concentrates on my lower lip and then my upper and I try to match him, but he's so smooth, so well-practiced. I sigh something like a purr and he slips his tongue into my mouth.

My fingers curl into a fist, gripping his shirt. I slide my tongue past his to take in his mouth as he tastes mine.

My eyes are closed and the vodka's starting to sink in, making me feel a bit like we're on a rocking boat, rather than solid ground leaning against a solid table. But I must do something right, because he groans, a soft little roar, really. His hands fall to my waist and he lifts me—like I'm featherlight, which I very much am not, which makes it really fucking hot—and presses me onto the table. He pushes between my legs until his erection is...*right there*, and he groans again, into my mouth this time.

Fuck, why am I still wearing pants? *Why is he?* The kiss stretches on, sensual and perfect, and I unbutton his shirt, yanking it from his pants to finish the last few. I slide my hands beneath his undershirt, feeling the warm, soft skin covering his oh-so-fucking-hard abs, and *this* is what's going to be above my body tonight? All night?

Yes, please.

He gives one slow lick inside my lips, making my skin stand on edge, and then his mouth is gliding over my chin and down my neck, his tongue fluttering against my pulse point and it's my turn to moan, because my insides are melting into hot caramel. I slip a hand between our bodies to stroke him over his pants, and he nips my skin with his teeth and a little growl. "Careful. I want to take this slow."

But I don't want to be careful. I don't want to take this slow. I run my fingers over the fabric, tracing him and massaging him until he grabs my wrist, stilling the motion and saying, "You are so fucking sexy, you're making it hard for me to take the time to explore you as thoroughly as I want."

My hand is still, held captive by his, but the room is not. When I open my eyes to grin at him, the poker table suddenly seems to be the world's slowest carousel ride. Slowly, slowly, slowly spinning to the side.

I steady myself against his chest and wrap my legs around him, pulling him closer to me, his erection pressing against me. "We have all night. Take it slow later. On the next round... Take *me* now."

He grabs my face and kisses me, fast and hard. "Here?" he asks, his mouth a whisper away from mine. "Or the bedroom?"

Poker table sex would be memorable for sure, but he has that comfortable-looking king-sized bed, and maybe it'll be steadier under my unsteady body. Maybe a more traditional start will be...easier. "Bedroom," I slur out the word and the next few, too. "This time. But I expect you to bring me back in here before the night is over."

I take his hand and pull him toward the door, but I stumble a little—so he swoops down and picks me up. Again, like I weigh nothing. I twist in his arms to face him and wrap my legs around his stomach and I take my turn now, tasting his neck, running my tongue along his skin, rubbing myself against his body while he walks. I slide a little lower along him until his erection is pressing against the very center of my thighs, making me moan. Making me so wet that if he doesn't have my pants off in the next few minutes I may be nothing but a fucking puddle by the time he tries.

He's making noises too—half pained, half something sexy—and I want to taste the sounds as they fall from his mouth. I let my lips travel along his sandpapery chin and I squeeze myself tighter around him when our lips meet again.

"This might be my new favorite way to walk anywhere," he says against my mouth and I kiss him harder in agreement, letting him carry me into his bedroom.

CHAPTER NINE

I'M IN FRANK'S bedroom.

I'm in Frank's bedroom and he's hard as a rock, pressing through his pants and mine.

I'm in Frank's bedroom and he's hard as a rock *because he wants me*.

We're standing here—actually, *he's* standing here, holding me up with my legs around him and his erection begging to find release, and he's starting to grind against me and all these warm sensations are shooting like fireworks through the lower half of my body.

We're really going to do this.

Holy shit.

I push myself away from him and slide down his body, stepping back.

Panic. Panic is lacing through those streams of fireworks.

I need a moment. I need a moment to gather myself. To gather *Cindy* and her super forward takes-what-she-wants ways.

"Can I use your bathroom?" I ask and then blush because what if he thinks I have to...do something embarrassing. I scramble to clarify. "To freshen up first?"

I don't even know what that means, to freshen up, but I know people say it in movies.

He's watching my face, amused. "Sure." He points to a huge set of double doors that I figured led to a huge walk-in closet. They're covered in thick, intricately carved wooden panels over panes of frosted glass. Or at least I think they are. All the vodka's definitely catching up to me now, and the maze of wood almost seems to be moving in my vision.

Still, I manage to push through the doors and let them swing shut behind me. I make my way to the sink and lean on it, dropping my head between my arms, breathing huge gulps of air.

I cannot believe I'm this nervous.

It's ridiculous. I'm a fucking adult. Kind of, anyway. I need to stand up, march out there, and take what I want.

I turn on the faucet and pause right as I'm about to splash water on my face. One, because I remember I'm wearing makeup, but two, because his bathroom is unreal. His shower's big enough to be a sauna and there's a huge, footed tub on the other side of the room. A new sort of longing blossoms between my ribs, sharper than the heat of the fireworks. One that tells me this'll be the closest I come to a tub like this. Oh, what I wouldn't give for a soak in there…

There's a dresser against the wall and I want to snoop through it so badly my fingers itch. But that'd be me getting to know more about Frank. And I already know too much for a one-night fling.

Instead I wash my hands, and I lift my eyes to study my reflection, maybe to give myself a mental pep talk—but there's no mirror. I find a small circular one, face down, on top of the dresser. A shaving mirror, but that's it.

I dry my hands and wipe them under my eyes to catch mascara smudges—and am filled with pleasure as Frank's scent hits my nose. It's his soap. A simple bar of soap has had my senses tingling every time he's been near me tonight. I almost laugh.

Instead, I take another deep inhale, and I turn and head into his room. Back to him. Back to exactly what I want.

He's sitting on his bed, looking at his phone. His shirts are still untucked, his button-up unbuttoned, his undershirt bright white and tight across his chest. I can't keep my eyes from dropping to his lap for a very, very brief glance. And he's still hard. Very, very hard.

He looks up when I pull the doors all the way open.

"What's with the no mirrors policy?" I ask.

"What do you mean?" But his tone is too carefully blank, so I know there's a story here.

"You know what I mean," I say, sauntering toward him. I step out of my shoes, kicking them to the side. I unbutton my pants, slide them slowly down my hips, past my knees, stepping out of them, too. Loving the bob of his Adam's apple when he swallows, watching my movements. Wish I'd worn sexier underwear, but at least these are black. That's kind of sexy, right? And I will not think about the shape of my legs. Not even for a second. "Who doesn't have a bathroom mirror?"

I climb into his lap, sighing when he wraps his arms around me. And...oh wow. Without my pants in the way, his erection is much more pronounced. *There.* I rock my hips back and forth, needing more friction. It's time for his pants to go. Like, now.

He groans, tightening his arms and angling himself against me in a way that has a noise I don't recognize slipping from my mouth, but he says, "Sorry, kitten, but you've reached your truth quotient from me for now."

"Please," I say, my tone as teasing as I can make it—because it takes most of my effort not to slur. "Two truths from a game we played hours ago? That's all I get?" I think back to what he said... "Your brother's getting married, and you wanted to take me home. That's it?"

"Four truths, actually." He confesses with a guilty little smile. "I wanted you to guess right."

"*Right.* The comic books thing. I should've known. You are such a cheater!" I shove his chest and he falls onto the bed, bringing me down with him. I giggle, loving the way his erection presses against me, but when we land, the world's tilting at an angle adjacent to where we lie. I have to roll off of him and I scoot myself backwards until I hit his headboard, needing it to steady me.

It helps, but not that much.

"You do not stutter," I say, focusing on his face. Even kind of blurry it's the sexiest face I've ever seen.

"Oh, believe me. I do."

"I think you're a cheater *and* a liar." But I smile and so does he.

"My next stutter is always at the tip of my tongue," he says, his lips still curved up, but the truth lies at the center of his tone.

"That must be hard." I fiddle with one of his many pillows, running the fabric through my fingers.

He shrugs, his smile gone now. "I had an excellent fluency coach for a lot of years. Perks of parents who accept nothing but the best."

There's a sour note buried under his words and I wonder if he means his parents expected the best of him, rather than the fluency coach, but we're falling into that trap of getting to know each other more than I'm comfortable with.

I lean toward him and I channel my inner Cindy, and I say, "I can think of something else you can do with the tip of your tongue."

"Is that so?"

I tilt my head. "Or there are a few things to do with the tip of *my* tongue..."

"I think I love the way you think." He stands, sliding his shirt off his shoulders. His arms, beneath his undershirt, ripple with tight, toned muscle. "But I want my turn now. I've been dying to taste more of your skin since the first sweet tease I got earlier."

"I thought you said I tasted salty?"

"That was before I sampled your pretty neck... Your tempting mouth..." He means what he says, I can tell, and it freaking *thrills* me. Like, literally, thrills are shooting through my veins. But it's hard to give in to the sensations when there's a shadow in his expression. I wonder if it's because I made him think of his stutter, of his parents. And he still isn't moving toward me.

And I'm still dizzy.

And I'd like for him to steady me.

Or unravel me altogether.

"Are you..." I swallow around the lump of nerves in my throat. "How often do you do this? Sleep with random girls?"

There's a bit of a pause before he answers. "I'm not a priest. But I'm very careful. And I'm clean."

If I can trust what he says—and I do, oddly, trust him, or want to, at least—maybe we won't have to do the awkward condom dance when things really get started.

"I'm on the pill," I say, pushing the conversation toward what we're about to do. Plus, it's probably the type of conversation you should have before sleeping with someone. "And I'm clean, too."

"Good to know." He's watching me, musing stretched across his features, and I have a feeling my own thoughts have been stretched across mine.

"Anyway, you gave me four truths," I say, hastily. "I must owe you a couple more. Here. I'll give you three. Three truths, no lies. Ready?"

He nods.

"First...my mom actually is famous. Well. Half-famous, maybe." The words trip right over my tongue, falling out easily thanks to all the alcohol coursing through my system.

"Really?" Curiosity replaces the shadow across his features, and I feel like I've achieved something awesome. "Who is she?"

"Nope. Nuh-uh. That's a truth I'll never share." It's been years and years and years since I've spoken her name out loud. I don't plan to ever do it again.

"What if I kiss it out of you?"

"You'd have to kiss me for a very, very long time," I say. "I mean, I still wouldn't tell you. I'd just like for you to kiss me. For a very, very long time."

"I have no problem with that." He crawls toward me, *finally*.

I scoot down to let him rise over me.

He takes his time.

Dropping kisses along the tops of my feet, my ankles, my legs.

Trailing his hands and then his tongue along my inner thigh, first one and then the other, and my entire body flashes with heat.

Oh my God did I shave this morning?

Wait. Is it tomorrow morning now? What time is it? My mind is so tired, but my body... My body is so alive.

His tongue is silk against my skin and my blood is rushing, magnetized directly to the lines he's licking like arrows, up, up, up my legs. His hands are calloused. Why are his hands calloused? What will they feel like when they're... *Right there.*

Slipping under my panties, drawing a line through the very center of me.

"*Oh my God, that feels so fucking good.*" Wait. Did I say that out loud? Shit. I did, didn't I? My mind is shutting down; I can't keep track of my thoughts. I can't keep track of anything except the way it feels to have his finger sliding through me, into me. Twisting, turning, curving until he's hitting a spot that makes me want to fucking sing and has all that heat shooting straight to where he's touching me. Liquid heat—I feel myself soaking into his hand.

I think I say something again. I think I repeat myself. I wonder if I should be embarrassed. Am I reacting the way I should? It doesn't matter; I can't control myself, not with what he's doing to me. And Frank doesn't seem to mind. In fact, he tugs at the skin of my inner thigh with his teeth, sending tingles everywhere, muttering, "Jesus, you really are sweet."

And then another long, slow lick along my leg, and when I force my eyes open, he's watching my face and I've never lived through a hotter moment in my entire life.

"Kiss me, please," I hear myself say, not sure where the words are coming from. "I need you to kiss me. Right fucking now."

"Where?" he asks, slipping in another finger and making me swallow so hard it's a miracle I don't choke. "Where do you want me to kiss you?"

"My lips."

"Which ones?"

And my toes fucking curl.

"My..." I struggle to get words out because of the pressure he's suddenly applying. With two fingers. And his thumb. I can barely breathe. "My mouth."

"As you wish." He plants one more kiss against my thigh and slips his fingers out of me—smoothly enough to make me shiver. He guides his hands under my tank top, trailing a bit of my own wetness along my skin. "I wanted an excuse to take this thing off of you anyway."

He lifts my shirt higher, trailing kisses along my stomach, until his hands are sliding over my breasts, his thumbs rubbing my nipples through the sheer fabric of my bra until they're so tight under his touch I might explode.

"I haven't told you all three truths yet," I say, starting to ramble as a pressure in my stomach quivers and expands, warm and fluttery. "It doesn't seem fair. It's not *even*. You know?"

Ramble, ramble, ramble. I can't shut my mouth.

He lifts my shirt over my head and runs his mouth up my neck and along my jaw.

I don't know what to do with what I feel. It's too much. Too intense.

And I'm too dizzy.

So I keep talking.

I keep talking; I keep talking; I keep talking until I lose track of every word that falls from my mouth.

And then I pass out.

And then I wake up with the sun hitting my face and I can't recall a single damn thing about anything else from the end of the night.

Fuck.

CHAPTER TEN

NOTHING. NOT A thing. I remember Frank kissing up my neck. I know I was jibber jabbering. And that's it. That's all I've got.

Oh my God, *Frank*.

I force my sandpaper eyes to open wider than their current narrow slits and I roll to my side.

And there he is. Sleeping. Snoring softly on his inhales.

How can I wake up so attracted to someone who snores?

Maybe because even with his mouth slack, slightly parted, he looks like a damn Greek god.

A Greek god I came home with. To have sex with.

Oh my God, *sex*.

Did we?

I gently roll onto my back and run a hand over myself. Over my underwear. I don't feel touched, or tender. Or stretched. Or...who knows what it'd feel like after sleeping with this way-too-beautiful guy beside me?

The point is, not me.

We didn't do it. He's still in an undershirt, and—I slowly lift the covers to peek—his boxer briefs. Holy shit he's got morning wood, though.

Yeah. No way that thing was inside me last night. I wouldn't be able to walk the rest of the day. Probably not tomorrow either.

Yeesh.

Frank sighs—and I freeze, but he only closes his mouth and settles more deeply into sleep. One of his arms is strewn out toward me, palm down like he's holding the covers in place, though he gave way easily enough when I lifted them. A strand of morning sunlight flows across his skin, highlighting an odd pattern of jagged scars across the top of his hand. I didn't notice them last night, though maybe I never looked. Plus, let's be real, every time he touched me with either hand, I lost a little focus. But I wonder what caused the scars. They're healed now, but the skin's still raised and whatever happened looks like it was painful.

My eyes catch on something a few inches from his hand—my tank top. I quietly rise and reach for it, holding my breath—and he clears his throat, shifting behind me. Panic pushes me out from under the covers. I move slowly, carefully, and once I'm free, I dart into his bathroom to get dressed.

At least from the waist up.

Not sure where my pants are.

No, wait.

The memory slams into me like a physical blow. I remember sliding them down my legs last night, stepping out of them, straddling him... His lips on my neck, his hands riding up the skin of my stomach.

How am I *this* turned on all over again from a memory—and while the dredges of a hangover are beginning to sink their claws into the sides of my skull? But the very skin of the very stomach he ran his hands along last night is quivering. And that is very much not from my hangover.

Okay. It was one night. It's over. And now I need to get out of here. And the point is that my pants are at the side of his bed. I must've walked right over them, and now I have to go out to get them and he's probably wide awake waiting for me. For my pasty, freckled legs in the light of day. And without the aid of alcohol to give them any sort of faux-confident swagger.

Plus my knees are wobbly from remembering all the heat from last night.

I splash water on my face and thank God there's an elastic around my wrist for me to tie my rat's nest hair up with. I find a tube of toothpaste in a drawer and squirt some onto my finger, rubbing it over my teeth and then rinsing some of the dried saliva out of my mouth.

Hoping I'm at least halfway presentable, I pull the doors open like I'm not at all intimidated.

And I nearly pass out with relief when Frank's no longer in the room.

I finish dressing in privacy, and try to figure out if I'm glad we didn't sleep together, or disappointed. But it's the sinking weight of disappointment winning in my belly, because when will I ever have a chance like this again? Last night was unreal.

Literally. Not real. He doesn't even have my name. He doesn't know anything about me, really. Everything he learned, he learned from *Cindy*...

And now I have to figure out how to get out of here without making it worse.

I should slip out. I should sneak down his stairs and let myself out the door.

But I want one more glance. One more peek at what might've been. One more mental snapshot of the most beautiful person who's ever wanted me. I'll say goodbye. That's it. A quick goodbye, and then I'm gone.

I sling my purse over my shoulder and tiptoe down the hall the best I can in last night's heels. I spiral myself halfway down his staircase, pausing when he comes into view.

He's sitting at his kitchen island with a tall coffee mug in his hands. There's a second one in front of the seat next to him. And the air smells like cinnamon rolls, making my stomach grumble. I choose to think it's my step down onto the next wooden stair that makes him look up, though.

"Good morning." Good. I'm the first one to speak.

He clears his throat and waits until I'm all the way down to respond. "Hi."

"Smells good." I walk toward him with a confidence I don't feel. It's exhausting. Especially hungover.

Mostly because the sight of him stirs things up in me I don't want to deal with, especially sober.

"I take mine black," he says, sliding the second mug toward me. "But I made yours extra sweet."

"Please, please don't tell me it's as sweet as I am or something similarly lame." I'm so proud of my careless tone right now I want to take it out for ice cream.

"You liked sweet drinks last night. I made an educated guess." He smiles, but it doesn't reach his eyes and that makes me a little nervous.

"Well then." I stop across the island from him, reaching to grab the coffee. "Your reasoning paid off. I do like my coffee extra sweet." And with the first sip I have to keep from moaning. It's perfect and creamy and smooth. Hot enough to burn the roof of my mouth, but I don't need taste buds after this anyway.

"We should talk," he says, his tone serious enough to cancel out the pride I felt for my own a few seconds ago.

"About?" I keep my gaze on his for approximately half a second before I can't take it anymore and I study the mug in my hands instead. Tall and blue, ceramic. Probably not dishwasher safe.

"About last night."

My chest tightens. He doesn't strike me as the kind of guy who'll be pissed we didn't bang... But I don't strike him as the type of girl who's named Teagan. We all have our secrets.

"Listen," I say. "About that... Sorry I passed out. I don't usually make promises I can't keep."

"You didn't make me any promises last night." His voice is sharp, and I can't help but look up. There's a muscle clenched in his jaw, his sexy, sexy shadowed jaw. "You don't owe me—or anyone else—anything."

"No shit." I don't get where he's going with this, or why.

I'm not sure he does either, because it takes him a few moments—and a few sips of coffee—to speak again.

"You told me—wait." He breaks off, shaking his head, and nervousness swirls into panic in the pit of my stomach. I told him what? A fake name? *Does he know?* When he looks at me again, his gaze is so direct it's startling. "You don't even know my real name. Let's start there."

Oh my God, he does want to discuss names. He knows I lied.

Should I tell him the truth? Laugh it off like I thought he knew I was joking?

He walks toward me and my stomach clenches for too many reasons to name.

I grip my coffee mug like it'll shield me from any awkwardness.

It's not working.

At all.

And then he's in front of me, watching me so studiously I slide a hand across my face in case there's something stuck there.

"I'm Alec," he says, sticking out his hand. I check for, but don't find, any scars on this one.

Don't tell me, is what I mean to say. But what slips out is, "I thought the girl last night called you *Alex*?"

"Probably to irritate me. We hold no particular fondness for one another." He says it casually, like it weighs nothing in his mind. Still, I wonder why—and am tempted to ask—but then he continues with, "Anyway. I'm *Alec* Chambers."

And his full name echoes through my brain, bouncing around and, instead of fading, growing louder with every iteration.

It's officially worse.

So. Much. Worse.

I know his name.

I know who he is.

"Cool." I take his hand, offering the limpest shake of my life and letting go as soon as possible. "Do you have any headache meds or anything?" I gulp my coffee so fast it scalds my throat. "Got a crucial hangover."

Got a crucial hangover? What am I? Some teenage surfer? Why don't I throw up a hang ten sign while I'm at it?

But he takes the bait. "Probably somewhere upstairs—I'll go check."

I don't even wait for the relief to hit. I get the hell out of his condo the second he's far enough away not to hear his door shut.

The glass elevator seems so much more appropriate this morning. Almost like the universe is handing me a dose of the snide sarcasm I use so spectacularly on my own. Everything I wanted to keep hidden is about to be made clear, whether I like it or not.

Fuck.

I went after a fairy tale, but I didn't get it—and the stupid fucking clock just struck twelve anyway. Here's my Cinderella moment, fleeing before I return to tatters before his eyes.

But this time, the prince won't need a glass slipper to find me.

Because Alec Chambers?

His father is the CEO of Chambers & Britt.

I know this for a fact because my starting position at the company is to be the second assistant to the CEO's son, while he's home for the summer, studying for his MBA from fucking Harvard. And that son's name? Yep. It's Alec Chambers.

I'll see him again on Monday.

CHAPTER ELEVEN

MAYBE I SHOULD quit... But I shake my head before the thought's finished filtering through my mind. I shove myself out of the apartment complex, squinting in the bright morning sun. I'm desperate for this job. Considering I was fired from my last one—and especially the reason for it—makes getting hired anywhere else pretty much impossible.

When Frank—or, no, *Alec*—figures out who I am, I'll probably be fired all over again.

This is bad. This is so, so bad.

But, like I'm being granted some sort of respite to the rest of this shitty situation, there's a cab waiting out front. The driver looks up when I exit, and I dash straight to him.

I open the door, breathless and nervous. Every second that ticks by gives Alec one more second to come after me.

"*Go,*" I say, slamming the door. "Please. The faster, the better."

I don't care that I'm stealing someone else's cab, but karma is a total effing bitch and we don't even make it out of the long driveway before I'm yelling for him to stop.

Because my cash is in Cassidy's blazer.

And Cassidy's blazer is somewhere in Alec's place.

The cab driver is not pleased and, understandably, refuses to even drop me off at Springs Corner right up the street. So I hoof it. In last night's wrinkled outfit, wearing a mangled wreck of a bun in my hair. And after the third honk from a passing car, I want to murder someone. Anyone. Maybe Alec. Mostly myself. Humiliation is hot and unforgiving in my veins.

I call Cassidy over and over and over again.

Finally, Gage answers her phone, his voice all groggy like I woke him up. Boo-freaking-hoo. He tells me Cassidy's in the shower. I tell him I don't care, get her out. She, at least, responds like a friend, telling me she'll throw on clothes and rush to come get me without even needing an explanation.

"I can't tell if this means things went well with that guy or not," she says before I've even gotten my seat belt on. "I'm thinking maybe not?"

"*That guy?* You mean the one you *had* to tell I hadn't gotten laid in a while?" I glare at her when she snorts. Her hair's wet, flung up in a bun, and I can tell she didn't stop to put on a bra under her T-shirt. I should be nicer to her. But I don't have anything nice in me at the moment. "Yeah. I went home with that guy. And guess what? Turns out he's my fucking boss for the summer." I'm suddenly furious all over again that she thought it was funny, then or now.

She pauses mid-giggle. "Are you kidding?"

"Why the hell would I kid about something like this?" Why the hell would I get myself into this situation? "He's your dad's CEO's son. Working for the summer until he returns to his Ivy League MBA program. I was hired by his dad's secretary to be *his* second assistant for the summer. Because apparently one isn't enough." Then it hits me. "*How could you not tell me who he was?*"

She blinks. "How would I have known?"

"Your dad is his dad's second-in-command. You can't tell me you've never met Alec before."

Understanding dawns across her face. "I haven't, Teag. I swear. Not once. There aren't, like, company family functions all the time. I've been to Mr. Chambers' house for dinner before but I've never met his kids. They're all out of the house, I think. Maybe if I'd paid better attention to pictures, or—oh my God, he does look like his father. There was something familiar about him, but I didn't place it. Because he's hot and I've never thought of his dad that way. But I should've re—"

"Whatever. It's fine," I cut her off, because she's spiraling into self-doubt when it's really not her fault. Not that it keeps me from being irritated with her anyway. "But what the fuck am I going to do?"

"Did you sleep with him?"

"Who cares?" I can't bring myself to lie to her about it. "He's my fucking boss and I lied to him about my name. And instead of coming clean, I split while his back was turned."

"Teag!" She shoots me a sympathetic glance, which would maybe mean something if her stupid lips weren't quivering to hold in her laughter. "What *are* you going to do?"

"Not talk to *you* about it anymore." I stare blindly out my window, hating how bitchy I'm being, hating how she's not grasping the seriousness of this.

Hating everything, basically.

Myself most of all.

"I'm sorry. I'm not laughing at you—just at how ridiculous this situation is." The sincerity in her apology makes me feel even shittier. "Is there anything I can—?"

"It's fine." My tone says otherwise, but it'll have to do. "Can we not talk about it for a while? I need some time to process." To stew.

No. To get over myself and this *thing* that lives inside my stomach, the one that has my hands in tangled fists across my lap, squeezing as hard as they can to try to keep some of the fury at bay—because this is my fault, not anyone else's. Not his, and definitely not Cassidy's.

"Okay." She says the word quietly and now I loathe myself. But it doesn't keep me from staying silent the rest of the drive. From muttering a thank you before letting myself out of the car and not looking back, even when she halfheartedly calls out to me that she'll see me later.

Angry or not, I can't look back, though. I never can, not when I'm this close to where I live. If I were to look back, I might go running after Cassidy's car, begging her to take me with her.

My house is two seconds away from looking like one of those rundown, boarded-up, peeling-paint shacks visible from the side of the road in bad neighborhoods. It's one more falling shutter away from being dilapidated, a word I know because it's been flung in my face several times. I got over the teases a long time ago, though, because the outside is such a perfect representation of the inside. And the people within.

My key is in my hand, but I can't bring myself to use it. I don't have it in me to deal with my grandparents on top of everything else. And... I can't stop flashing back to this morning. Frank's face. Alec's face, I mean.

Why didn't I laugh and confess who I was the instant I realized he was my freaking boss? Why did I flee? All I did was make things *so much* worse.

And before he even said his name...he looked so serious. What happened to the sweet and charming guy from the bar—from his game room...his bedroom?

Damn it. I wanted last night to mean something, to give me something to hold on to. A memory to cherish, to pull me through until I can afford my own apartment, to push me into a newer, better, more experienced me. Instead, all I have is anxiety and fingers itching to call Chambers & Britt to quit before I've even started.

Alec. I shape his name on my tongue. The name suits him way more than Frank ever did.

And that's as far as I get because Gran opens the door, in her uniform, anger in her eyes and the still-lit butt of a cigarette hanging from her lips. She doesn't speak, stepping aside to let me pass. I don't speak either, slipping through the doorway, holding my breath to escape the worst of the smoke.

And then I figure, fuck it. And I breathe it in. This, at least, is familiar; it goes all the way to my bones. Dirty house. Stench of smoke. Gran's contempt. These things bring me back to myself.

"You look like yesterday's trash." She's looking for an argument and my throat tightens. I pause on the bottom step to the upstairs and turn to face her. We've lasted weeks this time without speaking to each other. Guess this means Gramps fell off the wagon again. He's probably still sleeping it off. I bet if I inhale deeply enough, I'll smell the rank scent of cheap booze underneath all her cigarette smoke. I choose not to try it. I also choose not to give her the fight she wants.

Six more months, I remind myself, instead. If I save for six months, with my salary—even as small as it is—I'll be able to afford almost a year of a cheap apartment on my own. Clinging to this knowledge, all I say is, "You're right."

If it shocks her that I'm agreeing for a change, she doesn't show it. "Gonna turn out like your mama, knocked up before your time."

Maybe if I turned out like my mother, I'd be the one my grandparents taped once a week on a cheap TV tape player. The one on a reality series to be the next top LA socialite, pretending not to have a family anywhere.

Maybe I'd be the one who managed to escape this house and everyone in it. Sometimes I almost understand why she did it.

But, "I'll never be like her," is what I say. Because no matter what other path of hers I might follow, I would never abandon a newborn. Especially if it meant leaving her with my grandparents, people more likely to laugh when a child falls down than to help her up.

Gran cackles, a hacking sort of cough disguised as a laugh. "Keep telling yourself that, chub-doll."

"I'm going to shower." My voice carries no emotion. It's deadened and that same deadness creeps through the rest of me, weighing me down like my limbs and my stomach are full of wet sand.

She pulls on the last embers of her cigarette. "Hot water's off, but you look like you could use a cold one, anyway. I work a double at the grocery today, so make sure you feed your grandfather this evening."

"He can fend for himself," I say without much bite, heading up the stairs before she has a chance to respond.

My feet automatically skip the third and eighth steps; one's splintered, the other close to joining it. And I hold on to the wall instead of the railing, which is also splintered in spots. I dump my clothes in my bedroom, wrap myself in a clean towel, and head straight to the bathroom. I need to wash off this morning's humiliation, but more than that, I need to rinse Gran's words down the drain with it.

I turn the water on to mute my voice, and then I turn toward the full-length mirror hanging on the back of the bathroom door. I hesitate a few moments, but I know I have to do it, so I drop the towel. And I study myself. Hard.

"You are not a chub-doll." I glare at my reflection so that maybe the truth will sink in. There are bags under my eyes and my cheeks are a little gaunt. I force my gaze lower. My boobs are medium-sized and perky and *almost* symmetrical. There's pudge around my belly, and some cellulite on my thighs, but not a ton. *Not* a ton—the thought needs some extra force behind it. My feet are slender, my toes thin and pretty. I tell myself the truth every day. I'm honest with myself about my appearance, sometimes brutally. But I have to be. If I tell myself no lies, her criticisms won't sink all the way in. Not the way they used to.

"I am not fat. I am average. And sometimes even passable as pretty." I've said these words a thousand times, so I don't know why my voice is quivering this morning. I don't know why my eyes sting with tears, or why I find any of it so hard to believe now. "Even Alec thought I was attractive enough to take home."

Oh, God. Alec.

I wait for the surge of embarrassment to swell through me, but it doesn't happen. I'm too...heavy to feel anything with much force.

This is worse.

This is so much worse than all the anger.

Sadness has no outlet, no fury to unleash and relieve.

Even ice-cold shower water doesn't do anything to shock it out of my system, try as I might to scrub it all away.

I let my wet, sandbag limbs carry me to my bedroom. I let them crawl me onto my thin old mattress. I let them weigh me down into sleep.

CHAPTER TWELVE

CASSIDY CALLS ME all weekend. I ignore her.
Vera tries me, too. Same goes.
Clearing their calls makes me hate myself. But I hate the thought of speaking with anyone even more than that.
Gran doesn't bother trying to speak to me—neither does Gramps—the few times I stumble downstairs to grab water and the occasional snack. I think they prefer me out of sight.
I know I do.
When I'm not sleeping, I'm curled tightly as I can be on my side, squishing any feeling that tries to rise, wanting to be asleep. It's easier during the days. The nights? Nights are always the worst.
Nights bring the stomach ants. Anxiety. When I was younger, I only understood the tight, crawling sensation that circled in my belly to be ants. Marching nonstop. Biting the inside of my tummy. Making my breath come faster and my mind swirl.
All the things I've done, the ways I've acted. I never get to forget them; they're just around the corner of my mind, every time. External reminders. Internal guilt. The weight of it all is crushing.
And it's always there, a river of gasoline through my veins.

Plenty of times, it goes dormant. There, but manageable. Not forgotten—but abated. Happy days. Happy weeks. Happy months... Well, not *happy*. But not miserable, at least.

The thing about gasoline, though... It only takes a spark to explode. And every single time I fail at something, there's a flame.

When I let my friends down. When Gran's digs manage to get to me. When an inch of my belly hangs over pants that shouldn't be too tight.

When I can't understand the things everyone around me seems to find simple. When Gramps spends the money I pay them for bills every month on something other than what it's intended for, and our hot water gets shut off.

When I feel fat. Ugly. Bad skinned. When I notice my plainness compared to my friends in pictures. When my pudgy stomach's the first thing I focus on.

Such vanity. I wish I could let it all go and be happy with who I am.

But I can't.

And all that gasoline in my veins? And all those sparks?

They meet way too often.

Ka-fucking-*boom*.

I spend both weekend nights unable to sleep, tossing and turning and lost in thoughts that grow darker with each minute until I'm crying without tears.

Because tears would give me release, and apparently my chub-doll body hates me too much to let me have it.

Then, somehow, it's Monday morning and I don't have a choice anymore. I'm sleepless, disheveled, *gross*. And I have to get out of bed.

I reach in my closet and pull out a tilted old picnic basket. I made it in middle school home ec, and it was the first thing I'd ever created that wasn't a total disaster. Yes, it's crooked. And the paint's not thick enough to cover some of the newspaper print from the pages I cut up and rolled into tubes to weave into the basket.

But it's functional. It gets the job done. And that's what I have to do today. Be functional. Get the job done.

In the basket is the only other thing I have of value. A blanket I made, also in middle school, out of scraps of cloth—and sewn into the center is my baby blanket. The thing I came home from the hospital with, tattered and threadbare. I found it when I was younger, thrown in with dust rags. Gran laughed about it when I asked why it was different colors than the other white rags. Then she told me what it was, and when I got mad that she'd used something that was mine to collect dust and dirt, she laughed again.

Sometimes looking at these things, touching them, remembering the way it felt to make them, helps when I'm in a bad mood. Today is no exception, but the little rise in temperament they give isn't nearly enough to push through the weight of the fog holding me down.

CHAPTER THIRTEEN

ANOTHER COLD SHOWER—and the bite of anxiety coming through over seeing Alec again—helps to clear some of my fog.

At first, it's almost nice to feel something other than overwhelming nothingness. Little nips and jolts along my nerves... It's like remembering I'm alive. It's enough to push me into actually attempting to style my hair, which I'm sure I'll appreciate later. It's also enough to have me squandering away a few precious dollars for a drive-through coffee on my way to Chambers & Britt.

But once I'm there, my poor car sputtering her way into the parking lot, past the company's three towering glass buildings? Suddenly, as hard as I've been trying to avoid it all morning, Alec's face is in my mind. So in focus that everything else blurs away. So sharp I can practically *smell* him, that woodsy soap scent.

If my face wasn't numb from lack of movement for two days, I'd cringe. As it is, I schlep into an empty space and bury my face in my hands anyway. God. Right now, in his mind, I'm some girl who disappeared like an asshole. Big deal. But the second he sees me this morning? I'll become so much more than that. *A way bigger asshole.* A huge liar.

Possibly fired.

I wish I hadn't left.

I wish I *had* slept with him. Not that it'd make this situation any easier, but I bet the memories would be worth it.

I wish I'd been honest.

I wish—*shit*. The time on my dashboard tells me I really can't be sitting here making regret-filled wishes right now. I wish I wasn't about to be late for my first day of work.

I'm out of the car and halfway through the lot before I notice all of the sleek and fancy cars lined up around me. If I wasn't still so *blah* about everything, they'd make me feel so inadequate I'd turn around and sputter my little Toyota right the hell out of here. I don't have that option though. I need this job.

I need to figure out how to convince Alec not to kick me to the curb the second he sees me.

I want to pause for one last deep breath before stepping through the doors, but there's a woman rushing beside me and she pauses to hold the door, offering a halfhearted smile.

So in I go.

And, when I check in to ask for the badge that's supposed to be waiting for me, the receptionist at the front desk tells me I'm half an hour late.

"What?" I almost lean forward to grip the jutting top of the counter he stands behind.

"You're half an hour late." He says the words slowly, like he's speaking to an idiot. Which maybe he is, but his tone still pisses me the hell off. Another nice burst of *feeling* shoots through me.

"The email said—*confirmed*, actually—my start time was nine a.m. every day except Thursdays." I have to come in half an hour early those days to help set up for a weekly all-hands meeting that starts at nine sharp. I read that line ten freaking times to make sure I had it right—in a magnified print. I point to the clock on the wall behind him. "I'm exactly on time."

"For the record, exactly on time would mean you're in your desk at nine a.m., which you aren't." He's so smug I want to pinch him. "And the email also said that on your first day, you should arrive thirty minutes early for a brief orientation follow-up."

"Where?" My one word is full of enough attitude to make him blink, but I'm getting irritated. Or maybe it's the panic clawing at my throat at how much worse Alec's first—or, actually, second—impression of me will be. "In fine print?"

"It's in the line immediately after your regular schedule is listed." He waves to someone walking past me.

"How would you know that? Did you send the email?" It came from someone in human resources, so I don't understand. I also don't understand why he's being such a dick.

"It's the standard format for all new employees." He doesn't roll his eyes, but he might as well have.

And, fuck. I always do this shit. I try so hard to focus on what I think is important that sometimes other important things slip right past my eyes. I swear I read the email start to finish. The problem is, sometimes words blur over each other if I'm not really looking for them.

"Listen, if you're waiting for me to apologize, it's not going to happen," I say, because his expression's so impatient that now I want to pinch him and twist the skin. "So may I *please* have my badge?"

He pulls it out of an envelope, handing it to me without comment.

"Thank you. And now what do I do because I missed this morning's orientation?"

He shrugs. "Ask your boss."

Right. My boss. I turn, making my way toward the elevators, and just like that Mr. Way-Too-Much-Gel-in-My-Hair Receptionist is out of my mind. Replaced by Alec. And his dimples. And his hard, hard chest. And the knowledge of what I've done to make this situation so incredibly shitty.

Fake name? Check.

Run out while his back is turned? Check.

Late for my first day? Check.

I can't do this. Nope.

As the elevator door opens, I swivel around, weaving through the group of people waiting with me, and I head toward the exit.

Right as Mr. Evans—Cassidy's dad—walks through it. Damn it. His face lights up when he sees me and he waves, calling to me as he comes closer. "Happy first day, hon."

I nod, unable to find my voice.

"Nervous?" He walks right past the guy in reception, who's watching us like he's confused I associate with someone this high ranking. It makes me feel a little better—but not enough to stay.

"Mr. Evans, I—"

"Please. We're colleagues now. Call me Brad." He throws an arm around my shoulder, leading me toward the elevators again. "You'll let me take you to lunch today, won't you? First day celebration?"

How do I refuse?

Last summer, Cassidy was supposed to intern here, but she changed her mind at the last minute to work at a rock venue. He was furious. Like, *kick his own daughter out of the house* furious. Granted, his son had died six months prior and he was a wreck with grief. They all were. *We* all were. He seems to have come a long way in the past year, but still. I can't let him put his neck out for me and be the second hire to fall through after he's vouched for them.

Damn it.

"Walk me to my desk?" I ask, hating how timid my voice comes out, but if I'm staying, I can't go up there alone. I *need* someone by my side the first time I see Alec again, and Mr. Evans is almost as high up in the company as Alec's own father. Maybe it's dumb, but I think he gives me a little clout.

Still, it's not enough to keep my hands from shaking the moment we step onto the elevator. It's not enough to give me the incentive to press the button for my floor. Mr. Evans pushes the nineteen absentmindedly while jabbering on about restaurants in the area.

I zone him out because the thought of food turns my stomach.

Then the elevator doors open on the nineteenth floor and I think I'm going to puke anyway.

Because Alec is standing in front of me, waiting for the elevator I'm about to step out of.

CHAPTER FOURTEEN

I VAGUELY RECOGNIZE that there's a man standing next to Alec, but I can't force my gaze from the guy in front of me. Shock etches into his handsome face, in every dazzling feature. I'm pretty sure a similar shock is marring my own freckled expression. Because even though I was expecting to see him, my memory of how pretty he is did nothing to prepare me for the sight of him in a suit.

Sharp. Tall. Slender, but somehow overpowering. Hair swept away from his face, still destructured enough to make me want to run my fingers through it, but styled in a much more professional manner than the last time I saw him. It looks soft. He must use wax instead of gel.

So. Fucking. Hot.

After a moment that stretches out eons, his brows go down. "Cindy?" The disbelief in his voice is matched in strength only to the burning heat that floods my face.

"This is *Teagan*," Mr. Evans says, beside me, stopping the door from closing in our faces and pulling me forward, out of the elevator. Closer to Alec. "Your new assistant, I believe."

This time the pause lasts at least a millennia. Alec's face filters through so many emotions it's dizzying. Confusion, more shock, more disbelief, and back to confusion. And then...nothing. His expression goes carefully, purposefully blank. Guarded. I'm surprised what a difference it makes. I hadn't realized how easy he'd been around me, how free.

He sticks out his hand and, *yet again*, I take it. One quick shake and he lets go. His words are brisk, toneless. "Nice to meet you." After a pause, like an afterthought, he adds, "Teagan." My name is an accusation.

"And this is Philip Chambers." Mr. Evans motions, palm up, toward the man next to Alec. He's unfazed by the crackling tension in the air between Alec and me. I pull my gaze from the son and put my hand out to meet the father. Who, I notice with an extra little jolt of shock, is nearly identical to his son in features. Gray hair and a bit of a belly, but otherwise the resemblance is jarring. Fucking Cassidy. How she missed it the night we met Alec, I'll never know.

"Pleasure," he says. "I'm making your job a little easier this morning and taking Alec out for coffee." He squeezes my hand before dropping it. "But don't worry, I won't have them take it out of your paycheck." He laughs. I do, too. Mechanically. I'm still too lost in the aftereffect of everything going on to make it genuine—and, anyway, is he mocking me?

Yes, part of my job is to fetch coffee. It's been grating on me since I was hired. "Let's really turn the tables, then. Grab one for me, too."

There's a hesitation before his laughter this time, and the humor doesn't quite reach his eyes. I wonder if I took it too far, or if my tone was bitchier than I intended, rather than the playful I was shooting for. Mr. Evans, on the other hand, is cracking up. He puts his arm around my shoulder for a quick squeeze. Alec, I notice in my peripheral—and with every nerve ending in my body—doesn't respond at all.

"You go on ahead, honey," Mr. Evans says. "I've got to speak with Philip for a moment, but I'll come by in a few to help you get settled in." And to my absolute horror, he pulls Mr. Chambers aside, leaving me alone with Alec.

My eyes make it as far as his neckline, to the very neat knot in his very expensive-looking tie, tucked into the very crisp collar of his very pressed shirt under his very sleek suit jacket. I can't look higher than that. I can't. "Where do I go?"

"Take a left at the end of the hall." He points and my gaze tracks the motion of his arm like a lifeline. "My office is in the back right corner. There's a desk set up for you in front of it. There's a note with your name so you won't miss it. Unless you're confused about what your name is." He waits for me to look at him.

Well. Keep on waiting, buddy, because my eyes are statues pointed straight at the ground.

"You'll see Sam at the desk next to yours, if you need help getting settled in."

"Sam?" I ask, finally forcing myself to look at him. At his blank expression. The one twisting my stomach into one gigantic hangman's noose.

"My other assistant."

"Oh. Right. Because you need two people to get you coffee." My sarcasm makes him wince—which, in turn, makes me wince. Why do I have to be such a bitch?

"Is that the tone you want to set for this...working relationship?" Still impassive, but there's a muscle clenched in his jaw, and under the facade I sense his growing anger.

"I'm sorry." I hate apologizing, even when I know I've done something to make it necessary. Especially when I have so many other things to apologize for—which I should probably do now. Damn it. I take a deep breath and endure another jolt to my senses when his woodsy aroma floods through me. Double damn it. Now I'm turned on while mortified and the conflicting senses are making my stomach twist. "Listen. I should probably tell you—"

"I'll speak with you when I return." He's so brusque, so short, it's almost physically painful.

"Right. I'll just find my desk then." I wait for him to nod, but he's already turned toward his father and Mr. Evans, like I'm not even here anymore.

My senses have never been so awake, so completely aware of every little detail as I make my way down the hall. At least the fog of the weekend is gone. That's a good thing.

Isn't it?

Maybe not. Because holy shit feeling like this big of an asshole is not fun. And this is coming from someone who feels like at least a little bit of an asshole most of the time.

Sam. Samuel or Samantha? I have no right to feel a pending jealousy if his other assistant is female, but I do.

Plus, the air is heavy with the mixed scent of pencil shavings and stale coffee and for some reason it reminds me of high school, adding to the dread pulling my stomach into a black hole. Every step I take pushes my nervous system into something more appropriate to a teenage girl. Especially when I turn at the end of the hall and find myself in a huge open-space work area, the size of a miniature stadium, filled with desks and people on phones and the soft whirs of printers and...just...too much busyness to take in all at once.

I'm so far out of my element I don't even know what an element is anymore. But I plaster on an expression that says otherwise, like I did in high school—like I do most days of my life—and I step further into the space.

The deep timbre of Alec's voice plays back for me, my mind putting a friendlier twist on his shortness this morning, because *Frank* wouldn't speak like that—and in the farthest right corner, there's a glass office where he said it'd be. In fact the entire back wall is a row of beveled, frosted-glass offices, but the one in the corner is the biggest. Of course it is. Nothing but the best for the son of the CEO.

There are two desks in front of the door. One empty, the other occupied by an Asian guy who looks about my age. Maybe a little younger. He's typing furiously at the computer on his desk, completely in the zone. So professional-looking. I can't type half that fast.

I should glance around and try to force my numb lips into a smile as I make my way through the office for what seems like hours in a maze, but I don't. I can't. I'm too rattled, too out of place.

Too tempted to turn around, sprint back toward Alec, and jump him.

Or ditch him altogether and get the hell out of this office, out of this life.

But I don't want to return to the other one, to the old me. This is my step forward—I can't afford to look back.

"Samuel?" I ask when I'm finally close enough to get his attention, stopping in front of the desk I assume will be mine.

"Sam, actually," he says, looking up, his fingers pausing over the keys.

"Oh, sorry."

"No biggie." He lifts a shoulder like maybe he's used to it. "Sam's short for Osamu. My mother had high hopes."

I'm missing something, but he speaks so plainly, it's like I should know what he means about his mother. If I'm not born smarter in my next life, I'm giving up on coming back at all.

He must see the confusion I'm trying to hide because he offers a smile. "Osamu means ruler."

"Oh." Relief is a small thing compared to everything else going on inside of me, but at least it's something. I *wasn't* supposed to know. "And yet, here you are, an assistant."

"And here *you* are," he says, his words calm, his eyes narrow, his smile gone, "below even me. A kid fresh out of high school. And you must be what? Thirty?"

"Twenty-two," I say, rankled. I don't look thirty. I *know* I don't. This is off to a *great* start. I drag a finger along my new desk, admiring how sleek the wood is, how unsplintered. Trying to smile, and halfway succeeding, I start over. "Where are you from?"

"Delaware."

"No—I meant—"

"I know what you meant." He stares at the flat screen of his computer, fiddling with the mouse. "My parents are American, too. In case that's your follow-up."

"I'm not trying to be offensive." For once in my damn life.

"Doesn't mean you aren't." He starts typing again, saying coolly, "Anyway. Let me know if you need help logging in. Otherwise I have a ton of shit to do."

And I stand here with my mouth wide enough to let an airplane land. Great. I'm an asshole even when I don't mean to be. Everyone I have to work with hates me already. I search my mind for what I said to offend Sam. "Listen, I—"

"*Teagan.*" Alec's voice is a whip cutting through the air behind me, the force strong enough to whirl me around. "My office. Now."

My mouth grows wet at the sight of him striding toward me, all angry and sexy—and wearing his suit like it was tailored to highlight his height, the width of his shoulders, the narrow slope of his waist. I can't do this. I can't face him. Not now. Not every day.

People are staring at us. Sam's snorting behind me. My ears have cotton in them, and my blood is no longer flowing beneath my skin.

"Aren't you going for coffee with your father?" My question comes out barely a whisper, and still somehow he hears me, coming closer and closer and closer, until he's near enough for me to catch a whiff of that soap I love.

"I told him to go without me. I thought it'd be a better use of my time to meet with my new assistant." He storms past me, straight into his office.

"Jeff Santos called from Berkeley Group earlier—and Piper left a message for you," Sam says after him. "She wants you to turn your damn phone on—and that's a direct quote." Alec doesn't even acknowledge him, and Sam whistles, muttering under his voice, "In trouble already?" I'm pretty sure there's admiration in his tone. "I will need details of this as soon as you're done getting reamed a new one."

"Pretty sure I'm getting fired, so don't hold your breath." I smile at him, sweet as a lemon. "Or, maybe, do."

But my smile drops the second I step past Sam toward Alec's office. My stomach, too. He's standing in front of his desk, waving me in with a short jerk of his hand and a look that says the longer I keep him waiting, the more trouble I'm in.

I lift my chin and I meet his gaze and I force myself through the door into his office.

CHAPTER FIFTEEN

"SHUT THE DOOR." His tone is calm, and he's leaning against his desk oh-so-casually, but his knuckles are white where they grip the wood, and that same muscle is clenched in his jaw as before.

I shut the door. "You're mad at me."

"I'm confused." He doesn't sound confused, though. He's short, pointed, *pissed*. "Start explaining."

I try to smile, but I can't get the corners of my mouth to work. I aim for humor instead. "There are so many things I could start with... Hard to pick one..."

It falls flat.

Like a pancake-on-the-floor flat.

Not even a halfhearted amused twinkle passes through his dark, dark eyes. Not even the slightest hint of one of his dimples. Just his angular face, all stiff...and smoldery...and *lickable*.

Fuck. That last one is totally inappropriate.

"Try your name."

"Right." I swallow around the ball of nerves bunched at the base of my throat, glancing around the room. Rectangular table in the corner. Bold splashes of color in abstract paintings hanging on the two non-glass walls. One windowed wall looking clear out into the city. What am I doing here?

"Any time now."

Shit. Okay. "I'm Teagan—"

"Walker, I know." He shakes his head—and then starts to laugh.

"*What?*" I'm in no position to snap, but his laughter is directed *at* me. And I don't do well with that shit. "What's so funny?"

"Just... Walker?" His brows go up. "You sure it isn't Runner?"

I roll my eyes. "You're a trip and a half."

"And you're lucky I'm laughing instead of—" He cuts himself off, his eyes flickering away. He swallows heavily when they travel back to mine.

"Instead of *what?*" I shouldn't push him like this, but he's swallowing a second time and... I think he's not thinking about professional things right now. His stare is so intense, it gives me a total rush, and his cheek muscle's working overtime and his hands are gripping that desk harder, harder, harder until he lets it go completely, stretching out his palms.

I swear to God I think he was going to say I was lucky he didn't spank me.

And I get the oddest urge to giggle. It grows and grows and grows until I have to clear my throat to cover the noise that slips out.

A war battles its way across his face and in the end, a professional mask slips over his expression. He pushes off of his desk and walks around it, sliding into his chair. "Why'd you leave without saying anything on Saturday morning?"

I tuck a strand of hair behind an ear. "I—"

"Sit." He points to one of the chairs in front of his desk.

"I'm not a dog." I'm also not somebody who will ever learn to bite her stupid tongue, apparently.

"Are you always this defensive?"

"Yes. Since apparently me telling the truth is the point of this whole meeting."

It's gone so fast I almost missed it—but the side of his mouth undeniably quirks up.

Now he wants to smile?

The nerves making loops in my stomach unwind a fraction of an inch. I sigh and take a seat in front of him, conceding.

"I'm sorry I lied to you about my name," I say. "And I'm sorry I left without saying anything. But until you told me who you were, I never thought I'd see you again—and then I panicked."

"What do you think I did when you disappeared?" He flips the page of his desk calendar, running a finger over the paper, tapping it a few times without even looking at it. "And it's pretty fucked up you thought we wouldn't see each other again. I thought we had a connection."

We still do, I want to say. But this is about the truth, so that's what I'll give. "Come on, Alec. We come from two totally different worlds."

"Yeah." His agreement somehow both hurts and relieves me. Until he says, "One where I tell the truth and you're a total liar."

"I'm usually an honest person, actually," I say, my words clipped.

He laughs again and I want to punch him. Or kiss him.

Both, if I'm honest. "Fine. Maybe I haven't shown you that yet, but if you don't fire me, I will."

"Pretty sure I can't legally fire you for what we did—and didn't—do on Friday." He straightens a frame on his desk, a silver, square thing—and I'm suddenly desperately curious about who's on the other side. His mother? Fraternity brothers? Love of his life? Then he's looking at me again and there's so much fire in his expression, I almost start to sweat. He crosses his hands on his desk. "Pretty sure we shouldn't be having this conversation at all. But tough shit."

He waits, watching me intently, but… I didn't hear a question. Did I miss something? "What am I supposed to say?"

"You aren't finished explaining yourself."

"You know my name—and that I'm sorry. That's all I have to say at the moment."

"I told you, I didn't want to be some swinging screen door, and you—"

"We didn't even—"

"And *that's* the worst part." He clenches his jaw, that same muscle in his cheek flexing like he's trying to hold back—but doesn't succeed.

"That I didn't sleep with you?" If that's the case, it seems out of character for the guy I took him for. Granted, I probably shouldn't make assumptions about anyone's character when I can't keep track of the ones I play.

He shakes his head in short, sharp motions. "Are you playing dumb on purpose?"

"Fuck *you*." It's my automatic response to that sort of question, and rage funnels through my veins so swiftly I'm not even embarrassed to have said it. Barely, only *barely*, do I keep my voice from raising loud enough for it to filter out through the office walls. "I don't care if you're my boss. Go ahead and fire me. But don't you ever—*ever*—call me dumb."

"I know you aren't dumb, Jesus. You've got to be smart to be as slippery as *you* are." He drags a hand through his hair and focuses somewhere behind me for a moment before bringing his eyes to mine.

"Then what is it?" I'm actually grateful for my anger now; it makes this conversation easier. "I said I was sorry for misleading you and disappearing. And I am. But can't we laugh this off and move on with our lives?" Even if I'll spend the rest of mine regretting not sleeping with him because being this close to him is doing horrible things to my hormones. Through all the anger. Through all the embarrassment. Through all the *everything*.

If he were to pull me across his desk right now and have his way with me... I would have mine with him even harder. Without giving the slightest fuck that the entire office might be able to watch our blurred forms through the frosted glass walls of his office.

That won't happen, though, because there's no desire in his expression. Only anger.

"If you're worried I'll tell anyone I duped you or laugh about it behind your back, don't be. If this is some rage over your hurt masculinity, put it away."

"You think this is about my masculinity? Trust me, doll, with what I'm packing, I never have to worry about that. You think I'd be upset because you might hurt my *fragile* ego?" The sarcasm dripping in his words comes close to schooling the best I've ever had to offer, and he studies me so hard I instantly want to check myself over to make sure nothing's out of place. "Are you for real?"

"I am for real. But that girl you met on Friday? *She* was a figment of your imagination. Can we start over from right here, right now?" I should heed my own question. But he brought up what he's packing, and now the glimpse I got of his hard-on under the covers on Saturday morning is frozen in my brain.

"Do you really not remember?"

Do I really not remember what? I open my mouth but the question doesn't come out, because suddenly I'm nervous about what I might not be remembering.

"You were going to let me be your first and then you were going to walk out in the morning."

"Stop." My hand flies up to block his words, but they find their way to me anyway. Like a sledgehammer to the gut, stealing every last breath. It takes all I have not to double over. And I have to respond... Finally, lamely, I come up with: "That's bullshit."

"You told me the truth that night, so drop the act."

"What are you talking about?" *Oh my God. Oh my God. Oh my God.* "Nothing I told you on Friday was true—that's why we're here having this very conversation, remember?"

"You're the one who needs to stop." He says it patiently, like his anger with me is suddenly gone.

However, for me, panic is a rabid tiger with foot-long claws, slashing through my insides. "Alec—I don't know what you're getting—"

"You're a virgin."

And I drop dead.

Or at least I squeeze my eyes shut and wish I could. Because what he's accusing me of?

It's the truth.

CHAPTER SIXTEEN

"YOU'RE A VIRGIN," he repeats, making the entire world crash down around me a second fucking time. "And you weren't going to tell me before I fucked you."

He watches my face, scrutinizing me so closely he must be looking for any chinks in the armor of my reaction. But his words spin me around so roughly, I'm too dizzy to gather anything to protect myself with.

Virgin, virgin, virgin. The word echoes through my mind, through my limbs.

It's the biggest truth I've never told anyone.

Except, apparently, for him.

Fucking alcohol. I'm never drinking again. Like, ever.

"I... That's not true." Breathe. Why can't I breathe? "I've had tons of sex—ask my friends. Ask *anyone.*"

"So if I had *fucked* you—and trust me, Teagan, that's what we were building toward—something fast, something hard, something unrestrained..." Naked desire weaves through his expression, making my breath catch—it stays stuck even when he wrestles control over his features, contorting them into anger instead. "If we'd done that, you wouldn't have bled? It wouldn't have hurt you to be taken so roughly your first time?"

I should not be picturing him above me, *fast, hard, unrestrained*... *Rough.* Oh, God. I need to stop. I need to cross my legs to ease the fluttering happening between my thighs. Focus, Teagan. *Focus.* Now I can breathe, go figure, but it's happening too fast, too heavy. And he's watching my mouth. And, very, very deliberately, I'm biting my lower lip to keep his attention there.

Virgin, virgin, virgin.

The fact that he knows this thing about me should hit me like a freezing cold shower, should get rid of this damn attraction. But the way he's speaking to me, so rough, so purposefully graphic... It's heating me in a way a splash of water could never cool off. Hell, an entire tub of ice couldn't chill the rush burning through my veins. Even if he's using the language to try to freak me out. *Wrong route to take, buddy.*

"I don't think you're supposed to speak to me this way," I say, my voice *almost* steady.

"You're right." He breathes deeply, trying to rein himself in.

"I'm not saying you should stop. Just pointing out that you aren't perfect either." What am I doing?

"What are you doing?" *His* voice is strained, and for some reason it makes me want to giggle again.

"I don't know." But I do. I've dipped my toes into the quicksand of this attraction and instead of pulling my feet back, I want to dive in all the way. "I've regretted Friday night from the moment I opened my eyes on Saturday."

"If you'd told me, I wouldn't have been so—"

"So what? So aggressive? So demanding? So *hot?*" I almost smile when he starts to nod, but stops short with my last question, confused. "I don't regret any of that, you moron. What I regret is not sleeping with you."

His beautiful cheekbones stand out a little sharper when he presses his lips into a line before speaking. "Why?"

"Um, look at you." I let my eyes slowly drift down his face, his neck, his chest...and just as slowly, back up, my own body tingling with desire.

"Who cares how I look?" he asks. "You're beautiful, and you're funny. You deserve something spectacular. Something gentle for your first time. Not some drunk guy from a bar."

"You're clearly more than a drunk guy from a bar," I say, glowing too much from his compliments to stem the words falling from my mouth. "And I get the feeling you might actually be a semi-decent human being. Maybe the perfect kind of guy to be somebody's first. And if you ever tried to give me less than what you started to on Friday night? Something slower, something more *gentle*? I'd be so…not pleased."

"You'd be surprised by all the ways I can think of pleasing you, kitten, and if I were to go slow? You'd love it." Instantly the air between us is pregnant with something I'm not sure I can name. A mixture of hormones and nerves.

Or maybe that's just me.

Virgin, virgin, virgin…

"Fuck. That was insanely inappropriate." He slides a hand down his face. "I can't believe I fucking said that. I'm sorry."

"Don't be." I want to wipe his words away. The apology is dampening the rest of the mood. "I told you I didn't want gentle. I still don't…"

He clears his throat. "Are you asking me to—"

"No." I laugh, interrupting him before he can finish the question. *Completely chickening out.* "Get over yourself."

He smirks. "Really? 'Cause it sounded for a second like you actually wanted me over *you*."

He's giving me another chance to do it. Or maybe he's trying to ease the tension with a joke. Either way, I should go for it. Deep breath. "Maybe we could—"

"It's probably best we keep things—"

"What?"

"No, go ahead."

"Aw, you're such a gentleman," I say, letting my lip rise in a sneer. I know what he was going to say—which was the opposite of what I was going to say. Which makes my stomach close in on itself, and which means no way am I saying what I wanted to say in the first place right now. And if I keep thinking in these circles I'm going to get a freaking headache. "Friday night was a onetime thing for us. It'd be a mistake to try again."

"Right. Because now I'm your boss, and sleeping with you would be breaking a ton of ethical rules," he says, adding almost as an afterthought, "but mostly because I don't trust you."

"Because now you're my boss." I sigh, the tightening in my stomach turning sharper, more sour. "And you don't trust me." I pause, hoping he'll say something to make it still seem possible, but he doesn't. "Then I guess we've said all we need to say on the matter. Unless you wanted to sit there and judge me for a few more minutes."

"I'm not judging you," he's quick to say. "But you sell yourself short."

"I landed a job at Chambers and Britt. I'm doing all right."

He cringes at the name of the company, and I wonder why, but I won't ask. "I don't mean professionally, Teagan."

God. Why is he pressing this? Forget attraction. Forget regret. That slithery snake of anger is starting to stir in my veins. I stand, pushing my chair out with the backs of my knees. "No shit. But guess what, *boss?* It's none of your business."

He stands, too, his hands pressed flat on his desk, tension leveling his shoulders. "You want to play boss and employee? Fine. Start by speaking to me with a little more respect."

"Respect? After you basically call me a slut? Good luck with that shit."

He stares at me, his mouth agape. "That's not what I'm saying. Do you always put words in people's mouths? Jesus."

"My name's Teagan," I deadpan, too pissed to be proud of the quick retort.

"Could've fooled me. Oh wait, you did."

"We're back on that? Because if you're going to talk in freaking circles all day, I should sit down. These heels aren't comfortable enough to stand in for that long." I don't sit, though. Neither does he.

He sighs, loud, hard, his shoulders relaxing a few degrees. "No. That's...behind us. I don't know why I'm being such a dick. I can't keep myself in check around you."

"Actually, most people have that reaction," I say, shrugging off some irritation of my own. It's easier because he did it first. "Probably because I'm such a bitch."

I wait for him to tell me I'm not, but all he does is offer a small smile, and his honesty—or at least his lack of a lie—loosens more of the tight emotion in my chest. I'm out of breath, like I've run a mile while standing here. He's breathing heavily, too, and for a moment we watch each other without speaking.

And gradually, the rest of the tension—from the anger, at least—fades. His mouth quirks and, this time, mine follows.

"We'll start over," he says.

I want to say no. I don't want to start over—I want to finish what we already started. But he knows my truth. And more than anything, I want to return to a place where he didn't. Which means we're starting over. From scratch. So I stick out my hand, across his desk. "Hi. I'm Teagan. Your assistant. And I think we should discuss the proposal your father rejected on Friday. Put me to work and maybe we can get him to change his mind."

"I'm not sure how you'd know about that if this is our first time meeting," he says, a smarmy little smile across his mouth. "But I like your line of thinking."

I'm both relieved and disappointed when he doesn't hang on to the handshake longer than professionally necessary.

Mostly disappointed, though.

CHAPTER SEVENTEEN

ALEC'S PROPOSAL IS...well, basically I'm way out of my depth and suddenly beyond thankful I'm starting at such a low position because I'll have time to build up my understanding of the industry. But his proposal *sounds* smart, at least. Shit, the guy goes to grad school at Harvard. I'm pretty sure he knows a thing or two...

Chambers & Britt—built from the ground up by Alec's grandfather—is a family equity firm, and both Alec's father and grandfather have kept the firm's focus on financial and industrial markets. Alec has an idea to move toward investments in tech startups and small businesses. He wants to give dreamers the chance to build companies. (His Cinderella-style words, not mine.)

"My father always shuts me down," he says.

And, finally, here's a spot where I can be helpful. Thank God for my natural bitchy inclinations. "So?" I keep my tone aloof, kind of catty. "Don't let him."

"It's not that simple. There are a lot of considerations. My father—who's basically remote-operated by my grandfather—is old school. They want the focus on traditional assembly-line industries. They—"

"You're making my eyes glaze over," I say. "I don't know enough yet to help with the technical aspects, but I do know about getting what you want. Look where I am. I want to be here. I made it happen." Okay, it's not all that easy, but he doesn't need to hear that part of it right now. "I do know that you can either whine about your father rejecting what you proposed—or you can fight harder for what you want."

Alec blinks. Maybe he's never considered it. "I always go after what I want," he says. "I went after you, didn't I?"

Not hard enough, I almost say, biting my tongue at the last second. "And for one night, I went with it, didn't I? Because you were persuasive."

"You were pretty persuasive yourself," he says.

There's this sudden jolt of candy-coated tension sending shockwaves of sugar through the space between us. I bite my lower lip again, accidentally on purpose, to see if his eyes will drop to it.

They do.

He swallows.

I pull sweetened air into my lungs.

"This is not going to be easy, is it?" he asks.

"I don't know what you're talking about," I say. "Considering we decided to start over."

"Right. Starting over."

"And on to your daddy issues." I wonder if I've gone too far, but thankfully he laughs.

I probably have the bigger daddy issues of the two of us, all things considered, but I'll keep that little nugget to myself. Instead, I bring us back to his proposal.

It's a much, much safer ground.

Later, at Alec's instruction, Sam gets me set up on my computer—giving me the side eye the entire time. I don't have time to set him in his place though, because I have to mentally prep for my next official task. Note-taking.

Of all the fucking things I'm supposed to do, keeping notes at meetings is my number one priority for Alec.

I knew this this coming in—it was explained very clearly in my interview. I may have fibbed about my note-taking skills. Truth: They are abysmal. I can never read my own handwriting. I figured I could fake it, like I've always done—but I didn't realize I'd be working for someone like *Alec*. For someone I don't want to look like an idiot in front of. For someone who seems to see through anything I try to fake.

    So that's great.

    "Do you have a notebook I can borrow?" I ask Sam, who's at his own desk, typing away.

    "If you ask me nicely."

    I want to scream. "Please."

    "Come on." He stands and motions for me to follow. "I'll show you the supply room. Might as well get familiar with it, as we have to keep it clean. Break room, too."

I enter the conference room armed with tools that'll do me absolutely no good, but make me appear to have a clue, anyway. Paper, pens, and freshly applied lip gloss.

    Sam and I are the first to arrive, as we're supposed to be, to set everything else up. We un-lid platters of pastries and lay out napkins and plastic cutlery. We stack disposable coffee cups and fill containers with sweeteners and stirrers. We lay out pens at each seat around the long oval table and connect the dial-in contraption speaker things for people who call in to the meeting from off-site. We do a lot of other boring, mindless tasks that somehow still make me feel like I've accomplished something when, at the end of it all, the room is set up. Neat and professional looking.

    I smile at Sam. "It looks awesome in here."

    He blinks, surprised at my good mood. "Yeah. So?"

    "Feels good to actually get something done," I admit, guilt bringing me down to reality already. I fucking hate how shocking it is when I act like a decent person. And I hate even more that I do it to myself. It's all my fault. Why did I start off like such a bitch to him?

    "Got the new job jitters?" he asks, grabbing a muffin and shoving half of it in his mouth, speaking through it all. "I had those, too. But Alec's chill and nothing we have to do is ever really hard."

    The corners of my mouth fall to their usual spots, the rest of my good mood disappearing. How nice for him to think the job's easy. He probably has legible handwriting. He probably takes in emails on the first read...

"Here." He shoves out the chair beside him. "Sit next to me. I'll show you the kinds of things that we have to make sure to catch in our notes during meetings."

Relief is instantaneous and I work my way around the table to drop down next to him. "You're taking notes, too? Mine are only backup?"

"For the first few meetings, then you'll take over full-time and I'll be back to other stuff."

Yep. There goes all the relief. But maybe I'll figure something out, some sort of system, before Sam stops.

People wander in, greeting Sam, introducing themselves to me. I smile. Or I try to, at least. I write a panicky note to Sam on my pad asking for help remembering names. Usually my memory's great for names, but today my mind's blanking. He squints at the note, unable to read my handwriting.

Great. That makes two of us.

"Are we supposed to get everyone coffee?" I whisper.

"*Oh.*" He shakes his head, whispering back. "Just Alec, in the morning. And sometimes he wants one after lunch, too." He doodles something on his own notebook, adding a second later: "He takes it black, so it's easy."

"I know," the words slip out before I realize my error. How on earth would I already know that? "I mean, he seems like the type to take..." But I trail off because Sam's not paying attention. He's drawing some intensely detailed patterned thing. It's impressive. And distracting him.

Then Alec walks in and Sam's not the only one distracted anymore. He zeroes in on me almost as immediately as I do him. My palms start to sweat at the heat in his gaze—and then it's gone, replaced with the professional mask that hopefully mirrors the one I'm attempting to wear, too.

Yeah, right. There's no way to hide my attraction, or the things he stirs up in me. Plus...

Virgin, virgin, virgin.

Ugh.

Of course, he sits directly across from Sam, effectively right in front of me, too. He's messing with his phone, not looking at me, but still. I need to stop staring at him, except he's like a damn magnet for my eyes. He's all relaxed and gorgeous and sharp and *almost* close enough to reach out and touch... How am I supposed to pay attention to anything, much less attempt to take notes?

The woman in charge of the meeting makes it easier. Her name's Denise. She's beautiful, she's black, and she commands the room by stepping into it. She sits at the head of the table, smiling and shooting the shit for a few. Asking about one guy's kids, another woman's upcoming vacation... And then she starts the meeting and it's all business.

She's clear and concise and it's obvious everyone respects what she has to say. Even me. Not that I understand half of it, but the calm way she speaks and her clear enunciation makes it easier to record her words about financial contracts and client management in my notebook. And when anyone interrupts her, or disagrees, she listens and considers and answers with her own thoughts in a totally levelheaded manner.

I want to be her when I grow up.

By the time the meeting's over, I have pages of scrawl to sort through. People are laughing, grabbing the last few muffins, and exiting together. Alec sticks around to speak with Denise, not that I'm watching him or anything (yeah freaking right), and I make it to my desk still in one piece.

I can't believe I pulled that off. I managed to sit in that meeting, to follow it, like an actual responsible, capable person.

My hands are shaking.

Why are my hands shaking?

Why is my breath coming so fast?

Oh God. Is this a panic attack?

I sink into my chair, staring at my computer screen until it blurs.

This should feel good. This should feel *incredible*. Instead, I feel like a complete imposter.

"Uh, are you okay?" Sam asks, and when I turn to him, hoping for... I don't know what, but some sort of kindness, instead I find that his brows are furrowed, not in concern, but something more like half a sneer. The kind only a teenager can pull off.

I don't even have the energy left to try to match it. "I was fine until you started talking to me."

Now those brows shoot straight up. "You are the most hostile person I've ever met."

"Should I clear off space on my desk for that trophy?" I bite my tongue, a second too late, reminding myself he *is* a teenager, after all. And he helped me before the meeting. We even had an almost friendly start-over back in the conference room. "I'm…" I cough, choking over the next word, irritated that I have to say it even though I know I'm in the wrong. "Sorry. I don't mean to be such an asshole."

"You're failing." His dry tone and complete honesty makes me laugh, crumbling one of the bricks of tension in my chest.

I hold my breath, clicking on the little email inbox icon on my computer, sighing in relief when there isn't anything new. "I'm kind of overwhelmed."

"Really?" His voice rises in surprise. "But you're on break from college—isn't this a million times less overwhelming than that?"

Right. He assumes I'm in college. Because that's where I *should* be at my age.

According to the rest of the stupid world, anyway.

Alec must know I'm not in college.

I don't want to care. I usually don't.

School's not my thing. Hell, I spent my senior year in my high school's cosmetology vocational program—which boosted me almost all the way to my hairstylist license. Six months after graduation, I had the certification in my hands. I stood in the moment with absolutely zero intention of considering college. Nothing's changed since.

But… Alec's in grad school at *Harvard*. I mean… Let's just add another checkmark to the tally of things that make me feel small.

I stare at my monitor and press my fingers into my mouse so hard something flashes across the screen and disappears so fast I have no idea what file I opened. Or deleted. Or whatever.

Who the fuck cares?

"Where do you go again?" Sam asks, apparently caring.

Ugh. I cannot be a bitch again. No matter how much I want to.

No matter how hot anger boils in my veins.

"Levels of being overwhelmed are different in different situations." I don't know what I'm saying, but it's either talk nonsense or snap his freaking head off. Plus, out of the corner of my eye, he nods, so maybe I made sense after all. I'm the only one too dumb to get it.

Super fucking awesome. I sound smarter when I spew shit I don't understand than I do when I speak like myself.

Little prickles, both sweet and stinging, nip the sensitive skin of my neck and when I look up from my computer, Alec is striding toward me, through the office. The instant our eyes meet, he looks away, saying something to the guy he's passing, pausing to laugh at whatever his response is. He doesn't glance at me again, only stopping to ask Sam for any messages when he passes between our desks.

More awesome. Now he won't even look at me?

Sorry, he says in an email that pops up a few minutes later. *I was rude walking past you. Still trying to figure out how to treat you as a coworker. Forgive me?*

I almost reply with, *I get it. How can I think of you as my boss when I know what you look like with a huge erection?* But I don't have the guts to do it. Instead, all I come up with is, *Moonwalk into the office tomorrow, and we'll see.*

God, I'm lame.

But a hint of his laughter echoes through the glass walls of his office—I'm not sure I'd even hear it if I wasn't listening for it—and it melts like warm honey along my skin, making me resist the strongest urge to giggle.

Or stride right into his office and kiss some of that laughter right out of his perfect mouth.

It's enough to distract me for a good half an hour, thinking about doing that. Who knows how many times Sam has to say my name until I notice? He asks if I want him to walk me around and make introductions.

Obviously, I don't. Even if I enjoyed making small talk, I've met most of them, either today, or at the happy hour. But I do let Sam ramble on, telling me about his high school baseball team (he pitched) and the various scandals that happened over his senior year. It helps to keep my mind off of Alec, but not for nearly long enough.

Later, Mr. Evans drops by, reminding me of my promise to go to lunch with him. It's a relief to leave, and it's hard not to turn and glance at the shadow of Alec in his office as I walk away, but I manage.

When I'm back, stuffed with more pasta than I've ever eaten in one sitting, Alec is gone, out with clients for the rest of the day.

I hate it.

But damn if I don't find it a lot easier to do even the simplest of things without him in his office behind me.

CHAPTER EIGHTEEN

THE NEXT MORNING, after a restless night of sleep—with only Alec and the word *virgin* spinning through my mind until they became so connected I doubt I'll ever be able to separate them—I walk straight past the reception guy in the lobby. Pretty sure he rolls his eyes at me, but I refuse to look his way. Today's going to be a better, less insecure day.

I'm going to read things carefully. I'm going to finish transcribing what I can from my notes yesterday.

I'm going to convince Alec to sleep with me.

It's the perfect situation. He knows my secret. He's fucking gorgeous. And he leaves at the end of the summer to head back to grad school. So I don't have to worry about wanting more than a fling, if my mind's already aware of how unavailable he is. There's no way I'll end up like my mother, because he'll be gone, far enough away that I won't be able to cling to him.

Even if the thought of him leaving tightens muscles in my stomach with the anticipation of some longing I definitely have no right to.

But that's easy enough to ignore.

Or, at least, I'm sure it will be.

Sam's already at his desk—and there's a steaming cup of coffee waiting on mine. I look from it to him. "Did you poison this?"

He rolls his eyes. "It's a peace offering."

"A poisoned cup of coffee disguised as a peace offering?" But I smile when I ask, and this time he laughs.

"Ty—my boyfriend—thought maybe I should've been nicer to you yesterday."

This surprises me. "Why? I was the asshole."

"My grandparents were Japanese." He says it like an explanation.

"Okay?" I grab the coffee, wincing with the first sip—not sweet enough. And, when he doesn't elaborate, "So?"

"Both my parents were born in America. So was I. When you asked where I was from… People ask those questions to make me feel different. *Other*. But I'm not. I'm American."

I need more coffee to process what he's saying. I take another bitter sip. "I didn't mean to—"

"I try to believe that most people don't *mean* anything intentional with questions like that. But when you've been asked it your entire life, every time ends up a dagger, slicing me away from the ability to feel normal, like I belong." He sighs. "And now my instincts are to apologize to you for being a jerk about it, but that would be more—"

"You shouldn't." I shake my head. "Don't apologize. I'm the one who's sorry." I am, too. I don't mind offending people—but only when I do it intentionally.

"So you get it then?"

"Yeah." I'm tempted to admit that I feel out of place all the time. That when people say things they assume I'll understand, I either have to ask for clarification like an idiot, or nod along like I get it, feeling more and more isolated the longer the conversation goes on. It's a totally different situation from what Sam goes through, but the end results are certainly similar. All I say, though, is, "Thank you for explaining. I never would have understood that on my own."

"Now you can." He starts to say something else, but the phone rings and he sighs. "Here we go."

The rest of the morning he's busy. I try to appear busy, at least. I open my email, not expecting much yet. But there's a message from Alec. *Thought you might like to know…* is the subject line. Instantly, I'm nervous. Or maybe excited. Sometimes I have trouble telling the difference. Either way, my face heats, and I hesitate before opening the rest of the email, mentally counting down from three first. And then reading slowly to keep from missing anything.

Teagan, it begins, as I wrongly interpreted your two truths and two lies from the game on Friday, I thought you might find this video to be educational. On the other hand, I personally found it distracting.

A bit like I find you.

Alec.

On my first read, my stomach tightens painfully. I see the word *lies* and everything plummets. He's still upset with me. All I want to do is close it out, delete it, and leave. But I can't, and I need to pay attention to anything else he wants me to do, in case there are instructions here that I've missed.

On my next read, I'm interrupted because Sam laughs at me and I realize I'm sounding words out—not just in my mind. Shit. But I don't stop, because I don't want to make another mistake like I did yesterday, missing key information and showing up late on accident. I angle my face away from Sam, though, and keep the mouthing silent on the next read.

This time, his other words sink in. *The game on Friday. Distracting…like you.* I swivel in the spinning seat of my chair, biting back a smile, though its lightness makes the muscles in my face lift anyway.

He thinks I'm distracting? Like, *still* distracting? Like, even after everything he now knows about me?

A little thrill rushes through my veins.

Okay, that was a lie.

It was a huge thrill, and it's still rushing. And it grows fiercer when I notice the time stamp of the email and discover he sent it at ten p.m. *He was thinking about me at ten p.m.*

Or some educational video reminded him of me, at least.

What sort of person watches educational videos that late? I guess guys who have entire game rooms full of comic books and video games; the thought has me smirking.

Then I click on the link, and it's a fucking instructional video about how to tie a cherry stem into a knot with my tongue. "Oh my God."

"What?" Sam looks over and I click out of the video with almost superhuman speed. He laughs. "Watching porn on your second day? Ballsy."

"It wasn't porn," I say, my face boiling, an annoying smile forcing my lips apart.

"Right. Because that's why you're grinning like an idiot."

"Your sarcasm is on point today," I say, trying to get my expression under control, a weird giddiness making it impossible to get all the way back to my smirk, so I settle for half of that, half of the smile. "Dry enough to make me thirsty."

"Good thing I brought you a coffee then."

"Could've used some sugar." I hold it up in thanks, though, before taking a sip. Sam rolls his eyes, turning his attention to his computer.

I want to open the video again.

Badly.

Maybe something between us really isn't off the table after all.

Maybe he can take me *on* a table. Or over his desk.

Yum.

I might not ever have actually had sex—but I've definitely participated in the preceding events a time or two. And, regardless, not having done it doesn't mean I can't vividly imagine what it'll be like. Especially with Alec. If I close my eyes, I can *feel* him. His chest against my back, his thighs pressing my legs into his desk... His warm, soapy scent. His stubble rubbing the skin of my shoulder while his lips travel my neck...

I force my eyes open, sliding them toward Sam—thankfully, he's typing something and not paying me an ounce of attention.

I'm at work.

I'm at work and I should not be this turned on.

I should not be shifting in my padded mesh desk chair to ease the fluttering between my legs.

This is inappropriate.

I stare out at the rest of the office, zeroing in on a guy who's old enough to be my grandfather at the far end of an aisle. Wrinkled face, huge nose, receding hairline…

There. I no longer feel the need to shift back and forth.

So that helps.

But the universe is laughing at me, because behind the old man, Alec freaking appears, striding toward me. Gray suit this time. Hair slicked back. Stubble-less, but still sharp jawline.

He's looking at a paper in his hand, not at me, but I appreciate the private moment to…appreciate him.

A woman I recognize from the meeting yesterday steps in his path, drawing his attention to something at her desk. He leans down to study her computer screen. I shift to my side, wondering if there's any way to get a better view of the way his suit shapes his ass while he's bent over.

"Neck cramp?" Sam asks.

I snap upright, rubbing my neck, staring at my computer screen. "Yep. Slept funny last night."

"Are you sure it has nothing to do with our super hot boss?"

"Eh." I shrug—and then wince, like it hurt my sore neck. "He's all right."

"You're definitely lying about your neck, then." He's all smug.

"Does your boyfriend care that you check out your boss so hard?"

There. My turn to be smug.

But he laughs. "Ty crushes on Alec harder than I do."

I lean back in my seat, smirking. "That's weird."

"*Eh.*" He shrugs, mimicking me. "He's straight. Alec, I mean. Obviously not my boyfriend."

"No shit." My tone's dry, though the kid's kind of starting to crack me up.

"Who cares? It's like thinking a celebrity's hot. Doesn't mean there's anything real to it."

I make a noncommittal response. That's the thing. My attraction? Oh, yeah. There's something real to it.

And if Alec's sending me cherry stem tying videos, if he's thinking about me outside of work—enough to imagine me tying a cherry stem with my tongue… It's maybe not a one-sided thing, either.

I probably shouldn't be excited about this. It's probably a recipe for destruction. He's the son of the CEO. He's my *boss*, for fuck's sake.

But I'm excited, anyway.

Because... I can't help staring as he closes the distance between us, striding, striding my way, his eyes on mine this time... He's so, so pretty.

I've got it fucking bad.

"Sam, Teagan." He nods to each of us, his eyes lingering on me, my face. "You get your email set up all right?"

I nod back through my blush. "But I got the weirdest spam message last night. With the most random-looking link. I didn't click it, so don't worry. The company won't get a virus because of me."

"You didn't click it?" He shakes his head. "That's too bad. I thought you might enjoy clicking it. A few times."

"Well..." I bite my lip, my heart jumping into my freaking throat when his gaze drops to it. "Okay, I might have clicked it a little bit."

He snorts, clearly biting back a harder laugh. "Me too."

I have to look away or I'm going to die laughing.

Sam clears his throat, and Alec's gaze jumps straight to him, like he's late to remember we have an audience. "Any messages?"

Sam shakes his head. "A few meeting confirmations."

"Thanks." And then he's gone, past us, into his office. Not even a glance back.

But I don't need one. Because I got everything I wanted with our one little exchange.

Holy hell, it's freaking electric, flirting this way.

With the guy who knows more about me already than anyone I've ever known.

The one who knows all of it—and still seems to want me.

God.

Back to shifting in my seat again.

Damn it.

This is going to get uncomfortable, real quick.

"Uh, what was that?" Sam asks.

"Nothing. You're crazy. I mean, what do you mean?" But I say it all with a smile, because Sam already knows there's something going on.

"Holy shit, is your crush more than a crush?" He leans forward, toward me, his hands on his knees. "There's definitely some sort of leftover sizzle in the air right now. I want details. Spill 'em."

"What crush? No idea what you're talking about."

"*Sure...*" He studies me, clearly biting something back.

"What aren't you saying?" I really need to quit this grin.

"Jealous?"

He laughs. "Maybe a little." Then his face grows a little more serious. "Be careful, okay? Because I kind of think you might be fun to have around...but Piper'll skin you alive."

"Piper..." I hesitate to ask, my throat suddenly thicker than a moment ago. "Who's Piper?"

"Piper's his fiancée."

I blink.

I wait for his words to make sense.

It takes too long.

My smile turns brittle and cracks into pieces. Surely if the floor wasn't carpeted, we'd hear them crinkling like shards of glass when they land. "Alec's engaged?"

"Unless the definition of fiancée's changed, yeah."

CHAPTER NINETEEN

"OH, SHIT. YOU didn't know." Sam hasn't moved, but his voice is tinny and far away. "Whoa—are you okay? Your face is really white."

"Funny," I say through gritted teeth. "Because I'm seeing a whole lot of fucking red."

I am, too. I never fully understood that expression until now. My vision is literally blurry and I'm so furious that a red-hot sort of film is webbed over my thoughts, stretching out, reaching its way to the outer corners of my eyes.

I'm standing, somehow. My chair shoved back. And I'm turned toward Alec's office. Sam's saying something, or telling me to wait or... I don't know. Don't care.

And then I'm in Alec's office, without really even telling my feet to move me there. I shut his door and then I'm at his desk and he's glancing up at me in surprise—a fucking smile on his perfect, stupid lips. "Are you here for a knot-tying lesson?"

Like he's pleased to see me standing here.

Like I'm such a fucking idiot, I'd run in here over a cherry stem to flirt.

"You think that's what I'm here to use my tongue for?" I ask, my voice scathing.

But he doesn't get it. Dumbass. He's still smiling. Like maybe I'm being suggestive. Yeah. Let's nip that shit in the bud. "*How could you send me that fucking video?*"

"I thought you enjoyed it." His eyes dip in confusion—which is almost more infuriating than anything else. He's playing dumb, because he thinks *I'm* dumb enough to fall for it.

I take a few steps back, sliding behind a desk chair, needing to distance myself from him. Deep breath to keep from screaming. And to keep the swelling in my throat from closing it completely. "That was before I found out you have a fiancée."

Yep. That wipes the stupid fucking gorgeous smile from his face. "Piper."

"Piper," I repeat. The girl I should feel bad for, for being with an asshat like Alec—but I can't because apparently she'd eat me alive for flirting with him—and that sounds like a challenge and I never back down from one of those. So, instead, I want to hate her. And I hate girls who hate girls for that sort of reason. *Ugh.* Alec's watching my face, calmly, like I didn't just bust him on being a huge hypocrite. "You asshole."

"Now wait a second." He lifts a finger, his face stern. He's going to lecture me? Yeah. No. Fuck that.

"No. You made me—"

Sam's voice buzzes through the phone on Alec's desk. "Um, Alec?"

"What?" Alec snaps, his gaze hot on mine.

"Sorry to interrupt your...um...meeting, but Denise is on the phone."

"I'll call her back." Alec slams his palm against the phone, effectively hanging up on Sam, still not dropping his eyes.

I glare at him. "You made me feel like such shit about Friday. For lying to you. But you? You sleaze on strangers in bars when you're about to get *married*. Who's the bigger dick now?"

"You have no idea—"

"If I had any other options, I'd walk the fuck out of here. I'd quit. But I can't. Nobody will hire someone who got fired from a fucking hair salon." I'm too pissed off to be embarrassed about it, but that'll probably come. So that's great. "Get me transferred. I want to work for someone else, be someone else's assistant." *Like Denise*, I almost say. But everything I felt yesterday? Thinking I wanted to be her when I grow up? What a joke.

I'll never be her. I'm not smart enough. Not nice enough.

And it's too late, anyway. I'm already grown up. I'm already who I'm going to be. The fucking fool who's dumb enough to get fired from a hair salon. Who's dumb enough to fall for lies that come out of the pretty mouth of a pretty face.

Exactly like her dumb mother.

"Are you done?" he has the total effing gall to ask.

"Just getting warmed up, actually. Unless…" I pause, the tiniest glimmer of hope flaring. "Unless you're letting me make a jerk out of myself because you aren't actually engaged. Are you?" I ask, my voice steady. "Engaged?"

His jaw goes tense and his eyes drill into mine. "Yes, but—"

"Nope. No *buts*. I'm out. Find me a new boss."

"There's another side to this." His voice is annoyingly placid. His expression is too.

"Alec?" Sam buzzes in again.

Alec suddenly cusses under his breath, and his expression slips. He's closer to losing it than I thought. Well, good. "I said to tell her I'll call her back."

"It's Mr. Chambers. Your dad, I mean."

"Give him the same fucking message." Alec's snarling now, and there's a quiver in Sam's intake of air before the line's disconnected.

"You should treat your assistant a little nicer," I say. "Considering he's the only one you have left."

"You don't get to come in here calling me names," Alec says, standing, his voice rising in a way that makes my heart jump. "You don't get to come in here throwing accusations around when you don't know the entire story."

"You're engaged. You took me home. You got mad at *me* for lying to you. These are all the things I need to know. I'll be out there, at my desk. Waiting to hear from you who my new boss is. Unless you want me to do this through HR."

I turn to storm out, happy with the last word, but the steel in his tone spins me back around. "You don't get to play this both ways."

"Excuse me?"

"You want to make this an HR issue? I'll walk you there myself. But I think you're this pissed because you feel something for me and you're hurt. And if that's the case, you need to step off your high horse and listen to what I have to say."

"My high horse?" The words sputter out of my mouth and I search for something else to say, but I can't find anything. I'm too mad.

"Just listen," he says. "I'm not... I can't tell you certain things, but I can assure you, I wasn't *sleazing* when I brought you home on Friday. Or when I sent you that video last night. I have every—"

"Does she have cancer? Is this some thing where you're still with her because dying? Because that still makes you a huge douche canoe." I grab the chair separating me from his desk, squeezing—and, frustratingly, not even making a dent in the leather.

Alec jerks his head to the side once. "She's not dying."

"Then what is it? How the hell are you so okay with what you've done?"

"I can't tell you, but I s-swear, Teagan, I'm not doing anything dirty or...douche canoe-ish." He's pleading with me, but there's an underlying anger making him stiff and his words short. His stutter tugs at me, which is so fucking annoying. So does the clench of his jaw, and the way his hands are pressed so hard against his desk that his knuckles are white.

Why do I find him attractive still? Why do I want to press his buttons until he snaps completely? This is so messed up.

"I'm supposed to stand here and say, what? *Oh sure. Tell me there are things you can't share, but it's cool. Flirt with me, send me videos. I'll eat that shit right up.*"

"No, it's—"

"Girls who are always doing that in movies? They piss me the hell off. *Oh, yeah, keep secrets from me. I'll go along with it.* Uh, no. I don't fit that mold, never will. You can go screw yourself."

Of all the reactions he could have, laughter is not one I expect. But it's what he does. I frown. "This isn't funny."

He wipes his mouth. "It isn't. I know. But you're so fierce in your conviction."

"And that's laughable to you?"

"It's respectable, honestly." He sounds surprised. Surprised I'd be respectable in this situation? Fuck that.

"What the hell do you know about respectable?" I'm seething, staring at his stupidly calm face.

"Alec?" Sam's voice cuts through again.

"Goddamn it, Sam. Give everyone the same message." Alec hangs up on him again.

A moment later, Sam's knocking on the door. Quietly, tentatively peeking his head through.

"You seem determined to try my patience today," Alec says. His voice is mild but irritation tightens itself in the set of his jaw.

"I'm sorry, Alec. But your dad..."

"What?" Alec barks. "Out with it."

I turn as Sam steps into the room. He closes the door softly, not coming closer than he has to. "Your dad wants you to meet him at the hospital. Your grandfather had a stroke."

I spin toward Alec and the change in him is immediate. The anger is gone from his stance, the humor from his eyes. He looks...hollow. In shock, maybe. "Is h-he..." He clears his throat. "Is he still alive?"

"Yes," Sam's word comes out almost in a whisper. "But he was unresponsive when he arrived. Last night."

"Last night? Jesus." Alec sinks into his seat.

My own anger droops; it's still there, but hidden under the weight of Sam's message. I can't believe Alec's dad didn't demand to speak to his son. His son who, somehow, looks very much like a little boy right now. Lost and confused.

I should say something.

I should open my mouth and say something.

But what? A second ago I was telling him to fuck off—how will anything that comes from my lips seem sincere now?

"Should I call your driver?" Sam asks.

Alec starts to nod, but words push themselves through my mouth, finally. "I can drive you."

He looks at me.

"I mean, if you don't want to be alone. Not that you'd be alone because Miles is great, but I—"

"Yes. You drive me. Please." His voice is shaky. It makes my heart hurt in an entirely new way.

CHAPTER TWENTY

I AM SURE forgetting that my car's a total piece of shit until we're in the parking lot is some sort of karma biting me in the ass. I stop short half a row away. "Maybe we should call Miles."

"Just take me, please." Alec keeps walking, heading straight for the hunk of junk.

Right. Because I already told him about my car, and he knows it's the fugliest thing in the lot without my having to point him in the direction. I hurry after him, my face in flames, and slide into the driver's seat. I reach over to unlock his door, doing my best to ignore my embarrassment when he ducks into his side. "Sorry for the complete downgrade."

"I've always dreamed of riding in a ten-year-old Toyota with a broken taillight." He tries to crack a grin, fails pretty epically.

"How do you remember *every* little detail of everything like that?"

He closes his eyes, resting his head against the seat, though he's so tall he nearly misses. "I remember every little detail when it comes to you, it would seem."

"I..." Don't know what to say to that.

"Turning out to be a pain in my damn ass, though."

"I'm a pain in your ass?" I pull out of the parking lot, shaking my head. "Funny. You're the one who's—" I cut myself off. His grandfather's in the hospital. This fight can wait.

"Oh, no. Please, let me have it." His eyes are still closed, a whisper of a smile still trying to happen across his lips. "I know I deserve it, and the distraction will be nice."

"There's nothing nice about what I want to say to you." But it's hard to be furious with someone who looks so damn vulnerable. Especially someone who's usually more aggressive. Now, though, he has these little blue veins running across his eyelids and they...I don't know...make me want to make everything better.

Which is fucking annoying.

Literally every person on Earth has veins in their eyelids. His should have zero effect on me.

His eyelashes are almost long enough to rest on his cheeks. He seems so innocent.

He's engaged.

Okay, there. A little of the anger comes to a simmer. That helps.

"Which hospital am I taking you to?"

"Riverview."

"Are you sure? Do you need to check with your dad?"

"My grandfather funded a wing of the hospital—it's named after him. He only lives about a mile from it."

God. These people live on a level I couldn't even dream of. I know where it is, so I keep quiet and I drive, thinking he might want silence to process his thoughts or feelings or whatever. Until he says, "Talk to me. I can't stand sitting here in the quiet."

"What do you want me to talk about?"

"I don't know. You. Life. Keep telling me off about Piper. Anything."

Hearing her name makes my chest hurt, makes my blood rage. "Your grandfather had a stroke. I can wait on all the yelling I have left to do."

He doesn't respond, sitting there with his eyes closed, his face drawn.

"Are you close with him?" I ask.

"Sometimes." His fingers lace together in his lap, a casual gesture but there's tension in his grip. "It's complicated. He's complicated."

"Why?"

"I'd rather not get into it right now, until I know if he's going to be okay."

Right. That makes sense. God. I'm not very good at this distraction thing.

"Um..." What do I talk about? Why is my mind blanking? "I love movies. Do you watch them?" *Does he watch them?* I'm a moron. "I mean, obviously you do. Otherwise you're an alien."

He nods. "Mostly during summers. School keeps me too slammed."

"Have you seen *The Great Gatsby*?" I watched it two weekends ago. Stuck with me. I didn't cry, but that ending hit me so hard it still makes my chest feel tight—not that this is something I'll ever share with him, or anyone.

"Awesome score. The book is better."

Ugh. Books. "Okay—what about..." Think. What sort of movies would Alec be into? "*Fight Club*. Tell me you didn't love that movie."

He halfway unshutters his lashes to focus on me. "Good movie. Still not as good as its book."

"Get the fuck out of here. No way the book was better than that masterpiece."

"Read it and you'll see."

"Wow. You're a tough crowd."

Something kind of sort of resembling a laugh rumbles in his throat.

"No digs at my all-time favorite... *Interview with a Vampire*." I watch it at least once a year. There's something so horrible and sexy about it.

Finally he offers a real smile that has me grinning in return even if I'm still mad at him, even if after this I'm still done working for him. Done speaking to him.

"You're missing out," he says, "on some awesome books. I have all three—I'll lend you one, or all. Though *Fight Club* is so dog-eared, I should probably buy you a new copy."

"Reading's not my thing." I shrug, like it doesn't bother me. Like it hasn't always bothered me. "I can't lose myself in a book the way I can in a movie."

"But you miss so much of the story with movies." Great. He's ruining one of the few things I actually love.

"Music, then," I say. "Tell me your favorite artists—and I'll pull an Alec, systematically telling you why you're wrong to enjoy them."

I'm rewarded with a full laugh this time, and we spend the rest of the ride arguing over Franklin Charles and Castle Zero. Spinster Malady and Demi Jade. The merits of my favorite drummer, Norris Marshall, and why I wish he'd leave Gold Rush Standard. I might be a little biased. I know, personally, what a complete twat the lead singer is—via Cassidy and her mistake of a fling with him last summer.

"I met Norris last summer," I say, pulling into the hospital's parking lot. "He's incredibly sexy and genuinely nice and... I might love him a little." He's also very married and his wife is cool as hell, too.

"No kidding?" Alec asks. "I saw him solo once in Virginia Beach—one of the best shows I've ever seen."

"Get out." My heart does a funny little tripping thing.

He smiles, though there's tension etched into his face. "I'm not James Bond. You need to park first."

"No. I mean I was there. At that show." Norris was in Virginia Beach for one night, randomly, and threw together a last-minute solo gig.

He studies me and I can tell he wants to ask me about it, about the strange coincidence of us both being there. But a second later, he looks out his window and I can also tell his mind's splitting— weighted much heavier toward the fact that we're at the hospital. Because his grandfather had a stroke.

I want to talk about it, too. But he's engaged. And I shouldn't want to know him any more than I already do. The memory of that concert is something I cherish, and I don't want to weave Alec into it. Plus, we're here. I'm parking. We have to go in. Or, at least Alec does.

"I'll wait here," I say. "Or, I can drive you up to the entrance, if you want."

"Come with me," he says.

"I'm not sure that's appropriate." I hate how much I long to ease the anxiety in his eyes, in his shoulders.

"I get it." He opens his door, turning to me before stepping out. "I'll call Miles for a ride after. I don't know how long I'll be. You don't have to stick around."

I nod. And a minute later, I cuss, throwing my own door open, chasing him down the parking lot. "You don't have to walk in there alone," I say, halfway reaching out to take his arm, dropping my hand instead.

"Thank you." We catch eyes for a moment and I swear in his I see a world of conflict, a world of destruction. He's feeling things deeply enough to travel straight from him into my own heart, where it twists and aches and makes me wish I had the words to take away all the pain.

But I walk silently beside him into the building, and that will have to be enough for us both.

CHAPTER TWENTY-ONE

ALEC'S PHONE IS in his hand and when it buzzes he glances down, reading from it to me. "My brother's on his way. He spoke with my dad, and Grandfather's in a private room on the third floor in the family wing."

We head straight past registration because Alec knows exactly where he's going. Thank God, because I'm too blown away to think about asking for directions. *The family wing.* The casual way he threw the term out there is a shock to my system all over again.

The only wing my family's ever had is fried. And from a greasy, cardboard bucket.

While we wait for an elevator, a short black doctor walks toward us, a still-steaming cup of coffee in his hands.

"Dr. Greenwald," Alec greets the man, who smiles somewhat tersely before speaking.

"Alec, good to see you. Sorry for the circumstances."

We stop right inside the doors and he waits patiently for Alec to respond.

"How's m-m-my..." He shuts his mouth, swallows, and starts over. "How is he?" He shakes the doctor's hand without pause, but his expression shows what the stutter cost him, and I want to squeeze him. There's something about this beautiful man looking so broken that tugs at me in a way I haven't quite experienced before. This must be compassion. I wasn't sure I had it in me, before this. Which is really freaking sad all on its own.

But then Dr. Greenwald says, "He's up, actually. Speaking, even," and the relief in Alec is palpable. He exhales a long breath, as though maybe he's only been taking shallow ones for a while, and his shoulders lose some of their tension. Without thinking, I wrap my arms around him, feeling little vibrations in his body, the excitement of relief, maybe, and only a moment later do I catch Dr. Greenwald's frown. Which reminds me that this is totally inappropriate.

I apologize, pulling back. "Lost myself for a second. I'm happy for you... For him, I mean."

"Hello. I'm Charles Greenwald." The man shifts his coffee between hands and sticks one out to me.

"Teagan Walker," I respond, taking it.

"And how do you know Alec?" He's not asking unkindly, but there's a wariness in his expression.

"Teagan's my..." Alec trails off, glancing at me.

"I'm his assistant," I finish. Because it's still true. For now, at least.

"Right." Dr. Greenwald's tone is as weary as his face, but thank God the elevator opens right then, and we all step through, the conversation halted.

We walk down a long hallway, my skin feeling tighter and tighter by the second. I don't have good memories of my own hospital visit a few years back.

Obviously, my plan is to wait outside Alec's grandfather's room—no way do I want to interfere with the family. Problem is, I don't realize we're getting close to the right room until the door beside us is opened by an exiting nurse, and Dr. Greenwald pushes me through in his haste to get by.

Fucker.

I keep my back against the wall, trying to keep a pleasant expression, not quite sure how to manage it. The room—bigger than my entire living room at home—smells astringent, and everyone's faces match the scent. Tight. A little sour. Two women—one clearly Alec's mother, the resemblance is spot-on, minus the just-bit-a-lemon twist to her features—and Alec's dad. Plus, his grandfather. In a bed by a huge bay window.

Dr. Greenwald heads straight to the chart at the foot of Alec's grandfather's bed, studying it without comment.

Alec strides by me, but grabs my arm for the briefest of moments, squeezing it. Thanking me, maybe, for sticking around. "Grandfather," he says. "How are you feeling?"

"As though I've been in the hospital all night and am going to rescind every one of my donations if they don't let me out now." He glares at Dr. Greenwald, who seems to be impervious to the sudden chill in the air.

"Glad you finally made it," Mr. Chambers—Philip, Alec's father—says, his voice booming toward Alec. He looks at me for a moment, until recognition replaces his puzzled expression, and then his eyes slide away, much like they would over a piece of furniture.

Alec's grandfather's eyes are dark like his grandson's, but cold, like he's looking straight into me and finding me lacking. "Who are you?"

For someone who just had a stroke, he looks very out of place in a hospital bed. He's too commanding. Thick white hair, square jawline. A set to his mouth that says he owns the world and is not to be fucked with.

I want to cower, and it pisses me the hell off. I stand a little straighter. "I'm Teagan, Alec's assistant."

"Get out." He doesn't even have to snap his words to make me jump. So much for standing tall. "This is a family matter."

"Grandfather," Alec starts, but I shake my head, telling him it's fine.

"I'll be in my car." It really is fine, too. Hospitals make my skin crawl. And no way do I want to spend another second in this room.

So, instead, I spend thirty minutes in my car developing an ulcer.

I should hate Alec. He's engaged. He's a liar.

He's sexy. He's sweet. He's vulnerable right now.

I beat my hand against the dashboard until the radio kicks in.

Of course it's a stupid Gold Rush Standard love song.

I beat the dashboard again until it shuts off.

My thoughts chase each other like crushes on the playground for the next thirty minutes, until I'm actually glad when Alec shows up again, even if they've all been about him.

"Sorry he was such a dick to you," Alec says, sliding into his seat. "I'd say it's a side effect of his stroke, but that's all him."

"It's fine."

"It isn't." He drags a hand over his face.

"Will he be okay?"

"It was a mini-stroke," Alec says. "That's why his speech wasn't slurred or anything—but a few minutes in I swear his face turned gray from the effort of speaking. Naturally, he was even nastier than normal for as long as he could be before falling asleep. Weakness in any form is unacceptable. He has it in his paperwork that next of kin isn't allowed to be notified unless he's dead or unresponsive. He was in there, all night, fighting. But he'd rather struggle alone than let anyone see him defenseless. That's why he was such an ass to you. Because he's depending on other people to live right now."

"I needed a reason to leave anyway."

"Hate hospitals?"

"Nah, but being in one made me feel like my barely there bank account was about to deplete completely."

His brows dip when he looks at me, asking what I mean.

"Not having health insurance costs a whole lot of money if you end up in a hospital. I broke my arm when I was eighteen. I'm still paying it off."

"That's shitty."

"Yup." I back out of the spot. The last time I was at the doctors was...when I broke my arm. Not counting Planned Parenthood for birth control a few months ago, because I swore I would find a way to lose my virginity at some point this year, not that it's gone so well... Which I am *not* going to think about with Alec sitting next to me. "Anyway. Do you want to talk about your grandfather?"

"No."

"Well, there's not much else I'd like to talk about," I say. *Because I don't want to know you any more than I already do...* "Mind driving in silence for a bit?"

"If that's what you want," he says. But a after a short stretch of quiet, he speaks again. "Piper's wearing a ring I gave her, but—"

"Nope." Seriously. Nope. Can't go down this road. I'm conflicted enough as it is. "I don't want—"

"But we aren't getting married." He cuts me off, dropping that bomb, letting its explosion eat all of the oxygen in the now quiet air, until I turn to him.

"Explain."

"I'm helping her to keep her family happy. But we have an agreement, and I can still date—privately. And if things get serious, we break off the engagement."

"That...sounds like one of Gran's soap operas," I say, waiting for his words to sink in. They have an agreement? "And it also sounds like bullshit. I need you to clarify."

He sighs, his eyes still closed. "Piper's set to inherit a lot of money, but part of the stipulation is that she marries a...guy her family approves of. She has no interest in that, but to keep her family happy—to keep that inheritance on the line—she plays the role. Hell, she created the role."

His voice gives away how tired he is. How exhausted, how defeated. The anger gripping my spine begins to loosen—but not all the way. "What do you get out of it? Sex without strings?"

"I love her." Now, he opens his eyes, waiting until I meet them. "Like a sister. No sex. We grew up together. I owe her a lot." He flexes his palms, one at a time, in his lap. "And it makes my parents happy—my grandfather, too. He's stuck in the old way of thinking that a pedigreed—which is his word, not mine—coupling is good for business."

"So they can tout you around like dogs at a show?" It comes out sharper than I intend, but *God*.

"Pretty much." His eyes are closed again. He's resigned.

"Is she hideous?" I ask. "Because looking at you—I don't know why she doesn't go for the real thing."

"She's gorgeous," he says. "But I'm not her type. And I don't feel it for her, either. We tried years ago, ended up laughing the entire thing off."

If she's gorgeous and he's gorgeous, it doesn't make sense that they wouldn't live their perfect little money-filled lives together. Though I should know better than anyone that you can't force someone to love you if they don't. Romantically or parentally... Not grandparentally, either. Ugh. Not going down that particular slip-and-slide right now. But there's no good direction for my thoughts to go, because I'm jealous that this gorgeous Piper had him for real even for a moment. Which is stupid. He's not mine to claim.

But... maybe he could be. For the summer.

If he's really not engaged. Which is the real question. Do I believe him? He's rich. He's cocky. He carries himself like a typical playboy. This feels like something I could regret later.

But...

I'm good at reading liars, and there's nothing in his expression, in his tone, in... *him*, that feels off about what he's saying.

"I wasn't sleazing on you," he says. "I wasn't cheating on her. I was trying to get to know the girl who sparked my interest from the first word I heard her speak."

"Screen door?"

This earns me a small laugh. "Yeah, but not because you were talking about banging. Something about you stood out to me. Not just the way you look—everything. Your stance. Your voice... I had to know you. And now, you're so fierce in your conviction about how wrong it is to cheat—something I actually agree with one hundred percent... I think I like you even more, if that's possible."

"Why didn't you tell me right away? You could've saved yourself a lot of yelling..."

"This is more Piper's secret than mine. I promised her to keep it, unless I got serious about someone."

"I mean, we've known each other less than a week..." I'm not delusional enough to think he's serious about me. "And most of that time, you didn't really know who I was."

"The thing is, kitten, who you are shines through regardless of what name you gave me. You've got claws and they're hooked under my skin and, for some reason, I don't want you to extract them. I want the chance to know you. I want the chance to see where this could go. So maybe this isn't serious, but it was coming down to telling you or losing you, and you see which one I picked."

He didn't want to lose me. *He picked me.* This is a total first. I'm not sure how to respond—but my body feels like it's made of air. Or cotton candy. Or something else sweet and light and totally foreign. "But I've been such a bitch."

"Yep."

"And you haven't deserved at least half of it."

"Nope."

"And you still want—"

"Everything."

CHAPTER TWENTY-TWO

"EVERYTHING?" I REPEAT Alec's word, my blood beginning to swirl, beginning to *long*. He wants everything with me. And he's not engaged. Not really, anyway.

And then that big neon sign starts flashing in my mind... *Virgin, virgin, virgin.*

He doesn't mean *that* everything. But still...it's out there. "What do you mean, everything?"

"A date, at least," he says, opening his eyes, one corner of his mouth lifting in a lazy smile. "How's Friday?"

"I have plans." The words shoot out of my mouth and I don't know why I'm pushing back.

Wait. Yes, I do know why. *Virgin, virgin, virginnnnn.*

He blinks. "Plans with your girlfriends again, or plans with someone giving me some competition?"

"Plans with..." I sigh, shaking my head. "You make me nervous and I made it up. I'm free Friday."

He laughs. "I make *you* nervous? Pretty sure you've got that mixed up."

"I mean, obviously I can demolish you with my well-sharpened bitch. I get it. But you make me nervous, too."

"I wouldn't say *demolish*."

"How would you define what I was doing this morning in your office after I found out about Piper?" Saying her name brings a sour taste to my mouth. Not toward her specifically, but maybe I'm not all the way over Alec's secret yet.

"Fair point. But you're making *my* point at the same time. You're the one who makes *me* nervous." His lazy smile evolves into something cockier. "And pretty girls very rarely make me nervous."

"Right. Because you're God's gift to women?" I stop at a red light, lifting a brow.

"Maybe." He watches my face, his eyes dancing. "I'll take you to dinner on Friday so you can find out for yourself."

"I haven't said yes yet." I'm going to, obviously. But this teasing, this back and forth, it's pushing him out of the shade of sorrow he's been cocooned in since learning about his grandfather. Now that I know the truth about Piper, all I want to do is make him smile.

"Why do I make you nervous?" he asks.

"Oh, that."

"Oh," he deadpans, "that."

"You know things about me," I say, deciding on straight honesty, realizing how freeing it is to have someone who knows my truths. "One thing in particular that makes me a little…unsettled."

"That you've never…" He clears his throat. "That you're a—"

"Yep. That one." No matter how he says it, the virgin status of my vag isn't suddenly going to get sexy. Just awkward. I mean, not that my vag isn't sexy. Just that… God, now I'm even embarrassing myself in my own thoughts. "And, you know… You had morning wood on Saturday and I got a glimpse and… I can't quite compute how all of that will fit in—" Someone behind me honks because the light's green, and the blaring horn jolts me out of my ramble. "Never mind. Forget it."

I throw my hand up to flip off the driver in my rearview. Alec laughs and grabs my hand, tugging it into his lap. "One date on a Friday night won't lead to me asking for more than you're ready to give. One million dates on one million different days won't lead to that either."

Oh God. He's being sweet. And he's rubbing the pad of his thumb over the back of my hand and I'm suddenly super close to either giggling or…I don't know…moaning. "Pretty sure I made clear what I'm ready for. I would've done it if I hadn't passed out."

"Last Friday worked out exactly how it should have," he says, rub, rub, rubbing. I'm not sure how he's able to use his thumb here on my hand to send shivers all the way up my spine. But he does. "Maybe you're ready." Stroke, stroke, stroke. "But maybe I'm not. Maybe I want to take my time. Maybe sex on Friday is off the table."

He flips my hand palm-side up, tracing spiraled circles over the inside of my wrist, making my breath come a little faster, my shivers dance a little lower. "Maybe I want to touch you, tease you…taste you first." He lifts my arm until my wrist is against his mouth and his tongue takes a turn circling my skin and somehow he's taking this conversation and spinning it into a sensual realm I've never visited before.

"Oh…" Yeah, awesome response. But come on. Like I should have to be able to think about anything while he's doing what he's doing… We're lucky I haven't crashed the car.

"And if you're worried about my size," he breaks off, a cocky little chuckle, like he's aware of how worried any girl—virgin or not—might be. Which, fine, I won't even snark about because seriously. "If it gets to that point, I'll be gentle. You, kitten, aren't the only one with a talented tongue. I'll have you ready, wanting, needing." Another dart of his tongue against my pulse point. "Begging."

"Sorry, Charlie. This girl doesn't beg." I pull my hand away, placing it carefully on my steering wheel, before I make a liar of myself. Talented tongue? Yeah. Triple check that column. "And you might want to speak with someone about those self-esteem issues…"

"I'm being honest. Isn't that our thing? Honesty? Unless your name isn't really Teagan and you've got a whole different life you're hiding from me. Because that would be impressive."

A laugh pushes itself out of my mouth, but accidentally, "Trust me. I'd give anything for a different life," slips out behind it. "I'm me, I mean."

He doesn't respond until I stop at the next red light. And he tugs my chin toward him first. "See? Complete honesty. You be you. I'll be me."

"A pessimistic bitch and a guy whose ego almost matches the size of his…"

"Thing?" he says, his eyes laughing the same way they were when Miles was driving us home on Friday night.

"I can say *dick*." Even if my face bursts into flames when I do it.

"You see yourself much differently than I do."

"The pessimistic bitch thing? Don't worry. You just met me. You'll come around. Everyone always does."

"We'll see," he says in a tone that really says he doesn't believe it.

"Guess we'll see about a few things," I say in a tone that really says hurry up and make me beg like you've promised…

"Why were you fired from the hair salon?" he asks.

"I—wait. Are you asking as my boss or as my…something more personal?"

"This will have zero impact on your job. Though your resume didn't mention that you were fired. Funny, that." He gives me a look sarcastic enough to have my lips curling up. If I tutored him only a little, he could have the whole Teagan impression down in less than a day.

"Well… Mr. Not My Boss…" I glance at him, waiting to continue until he nods, confirming that this is off the record. "I had a client who was a total piece of work. I mean, nasty. Judgmental. Bitchy. Rude—and yes, I know, I'm practically describing myself—but she was on a whole other level. Cruel—and loved it about herself."

Casey Cantrell. I can picture her clearly. Probably will be able to forever. Especially the last time I saw her. "She thought her husband flirted with me when he came in to pick her up. Didn't happen, but she told my boss all these lies. Like that I was texting him, sexting him—never mind that I didn't have his number, even when my boss took my phone to check."

"Your boss took your phone?"

"Yup."

"And fired you even when she found nothing?"

"Not exactly… That wasn't when I got fired." Here's the tricky part. "The client made me keep doing her hair. Weekly blow outs. Monthly dyes. All the while spreading rumor after rumor about me. She did it to make me squirm. But I don't squirm that easily."

"Wanna bet I can change that?"

"Do you want to flirt—or do you want my story?" Oddly, I want to tell him what happened. Another first for me.

"I already told you. I want everything."

Thrills. Up and down my belly. His words—and the sincerity behind them—make me feel light in the middle of a story that usually brings me down.

"She wanted something different the day I got fired. She wanted to go from brunette to platinum blonde. And... I... At the end of the appointment, chunks of her hair were so ruined they crumbled into mush. Burned her scalp, too."

"Jesus."

"My boss asked if I did it on purpose."

"She's an asshole." There's no pause before his words. He doesn't think for a second before assuming I didn't do it, and those thrills melt into a gooier sort of happiness.

"The thing is... I admitted to it." I watch his face carefully, testing him in the most unfair way.

But—literally, the first person ever—he passes, and says, "So, it's not just me you lie to."

I can't remember the last time I cried, and I'm sure as shit not about to start because he has this sort of faith in me.

My damn eyes need to stop stinging. Immediately.

"What makes you so sure?" I ask, staring out the windshield now, avoiding his gaze. Blinking like a fucking madwoman.

"You're a kitten," he says. "Not a scorpion. You've got the tools to hurt people—but not the drive to really fuck them up."

"Not a scorpion," I repeat. "That's the strangest compliment I've ever received. But I'm not sure you know me as well as you think you do. Plenty of people would disagree."

"Because you lie," he says. "Because you present a version of yourself to push people away."

"Whatever you say, Dr. Shrink Man." I mock him, but the truth is—he scares me.

He forces a sort of...not happiness, exactly, but something closer to excitement through my veins. He gets me and I don't know why. One part of my mind whispers *finally*. But another is screaming *run*.

"Anyway," I say, my voice flat. "Whatever. No. I didn't do it on purpose. I mixed up the instructions. Added too high a level of peroxide and kept her under the lamp for too long. I told you, reading isn't my thing. So, for the record, if you could stop shoving books down my throat, that'd be great."

Slipping into asshole-mode is like rediscovering my skin, keeping my insides from feeling so exposed.

It also makes me hate myself.

He's quiet for the rest of the ride, but when I park, before he slides out of the car he turns to me and says, "Push me away all you want. I'm still taking you out on Friday."

"Can't you get in—I don't know—*huge* trouble for sleeping with your assistant?"

He lifts his brows. "Who said anything about sleeping with you?"

"Alec, come on." I'm not sure his answer will change anything, but I'd like to know what we could be up against.

"My father owns this company," he reminds me, though it doesn't really reassure me. "And I told you. I like you. I'm not a random sleazy boss trying to get in the hot chick's pants because I have some sort of power over you. You like me, too—even," he holds up a hand when I open my mouth to contradict him, "if you won't admit it. So I'm taking you out."

I was going to protest the hot chick comment, but I'm glad he stopped me. There's a flush in my veins making me feel way too light inside to ruin it by dismissing his compliment. Still, "I still haven't said yes."

"You will."

"Really, that self-esteem. Try to think a little higher of yourself, okay? Or maybe you should try talking to a professional." I laugh and he does too, and we get out of the car like nothing's changed, but I can't help wondering if he hears the tiniest bit of longing that slipped into my voice. He seems so observant about every little thing.

But it's weird, isn't it? That a girl might fantasize about affording professional help. Like, screw fancy cars. Forget designer clothes. I'll spend my adulthood in a one-bedroom apartment, if I have to.

Someday, I will have health insurance.

Someday, *I* will be the one to speak with a shrink.

Someday, I will stop hating people for no reason. I will stop being so goddamn angry over nothing, ninety percent of the time.

Okay, ninety-five, if I'm being honest. And that's the new goal, isn't it?

CHAPTER TWENTY-THREE

"YES, BY THE way, to Friday night," I say as we walk into the building. My voice is steady, as though my heart is beating at its regular pace instead of like it's chugged a gallon of coffee. "One condition, though. I meet you out. You aren't picking me up." Not in a million years is he laying eyes on my grandparents' place.

"No," he says. "I'm driving, like a real date. You don't need a car to make an escape. If you want to go home at any point, I'll take you."

Oh, God. He doesn't get it. It's almost laughable.

But maybe I can let him grab me at Cassidy's house. "Fine."

"Good," he says. "I like when you let me have my way."

"Don't count on it becoming a thing."

"I've been very clear about my...thing." He says it with a straight face and a low tone, and I explode into a firework and burn down the building around us.

Now how am I supposed to make it until Friday? How am I supposed to stay professional around my very sexy, very commanding boss?

How the hell am I supposed to stop thinking about his *thing*? Or the way he might use it to make me beg? Or his tongue? Or... God. I have to get a fucking grip.

It's just that he doesn't make it easy.

On Wednesday, I find a wrapped gift on my chair, hidden under my desk. And when Sam gets up to grab coffee, I tear into it, finding a fancy set of headphones attached to two cards: one in an envelope, the other face up with instructions written on it.

Download an app called AudioVectorEase on my phone. Enter the code listed on the instructions. Then read the second card. I do it all—a bit hesitantly, though I'm not sure why.

The second card reads: *I know books aren't your thing. But I think audiobooks could be. The code you entered pre-downloaded one of my all-time favorites. Figured you might enjoy it, given your love of vampires and violence. And trust me, you won't need a movie to enjoy this one. Alec.*

At first, I'm confused.

At first, I think, books? Reading on my phone will suck even more than reading across a page. He doesn't get me like I thought he did.

But a second or two later, I put it together. Not reading. Listening. *Audio.* Plus headphones.

Interesting...

And sweet.

Then stupid Sam returns with coffee and even though he has one for me, I hate him a little. I want to listen right away, but I want to do it in private. So I'm stuck in a workday with hours and hours to go until I can use Alec's gift.

Alec, who smiles when he sees me and asks if I *liked my assignment*, like he's trying to speak code in front of Sam—though Sam's expression says he knows there's something else going on.

"We'll see," I say, noncommittally. His smile turns smug, like he's so sure I'll love it. Which kind of makes me not want to—which is totally fucked up. "How's your grandfather?"

"Released last night," he says. "Home. Dr. Greenwald's staying with him for a few days."

A live-in doctor. It must be so weird and so amazing and so... I can't even come up with the right word, to have that much money.

It turns out, I do love Alec's gift. Listening to a book—all I have to do is close my eyes and soak it up. No actual reading. And the one he chose for me is perfect. *The Passage.* Post-apocalyptic vampires created in a government experiment gone wrong? Game freaking on. I'm up all night listening to it—to the point that I have to stop at a drugstore on my way to work, to find something to cover the bags under my eyes that are threatening to eat my cheeks.

I'm sluggish and dreading seeing Alec because I'm also all crumpled and not put together. I have half a mind to tell him it's all his fault, but he'd probably get a kick out of keeping me up all night. He's not in today, though. His grandfather is back in the hospital.

"He left a message this morning," Sam says. "And requested you set up your voice mail. Guess he tried to call you first?" His voice rises on the last word, like he's fishing, like he's hoping I'll tell him what's going on.

I'm tempted to, too. But my secret infringes on Alec's secret, which isn't mine to share. Instead, I nod. "Can you show me how?"

I email Alec with my cell phone number when Sam's done. It's on my resume, but I guess he didn't look there. Makes sense since he's not the one who hired me. It's weird we've never texted or spoken on our phones before—but it's also not, because we've known each other a whopping six days. It feels like a hell of a lot longer than that though.

Which makes me wonder if my mother's genes are starting to surface.

Am I letting myself get swept up the exact way I've always sworn I wouldn't? With a rich guy and a pretty face?

My heart tells me this is nothing like that. I do enjoy his pretty face, but I don't care about his money. Hell, had I known how wealthy he was when I met him, I'd never have bothered speaking to him. It's more of a deterrent than a turn-on. But my mind's too used to seeing the darker side of...well, pretty much everything, and I've all but convinced myself to cancel when he texts me.

Kitten, Looking forward to tomorrow. Wear something sexy to work. To our date, too.

How's your grandfather?

A cranky old man. Still kicking.

I'm glad.

I miss your face. Send me a picture.

I snap a shot of my desk.

Not what I meant.

    I let the conversation taper off here, because his flirting makes me smile—and, annoyingly, that makes something inside of me go sour.
    I'm not my mom. I know I'm not. And I'm not backing out. Alec has substance to go with his pretty face and sky-high bank account. I'm not even interested in the latter, anyway. *Wouldn't it be nice, though*, a little nagging voice—my mother's voice, again, what the fuck?—whispers in my mind, *to let him take care of you. Pay away all your worries. Buy you fancy things and—*
    "Earth to Teagan." Sam interrupts my brain spew.
    "What?" I snap even though I'm grateful for the interruption and immediately draw in a deep breath to chill out.
    "I asked if you could cover for me if I leave thirty minutes early."
    "Hot date?"
    "*Maybe.*"
    Taking on Sam's responsibilities might help me pass the time a little faster—until I get to go on my own hot date. "What do I need to do?"
    He spends the next while showing me how to work Alec's calendar in case anyone calls regarding meetings. Then, I spend the rest of the day trying really, really hard not to snoop through it. Even when I find a few times blocked out with Piper's name across them.
    She's not his real fiancée.
    I repeat the line so many times to myself it stops holding much meaning.
    But God, I wonder what they do when they're together.

Shit. Between his fake engagement, and my goddamn mother in my mind, this is pretty much doomed from the start. Even if it's only a summer fling—there's no way for it to end well.

I miss your face, he said. I stare at the text until my eyes blur.

Stupid. Every thought I've had today is stupid. I need to relax a little.

Ha.

Ha ha.

Because that's so freaking easy.

Sometimes it's like I'm only a projection of myself. Like the real me actually lives inside my brain, rattling around in there, pounding to get out. Some different, more positive version of myself. She's in there somewhere. *I'm* in there somewhere. But my brain's got a tight-twisted deadbolt and I don't have a fucking key to get out of it.

On Friday, I don't dress sexy.

First of all, I mentally prepare to tell Alec, *it's not appropriate.* He might be leaving at the end of the summer, but I want to keep working here. I don't want to get a reputation based on how I dress. Which is a bullshit thing to be judged on, but if my grandparents are any indication, that's how the current world works.

And, second of all... I can't help it, something in me rebels at the thought of following orders, even of a sexy variety.

I do, though, wear a black lacy bra and undies set under my blouse and skirt, which I have every intention of hinting at to Alec, to wet his tongue.

I forget all about it when I open my inbox and discover an email from HR telling me there's been a mix-up and that I'm eligible for company-sponsored health insurance.

And I clap so fucking loud a handful of people turn to stare. And then I drop dead right in my seat.

Because *health insurance.*

CHAPTER TWENTY-FOUR

"ARE YOU ALIVE?" Sam asks a few minutes later, when I'm still sitting frozen, my head tilted against the back of the chair, my eyes closed. Who knew so much relief would be like sugared air in my veins?

I take my time and then I smile so wide it's his turn to look shocked. "I'm fucking great."

"O-*kay*." He stretches the word out, and it makes me laugh.

"How was your hot date?"

He grimaces and I'm about to ask what's wrong, but Alec turns the corner into the room and the world goes a little off-kilter. God, he's fucking hot.

"He looks like a magazine ad," Sam says, pretty much reading my thoughts.

"Yup."

But by the time he's closer to us, both Sam and I are busy working at our computers like we haven't even noticed him.

"Sam," he says, his tone amused, obviously not buying our act. "Ms. Walker."

"Boss," I say, acting like it's hard to drag my eyes from my computer screen to him.

"A word?" He walks into his office without waiting for my answer.

I stay at my desk, smiling, smug with the upper hand.

"Um, are you going in there?" Sam asks.

"Eventually." I lean back in my chair, a relaxed pose even if my blood is beginning to surge beneath my skin.

My phone rings. I pick it up and hear Alec's cool voice. "Keep me waiting and you'll see what happens when I make *you* wait. And, kitten, I'm going to love to make you beg."

I slam the phone down.

Because, really, what the hell am I supposed to do with that?

Besides melt into the floor.

Or race in there and fucking jump him.

I swallow and hear the saliva travel down my throat like there are no other sounds in the world. I stand, my face flaming, my skin tingling.

Sam's wearing the superior expression I've just discarded. "Get in trouble?"

"No." And I freaking giggle.

"I *am* going to get this story out of you, you know."

"There's no story." But, because I can't keep the corners of my mouth under control, I turn and step into Alec's office. Not like that helps with facial control, but at least Alec's allowed to know why I'm smiling.

"Close the door." He's sitting at his desk, a smug expression across his face. "Playing games this morning?"

"You're my boss. You're bigger than me. Sexier. I've got to take the upper hand when I can get it."

"I am your boss," he agrees. "And I am bigger than you. But sexier? That's where you're wrong. Let's have a word about what you're wearing."

"I know I didn't dress in anything sexy, but I—"

"Have you seen yourself?" He cocks a brow, his eyes traveling my body, a slow smile parting his lips. "You're sexy as fuck, Teagan. I have half a mind to pull you over this desk right now."

"Then you should see what I'm wearing underneath this..." I aim for a sultry purse to my lips, but my face is so hot, it's definitely red, which messes up the rest of my expression.

He doesn't seem to mind, though, running a hand over his hair, his eyes flashing down my body. "Who needs coffee when you're around?"

"Speaking of, should I get you one?"

"Not until you tell me what you've got on under there."

"Black lace," I say. "And not a lot of it."

As far as exit lines go, it's pretty fucking awesome. And when I bring him his coffee, it doesn't bother me nearly as much as I think it will. I don't feel subservient. I feel powerful. Especially when he says, "I'd stand to take that from you, but I'm hard as fucking steel right now."

"Hmm," I offer, smug all over again. "Maybe I'll be the one making you beg tonight..."

Another awesome exit line, and before his office door closes behind me, his laughter fills the air.

I call HR to figure out the whole insurance thing, fill out some paperwork over lunch, and before the day's over, I've made a doctor's appointment, after choosing a primary care physician who's *in my network*. The knowledge that I have a network keeps a grin on my face almost the entire day. I make a dentist appointment, too. Granted, my teeth are in good shape because I'm fucking religious about taking care of them—kind of have to be when you don't have access to a dentist for years on end. But I make the appointment.

Because I can.

Alec emails me, even though he's sitting ten feet behind me. *I'm heading out in a few. I'll grab your address from your file and pick you up at seven. Hope you don't have a curfew.*

I respond with, *Ew, don't grab my address from my file. That's so creepy. Stay away from my file, stalker. Also, don't fire me for saying that. Pick me up here*, with Cassidy's address. Then I add—and hit send before I can chicken out—*I only have a curfew if you give me one. For your place.*

Fire you? Not likely. Name a different F-word and my answer might change. Related: will you still be wearing that black lace?

If you're very, very good. Though, on second thought... I'll pick up a new set after work, because I want fresh...everything for tonight.

By the way, I'm only flirting. There will be no F-wording going on this evening, in case you were feeling pressure. Or getting excited. Told you I'm making you wait. (I'll wait as long as you need.)

I'm about to respond when he sends another message. *But don't let any of that fool you into thinking I haven't fantasized about what it'd be like basically every second since I met you. Even when you were Cindy. Especially after.*

And again I don't get a chance to write back because it takes me too long to read his email, and a few minutes later he's breezing between Sam's desk and mine. He turns pointedly toward Sam. "Did you hear from Denise about Monday's schedule change?"

Sam shakes his head. "But I can call your cell phone if I hear from her before I leave."

Alec tells him not to worry about it and slowly turns toward me. "Have a nice weekend."

"See you Monday, boss." But I'm smirking as I say it. And then biting back a giggle when he gives me an *oh, really?* look before walking away.

Nothing can kill my mood. Not a thing. Even when I have to spend the last two hours of my workday filing things in our floor's supply room. Long rows of drawers that pull out into longer rows of dividers—which is my personal hell. It's impossible for me to easily read the labels and everything blurs together and I lose my place nine times out of ten. A lesser girl might break down in tears.

But that girl probably doesn't have health insurance. And she also probably isn't a few more hours away from a date with the sexiest guy she's ever known.

So yeah. *This* girl can keep her shit together.

This girl even smiles while she does it.

Cassidy's eyes widen when she answers her door, and she catcalls me loud enough for her far-off neighbors to hear. "Your makeup—wow. You look *hot.*"

"Shut it." I shove past her, but I'm still too high from the rest of my day to be embarrassed. Still too high to let the pictures of Jason surrounding me suffocate me. If I don't look at them, they won't have the chance.

"What's in the bag?" Cassidy asks, and I instinctively crush it to my chest, the plastic crinkling all loud and obvious.

"Nothing."

"It's totally lingerie." She knows me. I've talked about sexy sets before. A lot.

But I was never being honest, and now that I'm actually going for it, I don't want to talk about it.

"Don't you want to wash it first?"

"I don't have time. Can we please drop it? And can you please give me something to wear?"

She motions for me to follow her up the winding staircase leading out of her foyer. "We've got to find something hot enough to match your hair and face."

"Thanks." I blew out my hair, really took my time with it. Now it hangs sleek and straighter than I've worn it in a long time. Put extra effort into my makeup too. Only took me four tries to master the cat eye. Gran told me I look like a whore on my way out, but it didn't cut me as deeply as it could have. I feel pretty. I feel *good*. Which, being here in this house, is saying something. But I'm not letting my thoughts travel that direction. "I was thinking that black top you have, with all the beading on the shoulders."

She shakes her head, not turning around when she responds. "I have a green dress that's going to be fucking killer on you. That's what you're wearing."

I have my doubts about wearing a Cassidy dress. She has bigger boobs; I have a bigger belly. Sometimes shirts work because of the differences in space, but a dress? I can't picture it.

And then she makes me try it on and I can. In a mirror.

Her green dress is perfect. Somehow it isn't too big in the boobs. Somehow it makes my belly look flatter. Somehow I can still breathe in it.

"Yeah. That thing's not going to be staying on you for long," Cassidy says, circling me. "It hits you in all the right spots."

This should make me happy. It really does hit me in the right places. But the thought of the dress coming off—and what it means—makes my nerves ripple uncomfortably under my skin...

Then I remember Alec took sex off the table for tonight, and my nerves relax. A little, at least.

"He's a good guy," I say without really meaning to, my voice way, way too breathless for my liking.

"Oh," Cassidy says, pausing in front of me. "*Oh*. You *like him* like him."

"He's okay," I mumble. Cassidy's my best friend, but—because of it, because of how closely she can look right into me—it's like pushing a boulder uphill to get myself to open up to her. Or, if I'm honest with myself, it's like holding up the immeasurable weight of a secret weekend spent with her brother before he died. He blocks everything else that would maybe come out easier otherwise.

"Remember senior year?" she asks, tucking a strand of hair behind my ear. "I gave it up to Jackson Winters and he dumped me right after—two weeks before homecoming?"

Ugh. That prick. He convinced Cassidy to lose her virginity before the dance so they wouldn't be a cliche, doing it after, but he dropped her literally the next day. He'd been planning to take Cassie LeClaire the whole time anyway. I study Cassidy. "You think Alec's looking for a pump and dump? Because I promise you, he isn't."

"No." She shakes her head emphatically. "I think you're too smart to fall for someone's bullshit the way I did. But remember how you keyed the shit out of the side of Jackson's shiny cherry red Camaro before the dance—and forced me to come back with you afterward, to watch his expression when he discovered it? And he *cried*? And stood up Cassie because of it. And the entire thing was fucking awesome?"

"Yep." The memory makes me smile almost as widely as the actual moment did. It felt good, destroying his car after he'd destroyed my best friend. I swore that day—though it wasn't the first time—I'd never let some asshole dupe me.

"What I'm trying to say is that *if* this Alec hurts you, Teagan, I'll find whatever he treasures as much as Jackson did that stupid Camaro, and I'll destroy it."

I study her harder now, looking deeper in those wide green eyes. "What's with this sudden protectiveness?"

A pale pink sweeps across her cheeks. "You like him. He's not some fuck and fling-away like the others. I want someone good in your life—and if you're finally taking a chance to let him into more than your bed, I want him to be worthy of you."

"I have someone good in my life," I mumble, irritated that she's making me feel more touchy feely than I'd like. Irritated that she's reminding me of all the lies I've fed her—and everyone else. "You. And Vera."

"True." She squeezes me for about two seconds, which is as long as I last in her embrace before stepping away. "You know what I mean, Teag. Your skin is flushed, your eyes are sparkling... It's about fucking time you let a guy in."

"You are exaggerating," I say, ignoring my reflection when she spins me toward her mirror again. "You're trying to make me feel mushy and all that does is piss me off."

She sighs. "I know. But you've got this happiness in your face—I've never seen it there over a guy before."

It's been there, of course.

I need to tell her about her brother.

God. Jason.

The boy I once thought I could love.

The boy I once thought could love me.

The boy who fucking overdosed before I could truly find out.

God. *Jason.*

I open my mouth.

To say what? I once looked at your brother like that? But he swore me to secrecy? And then he died and maybe I should've seen it coming? Sorry? And sorry I've been keeping this from you for almost two years?

Cassidy's head is tilted to the side while she waits for me to speak. I shut my mouth.

I glance out her window, and Miles's town car is pulling into her driveway. "Fuck. He's here."

Cassidy grabs my arm. "Make him wait a minute."

"I'm not making him wait," I say, pulling her with me out into the hall. "I'm not playing games."

"You always play games," she says. Because I've always claimed to. The guilt from lying is heaviest in front of those misled, and I'm about to drown in mine.

"Not this time."

"Not this time what?" Mr. Evans is heading toward the stairs at the same time we are. Fuck. "You look nice, Teagan. Where you headed, honey?"

"Nothing," I say, my face heating. "I mean, nowhere. I'm—"

"She's got a hot date with Mr. Chamber's son," Cassidy teases and I want to punch her.

"Alec?" Mr. Evans blinks. "Isn't he..." *Engaged?* He doesn't have to say the word for it to ring loudly between us. He trails off, making his own assumptions. So this is fucking great. What do I say here? I can't tell him Alec's not really getting married; it's not my secret to share—but I look like a total whore, going out with an engaged dude. *Way to live up to Gran's expectations, Teagan...*

"Mr. Evans, it's not what you think, and I'm begging you not to say anything." How did I not think this through? Embarrassment and regret make good partners in the synchronized swan dive they take down to the pit of my stomach.

"Just be careful, sweetie," he says, his tone deep with warning. "The Chambers family is formidable. And Philip can be a bit of a bear when it comes to his business—which, in his mind, extends to his family."

"I'll be careful," I say. "Thank you."

"I had half a mind to see Cassidy with Alec, once upon a time," he says, his eyes shifting playfully toward his daughter. "Until she met Gangrene, or whatever his name is."

"Dad." But Cassidy smiles through the word, which shows some major progress, if they're joking together. They've had a rough relationship since Jason died.

"Anyway it's not a big deal, we're going to go over some work stuff," I ramble. "Don't make more of this than..." Than what? The thing I'm so clearly trying to pretend isn't happening? Mr. Evans isn't an idiot. "Work stuff, I mean."

"Right," Mr. Evans says, doubt clear across his expression. "He does have some interesting ideas..."

"About small business and tech startups?" I ask, the inkling of an idea blossoming at the back of my mind.

He nods, still frowning. "I've been trying to convince Philip to expand our focus for years now, and the directions Alec came up with are perfect."

"You should team up," I say. "With the two of you pushing for it, Mr. Chambers would *have* to listen, right?"

"Maybe," he muses. "But I'm not sure Alec's the kind of guy I want to get into business with." He gives me a pointed glance.

"Don't misread this," I plead. "He's—"

"Oh, please," Cassidy says, rolling her eyes. "Dad, stop being so overprotective of Teagan. She's a big girl. She can date whoever she wants. And Teagan. Come on. You're not borrowing my dress to discuss work things."

I glare at her. She's not helping. At all.

Probably my own fault for not telling her everything. But I'm so used to lying about this part of my life, I'm not sure how to be honest.

"Don't write him off," I say to Mr. Evans. "Anyway, bye. I'll dry-clean your dress, Cassidy. Thanks."

Cassidy laughs as I flee down the stairs. Her dad stays silent.

Jason's portraits watch me from the wall. And while looking at them doesn't make my stomach hurt the way they used to, I still miss him. And I hate that I'm rushing out of here while his father's judging me for something I can't refute.

Apparently regret and embarrassment were the opening act. Currently on deck, heavy on the board, is self-loathing. What am I doing? I'm an idiot. This will never work. Maybe Alec was lying about Piper. Maybe he's a total player and I'm falling for his bullshit, proving for the millionth time in my life that I'm dumb as a blank piece of paper.

Maybe I'm *exactly* like my mother.

Then I'm outside, and instead of Miles waiting by the car to open my door like I assume he'll be, Alec is striding toward the house. Toward me.

Crisp button-down. Crisp denim. Slicked-back hair and dark, dark eyes penetrating my armor of sadness like an arrow.

Everything else disintegrates into dust in the background.

I smile.

I *breathe*.

I meet him halfway.

CHAPTER TWENTY-FIVE

ALEC SLIDES A hand around my neck, holding me like his palm was created to fit just so. "You look... Wow."

I slide my gaze up to his face, my mouth suddenly wetter than before. "You smell like your soap."

He laughs.

"Or...something that comes off as a nicer compliment," I amend, because obviously he doesn't know what that scent does to me. He doesn't know my knees are turning to liquid and I might slide right into the ground if he lets go. "You look hot."

He doesn't know all I want to do is toss myself at him, wrap my rubbery legs around his waist, lick his mouth...

Oh, God. I'm in so much trouble.

"Thank you," he says, flashing his dimples. He slowly, slowly brings his face toward me, his eyes locked on mine, and says, gruffly, "I want a quick taste before we go."

He kisses the corner of my mouth, his lips lingering against my skin. One second. Two.

I try to remind myself that Cassidy—or worse, her father—could be watching right now. But... I close my eyes, inhaling. That soap scent hits me even deeper and something silky slides through my veins. I turn my face a fraction of an inch, until our mouths are flush, and I trace my tongue along the inner curve of his upper lip.

"Careful," he says, against my mouth. "I only wanted a hint of sugar before dinner, but you keep this up, we won't be eating tonight... Not food, anyway. I can think of something else I'd like to eat." His hand slides down my back, curving around my hip, and the heat of his palm sinks through the fabric of my dress and oh God my knees literally do slip an inch.

I catch myself against his chest, pushing away from him like I meant to do it, grinning, the whispered weight of his lips still echoing across mine. "Whatever. Told you I'd make you beg."

"You think this is me begging?" he asks, holding my chin, sliding his thumb across my lips.

I bite the tip of his finger before I answer, tugging at his skin with my teeth. Hard enough to make him wince a little. "I *think* you said you were driving, like a real date. But it's Miles behind the wheel..."

"I realized we might want to drink." He walks me to the car, opening the door for me.

"How responsible of you." I slide in, greeting Miles, who winks at me in the rearview mirror.

"Though maybe," Alec says, dropping down beside me, "we won't drink quite as much as we did last time."

And I doubt he means to do it, but I'm instantly reminded that I'm the moron who passed out after sharing too many secrets last time, and my mood starts to fall. "Yeah. Maybe I'll stick to water."

My hand is pressed flat against the seat and he runs his fingers over it. "Have I told you how sexy you are?"

"According to my grandmother, I look like a whore, so I guess that puts me somewhere in the middle of your opinions."

"Your grandmother's an idiot," he says without skipping a beat. "I have excellent taste. If I tell you you're hot, you're fucking hot. Understand?"

I stare out my window, watching Cassidy's posh neighborhood slide by, willing my brain to kick out Gran's words, to push away the embarrassment of my past mistakes. He grabs my chin, a little roughly this time, and pulls my face toward him. "Understand?"

And the way he's looking at me, the way his gaze drops to my mouth, the way he wets his own lips, I do understand. I nod and his grip turns to more of a caress.

"So, um, where are we going?" I need him to back away from me. Just a smidgen. Or I might eat him for dinner.

He leans back against his seat, watching me. "Clearwater Heights. I reserved a corner table."

"Cool." I scratch my neck, all casual, like it's not the nicest restaurant in southern Virginia and I've literally never known anyone who's been there—even Cassidy. Then...fuck it. I turn to him, letting my excitement show. "Why a corner table?"

"We'll have the river on one side and mountains in the background on the other," he says. It makes sense. The restaurant sits at the top of a towering business building and is all glass so patrons can look out over the water, or valley, for miles. Or, so I'd assume. And so I'll find out. *Holy shit.*

"Pulling out all the stops," I tease, cocking a brow—and then pausing to consider. "Unless this is a regular night for you."

He laughs. "No. I've only been there twice."

"Oh?"

"And never on a date."

I shouldn't be this pleased. I know better than anyone that it never lasts.

But damn, I *am* pleased. Too much to bother attempting to smother it.

And I'm even more pleased when we're seated in the restaurant and it's exactly as he promised. On one side of us, the river swirls below, and on the other, the mountains rise in the distance.

It's dizzying. It's... "Breathtaking."

"Yes," he agrees, but when I glance at him, he's studying me instead of the view. "You are."

I don't know how to respond, so I turn my face toward the river, watching gentle ripples dimpling the surface. And the sunset. The sky above the mountains darkens from a golden yellow into a bruised purple, stretching over the rolling peaks, and for the briefest of moments I wish I were better with words. Writing, reading. Anything to let me capture this feeling.

The waiter comes, and, after asking permission, Alec orders us a bottle of wine. I don't usually drink it, but there's no way I can't have it tonight. It's red and dry and...the least horrible wine I've ever had. Alec swears it will be delicious with steaks. When our orders are taken, he draws the waiter toward him and says something quietly in his ear.

"What was that all about?" I ask. "You're not having them sing happy birthday to me, right? Because I seriously doubt they do that here." I gesture subtly to the rest of the restaurant. Shimmering accents—on the restaurant decor and most of the women in it. Glistening crystal glasses, and twinkling lights and wedding rings, or earrings, or both.

"No," Alec says. "Wait."

A few seconds later our waiter returns, handing Alec a small bowl that I can't quite see into. Alec tips it forward, though—and I discover it's filled with cherries. I bite my lip to keep from cracking up.

The restaurant's darker now; they upped the ambient lighting as the sun set, and there's a whisper of something classical drifting out of hidden speakers.

And we're practicing tying cherry stems in knots with our tongues, trying not to die laughing.

"This is so not sexy," I say, snorting.

He shakes his head. "You should see your jaw—back and forth and back and forth. It's a lovely jaw, but it's moving as though you're chewing cud."

"Um, did you call me a cow?" I ask, feigning offense.

He backtracks so fast. "No, I meant—"

"Because that's sharp coming from someone who's impersonating a camel about to spit." I giggle, giving up the act, and humored relief relaxes his features.

When my filet arrives, it's almost tender enough to cut with my fork and no knife, and it practically melts like butter on my tongue. "You were right," I say, after swallowing and sipping. "The wine is awesome."

"I'm usually right," he says, sipping his own wine.

I roll my eyes. "Whatever you say, Mr. I Like Spinster Malady."

"Rich, coming from Ms. I Like Demi Jade." He takes another bite. He might've looked funny trying to tie a stem earlier, but the way he chews for real is somehow incredibly sexy. "Let's meet in the middle. Do you like Villain Complex?"

"Who?" I ask, though the name sounds familiar.

"Rock band, kind of alternative, a little indie." He waits for recognition to sink in, and it's hovering right there on the edge, but not quite making it. "They were on *The Sound*."

Oh. Right. Now I remember the name—and why I don't follow the band. "I don't watch reality TV."

"Because of your mom?" He asks the question quietly, but its impact is almost deafening nonetheless.

"What did you say?"

He doesn't drop his eyes, just dabs the corner of his mouth with his napkin. "I looked her up when I learned your real name."

"That's... I mean, that's..." I sputter, unable to force my emotions to words.

"I'm sorry if I crossed a line," he says.

"A line? You crossed an entire ocean." I want to stab him with my fork. Not really, but I can't believe he went behind my back the way he did. "That's my information to share—or to keep."

"When you left that morning, I was desperate to find you. Called the bar, offered to pay for your last name off of a credit card receipt. I went back that evening in case you were there—which I knew you wouldn't be because you hate pool—but you told me all these things about yourself and then left before I could tell you how much I wanted to see you again."

"That doesn't mean—"

"Seeing you again Monday morning was...indescribable. And the second I had the truth of your name, I was crazy for more grounding information on you, things to keep you *real* this time. So I did some digging and I looked her up." He shakes his head. "That logic is ridiculous. Hell, it's not even logic. But you made an impact on me. And I thought I lost my chance to know you."

The sweet sound of a violin plays through the silence between us while he waits for me to respond, and the music tangles around me, tugging at a bitter nostalgia I thought I'd buried.

Part of me feels so betrayed that I'm tempted to walk out of the restaurant, away from him. But... I also understand why he did it. Hell, even if he didn't want to know me, there's still a curiosity that comes with learning someone's mother is quasi-famous.

The problem is, it's embarrassing. The things my mother's known for are...gross.

"*Social Climbing* is only the show she's on right now," I say. "Before that there were others. Three of them. All about rising from nothing and digging for gold."

His eyes never leave my face. "I gathered as much."

"When she's interviewed, she says she doesn't have any family. That she's all alone in the world." I swish the wine in my glass, watching the burgundy liquid roll in circles. It matches the direction of my stomach.

"I'm sorry." He's watching me, concerned. I don't even have to lift my eyes to him to hear his expression in his voice.

"Don't be. I'm not." Anymore, at least. "The first show's producers did a little digging and discovered the existence of my grandparents and came snooping—where they also discovered me. And, in turn, *I* discovered who my mother was. I was sixteen." I take a sip of wine. "My grandparents threatened to sue the pants off the network if they exposed a minor, and so the show let her lies pass as truth." I take another sip. Then I gulp down the rest of my glass. "See? She's a liar. Like me. And she clings to people with money to get ahead. Aren't you worried I'll follow in those shoes as well?" I hate the acerbic edge to my tone, but something in me is cracking. What if I'm right? What if there's a part of me that's attracted to his wealth even if I'm not aware of it?

"You won't follow in her shoes." He says it so simply.

Yeah, because so far she hasn't managed to nab a rich guy, and it seems like I'm actually getting close.

Oh my God.

What the fuck is wrong with me?

"I might already be following." My words are shaky.

"You're nothing like her."

Two minutes ago, I might've agreed with him. Now? Now my thoughts are traitors and I hate myself. "You don't know that."

"My father's had at least four affairs, two of them long-term. My mother doesn't care." He drinks the rest of his wine, too. "And I can tell you here and now I'm not like either of them."

"I'm sorry." I'm always envious of people whose parents love them, but I also always forget that they have Big Things that suck in their lives, too.

"Do you think I'll have four affairs? Do you think I'll sit by idly if my wife cheats someday?"

"You don't strike me as either type."

"And you don't like me because of my money."

In the back of my mind, my mother laughs. *Hook him, sweetie,* she whispers to me. I shudder.

"Here's where you tell me I shouldn't be so sure that you like me." He flashes a grin and I try to follow suit, barely managing.

"Life is fucking unfair," I say, instead.

"And..." Something makes him hesitate and he takes another bite of steak before he continues. "What about your father?"

I study the cream-colored napkin in my lap for a moment, working to drown out the hint of self-pity that threatens to rise. "Don't know him either."

"Did you ever want to?"

"He didn't want to meet me. Laughed when my mother told him she was knocked up—and then disappeared exactly nine months before my mom did. Not a thing on Earth could make me search for that kind of man. I'd rather have no father than *that.*"

He waits, like he thinks I have more to say. Like he realizes it before I do, and suddenly the words come. "There's a part of me that doesn't believe what my grandparents told me. Maybe they lied, either out of spite, or because they didn't want to think about the guy my mom used to propel a disaster—aka me—into their lives. I thought about looking for him for a long time. But I'd rather live with the hope that they're liars and he's not a monster, than find out the truth. That they were honest."

"You'd rather be afraid of the unknown than live with the possible depression of reality," he says. "I get it."

And I think he actually does. "Anyway. Enough about me and my awesome home life. Tell me something about you."

His smile this time is slow to grow, but full enough to meet his eyes. It's on the verge of pissing me off. "What?"

"You're very strong," he says. "Stronger than anyone I've ever met."

"I can't even do a push-up," I say, purposefully misunderstanding him. Then, I sigh. "Thank you, but I don't want your pity. I don't want anyone's pity. That's why I don't talk about this shit."

I also don't want to get mad, but I'm still right on the cusp. I don't like feeling sorry for myself. I don't like anyone else feeling sorry for me. I stab a piece of meat, chewing it into nothingness.

"I don't pity you," Alec says. "I admire you."

It's the first time in my life anyone's ever said that to me—and, even more, he seems to mean it. My throat suddenly feels swollen and my eyes are prickling. I can barely swallow my next bite.

There are too many emotions; there isn't enough *me* to take them all in. I pour myself some more wine, taking a healthy swallow before answering. "And I admire...your ass."

I top off his glass of wine, too, and he takes it, swirling the liquid for a moment. "You don't have to do that with me, you know. Deflect."

"I also don't *have* to be thinking about how much I can't wait to get back to your place," I say. "But here I am, doing that very thing." It's the truth, now that I've said it. Enough talking. I'm ready for some action.

Annoyingly, Alec takes a bite of asparagus. "Tell me about meeting Norris Marshal."

I take a second to transition my line of thinking. "I met him last summer when Cassidy worked at Backbar Amphitheater and Gold Rush Standard came through on tour."

I pause, memories flooding my mind. Cassidy's summer was bananas. Mine was more like a circle. An endless loop of trying not to seem sadder than I should about Jason, and keeping the nasty black hole of anger in check (which rarely worked), and picking up as much overtime as I was able at the salon. But somehow, at the center of that circle, I found Norris Marshal. The one spot that shined brighter for me than anything else, regardless of how short my time of knowing him lasted.

"Norris is this...person-shaped being filled with endless amounts of sunshine." I blush, but it's impossible not to feel a little bubbly thinking about Norris. "That's stupid, I know. But I'm not sure how else to describe him. His wife, too. Like, somehow with one look he got to the center of who I am and wanted to break me free."

"Impossible," Alec says. "You're a maze, filled with twists and turns and *no entrance* signs begging to be cut down." He drinks some wine, his eyes never leaving my face. "And I hope you know I'm up for the task."

Don't blush.

Do not blush.

"It's easier for me to talk to people who don't really know me," I say, immediately regretting the words, certain he's finally going to look at me with pity. Like, *poor broken girl who doesn't have anyone close enough to really talk to. Has to resort to strangers...*

Instead he says, "Makes sense. It's easier to unload on people who can't turn around and hurt you with what they know. And it helps that you already held him in high regard."

"He told me the world was at my fingertips, if I'd reach out to take it," I say, swallowing the rest of my wine. "And that's what I want to do. With you." I reach toward him until his hand meets mine. "Take me home."

He clears his throat. "Are you sure?"

"I want to go to your place, Alec. Take me there."

CHAPTER TWENTY-SIX

ALEC PAYS THE bill, and I don't argue this time. It's probably higher than what I've got in my bank account—the menu didn't even have prices attached to the entrees. I try not to think about it as we take the elevator down and slip into the town car.

Alec tells Miles to play Villain Complex, and as the first strands of music unfurl in the air, I recognize them. I *do* know some of their songs—and like them. Yet another thing I have in common with Alec. Which is weird, considering how different our lives have been.

Before we take off, Miles sets up a tray for us with chocolate-dipped strawberries and glasses of chilled champagne. Alec thanks him, and I try to, too—but all I manage is a nod. I'm starting to get overwhelmed, and the echoes of my mother's laugh are still ringing in the distance.

Alec nudges me with his knee. "We can scrap all this and go get McDonald's sundaes if you'd rather."

His silly offer makes the entire situation easier. I sink my teeth into a strawberry, closing my eyes and moaning when the rich swirl of chocolate and berry plays against my tongue. "This is perfect."

"Almost," he says, and when I look at him, he runs his thumb over my lower lip. "You have a little chocolate right here."

"Did you get it?" I ask, pretty sure there wasn't any chocolate to begin with.

"Not quite..." He moves the tray and leans toward me, pressing his mouth gently against mine, murmuring, "God, you're sweet."

I part my mouth to give him a real taste, and he takes it, his tongue skimming the inside of my lips, teasing the roof of my mouth. I sigh into him, melting against him the best I can with a seat belt across my lap. I break away first, when the car stops at a light. "Let's—"

He pulls me back to him, swallowing whatever else I was going to say. Can't even remember now. Not with the way his mouth is taking control of mine. Not with the way his fingers are tangled in my hair, tugging with that perfect sort of pressure. Not hard enough to jerk my neck back, but firm enough to make my scalp tingle, the sensations shooting down my neck, across my chest, deep into my belly.

Fuck the seat belt.

I unbuckle it, clumsy in my haste, and climb into Alec's lap, my knees at his hips. My dress so high on my thighs it may as well not be there. He slides his palms against my bare skin, his finger grazing under the hem, his tongue forceful in my mouth.

I kiss him harder, taking all he'll give. His mouth is sweet like strawberries, and it makes me giddy that he scooped the flavor out of my own mouth. His palms inch higher, his thumbs pressing into my inner thighs.

Higher.

Higher.

Higher, until they're tracing the lines of my panties between my legs.

"Lace as you promised," he murmurs, dipping one thumb below the fabric.

"Mm hmm." It's the best I can manage because he's tracing places with the pad of his finger that have me unable to do anything other than moan while the most delicious sensation flows along his path.

Miles clears his throat, loudly. "Accident up ahead. Cop cars everywhere. Might want to, um, buckle your seat belts again."

"Oh my God." I fly off Alec's lap so fast it's a wonder I don't hurt myself. I forgot about Miles. Blue and white flash ahead of us in the distance, followed by sirens. I flash a panicked glance at Alec, wondering if he's as mortified as I am, but all he does is grin a wicked little grin—and then lick the pad of his thumb.

Oh my God.

Somehow we make it to Alec's condo without me spontaneously combusting.

Somehow we make it up the elevator—and he remembers to press the button this time.

Somehow we make it through his front door.

But where we don't make it is anywhere else.

He tosses me up onto the foyer console table. The wood presses sharply into the backs of my legs. I part them to give him access and he takes it, sliding between my knees and pressing toward me until there's no space between our bodies. And his mouth…his mouth takes mine, teasing, tasting, biting. He slides kisses along my jaw, down my neck, across my collarbone. His hands are at my waist. Mine are in his hair. I yank his head back up, needing the strength of his kiss again.

I will never not need this.

It's a sobering thought—but it doesn't have enough time to really sink in, because Alec's hands wrap around to my ass and he pulls me toward him, lifting me off of the table. "Told you this was my favorite way to walk," he says, nipping my lower lip. He pauses, though, at the foot of his staircase.

My pumps clatter to the ground. "If I'm too heavy you can—"

"Shut your beautiful mouth." He kisses me to make sure I do, and his body rises and falls as he slips his own shoes off. "I'm having a struggle with my conscience. Do I offer you something to drink—or do I toss you on my bed and show you everything I've been fantasizing about doing this entire week?"

"The second one."

He laughs, maybe because there was not a single moment of hesitation before my answer.

"Don't you dare laugh at me," I say, smiling. And then I kiss him to make sure he doesn't.

He carries me up his stairs, down his hallway—and tosses me onto his bed. Without a chance to catch my breath, he's on top of me, his knees on either side of my hips, his lips trailing along my neck, up my jaw, finding my mouth. His hands drag mine above my head.

I yank from his grasp, pulling them right back down.

In one motion, he flips us so that I'm straddling him. "You want control?" he asks over my gasp. "Take it, by all means."

I only wanted my hands free so I could strip him of his shirt. But I lean down and sink my teeth into his earlobe, whispering, "Good."

I've never felt sexier. And when I lift his shirt, peeling it off of him, the feeling only grows. All because of him, this guy, this sexy, sweet guy with a body harder than iron. Abs like they're carved from marble, and you better believe I let my fingers drift over every hill and valley, the warmth of his skin tingling against my palms.

His hips flex beneath me, and I feel how hard he is, and I shiver because oh wow. *I* did this. I made him this rigid, this thick. It makes me grin. It makes me powerful. I lean forward to kiss his chest, flickering my tongue over his nipples. He groans, his hands tightening around me, his fingers squeezing my ass.

I drag my lips up his neck and over his jaw, loving the texture of his stubble against my tongue. I hold his hands, this time, and pull them above his head. He lifts his chin, capturing my mouth with his, and the kiss is instantly intense. Lips pressing, tongues swirling, whispered breaths between our two bodies.

He threads his fingers through mine and beneath me, his abs go rock solid as he sits up, cradling me in his lap and breaking the kiss a moment later. "I want you in nothing but your lace. And I want to strip it from your gorgeous body."

My stomach jumps. My body is not gorgeous, I almost say. I'd give it a C at best. (And that's probably only because Bobby Fields gave it a D in high school. I mean, I kicked him in the balls so hard I'm pretty sure he still sings falsetto—but I'm not delusional enough to go higher. I'm a realist.) What I say instead is, "How about a little mood lighting?"

He gives me one of his soul-grazing stares, but he doesn't press it. He slides out from under me, lowering the light to a dim glow with a dial on the wall. Needing to gain back some of my momentum, I add, "Lose your pants while you're over there."

He snorts—and drops them to the ground.

"Why," he says, sauntering toward me, "am I not surprised you're bossy in the bedroom?"

I shrug and motion for him to join me, but he curves his own finger for me to go to him at the base of the bed. "Come here."

"And you say *I'm* bossy?"

He grins, his teeth gleaming in the low light, his dimples darkening into sexy shadows at the edges of his lips. "Teagan. Come here. Now." And something in his tone has more than my stomach jumping. My heart. My breath. The blood in my veins.

On shaky limbs, I crawl to him. At the edge of the bed, I rise to my knees and he touches me, one hand on my shoulder, the other on my hip, twisting me until I face away from him. I almost lose my balance in the plushness of his bed, but his hands catch my waist, and when I'm steady, they drop to the backs of my legs, the bases of my knees. He slowly, slowly runs them up the insides of my thighs. I widen my knees and roll my hips back, hoping a finger, or two, will find the spot where I most need to be touched under my dress. Under my panties.

Instead, he drops his hands from my legs, and I bite back a disappointed groan.

"Alec?" slips out of my mouth, though I'm not sure what I'm asking.

"Kitten." He brings his palms to the back of my neck, twisting my hair in his hands, winding it over one of my shoulders—and dropping his mouth on my bared skin, his tongue working along my neck in ways that have my head rolling further to the side.

His lips never leaving my skin, he unclasps the top of my dress and slowly, slowly tugs the zipper down. Inch by inch, past the middle of my back. Slower, slower, below the waist of my panties. When he lifts his head, the air hits my neck, cooling the spot where he's left the slightest trace of saliva against my skin.

"Jesus," he growls, nipping at me once more. "You have the sexiest fucking back I've ever seen, the sweetest skin I've ever tasted, and I never want you in anything but lace from this point forward."

I shiver, and it's not from the cool air on my neck. He jerks the straps of the dress over my shoulders, pulling until the fabric is puddled around my knees. He smoothes his hands along the skin of my lower back, pushing gently, until I'm on my hands and knees.

"Alec?" I ask again, still not sure what I want.

He shushes me. And even still in underwear, this is the most erotic thing I've ever felt, his presence behind me, his palms transferring heat up and down my spine. The dip in the bed when he climbs up, the charged space in the air that hits me when, from behind, he pulls my panties to the side.

The shocked pant of breath that leaves my mouth when he does.

The wetness of his tongue when he trails it along every exposed inch of me.

I can't keep the moan silent this time. I can't keep my hips from rolling. I can't keep this absolute *need* I feel from baring itself. And when he grabs my hips and plunges his tongue straight into me, I make a sound of pleasure closer to a song than anything else.

And I very nearly fall flat on my face.

Too much, too fast.

Or the opposite.

I need *more*.

I twist toward him, and after another dance with his tongue in my body, he allows it, letting me curve my body until I'm on my back and he adjusts himself, one of his knees sliding between my thighs, rising higher, higher up my legs, until I'm close to grinding myself against him for more relief.

"You taste incredible." He licks his lips, wet and shining in the shadows. He shoves his knee deliciously against me and grips my thighs, pushing them wider, wider. "I hope you don't expect me to stop for very long."

I open my mouth, the question I've been wanting to ask finally forming in my mind. I hesitate, a little nervous... A *lot* wanting. "Do you have a condom?"

CHAPTER TWENTY-SEVEN

ALEC HOLDS HIMSELF—holds *me*—very still, his arms all sinew and muscle even in the dimmed light. "I do have a condom."

But he doesn't move.

"Should you get it?" I ask. His knee is between my legs and my underwear is shoved to the side, and it's still taking all that I have not to roll my hips, not to rub myself against him.

He lets one hand drift down my inner thigh, tucking it between me and his knee, his finger dipping the slightest way into me. I moan. I roll my hips.

"Are you begging?" he asks.

And, absurdly, I giggle. "No."

He tightens his grip, harder, harder, one finger—two—slipping into me, then he *clutches* me until I gasp in pleasure. "And now?"

"No." But I'm not giggling anymore. And my hips are rising to meet the movements of his hand. "Actually, maybe I am."

He lowers his face until his lips are at my ear and my entire body flutters, waiting for what I know he's going to say.

Except he doesn't say it. "Told you that wasn't going to happen tonight."

Way more nervous to do it than I should be, I drag my own hand between our bodies, sliding it below the band of his boxer briefs and tentatively gripping him. He picks his head up to watch my face, but I'm much more interested in his. He winces in a pleasure-filled way, and does it again when I glide my hand along him.

"Pretty sure your body disagrees." I'm also pretty sure the long thickness of erection will never, ever fit all the way inside me, but I keep this thought to myself. Because every fiber of my body wants him to try anyway.

His breathing is so satisfyingly ragged, but still he says, "There are other ways to fill our time."

"Alec," I say, as sexily as I can drag out his name. A bit smugly, too. "I'm not interested in your game room right now."

"Neither am I," he says. "I'm going to spend the rest of tonight tasting every single inch of your skin."

His words leave my body a life-sized collection of fiery sparks, filling my skin, filling my mind, filling the space between my legs with the most electric sizzles.

He grabs my hand, pulling it out of his briefs and above my head. I nearly clench my legs around him, desperate to fill the void he left when releasing his clutch.

"Give me your other hand," he says. And I do without even the slightest temptation to fight him on the power imbalance between us right now. In fact, if my erratic heart is any indication, if the way my breath is caught below my throat means anything... If the wetness pooling between my thighs is a sign... He can have all the power. All night.

"Good girl," he murmurs, lowering his mouth to mine. His grip on my wrists is unyielding. His lips are forceful, and when his tongue leads my own in an intricate dance, it tastes of the salt of my body.

"Good girl?" I ask, running my teeth along his lip. "That's not how you want to speak to me."

"If I didn't want to speak to you like this, I wouldn't." His next kiss has so much force behind it, I have no choice but to shut up.

No choice but to give in.

No choice but to *shiver* along the path his free hand traces. Down the inside of my arm, along my ribcage, trailing the cups of my bra— and then sliding under the material. He takes his time, back and forth along my skin, and when his fingers find my nipple, he rubs the pad of his thumb over it until I gasp. He swallows the sound, scooping it from my mouth with his tongue. And then he moves to the other side and brings me to the point of moaning. My nipples are so hard, so full of anticipation, I'm all but pushing myself into his hands.

He releases some of the tension from his grip on my wrists. "Don't," he whispers between sweeping kisses, "move."

But how can I not move with the way my blood rushes under my skin?

How can I not move with the buildup of tension pinging me everywhere, needing his touch?

He lets go, and I bring my hands around his neck, pulling his face harder against mine, sweeping my tongue more deeply through his mouth. He lets me do it, but only for a moment.

He ducks his head under my grasp, breaking the kiss and laughing, a sound somehow full of humor yet also a warning. "What did I tell you?'

"When have I ever taken orders well?"

He grabs my wrists and slams them above my head, his chest over mine, shoving his knee between my legs again, making me writhe. "Start now and I promise you'll be rewarded for it."

He nudges my face to the side with his chin and slides his teeth over my earlobe, his tongue flickering along my skin. I sigh, melting into the bed. "Fine. You win."

"Get used to that," his voice is raspy in my ear. And then he gets to work and I forget how much I want to fight him on it because as long as he uses his tongue the way he does, he can get me to agree to whatever the hell he'd like.

He *bathes* me with his mouth, not missing an inch of skin.

Hands to shoulders, feet to knees to hips, breasts to belly...until I'm fully baptized in the church of Alec.

His tongue is my drug, my addiction, and when I can't stand another moment without more of a connection, when I think I'm going to have to break my promise and use my own hands, he shoves my knees up—and then nudges them apart. His eyes are on mine, glinting in the darkness of the room.

I'm thankful for the obscurity. I might not be able to fully enjoy this in the harsh reality of a world filled with light. In the darkness that yawns over us, when flesh blends with shadow, when my flaws are safely tucked away, it's easier to let my mind free. It's easier to tell him what I want.

"You," I say. And when a hint of amused confusion crosses his features, I clarify. "I want you, Alec. Now. The rest of tonight." *Always*, is on the tip of my tongue, but he slides up my body and captures my mouth in a kiss before I can say it.

He reaches between us again and curves his fingers into me, pulsing them through me until I cry out into his mouth and then sliding them back up my body, feeling me everywhere. Twisting my skin, pulling at me. Massaging me. His mouth never stops moving over mine. Not once.

Always always always reflects its way around my mind like a shattered mirror, like it's the only word I've every truly known the meaning to. And it flashes brighter, a neon glint, when he drags his mouth over my chin, down my neck, across my chest. He tongues one nipple and then the other, until I'm moaning with how tight they are, how ready I am for him, how desperate. My hands twist through his sheets above my head, my legs rise to wrap around him, my feet crossing at his back.

And he's *right there*.

His erection.

So. Fucking. Hard. Pressing through the fabric of his boxers. My hips writhe, and I press myself harder against him until I'm not the only one moaning.

Frustration rumbles up from my throat in a whimper. I want more.

He slides lower, planting kisses along my belly; the friction of his body slipping through my legs is unparalleled by anything I've ever experienced. He hooks his fingers through the top of my underwear and my breath catches.

He slowly, slowly slides the fabric lower, alternating a path of cool air and kisses along my skin as it's bared.

Pushing one of my knees closer to the other, he tugs my panties over my hips and slides them down my legs, down down down over my feet. And they land on the floor in the darkness with a soft rustle.

And then there's silence.

Though is silence the right word when, through the quiet, the air is so charged, electricity crackles deafeningly without making a sound?

His hands are at my ankles. They're sliding up my shins. Caressing my knees. Pushing my thighs apart. He flattens his palm against me and then drags it through my wetness.

His fingers press down like piano keys, pressing pressing every note there is to make me whisper, moan, scream his name.

His tongue is on my inner thigh. He's looking up at me. I'm forgetting how to breathe.

Higher, he licks. Higher, his fingers never stilling.

He laps at the crease where my leg meets my hip, and he slides his hands down to lift my knees. I am bare before him, his face is there, and then his breath. Hot. Cool. Hot cool hot cool *hot-cool-hot-cool.*

"Please." I whisper his name, begging. The sampling I had of his tongue inside my body seems so long ago.

And finally, *finally*, so perfectly I almost want to cry, he licks me again. Once. Slow and long, he presses the flat of his tongue against me and then curves it, along me, through me, into me. He shoves his hands beneath my ass, lifting me toward him, onto his face, his mouth, his tongue.

I'm moaning now—maybe have been the whole time, I don't know. I don't know anything except the pressure of his lips and the swish of his tongue as it enters me. Circling into me and out. Again, and again, and again. His face is pressed entirely against me, his nose, even, nudging me, and he twists his head from side to side, pulling me back and forth and... I'm going to fucking explode.

My hands are in his hair. His thick, thick hair; it's soft and glorious and the room is spinning. My legs are around his head and his tongue, his thick, thick tongue is lavishing me in a way I've only ever imagined—and I'm learning quickly my imagination is lacking.

He licks higher, using his tongue to press my skin down flat enough to make my moans grow feral, and his fingers tiptoe into me, slowly at first and then faster, heavier.

Something is building in my limbs.

A light sort of pressure.

It's soft, but full.

Swift, but lingering.

My legs are full of feathers, somehow, spinning, and my belly too. My breath is erratic. My heartbeat, too.

His fingers pump into me. Ruthlessly.

Perfectly.

His name falls again from my lips in a whisper, a sigh. The flutters spiraling through my belly explode into something so much more powerful, dropping like gusts of a tornado, gaining density, gaining speed, lower, so much lower, mingling with the pressure of his fingers, the rhythm of his tongue. His name becomes a chant and my entire body clenches and then *bursts*.

I am grains of sand in a storm made of Alec, scattering in his fierce wind and spinning back. Out to my limits and then retracted. Billow and fall.

But the wind gusts into something even stronger, something *more*, and with one final, unstoppable spiral out, I dissolve into absolutely nothing but a leftover pulse of a girl that used to exist.

And an exhausted Cheshire smile.

CHAPTER TWENTY-EIGHT

I'M SWEATY.

At some point, I reform into some semblance of myself. My skin is slick, damp. *Glistening*.

Then, I notice Alec. Feel him, really. The weight of his head on my thigh, the sharpness of his chin digging into my muscle. His lazy smile takes my breath away.

"Um." I don't know what to say. I'm out of breath, like I've run a marathon. My heart's beating as if that's the case as well.

"Um?" He lifts a brow, amused.

"Thank you?" I mean to say it with less of a question mark, but I'm suddenly a little too aware of our positioning, of how very naked I am, of how high on my thigh his head is… I shift, curving onto my side, facing him, and letting his head slip onto the bed.

His shoulders shake in a silent laugh and he crawls up over me, kissing his way up my body, sweet and silly this time, the intensity of before a nearby memory. "You," he says, between kisses, "are very," kiss, kiss, kiss all the way up to the side of my face, "welcome."

I twist my head toward him, kissing him on the mouth, again tasting the salt of my body lingering on his lips.

"Want some water?" he asks, quite some time later.

"How about a shirt?"

He rises over me, the heat from his body soaking into my own. "And cover all this up? Yeah, right."

"Alec," I say, teasing, both turned on and uncomfortable all at once. "I'm cold."

His expression says he doesn't buy it for a second, but he sighs and rises, striding to a dresser and tossing me an undershirt. I slip it on, pretending I don't suddenly feel awkward. It's soft and smells like detergent and fits me like an oversized trash bag.

At least I'm covered now. I clear my throat. "Water sounds good, actually."

"You still look beautiful," he says. "In that shirt. Out of it. Shit. If I didn't think you'd be terrified, I'd rip that thing right back off of you." He shakes his head, leaving the room.

Leaving me reeling.

I cover my face with my hands, falling onto the bed. What is wrong with me? I just had the most mind-blowing orgasm of my life and now I...what? Am uncomfortable about it? Shaking. That's what I am. Trembly. "Come on, Teagan, get your shit together."

Still, when he comes back to the room, it's as though I've reverted to a teenager and I can't make myself look at him. I reach out for the water, but he holds it hostage.

"Look at me."

My face is so hot I'm almost in pain. "I am."

"You're looking over my shoulder."

"That's definitely not the case." Yes, it really freaking is. "It's dark. You can't tell."

"Come here."

"No. You come here."

He stares me down until I can't keep from looking at him. But even when I meet his gaze, he refuses to come to me.

Well.

Two can play this game.

All night long.

Finally, I'm able to grin. I sit on my heels.

He crosses his arms.

I toss my hair over a shoulder.

He says, "Your nipples are hard and I suddenly fucking love that shirt on you because seeing them push out like that? There's nothing else like it."

"Well your…" Ugh. Why can't I say it? And I'd rather die than reference his erection as his thing again. "*You're* hard. And…" And why don't I have a follow-up here? "God, Alec. What did you do to me?"

"You mean like a few minutes ago? Or… metaphorically?"

There's no doubt my face is neon red even in the dark room. "The second one."

"Pretty sure I've made you like me." He takes a long sip of water. My mouth goes a little dry. And not from the thought of the water. Just… Wow. His body. His thick neck, bobbing as he swallows. His waist is narrower than his shoulders, giving his chest that perfect vee down toward his legs. And his erection. He's so hard it makes me bite my lip almost deep enough to draw blood.

"Is that uncomfortable?" Oh. Right. Because now's the perfect time for words to slip out all unfiltered.

"This?" He gestures toward himself, a wolfish grin flashing through the dark.

"I mean…do you want me to—"

"Stop." He pauses before continuing. "The thought of you touching me in any capacity makes me so fucking hard I could break concrete. But you need a break. So let's lie here for a while. All night. I'll be fine—*he'll* be fine."

"You would do that?"

"Why are you surprised?"

"Because…you're… I mean, you…did what you did and… God, I suck at this. I'm sorry. I *do* like you."

"Ah." He nods, and finally, finally moves toward the bed, handing me the water. "You saved yourself at the end. You were pissing me off for a second there, thinking I'd expect more than you're ready for. But if it's because I fluster you, because you *like* me, then I guess it's okay. Just this once."

But I can't leave it at that. "I'm not selfish, Alec. Or…I am. But I want to please you. It's not fair for me to get all the—"

"*Stop*," he repeats, the word sharper this time. The bed dips when he sinks into it, languidly crawling toward me to press a finger against my lips. "Don't you get it? Your orgasm—getting to tease those noises from you with my fingers, with my mouth, feeling you throb around my tongue like that? It pleases me more than anything I've ever done. More than any blowjob I could ever receive—even from you."

His words bring a glow to me so intense I'm surprised I'm not lighting up the room. "Really?"

He leans against the headboard, pulling me into his chest. "Those noises? The purrs you made—the way you called my name. Christ, Teagan. They'll be on repeat in my memory for a long time. I'm tempted to record you on the next round, so I can play it back whenever I want to, forever."

"Whenever you want to, forever?" I wish I could come up with something more clever than an echo of his words, but I'm too full of a grin. It hits my lips and zooms down the rest of my body. *More than just this summer?* I catch the question before it escapes, but I'm not shocked by how tempted I am to ask it.

His erection is pressing into my back. All I have to do is turn around, twist in his arms, kiss down his body... The thought has me flushing—but something's holding me back. I chug some of the cool water, using the moment to gather my thoughts.

"As perfect as tonight's been," I say, surprised I can admit what I'm about to, "I might have hit my capacity for perfection. I...need a breather." Otherwise, I might explode. Or implode. Or, worse, I might ruin everything. "I'm not great with...too much too fast."

The closest I ever came to letting emotions pile on this fast was with Jason. And that ended before it could really begin. I don't know what to do with happiness when life hands it to me. Not that I can share that with Alec. Not that I should even have the thought right now.

"We have time, kitten." He tugs me tighter against his chest. "I want you to know my body as well as I've mapped yours, but when you're ready."

I don't bite back the next question that thrums through me, alongside all the pleasure rushing with his words. "Are you too good to be true?"

"Are *you*?"

"You're talking to the girl who lied about her name, lied about who she was, got too drunk to offer what she arrived to do—and then showed up at your office with a completely new identity."

He takes the water from me, leaning away for a second to place it on the nightstand and then sliding behind me, nibbling at my neck. "You keep me on my toes."

"But I—"

"Will you shut up?"

"Don't tell me to shut up!" I grab his thigh, right above his knee, and I squeeze until his leg jerks and he laughs.

"That *tickles*." He digs his fingers into my ribs, and I giggle.

"Say you're sorry," I say, squirming—and resisting the urge to sigh when he slides his hands around my stomach, holding me, making me wish he'd slide them higher... Or lower.

"I apologize," he concedes, a pompous smile in his tone.

"Good. Because I have an idea."

"Oh yeah? I thought we were taking a break?" He grins when I turn to swat at him and tightens his grip around my stomach.

"We are," I say, kind of wishing we weren't... "This is business-related."

"From pleasure to business—isn't it usually the other way around?"

I laugh and twist toward him, loving the pleased glint of agreement in his eye when I tell him I think he should team up with Mr. Chambers.

He talks, excitedly, for a while, and I listen, adding an opinion here or there. But it's hard to focus on business for any length of time because I'm in Alec's bed. Because he's stroking the skin of my arms, the muscles of my thighs. Because he can't seem to keep from dropping kisses along my shoulders.

I slide my hand over the one he's left across my stomach, running my fingers along his skin. It's smooth, but not soft, somehow all guy. His knuckles are covered in raised spiderweb patterns of scarring. I want to ask him what happened, but I hold back. Sometimes people don't want you picking at their scars—visible or otherwise. I sure as shit don't. And I also don't want to risk ruining the night by opening my mouth about it.

At some point, Alec surprises me, pressing a small remote—which plays the audiobook opening of *Dracula* through a few speakers on the walls I hadn't noticed.

"I love this movie," I say, grinning into the darkness.

He kisses my neck, running a hand through my hair. "It's a book. Now keep that beautiful mouth closed."

But I turn my face toward him, stealing a kiss first. "You're kind of cool, you know?"

He grins against my mouth. "I know."

And so we listen.

He asks if I want popcorn, or something else to drink, but I shake my head. "Don't move. Don't do anything. This—this moment right here—I'm tempted to record it, so I can play it back whenever I want to, forever."

A laugh rumbles in his chest and he squeezes me tighter, and pressure from the weight of his arms somehow makes me *lighter*.

There's no anxiety tonight. No tossing and turning and traitorous, torturous thoughts funneling through my mind. There's only a gentle relaxation that comes with the beat of Alec's heart against my back, the soft rise and fall of his chest beneath me. I don't mean to fall asleep so quickly, but I'm out before Jonathan Harker even realizes he's Dracula's prisoner.

CHAPTER TWENTY-NINE

WHEN I OPEN my eyes, dazzled by sunlight streaming across the bed, Alec is watching me.

"That's creepy," I say, but a wave of pleasure washes over me anyway.

He taps my nose. "I missed these freckles last night."

"I had a lot of makeup on," I admit. Then, horrified, I see half of it's smeared across his pillowcase. "Shit—it'll come out, I promise."

He watches me, puzzled until he glances down at the orange-looking stripes across the otherwise stark white. Then, he laughs. "Who cares? I have more than one pillowcase."

"I care," I protest. "Your house is nice. Your stuff is nice. I don't want to make it all dirty."

Annoyingly, he laughs harder. "I like you here. With makeup. No makeup. In my bed. Out of it... Any which way you're here, you make my place a million times better."

Oh God. My brain's not awake enough to respond. My body is, though, trembling in all the right places. Who knew you could be so happy, so *turned on*, so soon after waking up. I sigh—and then I cover my mouth. "I need to brush my teeth."

"There's an extra toothbrush already out in the bathroom for you."

A blush warms my cheeks. "I brought my own."

"How presumptuous," he says. "I brought your bag up earlier." He points to it on my nightstand and rolls out of bed. Still in boxers. Still with abs formed from ridges and valleys.

Still mouth-wettingly appealing.

I scoff. "Like we both didn't know I'd be staying over." I reach out to him. "Come to bed."

He kneels on the mattress, letting me pull him toward me. "Thought you wanted to brush your teeth?"

"I do," I say, deciding in the instant to go for what I actually want. "But you stay right here."

"I was going to make us coffee."

"I have a different method of waking you up in mind," I say, forcing the words out so I can't back down, and slipping out of bed. I tug his undershirt down to cover my thighs.

He watches me. "What is this method you speak of?"

"Use your imagination," I say, "and picture my mouth on your body..." I smile and grab my bag, closing myself into his bathroom.

I'd love to study myself in the mirror, have a truth talk with my reflection. But his serious lack of mirrors issue makes it hard. Still, I brush my teeth. Splash some water on my face. Take a few deep breaths.

Remind myself of the ways he teased my body into bliss last night.

He deserves a turn now, too. And not because of some quid pro quo balance restoration thing, either. I want to start his day with a smile. I want to be the girl he thinks of, the flashbacks he gets when he closes his eyes all day.

I can do this.

I *can*.

Literally, I've done this before. Still. Everything's different when it's with Alec, more nerve-wracking. More significant.

One last deep breath, one last stern glance in the imaginary mirror, and I let myself out into his room. Where he's waiting. On the bed, his hands behind his head, a smarmy twist to the corners of his mouth.

"Christ, you're sexy in that shirt," he says.

"You're halfway decent without one on at all," I say, climbing over to him.

Straddling him.

Feeling him stiffen beneath me.

Oh, Lord.

His grin turns cockier, if that's even possible. And I find it annoyingly attractive. So attractive, in fact, I'm tempted to lean down and lick the corners of his mouth.

I give in to temptation.

And when I rise again, he slides his hands up my thighs, hoisting the undershirt higher, higher, until it barely covers anything. "Well," he says, his gaze steady on mine, "good morning."

"It's about to be."

"Is that so?" His thumbs inch down the insides of my thighs, tracing lines through the center of my body, bringing a cry to my lips. "Ah—there we go. Now it's a good morning."

Focus.

I need to focus.

I force my eyes open only to discover he's not looking at my face. He's...watching. His fingers. Flickering them over me.

Into me.

"*Alec.*" I fall forward, my face tingling painfully.

It feels like the kiss of a gentle breeze compared to what's happening between my legs.

Wet.

Heat.

A sudden desire to let him play with me all morning.

All day. All night.

Forever.

He smoothly slides his hands around me, curving over my ass, and between my legs from behind.

I press my hands beside his face, kissing him, slipping my tongue through his lips, tasting him, biting him gently. "This," I say, speaking against the kiss, my words trembling the way my blood seems to be too, "is supposed to be *my* turn to play with *you*."

"My house," he says, gnawing on my lower lip, "my rules."

"Is that so?" I ask, ready to play, ready to push. I slide a little further down his body, but his grip tightens between my legs, keeping me from drifting further.

Oh, God.

"Yes. And my rules are simple." He twists two fingers into me, circling, pulsing, making my blood jump. "Nobody comes before you do."

"Wanna bet?" I slide my tongue down his throat, shifting to trail kisses across his chest. He flicks his fingers and my entire body pulses around him.

He sighs, warm and lazy-sounding. "Believe me, I'll be delivering what I promise before you can count to—"

"To what?" I slide my teeth around one of his nipples. I mean to make my way to the other, but, as he groans, he tightens his arms around me, his fingers growing harder, more forceful.

Thrusting into me.

Again.

And again.

A lightness spins through my chest, sliding down my belly, lower to where his hands are playing. I can't control it, can't control the way my limbs are jellying, can't control the whimpers building in my throat, pushing through my lips. "Alec—wait."

But he's pulling my sensitive skin apart, pushing the pad of his thumb against me—somehow gentle, somehow rough—tugging me in circles and my world starts to tilt. Instead of his shoulders, my hands grip his sheets, twisting through the fabric, winding tighter and tighter, matching the sensations that shoot through me.

I manage to whisper, "Not fair," before I come completely apart. Before the warmth pooling between my thighs ignites like a firework finale, *booming* through my veins, through my belly, down my legs, my arms.

Boom, boom, boom.

Boom.

I collapse on top of him, too flushed with pleasure to give him shit for the laughter shaking his chest.

"Told you," he whispers in my ear. "I get my way."

"Shut up," I say, breathing heavy. Enjoying it. Enjoying *everything.*

His hands are on my ass, pressing gentle circles over my cheeks. He moves them up my back, smoothing my skin, up and down and up and down. It's almost enough to lull me to sleep again.

Or, it would be, if he wasn't hard as marble beneath me.

If I wasn't determined to do what I set out to do, even if he beat me to the game.

Lazily, I push myself off his chest, kissing his neck, kissing his jaw, his cheek, his mouth. I dip my tongue through his lips, tasting him, all masculine and mint. "My turn," I murmur, and this time when I lower myself, he lets me go, watching me, a jaunty curve across his mouth.

"You look like a cat who's captured the canary," I say, ducking down to plant kisses along his stomach. "So pleased before I've even gotten started."

"This is just icing, kitten," he says, drawing his hands behind his head. "I've already had the cake—and believe me, there's nothing sweeter than hearing you cry out."

"We'll see," I say, smug. I may be a virgin, but I spent one long, secret weekend with Cassidy's brother before he died, and we made sure... Well, we made sure my tongue was expertly trained to bring out the *icing*.

And when I place my mouth around Alec, I don't hold back.

I grip his thighs. I use my tongue, the gentle edges of my teeth, the back of my throat. The angle of my neck, the sweep of my hair across his abdomen, the squeezes of my hands. My breath, hot and cool.

His hands come down to grab my head, to tug my hair, and his breathing fills the room, ragged and uneven. Harder, faster, his hips rise and fall to meet my rhythm.

I start to hum and when he comes, it's with a roar, and only the thought of watching where my teeth go keeps me from grinning around him.

"Remind me," he says, sometime later, the tenor of his voice a bit hoarse, "to get a standing mirror for the foot of my bed. All I have to do is imagine the view behind you... Your ass in the air, my undershirt sliding up your back, no panties—Christ, the thought's enough to bring me back to the edge. Next time you do this—and please, God, let there be a next time—I want to watch you while you do it."

"That'd be kind of hard, given your fear of all mirrors," I tease without thinking about my words.

His lips fall into a flat line, his eyes lose a bit of their shine. His expression remains poised, but too polite, suddenly. He's shutting down before my eyes. Panic stirs in my chest. "I'm sorry," I say. "I didn't mean to—"

"Nothing to apologize for. Why don't I go make us that coffee?" He gently slides out from underneath me and sits up, stretching as he stands. He glances at me. "Seriously. No worries."

But yeah. Right. He's going for lighthearted and he's so far from pulling it off it's not even funny.

He slips into his jeans from last night, pulling them up, not bothering to button them.

"I'll just..." I motion aimlessly from my spot in his bed. "Get dressed, too."

"You sure you don't want to stay in my shirt? It really does suit you...and my imagination." He winks, and a bit of the balance shifts back between us to what it was before I opened my stupid mouth.

And when I meet him downstairs, dressed in last night's dress—though I may have slipped his undershirt into my bag as a keepsake—he's completely back to himself, handing me a coffee, the scent of bacon sweetening the air. "Eggs or pancakes?"

"Pancakes, obviously," I say, shaking my head. "Do you know me at all?"

"Every curve, every crevice," he says, tugging me into him for a long, slow kiss. I slide my fingers through his hair, sleek and soft. God, I love the access I have suddenly. He's amazing. And not just his hair. I twist the kiss into something heavier. He slips his hands down to grab my ass, pulling me harder against him. "I do love this dress, but I love it even more when it's off of you."

I could get used to this.

He gives a light growl when he releases me. "Maybe instead of food, I'll have more of you for breakfast."

My stomach does a weird hop/twist/turning thing, but I smile, smugly. "Tempting, but you lost the battle when you mentioned pancakes."

It's true, too. I'm starving.

And I love pancakes.

"We can't tell anyone about this at work." I'm surprised I'm the one who has to say it.

His brows rise in surprise, too, like he hadn't considered it. "There are papers we could sign for HR."

"No." I shake my head. "I don't want a bad reputation." Not this time. Not at this job.

"I don't think you'd get one," he says. "But, for now, we'll keep it our secret." He takes another bite, chewing. I could watch him chew for hours, the way his jaw sharpens, the sensual motion of his lips... He catches me staring—and I don't even care. I slide a slice of syrup-saturated pancake into my mouth, still enjoying his.

"The next few weekends, I'll be gone," he says. "Family stuff. A yearly summit in Palm Beach, not to be confused with a vacation, trust me. Vegas for my brother's bachelor party—not," he says, lifting his brows, "that you have anything to worry about. No strippers. Just gambling."

My mouth quirks. Then falls. "Will Piper be at any of these things?"

He shakes his head. "But she does want to meet you."

Boom. A bomb. Right in my stomach. "You talked to her about me?"

"Right before you came downstairs, actually."

"Why?" Beneath the explosion in my system—or maybe what remains now—is a sort of relief. He told her about me. She wants to meet me.

He wasn't lying about not being engaged.

I believed him—I believed in myself enough to believe him, but this seals it.

"Because I told her it's time to break off the engagement. Because I told her I'm falling into something serious."

CHAPTER THIRTY

HAPPINESS IS A glow beneath my skin, so bright, so light, I'm not sure how my feet stay on the ground. I literally can't remember the last time I felt this way. I'm not even one hundred percent sure happiness is the right word. Charged, maybe. Or passionate.

Flushed is a definite. From my head to my toes and all the spaces in between. Aching, too, for more of Alec. His time. His mind. His tongue...

I even say good morning to my grandparents when I walk into their house. Gramps' baggy eyes widen in shock. Gran stares at me like I'm something on the bottom of her shoe.

Oh well. Don't care.

I don't skip up the stairs, but it's close.

I close my door and spin myself onto my bed, staring at the ceiling, grinning like a fucking idiot.

Oh well. Don't care.

My grandparents start to yell at each other below my room, so I put on my fancy headphones from Alec and dive back into my post-apocalyptic vampires. And then I download a book on persuasive reasoning so I can better help Alec with his investment proposal.

I'm still so happy by the end of the weekend, I actually consider canceling my doctor's appointment. I don't, though. I've been through the cycle enough times to know that the darkness always finds its way through. The anger. The sadness. The...blah.

But when I walk into my early Monday appointment—one I still can't quite believe I have, even being here—I feel like an imposter. It's like being sick—and knowing it'll return, but all the symptoms have disappeared right in time for a visit. What if the doctor doesn't believe me?

Guess that's an answer in itself. She'll see how pissed I get if she doesn't believe me and immediately understand I need help. I bite back a snarky laugh. Who knew my anger could be a failsafe...

A nurse brings me to a shabby yellow room and weighs me on an ancient scale and asks a few questions about my visit. I'm up front with her. "Don't tell me what the scale says. And I'm here because I have anger issues and I want pills to make them go away."

She blinks, her pale blue eyes growing amused. "That's not exactly how it all works, but you're on the right track. Dr. Jones will talk to you about all of it."

Dr. Jones turns out to be a chubby man with a sharp gaze. I thought the picture of Dr. Jones on the network's website showed a woman, but I'm sure I mixed it up. I'm tempted to ask to speak with a woman, but find it difficult to say the words. Which is weird, because usually I have no problem with this sort of thing.

Instead, I stay silent and he begins the appointment, sitting on a stool with a thin laptop on his knees, asking me a series of questions. I answer, shortly but honestly, and eventually I slip into feeling a little more comfortable.

Until he asks if I've ever had thoughts of self-harm or suicide.

For some reason, it pisses me the hell off. "*No*. I have anger problems. I get sad sometimes. But that doesn't mean I'm suicidal."

Compassion crosses his face. Maybe it's been there the entire time. Or maybe it's pity. I can't tell, and that pisses me off, too.

"I'm sorry," he says. "I have to ask. And I also have to ask, if you ever do feel those things—will you promise to call 911 to get help first?"

"Yes," I say. "But it's not going to happen. Growing up with my grandparents... If that was going to happen, it would've happened a long time ago."

He opens his mouth, but I can tell by his expression he reconsiders what he's going to say at the last minute, and instead asks, "Do you ever have thoughts about harming other people?"

God. Enough is enough. "Well, I wanted to stab my dinner date with a fork the other night."

And he makes a fucking note on his little laptop.

"Wait—I'm *kidding*. You get that, right? Sarcasm?"

"I get it." He makes another note.

"What are you typing?"

"Tell me why you're here."

"Tell me what you're typing."

"Notes to make sure I don't leave out details that might be helpful with your treatment."

It's almost physically painful not to roll my eyes. He knows why I'm here. I told them when I made the appointment. I told the nurse who brought me here. But all these annoying notes of his are making me feel like I'm skating on thin ice—and he mentioned a treatment, which is my entire reason for coming. So I go with blunt honesty. "I want a drug to help control my anger... And when I get sad. And the way my thoughts spin at night, keeping me up. Sometimes so much I get stomachaches."

He considers me, thoughtfully. "Sounds like maybe you have some anxiety in the evenings?"

I consider him, blandly. "No shit."

"Anger and sadness are often symptoms of depression," he continues as though I haven't just acted like a total asshole, which makes me feel like an even bigger one.

"Okay," I say, trying to keep my tone kinder. I wish it wasn't so hard. "But what can I take to make it all go away?"

"There are several things you can try before we move on to a medicinal approach. Have you tried other methods?"

"Mood journals? Free counseling?" I wait and when he nods again, I say, "I'm not an idiot. I looked up every possible method available to me without health insurance years ago. I tried journaling—but my handwriting pisses me off. I tried books—but reading's a huge part of what started all of this in the first place. Everything blurs together. Instant anger trigger, believe me. I started going to church for free counseling. Didn't help—they tried to bring religion and prayer into helping me make myself feel better. Not against those things, sometimes I halfway believe in God myself, but they didn't do it for me. I can go on and on here, but I promise—if you name it, I've tried it."

Even right now, having to list these things, having to prove to him that I need something stronger, is making me clench my teeth. I have health insurance now. I want a fucking pill that makes me happy.

He makes another note.

My annoyance roars.

But finally, finally, he says what I've been waiting to hear. "There are medications that can help stabilize moods, but—"

"No buts. I want to try."

"*But*," he says with a small smile. "There's no one stop fix-all solution."

"I get it." I lift a shoulder, not to imply that I don't care, but that I know there isn't anything I can do about what he's said. "But anything will help at this point."

"Okay," he says. "I'll recommend a starting dose of fifty milligrams of Zoloft. It's an antidepressant that helps with anxiety too, which may help you fall asleep easier in the evenings. We can see how you do on that, and go from there."

I've waited so long for this moment it actually takes a few seconds for his words to sink in. And when they do, relief is instant; it punches me right in the tear ducts. I blink away the wetness. "Thank you."

"Don't expect immediate changes," he warns. "And start with half a pill for the first week or so, to give your system time to get used to the drug."

I nod, but think *yeah fucking right*. I'm tempted to take an entire bottle at once.

Then, though, I nod a second time, really agreeing. I want to get better. I should follow his directions.

"The Zoloft will help with many of your symptoms, but I also suggest a mild over-the-counter sleep aid for at least the first few weeks because before the medication begins to help, it can enhance a few of those feelings," he continues. "I also recommend that you set up an appointment with our onsite psychologist, Dr. Reyes."

"Psychologist?" My emotions, previously so happy and forward-moving, rebel, scattering in all directions. "Is this because of the fork-stabbing comment? Because I swear I was joking."

"No." He shakes his head. "It's because an antidepressant will help with much of what you describe, but combining it with therapy will make a world of difference."

"Can't I try the pills first?" I've wanted medication for so long—I thought a primary care physician would be all I needed.

"You took the first step in coming here," he says. "You want to feel better, to get better, right?"

I study a painting on the wall, a sailboat, while contemplating his words. "But a shrink? I'm not good at talking about things."

"You've done fine with me."

I wonder if he'd change his answer if he'd been able to hear my thoughts. "You're a doctor and can't judge me."

"Dr. Reyes is trained to listen even better than I am."

Fuck. He has a point. And maybe pills plus talking will help me figure out how to break out of my own mind sooner.

Because, really, the quicker the fucking better.

Even these thoughts are pissing me off.

Which...just...*why?*

Knowing my feelings are ridiculous makes me furious, which makes my feelings even more ridiculous which... Spiral, spiral, spiral. This shit has to stop.

"Fine," I say. "I'll set up an appointment."

"I can do it on my computer."

"Making sure I don't back out?"

"Making sure it's as easy as possible for you to do this," he counters, tapping away. "She had a cancellation, so she has an opening in half an hour. Can you stay to see her?"

I have the first half of the day off. He doesn't know that. I could say no and walk out with my prescription. But...as tempting as that is, I should probably give this a try. I blow air out through my lips loudly, probably rudely, before I respond. "Fine."

CHAPTER THIRTY-ONE

"TELL ME WHY you're here."

Oh my fucking God. If one more person asks me this... "Because you had an opening."

Dr. Reyes looks at me from her faded leather armchair, her expression annoyingly patient.

I lean on the ratty couch she directed me to sit on. "Because I'm starting antidepressants, and Dr. Jones thought talking to you could help in conjunction with that." This is so uncomfortable. Three times today I've had to say what I want. I've had to share that I have issues and I want to fix them and it makes me feel so fucking weak I want to scream.

"You feel angry a lot, sad sometimes, and anxious when you try to fall asleep." She doesn't make me repeat myself again, and I start to unwind. "You've tried non-medicinal methods in the past and have been unsatisfied with their results."

"Tell me something I don't know." I crack a smile. She smiles wider. I start to like her.

"How about you tell me when these things started to happen? Were they all together, or one at a time?"

This gives me pause as I try to remember. "The anger first, I think? It was forever ago—before high school even... Maybe in elementary school. I was kicked off my soccer team in middle school for my temper. And again in high school." I sigh. "Feels like I was born pissed off, to be honest. Which might be the case, considering my mother barely stuck around long enough to give birth to me. And ignored every attempt I made to contact her when I found out who she was a few years back." Which is so much more than I meant to say.

She waits for me to go on, and when I don't, she asks, "You were raised by your grandparents?"

Deep breath. "Yep. And they suck. And I'd rather not talk about them."

This time, she doesn't respond when I wait, so I grudgingly add, "Right now, anyway."

She continues to wait, but I can play this game, too. Finally, she says, "Dr. Jones left a note that sometimes when you read, things blur together—and this can be a trigger for your anger?"

"Can be? Try always. And mostly anger. Sometimes attempting to read only a paragraph makes me feel like giving up on everything. Which I know is lame. Which makes me pissed off—or, sometimes, sad... Like, blah. Can't get out of bed. Because I'm too old to still have trouble reading. I mean, I don't have bad eyes or anything. I don't get it."

She asks me a bunch of questions about my reading difficulties—and other things I've always struggled with. I'm halfway furious having to think about it all, and halfway relieved to get it off my chest to someone I won't worry about looking dumb to.

"Imagine," I say. "Just imagine being forced to read the same book every day, but the book's written in... I don't know, Ancient Greek or something. But you don't get it. And nobody explains it in a way that makes it readable, the letters are all squiggly and impossible to capture—yet somehow *everyone* else is moving on to the next level of Ancient Greek and you're not and your teachers are getting irritated and your grandparents don't care at all. So you know what happens? *You get passed up.* To the next level. Where you're someone else's problem. Where you're even more confused.

"Even teachers who tried to be positive were all *you can do it, you can do it.* But no. I really couldn't. So I stopped trying. Because I kept passing. It didn't make a difference. And maybe I wanted someone to pick up on it. Maybe I was *dying* for someone to notice. But that was back then. Now? Now I'm fine. I can read at a functional level. All I want is not to have to think about it anymore."

At this point, I'm out of breath and out of steam. Dr. Reyes stands and pours me a cup of water from a pitcher on her desk.

"Anyway," I say, embarrassment making my mouth even drier. It helps that Dr. Reyes doesn't allow any judgment to cross her face. "What does any of this have to do with Zoloft?"

She sits back in her chair, her eyes still assessing me. "Were you ever tested for a learning disability, in high school or before?"

I take a long swallow of water, my face suddenly numb. "Excuse me?"

"The way you describe your difficulties reading, and with note taking, is indicative of a visual perceptive learning disability."

Little trembles, a lot like fear, ripple under my skin. I place the glass on her desk. "In English please?"

"The things you're mentioning, the way you answer my questions, leads me to believe you have a learning disability that affects how you understand information that you take in visually, and, often going hand-in-hand with a visual perceptive discrepancy, a touch of dysgraphia—which affects handwriting ability."

"In dumber English?"

She gives me a chastising look. "You have difficulty processing communication that you see. It's easier for you to hear things."

This.

This finally clicks in.

I'm sure I should find this information upsetting. I'm sure it means I'm dumb...but, amazingly, the corners of my mouth refuse to stay down. Those trembles weren't fear. They're *excitement*. "That would explain a lot."

"I can schedule a formal assessment for you; however, I'm not sure you'd find it extremely beneficial. At this point, there's not a lot the paperwork will do for you—and it can be costly. If you'd like to delve in further we can certainly discuss it."

I shake my head, still smiling. "Just knowing what you think, just understanding there's a reason for the problems I've had..." I trail off before I can say that it's enough, because my throat is tightening and my nose is stinging and my eyes are growing wet. "It's enough."

So many memories swirl through my mind. Frustrated teachers. Books unread; tests failed. Handwritten English assignments with more big fat red Fs across the top because they were unreadable. For years, I tried to convince my teachers I wasn't lazy like they all said. Eventually, I stopped bothering. Let them believe whatever they'd like. I stopped caring...

"You must think I'm weird to be smiling," I continue. "And I'm sure later I'll be doing the opposite, when it sinks in that I'm dumb. But knowing there's something legitimately—*medically*—wrong with me? It's...*freeing*."

"A learning disability doesn't mean you're dumb, Teagan," she says. "I have no doubt you're a capable, intelligent young woman—especially given how you're reacting. All this means is that you process things differently. That you might need different avenues to help you when you need to read something, or write something."

"Like audiobooks?" I ask, thinking of listening to *Dracula* on Friday night, of *The Passage*, of the other books I've listened to ever since Alec set me up with the app for my phone.

"Exactly."

But... "That won't help me at work, though. And, as much as I love listening to stories—I need my job. I want to succeed." Wow. Saying it makes me understand how true it is. I want to succeed. I want to be Denise. Or higher.

"There are tools that will help, though. There are text-to-speech readers available. Or, if you don't have access—increasing font size, say in your email folders, may help. Perhaps you can request a laptop to take notes on at meetings, as your handwriting troubles you."

Imagining it all is...thrilling, to be honest. "Oh God, that would help me so much."

"Because you're an adult, Teagan, for much of this you'll have to be your own biggest advocate. Do you feel comfortable asking your boss, or the HR department, for some of these aids?"

Alec's face flashes through my mind. He's already helped me so much without realizing it. "Yeah, I do."

She nods. "Good. I'll give you a printout before you go, listing some of the available options to consider."

"Does this mean I'm not actually depressed?" I ask. "That I'm just dumb?" I smile wider, so she'll know I'm joking (mostly).

"Not dumb," she repeats, anyway. "But much of what you describe sounds, on the top, like clinical depression. We can delve a little deeper for the rest of the hour. There is frequently a link between the two, learning disabilities and depression. Does depression run in your family?"

The urge to smile is gone. "I don't know my parents, and my grandparents would never admit something like that." And this time, I find myself telling her everything. Never knowing my father. A mother who claims I don't exist and who's returned, unopened, every letter I've ever sent. The words tumble like drunk gymnasts from my mouth, and I let them.

So we talk.

And we talk.

And we talk.

I'm more candid, more *open* with Dr. Reyes than I've ever been with anyone.

We talk about what it means to be realistic and to stay honest with myself. I tell her I'm always honest with myself, not mentioning my mirror reality chats. She says that's good, that I've been helping myself—but when I'm feeling down, I need to be careful not to be too hard on myself.

"Depression can make people see themselves through a distorted lens," she says.

I laugh, a little bitter. "Trust me, I'm way harder on most other people than I am myself. That's a huge part of the reason I'm here. To be nice."

"Are you sure it's not yourself you need to be nicer to first?"

"Aren't you supposed to tell me if that's the case?"

She smiles. "We can determine it together. However, I do have another client scheduled in about five minutes. So perhaps we can start here next time."

"Next time?"

"I'd like to see you once a week," she says. "We can drop the regularity after the first month, but it's beneficial to start therapy with an accelerated frequency at first, especially in combination with medication."

"I would come that often," I say, surprising myself with the truth. "But I started a new job last week. It's half an hour from here, so lunch breaks are out, too." And I know from the office hours listed on their website that they're not open late enough for me to get here after work.

"I understand. But I would like to schedule quarterly check-ins then, will that work?" When I nod, she continues. "And in the meantime, I'd like for you to consider a therapy site called Straight Talk No Jacket."

I laugh at the name and she twists her mouth, admitting she doesn't love it, though the wordplay is clever. She explains it's an online counseling center, where I can speak with licensed therapists via video chat. "They don't take insurance," she warns. "But it's affordable—and sometimes insurance companies will offer reimbursement. I'm happy to write a referral on your behalf."

I can't stop nodding today. It's...weird. I'm used to the opposite. "I'd appreciate it."

And so I walk out of the building a changed girl. A prescription in my pocket. A small amount of understanding for all my years of failure. A sort of hope I'm not sure I've ever encountered before, one that brings a new outlook, a positivity toward the future I *know* I've never had.

Today is going to be a good day. The truth of it is beating with every pump of my suddenly full heart.

CHAPTER THIRTY-TWO

WHEN I GET to work, I walk straight into Alec's office. "You made them give me health insurance, didn't you?"

"Hello to you, too," he says. "I missed you yesterday—why didn't you return my text?"

Because, like a total lame-ass, I couldn't think of a clever response to *Hey kitten*. I was too focused on my looming doctor appointment.

"Tell me." I can't believe I didn't put it together sooner.

"It depends on if you'll be pissed at me or not." He offers a faux-nervous grin, and it makes me laugh.

"Thank you," I say, literally never having meant the phrase more than in this moment. I have pills in my purse. I have my first Straight Talk No Jacket appointment booked for two weeks from now. And actually being *heard* at the doctors' office today—by three different people, no less—makes me more hopeful than...ever. "You seem determined to change my life."

Then, because all of a sudden the air is filled with too much cheesiness for me to allow, I add, "Or maybe I'm still reeling from Friday night."

"You aren't the only one. When I close my eyes, I hear you purring, moaning. I can hear it when you speak now—those perfect little noises are right there waiting to be coaxed out of you."

I open my mouth, but find I'm too self-conscious about my voice to actually speak.

"Jesus, kitten, watching you... You have no idea..." He breaks off, cringing. "Shit. I have a meeting in ten minutes and I'm halfway to wood just thinking about Friday."

"So," I say, grinning, "I shouldn't ask you to remember what it felt like when I had you in my mouth? When my hands were gripping your ass? Your balls? My tongue flickering over you—"

"Teagan," he groans, leaning forward. "If you don't stop, I'm going to break a hole through the bottom of this desk."

"Let's not flatter ourselves, Alec. You're big—but nobody's got that sort of reach."

His laugh booms through the room. "Trust me, kitten. You give me all the reach in the world."

I drag my tongue over my lower lip, loving the way his eyes track the motion. "I'll leave you with this then." I lean over his desk to whisper closer to his ear. "I can still close my eyes and remember your flavor. And I'm desperate for another taste."

I exit his office high from the strangled noise my words force out of him.

And I giggle when he leaves late for his meeting, his expression pointed when he passes my desk.

Sam also shoots me a telling look. "What gives? Seriously. I need to know."

"I got a funny email," is all I say. He rolls his eyes.

I take my first Zoloft the next morning, breaking the small oval pill in half, like Dr. Jones suggested. I know I won't magically be super happy, but a tiny part of me can't help wishing maybe I'll be the first person ever to be affected that way.

All I feel, though, is a little spacey a few hours later. Sleepy—but not so much that it affects my work. Or my ability to flirt with Alec—thank God.

Most of the week passes much in the same way.

Reading long emails still really fucking frustrates me.

Filing still makes me miserable.

And it still takes me literally days to decipher notes I take during meetings. Which pisses me off more than everything else combined. Well, not including the fact that Alec hasn't asked me out again, and I've been too chickenshit to do it myself. It's so much fucking easier to take initiative with people who buy my act than it is with someone who sees through it the way he does. Actually, it's not that he sees through it—he doesn't even let me start the play.

Whatever.

Maybe the pills are kicking in, or maybe it's my own mental state feeling relieved because I'm at least taking pills that will help, but even when I'm pissed off, I only snap at Sam like fifty percent of the time.

Alec's out of town for the weekend—so I spend most of it in my room, listening to books and maybe, possibly, starting to fall for my boss for real. Because he gave me books. He gave me health insurance. He didn't run away from my crazy. Any guy who does all that seems like he'd be worth loving. At least a little.

Or maybe it's specifically because he's Alec. All I have to do is picture his face, imagine the timbre of his laugh, the weight of his hands on my body, and I start to melt. My body's ready for another interaction with his—so much so that I'm constantly in a state of anticipatory tingling—but he pushes on my heart, too, making it feel swollen beneath my ribs. His presence is there, on the sides of my neck that tighten when I can't fight a smile. In the tapping of my fingers when I'm counting down the hours until I see him again. Through my mind in the late hours of the night, while I toss and turn.

By Monday morning, it's clear. I've got it bad.

That sneaky motherfucker snuck his way into more than something physical, into feelings that travel under my skin like a lifeline. I'd give him a piece of my mind about it, if only I could stop grinning long enough to do it.

The next week, we're slammed.

Well, Alec is slammed. It's business as usual for me and Sam. But Alec is in constant meetings and out of the office half the time, and I hate it. I keep waiting for him to ask me out again.

I keep telling myself *I'm* going to ask *him*.

I keep chickening out.

Miss you, kitten, he texts me toward the end of the week, while I know he's meeting with his father.

Who is this again? I respond, smiling.

Don't act like I haven't heard you purr, he sends back. And a second later: *Can't tell you how much I'm dying to do it again.*

Oh, this must be Alec. Sorry. Hard to keep track of all my suitors.

You better be joking.

And if I'm not?

Sam snatches my phone out of my hands, and I whirl around in my chair. "Give that back."

"No. No way." He dances away from me, holding my phone out of reach. "You have a secret—and I know Alec's involved. If you won't spill it... I'll have to dig for it myself."

I'm up and in his face without thinking about doing it. "Give me my fucking phone."

"Teagan—come on."

"Ask me for my stories," I hiss, "and I might give them to you. But don't you take my shit. Don't you go digging where you have no right. *Give me my fucking phone.*"

Someone clears their throat, and I turn, realizing we've made a bit of a spectacle for the rest of the office. People are staring, people are smirking, people are avoiding my gaze. And good for them, too, because I'm ready to fucking roast anyone I catch looking.

"I was only joking." Sam shoves my phone into my hands, as the rest of the office begins to filter back into their regular routine. "I wouldn't really go through your phone."

"How the hell would I know that?" I ask, softening my tone when I notice how red his face is.

I...have issues with my privacy. Probably something to discuss with my therapist. But all I had growing up were my secrets. My life. I could share it with whom I chose—a select few people, and mostly just Cassidy. Sometimes Jason, but never all the way.

In fact, Alec knows me better already than anyone else ever has. I can't decide if that's sad, or if it means something more.

I sigh and walk to Sam's desk. "Here." I drop my phone in front of him, text messages opened. Alec's most recent one reading, *You're my only one if that makes a difference.*

"You're his only what?" He scrolls up through the conversation. "Suitor?" He glances at me, his eyes wide. "Okay, first of all, who the hell even uses that term anymore?"

"Don't be a dick. I couldn't think of what else to call it."

"Date. Boyfriend. Paramour. *Lover.*" He ticks off his fingers as he names all the words. So annoying. "Pick one. This is not the 1800s, Teagan."

I snatch my phone from him. Again. "And this is why I don't tell you things." It's why I don't tell most people things.

"Don't be all huffy," he says. "The more important thing here is—"

"*Huffy?* Now who's using outdated terminology?"

"Point made." He grins, but only for a moment. "But what about his fiancée?"

"Wipe that judgment from your tone," I say, quietly, glancing out to make sure nobody's paying us attention. "It's not what you think."

"You're not sleeping with him?"

"Well, no. But also, his situation with Piper... It's not my call to share, but..." What am I doing? I wanted to open up to Sam, but I can't do it by giving away a secret that isn't mine to share. "You know what? Forget it. I can't talk about it."

"No way. You have to dish, Teagan."

"This isn't some fucking reality TV show drama for you to sit back and munch popcorn with."

"Let me rephrase." He scratches his lower lip, hard enough I'm nervous he'll draw blood. "I'm in a huge fight with Ty, and I could use a distraction. And as *bitchy* as you are, for some reason I kind of like you, and I wouldn't mind getting to know you past that annoying exterior."

He's eighteen and talks like he's thirty. And I don't know whether or not his words piss me off. "Is this where I punch you or where I hug you?"

"How about don't touch me at all," he says. "You scare me."

A laugh expands in my throat, throwing itself from my lips. But it barely cracks a dent in his wounded expression, and I add more sedately, "Tell me what happened with the boy-toy."

Apparently, Ty doesn't want Sam to meet his parents. Which Sam would be fine with—except it's because Ty doesn't want to introduce a guy to them until he knows things are serious.

Sam's been under the impression they've been serious for months.

"Oh, honey," I say, wanting to cross the space between our desks again, but holding back because I know better than anyone what it's like to not want the pity that comes with physical comfort. "He's a moron."

"Too bad that doesn't make me want him any less than before." Sam stares at his computer screen, but I'm pretty sure his world's too bitter right now to take in much of what he sees.

"What are you going to do?"

He drops his face into his hands, smearing his words. "I don't know."

I mentally run over my bank account, knowing the balance down to the penny. I get paid tomorrow, which means I can splurge today. Or, at least, offer to buy the kid a meal. "How about I take you out to lunch, and you can tell me more—or not. Whatever. But let's get out of here, get some fresh air, get some—"

"Okay." His smile trembles when he looks at me, and he seems so young, so innocent. He's not that much younger than I am, but at the moment it feels like we're eons apart. Or maybe it's because he's wearing his emotions across his face and I keep mine trapped in my teeny, tiny heart.

I wish I hadn't been such a bitch to him before this.

I wait for self-loathing to set in, for anger to snap in my veins—and it *does* happen, but...it's muted. My mind manages to box up the self-loathing, pushing it away, and my blood quickly reduces to easy waves instead of tsunamis. Easy to ignore.

My smile doesn't tremble at all.

I wear it all the way up to when Alec strides toward us, his shoulders tense, his arms tight at his sides. He greets us, but his words are as stiff as his body language. Granted, his eyes soften when they land on me, but he doesn't linger, heading instead into his office, shutting the door slowly, with so much control I can tell it costs him.

Sam's chair squeaks when he swivels toward me. "Need a rain check on lunch?"

I'm already standing. "Give me ten minutes."

"Take as long as you need. I don't have much of an appetite anyway."

"We'll fix that," I tell him. And then I step into Alec's office.

CHAPTER THIRTY-THREE

INSTEAD OF SITTING behind his computer, Alec's slumped in a chair at the table in the corner, tapping—slamming—a pen up and down and up and down on the table. His suit jacket's strewn across his desk. His leg's jumping so hard the table's shaking.

"What's wrong?" I cross to him, intending to take a seat next to him, but he grabs my wrist, fast as a snake, and yanks me into his lap. "Alec!"

"What?" His question is surly, his tone raw. His thighs tense beneath me when he shoves his chair back further from the table. "The glass is frosted. Nobody can see us."

"They might be able to see one blurred shape at the table now, instead of two," I say, struggling—and failing—to escape from his arms.

"Nobody's paying that close attention. If you want me to stop, tell me. Otherwise, let me fucking touch you. I need to fucking touch you." He sinks his teeth into my earlobe, clamping a hand down on my thigh, forceful enough to make me jolt.

Deep down in my belly.

"HR probably frowns on this," I say, while also giving in, turning my face toward him and leaning back against his shoulder. "Did the meeting go badly?"

"You could say that." He pushes his nose into my neck and when he lifts his face he trails his tongue along my skin.

I shiver. Hard. And a longing unfurls between my legs, so full, so strong I'm tempted to widen them, to see what he does. But he's unhappy. And he's not getting out of talking this easily. I keep my legs where they are. "Upset client?"

I can't imagine that's it, though. A dissatisfied client wouldn't have Alec so tense his ab muscles are practically concrete against my back. That wouldn't have his shoulders so rigid it's a wonder he's not bursting through his shirt.

"Bullheaded father," he says. He's quiet for a moment, staring past me, but his thoughts swirl through his expression, so I wait for him to settle on the ones he wants to share. When he does, his words come out spiked as hammered nails. "He turned down my proposal again. And was pissed I don't want to let it go."

"Why didn't you tell me you were meeting him about that?" I ask, shock mingling with annoyance in my tone, in my gut.

"I wanted to tell you when I'd done it. Made it happen on my own." He works his jaw, his expression angry—but not with me. It costs him, I can tell, to admit defeat.

And his reasoning helps to melt my annoyance. "I'm sorry."

"I was captain of my lacrosse team in high school. Undergrad, too. President of my fraternity my sophomore and junior years—and my business fraternity now. In almost every aspect of my life, I'm a *leader*. I take charge. Yet my family... Jesus. I can't believe how much I roll aside to give them what they want. I've done everything my father's ever asked of me, everything Grandfather's ever demanded. A puppet, dancing whichever way they pull my strings. Pathetic."

I cover his hand with my own, needing a connection, hoping the contact will push the truth of my words into him. "Not pathetic. At all. And if they aren't pleased with how hard you work to make them proud, maybe it's time to cut some of those strings."

"Funny," he says, squeezing my fingers. "I was thinking the same thing. There are other investors I can go to."

"Or, you could talk with Mr. Evans," I remind him. "If the two of you joined forces on this, your dad would have to listen. He respects you both."

"He respects Brad, yes. Me? Not so much." There's not a single thread of self-pity in Alec's tone. Only a dry sort of acceptance.

I start to hate his father. But not everyone's family is as fucked up as my own. Maybe he deserves the benefit of the doubt, for a little while longer, anyway. "Maybe he'll respect you more if you don't give up."

"Maybe," Alec says. "But it's not only the proposal he's upset with me about."

"What happened?"

"You." He says the word so simply it takes a moment for my breath to disappear from my lungs.

"You told him about—"

"No." He shakes his head, nuzzling it against the side of my neck in a way that's probably meant to reassure me, but doesn't. "I mean you make me want to cut some strings, Teagan. But I've needed to cut them for a long time anyway."

"Okay...?"

"I told him Piper and I are ending the pretense of our engagement. He had opinions about it. Insistent opinions. He wants me to wait. Says it'll be bad for business right now. Says..." The size of the breath he takes pushes his chest against my back. "It doesn't matter."

It does, though. Discomfort rolls through my stomach like lava. "He has a point. It's stupid to throw away something that benefits your families on a whim. We've barely known each other a month."

But instead of looking relieved that I'm giving him an out—his expression darkens. "You're kidding, right?"

"Alec, I—" I freeze when he slides his hand up my leg, pushing my thighs apart. I tighten my hand on his to keep him tame—but he's a million times stronger than I am and drags both our hands under my skirt until he's cupping me against my underwear. Until *I'm* cupping his hand, while he cups me against my underwear.

"Um..." I can't remember how to breathe, how to say no, or why I'd even want to.

"This is not a whim. *You* are not a whim." He lays his palm flat against me, holding it still, heat transferring from his hand to my body. I start to pull my hand off of his—but he grabs it, covering it with his own, and presses it back against me. Pressing me...against myself.

I will not squirm. I will *not* squirm. "You can't know that."

"Yes," he says, curving his finger—and mine—over my panties, making me, damn it, squirm, "I can."

"How?" I mean to sound derisive, but he's using my own finger to tap out a rhythm beneath my skirt, and the word comes out in a whimper instead.

Tap, tap, tap. He leans closer to me, the pressure increasing, his mouth directly next to my face. "Because..." he says. *Tap, tap, press.* "You've been the first thing on my mind every morning since I met you."

Tap, tap, slap.

Oh my God.

I should tell him it's the same for me. He deserves to know.

But I can't make the words come.

"Show me what you like, kitten," he says softly in my ear. "Teach me how to touch you."

I swallow past the rise of nerves in my throat, past the flutters of excitement. "You've already proved yourself an A-plus student."

"This time I want a guide." He slides his thumb beneath the edge of my underwear, lifting it from my skin. "Show me."

"I can't." But there's an electric spark striking under my hesitation, telling me not to stop. I like this, touching myself for him.

"You can." He pushes against my hand and I let him, both our fingers creeping beneath my underwear. I'm wet already, no surprise, and *aching.*

"Alec," I beg. I always beg with him. For things I can't name. Somewhere in the back of my mind it annoys me, but the rest of my body's too turned on to care.

He reverses our hand positioning again, sliding his beneath mine. "Show me."

He's begging, too.

I can't believe I'm fucking doing this. What if someone walks in?

I twist my neck toward him to ask, but change my mind at the last minute, capturing his mouth with my own in a sharp, biting kiss, pulling at his lower lip with my teeth.

"I like this," I murmur, deciding on the spot to fucking go for it.

I press his finger, one, then two, into me.

"And this." I press his palm against me, showing him the pressure I like best. "Hard. Like this."

"You're so wet, so warm," he says, his voice rough. "So fucking sweet. You have no idea what that does to me, feeling you respond to me."

"Maybe I'm responding to *me*."

"Even fucking better." He picks up the pace, the pressure, the…everything, making my hips roll forward, so I can press myself harder against his fingers—against *our* fingers— moaning. "Shh," he teases. "Can't be too loud in here, kitten."

He tugs my skin, pulling it apart, and when he masters the rhythm I best respond to, he takes it on solo because I'm beginning to shake so hard, I need both hands to grip the table in front of us.

He shoves my underwear all the way to the side, dragging his fingers across me at the same time, making me gasp. The air hits me coolly and then his hand is back against me, and I swear to God I want to weep at the tumbled, erotic mix of sensations.

"Do I have it right, then?" He hooks one finger into me, sliding it, twisting it, hitting my spot—and new ones that turn my gasp into another moan. And another. And another.

He bites my mouth this time and yanks on my tongue with his teeth, pulling back with a pleased little smile, forceful enough to travel fluidly through me, a lightness twining with all the heat.

He's grown hard beneath me, pressing through his pants. When I shift my hips directly over him, he shudders and grabs my hip with his free hand, shoving me more roughly against him. "The things you make me want to do…"

"The things I want to let you do," I say. Grinding, grinding, while his fingers never stop fondling me, pushing into me, slipping along my slick skin.

The air is syrupy between us, weighty and fluid and sweet, and when he flattens his palm against me—pressing down harder, harder, pushing in another finger, deeper, deeper—I tingle so powerfully it's almost painful, and my head loses a battle with gravity, falling back to rest on his shoulder.

He lets go of my hip to rub his hand up my stomach, over my breasts, caressing, squeezing, tugging at my nipples until they're tight and sticking out through the thin fabric of my bra, of my shirt.

"You like this?" he asks, and when I nod, biting back the volume of the moan building in my throat, he captures my chin and tugs my face toward him. "I want to watch your face when you come."

The warmth of self-consciousness floods my cheeks, but it's nothing compared to the heat between my legs, and I don't look away. I bite my lower lip, my hips rocking, his wrist twisting.

We're in his office. We're supposed to be *working*. He's fucking me with his fingers so hard I can't keep from crying out.

This is so wrong.

I fucking love it.

He watches my face, his own so smugly intent it's almost enough to drop me over the edge. But it's more than his expression... It's this entire moment.

It's electrifying. And not because we aren't supposed to do this here.

It's this thing between us—between his hand and my body, between my heart and his mind; it's all connected and it *sizzles*. My breath is coming in little moans. My eyes close and my head starts to roll again, but he yanks my chin back in place, the short, demanding motion tipping me over the edge.

I've never been held so captive; I've never been regarded with such warmth.

His eyes are bright and determined. His fingers are quick and hard and demanding.

My body is trembling out of my control, and goose bumps rise along the base of my collarbone, a whirlwind sensation whipping through my body, spinning so fast I lose my breath.

"Look at *me*." He tightens his grip on my face, and when I open my eyes he's staring at me so intensely, my belly constricts and releases so fast, with such a physical blow, a cry that's more like a pleasured sob escapes my mouth.

And then it's not just my stomach pulsing. It's everything, everywhere. An orgasm funnels through me, taking up the space where my stomach used to be and slamming me lower, lower, until my legs squeeze shut around his hand, which he never stops moving.

His fingers nimble and fast, exploring me, his thumb pressing, pressing, smearing me in circles, while he whispers, "Fuck, that's it, Teagan, let it go, let it go," until I do. As quietly as I can, which is to say, not that quietly at all.

He releases my chin, sliding his hand up my face and into my hair, yanking my head to the side to capture my neck with his mouth and his foresty scent invades my senses, intensifying everything.

His fingers don't stop, tugging, piercing, twisting until there's not an inch of me left unexplored and then he starts again a second time, a third, and pressure like a deluge beats first in my chest then floods into my belly.

"Good girl," he growls, and I go completely under, lost, lost to the final crash of the orgasm. I squeeze my eyes closed—and, *oh God*, my mouth, to prevent any overly loud moaning—and it's like there's an entire ocean inside my body, whipping through me to the rhythm of his fingers in wild, biting, pleasure-filled waves, crashing, *swelling* through me.

Eventually, it slows, flowing more like water pushed by a breeze, lighter, lighter, until all that's left is a hollow, glowing memory of the motion that rocked me only moments ago.

Even still, I tremble.

Tremble.

Tremble.

CHAPTER THIRTY-FOUR

WHEN I FINALLY open my eyes, the light of the office somehow shocks me.

And then...

I nearly slide right off Alec's lap.

He locks his arms around me, keeping me from slamming into the table.

Holy hell *I may never be able to walk again*. My limbs are made of liquid, sloshing everywhere. I wonder if people heard me come. I tried so hard to stifle myself, but... I glance out at the office, but everything's so blurred I can't tell if anyone's looking.

"That was so fucking hot," he says a second (minute, year, century—who knows, who cares?) later, pulling me tighter against him.

"My clumsy ass?" I ask.

"The way you drenched my hand and moaned my name," he says, tossing a big ball of heat right back between my legs, holy hell.

"Oh... That..." I slowly, subtly pull my underwear across my still-exposed skin, doing my best—and failing—not to shiver in the process. When I'm covered, I stand, turning to face him, the table at my ass. Guess I can stand after all. But what I can't do is find the right words to respond with.

He runs his palms up my thighs, over my skirt this time. Which is a bit of a letdown—although I doubt I could handle a second round. He smirks, knowing exactly what I'm thinking. "If I thought you could handle another go, I'd bring you back to my lap. There's nothing I'd like more than getting to keep my hands on you—in you, the entire day. Fuck. I want you, Teagan. In every way. I want you."

I shiver again. And then... *Why?* I almost ask. Because I don't get it. But I'm still glowing, and I don't want to burst this bubble. "You want me...on my knees?"

"Stop." The word is quiet and deafens me all the same. "Don't purposefully twist my meaning into something less."

"I'm saying—"

"This is why I've worked so hard to keep my hands off of you recently." He stands, too, stepping away from me, toward his desk. "Don't you wonder why I haven't invited you back over?"

"Maybe." Yes. "Don't you wonder why I haven't asked *you* over?"

"I know why you haven't. It's for the same reason."

"Which is?"

He sweeps his jacket off his desk and shrugs it on, making the everyday motion sexy as hell. "Because, sweet Teagan, *I* know what this is between us. But I can't have you, not in my house, not in my bed, until *you* know it, too."

"I know what this is," I say.

"Tell me."

But I can't make the words come. Maybe I don't have the answer. Maybe I'm scared. Instead, I twist the silver picture frame on his desk... It's a toddler. Cute little girl. "Um. Do you have a kid?"

I don't know why the thought shocks me so much—but his expression drops down to something dark and he shakes his head. "That was my sister as a child."

"You have a sister?"

"Had." He closes his mouth and tells me more with his eyes than anything else that the conversation is closed as well.

"I'm sorry," I say, my heart twisting, an autumn leaf dropping from my chest, falling, falling.

"You still haven't told me what this is," he says.

I search his expression, but it's calmly unreadable.

"See," he says when I hesitate. "You can't."

I'm not sure which is more frustrating, my inability to articulate what it is between us, or his annoying determination to make me. "Why does it matter so much?"

"Pride, maybe," he admits with a shrug. "I want all of you, Teagan. Your body. Your mind. Your heart. And until you're ready, I don't want to take the risk." I open my mouth, but he speaks again first. "And let's clear the air about it because I know you won't tell me if you're thinking it—I'm not talking about sex."

"What if I want to talk about sex?" Because, suddenly, I do. "What if I want to do more than talk about it?"

"What if I want to invite you to my brother's wedding?"

"What if you didn't avoid my questions?"

"What if you said yes to mine?"

"Come on," I say, exasperation pushing my tone into something sharper than I intend. "Your dad's pissed that you want to break it off with Piper. You think he's going to allow your *receptionist* on your arm at your brother's wedding? When is it?"

"My assistant, not that it matters. Next weekend—and who cares about my dad?"

"Next weekend? Are you nuts?" Even if this were a good idea, I can't find a dress that fast. And, more importantly, "*I* care. And I'm pretty sure deep down you do, too."

He strides toward me and grabs my hands. "That's the thing. I don't. I've spent my entire life coasting along the path they chained me to. But I'm changing. *This* is changing me. And they need to know they can't control me anymore."

"I don't want to be used as a slap in your family's face."

"You're not a slap to them—you're a prize, a treasure, for me. I want to see you all dolled up and spend the night imagining what you're wearing underneath. I want to dance with you, to watch you whirl on my arm, and to catch you, all night. I want to taste the champagne toast still on your tongue when I kiss you."

It makes my head spin, everything he's describing. "God, what are you? A poetry major?"

"Don't snark your way out of this."

"Don't fill my head with fairy tales. I'm not your Cinderella."

"No. You're a kitten with a mighty roar." There's not a trace of mockery in his tone. I'm not sure how he does it. "Fuck Cinderella. This is our own story."

"*Fuck Cinderella*? Now you've gone too far." I try to smile, but it falls limply across my lips, dissolving into something closer to a frown. I'm...dazzled. He's stunned me with this sudden bout of intensity. "I'm not going."

"Because you don't want to—or because you're scared of my father?"

"Does it matter?"

"To me? Yeah."

"I don't want to get fired. Getting in the middle of a family battle when your father runs this company? It's not smart."

He laughs, a bitter sound, and trails the backs of his fingers down my jaw. "Don't you get it, Teagan? This thing between us? It guarantees you won't get fired. My father'd be setting himself up for such a huge lawsuit."

And immediately, I see it. If Alec tells his father about me—I'll keep my job.

For the *worst* possible reason.

The lava, long settled in my stomach from earlier, erupts in flames. "I don't want to blackmail my way into keeping my job." I slap his hand away, the sound ringing through the room. "And I'm pretty fucking offended that you think I would."

His sigh's so heavy, it sounds like it's attached to the weight of the world. "Do you hear yourself?"

"Do you?"

"Give me a little more credit." He laughs again, as sharp as the last time, but not as harsh. "We both know you'd never do that."

"Then why would you mention it at all?" I don't know what to do with my hands. He's standing here in front of me, one hand in his pocket, all casually cool, and I'm looking up at him like, I don't even know what. A moron. "Back up, would you? I can't think with you this close."

He lifts an amused eyebrow, taking a step back, and with distance between us I really do find it easier to sort through my thoughts.

"Thank you." I offer the words grudgingly.

"My remark about my father had everything to do with my frustrations with him and absolutely nothing to do with you." He reaches for my hand, stopping an inch short until he sees the permission in my expression. "Will you at least consider saying yes?"

As if any girl could resist the way he weaves his fingers through my hand, so gently—after I know how rough he can be with them? After very specific parts of my body are still halfway on fire from the way he hammered them against me?

"Will Piper be there?"

"Her whole family will be—but I can ask her to stay home. She might appreciate the time away from her family, away from mine..."

"No." I wait to feel nervous over attending the same event as Piper and her family, but I don't. Probably because I won't be going. "I thought we agreed to keep this secret—bringing me to a wedding kinda blows any sort of cover."

This stalls him. "I want to say I don't care, because for me, I don't. But I don't want to make things uncomfortable for you."

"Thank you," I say, annoyed at the disappointment running through me. He's being considerate. I should appreciate it.

But I don't.

He grins a cocky grin, like he can read it in my expression, though I'm trying so hard to keep it blank. "You want to go."

I do. I really do. "No, I don't."

"Say yes," he says, all demanding.

"I'll think about it," is all I'll promise, letting my gaze wander the office to avoid the pressure to give in.

"I get what I want, you know. Might as well say yes now." His smirk widens when I scowl at him. It'd be annoying if it didn't bring out his dimples. If it didn't fit the features of his face perfectly, all angles and smooth skin.

"I'll *think* about it." I turn to leave because I'm discovering that sometimes being near Alec, speaking with Alec, touching Alec, stirs things in me too...*full* to handle. I need space. Before I exit, I glance back. "But don't get your hopes up."

It's a weird thing, though, that my own hopes are raised. Not sure why. But the moment I step out of Alec's office, I'm buoyant.

All the way through lunch with Sam—who didn't seem to hear anything from Alec's office, or is too polite (or scared) to mention that he did.

All the way through the rest of the day.

All the way home, and even after that for a while, too.

"It's because he's totally falling for you," Cassidy tells me later, on the phone, her voice annoyingly confident.

I search for a way to argue against her point, but come up blank. "Shit. I mean, I wouldn't say he's *falling* for me. But he cares for me. Enough to upset his family by bringing me to his brother's wedding. You're right."

"Wouldn't be the first time."

"Keep telling yourself that." I scratch at a piece of chipped paint on my ancient cheap-o desk, the small familiar thrill when it lifts from the wood mingling with the much, much bigger thrill of the realization that Cassidy has a point.

"Doesn't change the fact that I can't go."

"Oh, come on. You know you want to go."

I roll my eyes hard enough she might actually see me through the phone. "No shit. But I don't want to lose my job—*or* keep it because I spread my legs for Alec." My stomach literally rolls with my words. I hate cheapening what's between us. "Not that that's all it is," I say, quickly.

"I *knew* it. You're totally into him, too."

"Whatever." Suddenly I feel like the exposed piece of my desk, her words scraping at the cheap paint I usually cover myself with. "That's not the point."

"No, but it's *a* point. And a pretty big one, too."

"You're not helping."

"Go to the wedding," she says. "It'll be huge and fancy and perfect. How can you pass that up?"

"You mean how can someone like me, from the slums, pass up the opportunity for a ritzy evening?" My tone would slice a lesser person into millions of slivers. Not Cassidy, though. I have no doubt she's rolling her eyes almost as hard as I was a second ago.

"You're impossible."

"So are you." A smile works its way through my tone, because she's driving me nuts—but I don't want to rip her head off like I usually do. "Anyway. Where are you off to this weekend?" She travels almost every weekend for her travel blog.

"Uh..." She pauses for a moment, probably in shock because I neglected to blow up at being called impossible. I can't blame her. I'm a little surprised myself. "New York, there's a small indie film festival right outside the city."

Part of me wants to tell her about the Zoloft. She'd want to know. But she'd also be *too* happy for me. And as much as I love her, I'm not ready to come clean. About that, or the learning disability, or...being a virgin. Still, when she asks, so casually, about how Alec measures up in bed, I can't lie to her.

"I'm keeping this one to myself" is all I say, fighting a wave of irritation that she'd ask like that. Like sleeping with Alec would ever be some easy offhanded thing to do or talk about. This irritation surprises me. It's my fault she doesn't know sex is a big deal for me. I'm the one who spent years letting her think—*leading* her, and everyone else, to think—I bang basically anything that moves. Funny, at one point I felt like it gave me so much power.

It no longer makes sense to me. All I feel is regret for not being happy with myself as I was.

"You have it *so* bad," she says.

This time, I don't deny it. I'm done lying about my romantic life. Right now. But I move the conversation on to other things because I'm not ready to come all the way clean about everything else. Not yet.

When we hang up, I still don't know what to say about the wedding. I stare at my ceiling the rest of the night, conflict eating up all the space in my brain that's otherwise become reserved for listening to books.

In the morning, I know what I'm going to do.

CHAPTER THIRTY-FIVE

I'M NOT GOING to the wedding.

I don't want to risk my fledgling career. Denise came to mind a few times during the night—how powerful she is, how efficient, how she runs meetings without breaking a sweat—and if I fuck it up with Alec's family, I may never get to be her.

Hell, I may never get to be her regardless, but I don't want to stack the odds higher against me.

I can't go. What I can do, though, is revel in how hard Alec tried to convince me to change my mind yesterday.

I mean, he really tried to change my mind.

And told me he wanted me.

Like, not just in bed. Which—even if that was all—would still be more than anyone's seen in me in a long time. But he wants more.

And he can have it.

He thinks I don't know what this is, but I do now. I get it.

I leave my room, ready for work, with this grin that my facial muscles are growing all too familiar with. The Alec-inspired grin. Both annoying and wonderful.

He'll be pissed when I tell him no, but I'm not worried. Because he cares for me—enough not to end things over my decision. What's one missed social event? And, plus, maybe I'll sweeten my answer with...a trip down south, under his desk.

Yum.

My breath skips a few beats, imagining it. I want him in my mouth.

I want him in my life.

And instead of scaring me, this *thrills* me.

Enough to have me practically hopping down the hallway to the stairs—I mean, obviously I don't hop, but still. I haven't even had the urge to do so since...elementary school?

That urge to skip disappears real fast, though, when I get to the stairs.

Because Gramps is lying at the bottom of them, prostrate.

Panic chainsaws through my throat, but I breathe past it. He probably got drunk last night, couldn't make it up the stairs and passed out there.

But the rationalization doesn't keep me from sprinting down the stairs, splinters scouring my palm against the bannister.

"Gramps?" I nudge his face. Nothing. I shake his shoulder with enough force to bruise him, turning him onto his back. Nothing.

"What the hell are you doing?" Gran says angrily from the steps behind me. I didn't hear her approach, but she doesn't startle me. I'm too numb in the moment. This can't be happening.

I slap Gramps' face...

And he wakes up like a fucking caged animal, yelling and thrashing—and nailing me right in the damn cheekbone. So hard my ears ring.

"Goddamn it, Teagan." My grandmother's words float to me like they're filtering through cotton.

I shake my head. "What?"

He's on his feet now, bellowing and still swinging and staggering to the couch, falling over the armrest and snoring immediately.

I'm numb on the inside.

Not the outside though. My cheek hurts like a bitch.

"Frozen peas in the freezer if you're going to complain." Gran's voice comes through clearer this time from her perch above me in the stairwell.

I spin toward her, spitting, "Did I say anything?"

"I see you rubbing your face, like a timid old man could actually do any damage." She's looking at me like I'm a piece of trash, and the steel in her tone is stronger than any compactor.

Thankfully, I'm used to it. "He fucking clocked me. No shit I'm rubbing my face. It hurts."

"See? Complaining." She pats her hip, probably for her pack of smokes, forgetting she's in her nightgown. "If you'd left him alone, your face wouldn't be smarting now."

I blink. I blink again.

I blink like the wipe of my eyelids on my eyes will somehow cover my ears as well. "Are you kidding?"

"You know what he's like when he's drunk."

"Yeah, he's an idiot. Clumsy. Not violent." I've never been hit before. No matter what else my grandparents have done to make me miserable, they've never been physically abusive.

Five more months. I have to hold on for five more months, when I'll have saved enough to be comfortable on my own.

But... I can't keep waiting.

Maybe it's the Zoloft. Maybe I'm changing at my core anyway. Maybe it's a combination—but whatever it is, I'm looking around the place I've always grudgingly called home, with fresh eyes. Peeling paint. Stacks of cigarette butts shoved in ashtrays on end tables that wobble next to sagging furniture. The hole in Gramps's sock and his disgusting yellowed toenail sticking out of it. Not that I didn't notice how gross this place was before, but for the first time, it's too much to stand. Getting out is more pressing than saving money.

"How have we lived like this for so long? It's vile." The question is more for me than her, because I can't believe I have.

Saving money is a valid reason, but maybe it's not the room I'm seeing with fresh eyes. Maybe it's the truth in my heart. Saving money is also an excuse to stay in place. And it's not cutting it anymore.

She pats her hip a second time and grunts, shoving past me and grabbing an old butt from a side table, lighting it. "Don't you insult the roof I've kept over your head. You're no better than we are."

"Yes," I say, allowing this truth to sink all the way in—for me, for her—before I continue. "I am."

"Get out of my house." She points toward the door.

A bitter laugh escapes my mouth. "That's it, though, isn't it? This is your house. Never mine. Never a home."

"Show some gratitude," she says, sneering so hard I can't figure out how the cigarette's not falling from her lips. "We took you in when—"

"Nobody else wanted me," I recite tartly. This line's been thrown at me so many times it's on permanent repeat in the back of my mind most days. Louder on the bad ones. "Why are you such a nasty person? Why are both of you this way? What did I ever do to deserve this?"

You were born, I hear her thoughts as loudly as if she speaks them. *You were born and your mother—the one person we actually loved—left because of it.*

But we don't talk out loud about my mother here, and so she doesn't say the words. And if she has another response, I don't stick around for it. "I am better than you," I repeat, walking to the door. And, before I close it on my way out, I add, "Or, at least I'm on my way."

It takes a few moments on the road until I notice how hard my hands are shaking. It takes longer than that to figure out exactly what it is I'm feeling.

Fury.

Reckless with it, I text Alec at a red light. *You want to use me to slap your family, go ahead. I'm in for the wedding.* Because I'll be using the event to slap my grandparents too. Fuck them for thinking I'm not good enough. God. Fuck everyone.

Let's skip over the part where I remind you I'm not using you as a slap to where I tell you I'm thrilled you've accepted my invitation. I'll be smiling my entire flight to Vegas.

Right. His brother's bachelor party. He won't be at work today.

I'm taking off today since you aren't there.

A pause, and then: *Playing hooky while the boss is gone. I like it.*

Shit's not always about you. I hit send and then hate myself for it.

He calls me and I clear it, because what the hell can I say after that?

He calls me again and I answer because I know. "I'm sorry."

"What's wrong, kitten?" His tone is low and tender enough to make a sliced onion cry.

Not me, though. "Fight with my grandmother. Pretty sure she

threw me out. Pretty sure I was leaving either way."

"Go to my place. I'll have Matthew give you a key."

"Um…" My mind circles his words like a vulture. His huge condo. I can see myself there. It's tempting. It's too tempting. "No. I have somewhere else I can stay." Probably.

"You sure? I kind of enjoy the thought of you in my place. In my bed. In my T-shirt again…"

Don't pass up such a golden opportunity, my mom's voice invades my conscience. So I say, "Have a good trip. I'll see you Monday," and I hang up before he can say anything else.

Before *she* can say anything else.

CHAPTER THIRTY-SIX

CASSIDY'S IN NEW YORK, and even if she wasn't, I don't want to stay with her. I can't be surrounded by the echoes of Jason without going crazy. Also, I'm pretty sure Mr. Evans is disappointed in me for going out with Alec.

It's Vera's place I drive to. She likes her sleep, so I doubt she has any classes scheduled this early. I'm assuming I'll catch her before she leaves. I huff it up the stairs to her apartment, and I lift my hand to knock right as the door opens and I find myself face to face with a brown-haired guy who looks familiar, but I can't place him.

"Oh. Hello," he says, his tone as surprised as his expression.

"Slinking out at eight a.m.," I say, giving him the look that feels right at home across my face. Disgust. "Classy act, dude."

He cocks his head to the side, his own expression cooling. "Actually—"

"*Teagan.*" Vera walks up behind him in tiny pajamas. "Quit it with the third degree." She slides a kiss on his cheek from behind, gently prodding him out the door, past me. "Have fun in New York, Jeff."

His eyes slide over me when he turns to take one last look at her. "See you when I get back?"

"Call me." Her smile's wide, but it doesn't reach her eyes.

Then he's gone and she's ushering me inside and I'm watching her cute little butt in these shorts tinier than underwear and wishing, not for the first time, I had a nicer ass. "You wear those shorts around any guy, they're going to beg you for another round."

"I wear these regardless of whether I'm sleeping alone." She drops into a seat at her dining table, back to a half-eaten bowl of Cheerios. "And speaking of sleeping, I was planning on getting back to it, so why are you here?"

"I'll leave," I say, ready to turn around, but she holds up a hand to stop me.

"No," she says, her mouth full of cereal. "Stay. Sorry. I'm tired and Jeff…makes me tense."

"Why was he here?"

She gives me a cynical expression. "Because he's also kinda helpful at relieving tension."

"Where do I know him from?"

She spoons more cereal into her mouth. "He's a roadie for Gold Rush Standard. You met him with me last summer."

"*That's* it. Guess he has some free time with Luca James in rehab?" I snort. The poster boy for the anti-drug movement had everyone fooled. Especially Cassidy. She almost lost Gage last summer when she went off gallivanting with Luca. She still beats herself up for what she did—even though she and Gage are annoyingly happy. Personally, I think they're a stronger couple now because they know how miserable they are apart.

And let's be real. Who *wouldn't* run off with the sexiest rock star alive if they had the chance?

Although, I think of Alec and… I'm actually not sure I would. Granted, I don't have the offer on the table, so who knows? Plus, Cassidy was all fucked up from Jason's overdose.

She ran away with a rock star to deal with her grief. Mine took my natural inclination toward bitchiness and set it on a steroid cycle. Pretty sure she got the winning hand in that fucked-up card game.

"What?" I ask Vera, who's waiting for a response to something.

"What happened to your face?"

I touch my still-tender cheek. "Long story."

She waits, a pointed expression on her face.

I sigh. "Gramps. But it was an accident."

She watches me a few seconds longer, as though trying to weigh the truth of my words.

"I swear. It wasn't on purpose." I wave away the box of Cheerios she offers me, taking a seat across from her. "How was your mom's visit?"

"Weeks ago," she says, snapping in a very un-Vera-like way.

"I started a new job, Ver. I've been busy, if you're pissed I haven't checked in sooner."

"You had time to talk to Cassidy. Even stopped by her house before a date."

"Your mom was here then," I remind her, but it only makes her eyes flash.

"And I could've used a break."

We can keep going down this rabbit hole of sniping, or I can apologize... Which, oddly enough, doesn't make me want to murder her for considering. "I'm sorry. I should've called you."

"You don't have any—" She cuts herself off, brows furrowed. "Wait. What?"

"Believe *me*, I'm not repeating myself," I say, grabbing my phone from my bag and placing it on the table. "And before you keep grilling me, don't forget—these things work both ways."

She stares at me like I've grown antlers. And then, surprising the hell out of me, she giggles. "I'm itching to fight with someone and I would've bet millions you'd be an easy target to practice with—and yet, here you sit, all calm. Way to ruin my ability to be irritated. Who are you and what have you done with Teagan?"

"I didn't know you had the ability to be irritated to begin with," I say, reeling inside from her words. She's right. I should be an easy target for verbal sparring—but I bit back my desire to punch out. And apologized instead.

A grin yanks my lips apart, and despite everything shitty that this morning started with, happiness looms in my chest like an overfull balloon. I was nervous I'd feel different taking an antidepressant, but I don't. I'm still me—but I'm also a version of myself I can actually almost stand.

"How's this?" I ask, loving the way her eyes are all wide at my expression. "I'll tell you something I haven't told Cassidy. Or anyone."

She leans forward, her elbows on the table. "Like you have to really ask a journalist if they want an exclusive?"

"Calm down, Ms. Journalism Major," I say. "This is so far off the record it's like pen and paper have never been invented."

"Obviously," she says, huffing, offended. "I'm just so glad you're actually ready to open up to me about something—anything."

"Do you want my story or do you want a box of tissues for the tears you seem about to burst into?"

"*There* she is," Vera says, her voice dripping with the smile she's trying not to wear. "That's the Teagan I love."

"You care about me. You love me. I mean, my God. You're smothering me."

"Watch it, or I will." She points beyond me to her living room, the furniture all dressed with hot pink pillows.

"Death by girly-ass pillow? I literally can't think of a worse way to go."

"Just shut up and tell me what's going on with you."

So, I do. I tell her about the Zoloft. And about the learning disability. And it all comes out so much easier than I expect.

And Vera doesn't even blink. I couldn't ask for a better reaction.

"Visual perceptive learning discrepancy," she repeats, slowly. "My best friend from high school had an auditory processing discrepancy... I wonder if they're similar." Then she shakes her head. "No—probably the opposite. He has to write everything down—or read instructions rather than hear them."

"Yeah, I'm the opposite," I say, agreeing. "I need to hear things."

"And you feel like knowing that about yourself makes life easier?"

I nod. "Don't get me wrong, life's not perfect. Hell, I'm here because Gran kicked me out of her house. But, I handle situations better now than before. And knowing *why* things aren't always easy for me helps."

"Obviously, you'll move in with me," she says, all nonchalant.

Some of the tightness in my chest unravels. "I was going to ask if you wanted a roommate."

"Yes. Please," she says, excitement lighting her face. "I've been so lonely since Cassidy moved out."

"But Cassidy's fun," I remind her. "And I'm—"

"A total bitch sometimes," she says. "I know. But I could use someone like you around, helping me toughen up a bit. I'm sick of people seeing all my fluff and no substance."

I gesture toward her pink pillows. "You kind of set yourself up for it."

"I'm allowed to enjoy girly things and still kick ass."

And to this, I have no comeback. "True. I got paid today. I can give you rent and a deposit." I'll be back to pennies in my account afterward, but...worth it.

She stands, dumping her bowl in the sink. "Please. My mom pays for this place. I don't want your money, just your company."

"I'm not going to live here for free." I stand too, leaning on the table.

"The only things I actually pay for are cable and internet. You can split those bills with me."

"I'll pay them fully," I counter.

"Fine. Then with my extra cash, I get to take you out to dinner once a month."

I definitely have the better end of this deal. "I love you too, you know." Ugh. My stomach twists. Pills or no pills, this fluffy girly stuff is so not ever going to be my style. "Don't get used to hearing it."

"Hearing it this once'll keep my soul lighter than air for...gosh..." She slams a hand dramatically over her heart. "*Years*, at least."

"Shut up," I say. "Show me my room. Then you can go to sleep."

"Do you need to get your stuff from your car?"

This deflates a bit of air from my bubble. "I didn't think to grab anything when I left. I was too mad. And I really don't want to go back there." Then, though, I discover the perfect Band-Aid. "But I got paid today. And I'm skipping work. So I'll go buy new things for now."

"In that case," she says, "fuck sleep. I hear the word shopping and I don't even need coffee anymore."

I glance around her apartment. Splashes of pink and black and gold. Feminine and bold. "You do have an eye for pretty things. Maybe you can help me find a dress."

"For what?"

"Get changed," I say, grabbing my keys. Springs Corner won't be open yet for the best shopping, but we can hit other, less expensive stores for necessities like underwear and a toothbrush first. "Then I'll drive. And I'll tell you all about Alec in the car." I use my palms to push up from the table and wince at the pain. I forgot about the splinters on the banister in my haste down to Gramps earlier. "Also, do you have tweezers I can borrow? I've got a few slivers of wood to pull from my palm before I do anything else."

She brings me tweezers—and rubbing alcohol, which stings like a motherfucker. But other than that? My day finishes a hell of a lot better than it started. I end up with the things I'll need to survive the next couple weeks, plus several cute new pairs of pajamas, almost as tiny as Vera's—and a fucking amazing dress. And the bruise on my face fades so much by the end of the day, I bet it'll disappear by Monday and I won't have to answer any stupid questions about it.

I can't believe Gran kicked me out.

I can't believe how *relieved* I am to be away from there. Well. Yes, I can.

Mostly, though, I can't believe how lucky I am to have someone like Vera in my life to make it all so much less horrible than it could be.

Cassidy, too. Who knows better than to offer sympathy even all the way from New York when I fill her in on everything. All I get is a series of texts making plans for all the girls' nights we'll have in the future.

And drinks. Lots and lots of drinks.

CHAPTER THIRTY-SEVEN

ON MONDAY BEFORE work, I borrow Vera's laptop for my first online therapy session. Vera fixes me with a stern expression. "You break that laptop, I break you. *Capisce?*"

"Being tough only works if the other person doesn't know you well enough to know you're full of shit."

"Oh. I guess that's why you're not scary anymore." She lets her features fall into the closest thing to smug I've seen her wear.

"Blah, blah," I say, waving my hand through her words. "You'd still be scared if I wanted you to be." She starts to retort, but I'm running late, so I cut in before she can, gently patting the laptop in my hand. "I promise to take care of your baby."

"Have a good appointment." Vera loved the idea of an online therapy site. If mine goes well, she's going to sign up, too. Knowing I'm not the only one who could use someone professional to speak with makes it easier for me to close myself in the guest room—or, *my* room now—and log on to the site. While I wait for the video component to load, I pull my headphones from Alec out of my purse, connect them to the laptop, and slide them on. By the time I'm done, my therapist is logged on as well.

Dr. Wú looks like she's in her late thirties and has a friendly face. She's thrilled the Zoloft is working already. "So many people have to try different combinations to find something that helps," she says. "It's easy to get discouraged—I'm glad you won't."

"I've been wondering if it's partly a mind over matter thing," I admit, leaning against the headboard, cringing when it squeaks. "Like I know the pill should help me, so taking one every day puts me in a better mental place before it even takes effect."

"I'm sure that helps," she says, a strand of hair falling forward when she nods. She tucks it into place. "I went over your questionnaire last night, so before we go over that—is there anything in particular you'd like to speak about?"

That damn questionnaire took me hours to fill out. And I'm sure it was riddled with spelling errors and incomplete sentences and…whatever.

My mind flashes to my grandparents. Who raised me on permanent thin ice.

To my mom. Who never wanted me.

To a blank spot where my father's face would be if I knew what he looked like. Which is stupid to wish for because he never wanted me either.

My throat strangles itself when I try to find the words to bring him up. "No. I'll let you lead, if that's all right."

She tucks more hair behind her ear and takes the conversation in a direction I'm much more comfortable with. "How have you been dealing with Dr. Reyes' suggestion of a possible learning disability?"

"I haven't really been dealing with it," I admit. "It's nice to know, but the thing is I don't want my life to be about depression. And I definitely don't want my life to be about a learning disability."

"It doesn't have to be," she says, glancing down from the screen for a moment. "Is your life about having red hair? Is your life about enjoying horror movies?"

"Those aren't the same."

"They're a part of who you are."

"Still. Not the same."

"Would you say you've felt much of your life *has* been about your anger?" she asks.

The answer is simple. "Yes."

"You wrote on your questionnaire you believe that anger stems from depression and your learning disability. Which means, by addressing them, you're fighting the thing that's made you most upset. Maybe having days where your life is about those things is preferable to the days in the past when it's seemed to be all about anger. Because you're treating all of it now."

"I don't want to think about it all the time, every second of every day."

"And you won't. But even with Zoloft, even with therapy, some days, your life will be about your depression. But some days it won't. That's the way this illness works. The good news is you're helping yourself now—and hopefully we can maintain things so that *most* days it's not at the front of your mind."

"I need some time to swallow that," I say. "I get that it's true. I knew it coming into this. But...hearing it so black and white is a lot to chew."

"I understand." She glances down again at something off screen before saying, "Then let's move on to some of the ways you can best help yourself."

Uncertainty has its grips in me, though, sliding doubts under my skin. Maybe therapy is stupid. Maybe Zoloft is stupid. If I can't get to a place where I never have to think about depression, what's the point? My mind is forceful enough to move the thought to my mouth. "What's the point?"

"You can do nothing and let your depression bring you lower and lower—or you can fight it and let it make you stronger in the process."

I appreciate that she didn't miss a beat, didn't need clarification. "Tell me how to help myself."

She wants me, it turns out, to more actively deal with my learning disability.

I'm not surprised. One of the reasons I selected Dr. Wú was for her description on the website. She specializes in depression—and learning disabilities. Also drug use and career guidance and grief counseling. While the time that's passed since Jason's overdose has really helped me heal, I could probably use a bit of retroactive grief counseling anyway.

I thought Dr. Wú and I would be a good fit. And she's starting to make me think I was right.

"Self-determination is important when you learn differently than others," she says, her words easy and mild-mannered enough to keep me from feeling bad about myself for being different. And she goes on to discuss the different aspects of self-determination.

Understanding myself and the ways I learn differently and how it all might affect my performance in daily life. Setting goals to keep myself on track with the ability to complete tasks. Learning from my experiences, tweaking and improving processes as time goes on, to make my career—my life—more manageable.

"Eventually," she tells me, "it will all become second nature. So you won't be living it every day. Or, rather, you will be, but you won't be so aware of it. You'll have set the stage for your own success."

I can't decide if the work ahead of me makes me excited—or full of dread. When I mention how sometimes I confuse the two, how sometimes I should be thrilled, but get angry instead, she tells me it's common.

"Sometimes depression or anxiety can make it hard for your body to understand what you're feeling," she says. "Your system can mistake excitement for anxiety, or regret for anger. But this is part of self-awareness, and knowing these things will help to temper them."

Our session's up after that, but I set my next appointment before closing out. Because while she makes it all sound so easy, I'm sure the moment I'm out the door today, I'll forget it all. Or twist it. Or think of a zillion questions about everything.

Funny thing, though. When I step out the door, I don't forget it all.

I drive to work reliving the conversation. Helps that it was face-to-face and I didn't have to read anything.

Which is a strength I should focus on. I hit the brakes, skidding to a stop behind the car in front of me, which is doing the same thing. Ugh. Traffic. But I have a good memory. If I hear something, I understand it a lot quicker than if I read it.

I should ask for a tape recorder for meetings, instead of taking notes. Or whatever the modern equivalent is for a tape recorder. Suddenly, excitement dances in my stomach. And this time it doesn't feel at all like dread.

"They're called voice recorders," Sam tells me later, as we start our computers. "But you don't need one."

"Actually, I do," I say, snarking a little because ugh. He doesn't get to tell me what I do or don't—

"No, I mean you can get an app for it on your phone."

"Oh." I offer my cringe as an apology. "I can't believe I didn't think of that."

"Here." He spins his computer screen toward me. "These are the top-rated ones."

I can't read them from where I'm sitting, and I lean back like I'm too lazy to get up. "Tell me which one I should get."

He studies the selections for a few moments and rattles off the name of the one he thinks will be best for recording meetings instead of personal thoughts or dictation.

"Where's Alec?" I ask, glancing at the clock. "He's late."

"He's out until Wednesday for his brother's thing in Vegas."

"Till *Wednesday*?" A whine forces its way into my tone. Yuck. But I didn't realize he'd be gone so long.

Ugh. Now I miss him.

"Yes. So that gives you two full days to catch me up with what the hell is going on with you two."

I pull my phone out of my bag to download the app Sam named—and, obviously, to avoid answering him. But as if on cue, a text from Alec buzzes in my hands. *What are you wearing?*

I bite back a laugh. *I'm at work, weirdo. Nothing to see here.*

You're always worth looking at. I need a visual.

What are you even doing up right now? Isn't it before 6 am over there?

Haven't been to bed yet. Caught up in gambling. And then maybe a comic book or two. Send me something for sweet dreams.

Nerd. I shake my head, but I also hike up my skirt. Just a few inches. Just showing a bit of thigh. And I send him a picture of my knees.

Jesus. Can't want to spread those gorgeous legs again. And a few seconds later: *I need to see your face.*

And because he makes a grin start all the way in my chest before it travels to my lips, I give him one. It's harder to take and Sam snickers when he catches me, but I'm too happy to care.

How are things at home?

New home now, I write, wondering how to send a tone through text message so he'll know I don't want to talk about it.

Are you all right?

I send him a picture of my middle finger.

A minute passes, and then Alec responds with a picture. His face, his hair all spread out and messy on his pillow, smudges of shadows under his eyes, but a smarmy twist to his mouth. *You didn't ask, but here I am anyway.*

Send me something a little lower, I respond, my fingers shaking with the sudden flash of hunger for him. And when he does, the image comes in of his bare chest, sculpted abs, the start of his happy trail…and the rest of him covered by a comic book. I take a closer look just in case—but all I get from it is the name of the comic book. *Silver Surfer.* I crack up because he's such a nerd, but nothing about his reading tastes keeps me from taking another look. And another. And that flash of hunger erupts into something much, much stronger.

Have to turn my phone off, I say. *Otherwise I might combust. Hurry up and come back to me.*

I do turn it off, too, because I'm not sure how I won't spend my entire day staring at those photos. And I swear the deep timbre of his laugh reaches me all the way from the other side of the country.

I'm eating lunch in the break room when Denise walks in. She acknowledges me with a quick nod and half a smile before hightailing it to the coffee pot. Which, thank God, I've refilled. She adds creamer and sugar and without even waiting for it to cool, chugs.

"Thank God for caffeine," I say.

"Back-to-back-to-back meetings all day—all week. I'd be dead without it." She fully smiles this time. "You're Teagan, right? Alec's assistant?"

"I am." It's like a high school crush, the sort of thrill that jumps through me because she knows my name. I place my fork carefully on my plate, not wanting another bite of salad in case it gets stuck in my teeth. "And you're Denise?" As though I haven't had her name tattooed in my mind from the first meeting she ran. But it doesn't do me any favors to play dumb. "I mean, I know who you are. Sorry. Nice to meet you, Denise."

Awesome. Rambling on top of wishy-washiness. Her expression's amused, and she leans against the counter, not speaking. Probably waiting for me to keep adding feet to my mouth. I should go back to my salad.

Then I remember Dr. Reyes telling me to be my own advocate.

I stand, instead, to face Denise. "I wanted to tell you that... I think the way you run meetings is brilliant. And it seems like you're brilliant in every other area of your job, from what I hear in those meetings anyway."

"Thank you." Her amusement turns to something else. Surprise, maybe?

I don't know how to take it, but I keep going anyway. "And Alec's leaving at the end of the summer to return to Harvard..." This gives me pause. I haven't been focusing on it at all—but now my stomach's dropping with the weight of an eighteen-wheeler. He's leaving... I'm staying.

"And?" Denise prompts me with a kind, but firm, tone.

Right. Take it one thing at a time. *Deep breath. Eye contact. Don't wipe your clammy hands on your skirt... Whoops.*

"And I'm not sure what my responsibilities will be when he goes, but if you ever need an assistant—or any position that would give me the opportunity to work for you—I would love the chance."

She takes a long glance around the break room. "This place has been a lot cleaner the past few weeks—are you responsible for it?"

Now it's easy to look her square in the eye. "I am."

Sam's squeamish about cleaning up after other people, but even at its messiest, the break room is practically sterile compared to my grandmother's house. So I clean it, and he organizes the supply room. It works. And now, I'm even gladder for it.

"I already have an assistant," she says. "But I like your initiative. I'll see what I can do."

Her words keep me floating through the rest of the day—and the next one too.

Then Alec doesn't return on Wednesday.

My grandfather's doctor had to go out of town, he texts me. *I'm on babysitting duty the rest of the week. But I'll be there to pick you up Saturday. Can't tell you how much I'm looking forward to seeing you... Touching you...*

I shiver when I text him Vera's address and tell him I hope his grandfather feels better soon—and that I'm sorry he has to miss work.

It hits me a few minutes later—Alec is a good person. Down to his core.

He's demanding and arrogant. He's got more talent in the tip of his tongue than I ever knew was possible—definitely more than any other guy I've ever known. And his family's got some serious issues...

But through it all, he's good. His heart is good. He's the kind of guy who'll miss work to spend his days with his sick grandfather—who, let's be real, seems like a total asshole.

I *admire* Alec.

I'm going to miss him so much when he's at school. I'm not sure how I'll function. The thought makes a fist in my stomach, clenching so tight I stop breathing. It hurts. The thought of being without him hurts.

Fuck.

I tap my fingers against my coffee mug so hard it sloshes onto my desk. I wipe it up with my hand, too distracted to do much else.

I don't want to run away. I don't want to push him away.

These are the things that usually define who I am.

I'm changing. And he's part of the reason why.

CHAPTER THIRTY-EIGHT

VERA HELPS ME get ready for the wedding, and the more she grins the harder I frown.

"You're allowed to be excited, you know." She tugs another strand of my hair around her curling iron.

"How the hell am I supposed to be excited when I can barely breathe?" I press my hands into my stomach as the lid of the toilet, where I sit, digs into my tailbone. This is stupid. I never should've agreed to go. "His pretend ex-fiancée is going to be there. He told his family he's bringing me. His father. His *grandfather*." I wish I'd never texted him to ask if his family knew. I wish he'd told me how they reacted, so I had a better grip on what to expect, but he's too *Alec* to do that. Too polite. Too considerate of my feelings. Which pretty much tells me all I need to know about how his family took the news.

Oh, God. I can't do this.

"So what? It's not like they wouldn't know you were there when, you know, *you show up with him*." Vera doesn't get it.

"So his family doesn't like me." Which, okay, *might* not be true—but I can't imagine they're thrilled, considering I'm the reason he broke off his perfect, business-favorable engagement. "I've never met the fiancée—ex-fiancée. Ex-pretend-fiancée. Whatever. I haven't met her—so it's been like she doesn't exist. But she *does*. And it's weird that I'm going. And to the rest of the world, I'm a fucking cliché. Like he dumped her for his secretary."

"When have you ever cared what other people thought?"

"His dad's the CEO of my company," I say, seething because I have to explain. "What he thinks of me matters."

"Then don't go," Vera says, laying the curling iron down on the sink. "If it's such a huge mistake, back out."

"Maybe I will." I stand, irritation wrapping around me tighter than the curls she's created in my hair. I start to stride out of the room—but I catch a glimpse of my reflection from the corner of my eye and…

Wow.

"Vera," I breathe. "What did you do to me?"

Her reflection regards mine smugly. "Not much. Just played up on your features a bit."

It's so much more than that.

My eyes are huge, and my skin glows. My cheeks are softly rose-tinted and my lips are halfway parted, pretty and pink.

"You're a fucking genius," I say.

"Tell me something I don't know." She puts her hand on my shoulder, pushing me toward my seat on the toilet. "And imagine the final product when you're actually in the dress."

I let her guide me, because now I'm imagining Alec's face when he sees me for the first time in a week, all done up. And when I have my dress on?

How can I pass up the dress?

I imagine how it'll feel to dance with him, to let him kiss the champagne toast from my mouth.

He's worth this.

How can I pass *him* up?

Short answer: I can't.

I don't want to.

I won't.

So I let Vera finish my hair and add one final coat of mascara. And then I put on the dress. It's long and burgundy and instead of clashing with my hair, it complements it. The material starts with a high neckline and drops all the way down to sweep the ground behind me. One long slit goes almost all the way up to the top of my thigh. There's beading along the shoulders and the back is open halfway down my spine, barely covering the sexy low-back bra I bought to go with it.

"Whoa," Vera says when I step through my bedroom door into the living room.

"Right?" I twirl. "I've literally never been this fancy. Ever."

"I was going to beg you one last time to let me dust you with glitter." She holds up her bottle of it with a guilty expression. "But you don't need it. You're perfect."

"Considering I practically went into debt for this dress... I hope I make an impact in it." I couldn't pass it up. The second I laid eyes on it, I knew. And it fit. And it was perfect.

And it still is.

With timing that is, of course, impeccable, there's a sharp knock at the door.

"He's here," Vera hisses in a whisper.

"No shit." Panic is a funny thing, squeezing my windpipe. "Where are you *going?*"

She turns on her way to her bedroom. "This is your thing, your moment. I'll meet him again some other time."

She gives me a thumbs-up like a fucking nerd and then tucks herself away in her room.

I fill my lungs with so much air I can't believe they don't pop. Then I slowly let it all out.

Then I open the door.

Alec.

He looks at me and his smile is a carnival ride, dropping my stomach with the force of suspended gravity. His eyes drop down and then rise against me, slowly, slowly reaching my face. "Damn, kitten."

But while he's noticing me, I'm noticing him. And... "Damn, Alec."

He cuts his tuxedo like it was invented solely to fit around him, all sharp and elegant.

His hair's slicked away from his face, and his smile's blinding. "You are so fucking beautiful."

"Do you want to come in?" I ask, flustered and gesturing to the rest of the apartment behind me. It's disconcerting to be this turned on while in formal wear, while standing in a shabby doorway. "For a drink?"

He swallows, but I don't think it's because I've offered a beverage. "If I come in, we won't be making the wedding."

"You mean," I say, a grin tugging at the corner of my mouth, "you'd have me waste this dress? Vera would be—"

He grabs me and yanks me to him, crushing his mouth over the rest of my words. His hands curve around my back, his fingers trailing my exposed skin. I hold his shoulders, not sure if it's for my own balance or to keep him in place. His tongue is gentle at first, sweeping through my mouth, growing more demanding.

He tastes like mint and whiskey.

He smells like soap and leather.

He feels like home. Like trust.

I slide my hands up his neck to hold his face, my own lips more insistent than his.

He cups my face, too, then gently breaks the kiss, which, however disappointing, is probably a good thing considering how fast I'm breathing.

"I've missed this. I've missed you," he says. And with his next words, he takes my breath, tossing it away like it's nothing. "I'm addicted to you, Teagan. I crave you when I don't have you. I crave you now that I do. You're the sweetest drug I never knew I needed. I will never not need you."

"Alec..." I stammer over his name.

"You don't have to say anything," he says. "I wanted you to know—needed you to know. I'm yours. However you'll have me. I'm yours."

"If I wouldn't ruin this dress, I'd be jumping you right now. You get that, right?"

The grin that splits his face is dazzling. "If you wouldn't kill me for it, I'd be forcing the issue anyway."

"I'd like to see you try." Words come easier now that we're back on familiar ground.

He holds out his arm. "Shall we?"

I take it. "Let's."

At any other time walking down a concrete stairwell in muggy Virginia summer heat might feel ridiculous in formal wear, but…nothing about standing next to Alec looking the way he does is ridiculous.

The only thing that's ridiculous about the situation is when we step into the parking lot and I discover a huge, long limo waiting for us. The limo's not the ridiculous part. My mother's voice in my head is. The one that tells me I've made it. The one that cackles at the way the sun shines like diamonds against the car's exterior. She's as smug as it is humid outside.

I try to drown her when Alec hands me a tall flute of champagne inside the limo. He sips a glass of whiskey, watching me.

With the second flute, I finally succeed. The coolness of the air conditioning settling over my hot skin helps too.

"How's your grandfather?"

"Irritated," he says. "Irritating. On bedrest, but still well enough to destroy me at chess."

"Comic books, chess… What's next? Model airplanes?" I tease, but my tone is weak. He's rich. He's smart. He's cutting a tuxedo like nobody's business.

He's a fucking catch and a half.

I wish he wasn't.

"What's wrong?" Alec asks, concern dampening his features.

"Nothing. This is perfect," I say, stronger this time, putting my empty glass down across from us and taking his face in my hands. "How could anything be wrong?"

"I know you're lying," he says. "But you look like you're about to kiss me, so I'll let it pass. For now."

If I were my mother, she'd kiss him fiercely, recklessly, really driving home the point of how much she wanted him.

I kiss him sweetly, teasing him with my tongue and keeping my lips gentle over his. He's the one to pull me tighter against him, to press our mouths harder together. I let him.

I revel in him.

I'm going to spend the rest of the night doing the exact same thing.

CHAPTER THIRTY-NINE

WE KISS AND kiss and kiss so long my mouth goes numb. And then we kiss some more.

But my mother won't shut the fuck up, laughing in the back of my mind.

I'm the one to break away because my brain's about to split in two. I'm going crazy.

"I'm in therapy," I say, suddenly panicked. Because who doesn't love a good mood ruiner? "I have a shit-ton of issues. Like, I was practically in love with Cassidy's brother—who overdosed almost two years ago—and I never even told her."

Comprehension filters through his gaze. "You're talking about Brad's son. That was an awful situation. I'm sorry for your loss."

"Well..." I struggle to come up with something else to say. "Whatever. It was a long time ago. I don't know why I brought it up." Of course I do, though. To ruin the moment. It's my super special talent.

Alec studies me, hawk-like in his expression. "It's good. That you're still in therapy, I mean."

"So you agree I need therapy?" I ask, challenge rising in my tone, moisture rising in my eyes. I watch out the window across from where we sit, letting the blur of the landscape distract me until it defeats the sting of tears. Of course he thinks I need therapy. I'm nuts. I broke off from kissing him to talk about a dead boy I used to almost love.

"I think most people would benefit from therapy," he says, calmly. "And maybe while you're there you can figure out how to stop trying so hard to push me away. I'm not going anywhere."

"I doubt you've ever been to a shrink," I say, unable to stop myself. Literally. I try to bite back the words, the bitterness they're laced with, but they come tumbling out anyway.

He drags a hand across his face, not meeting my eyes for a moment. But when he does, his expression is both full of steel—and, somehow, vulnerability. "You see these scars?"

He raises his fist toward me and extends his fingers, slowly, the web of scars stretching across his knuckles, over his fingers, and down the back of his hand.

"I'm surprised you've never asked about them," he says, his voice steady.

I force my eyes to his. "I figured if they were something you wanted to talk about...you would."

"Well," he says, a twisted, disarming smile across his lips, "here you go. This is what happens when you punch a mirror with a cabinet behind it. You don't just bust up your knuckles, but your entire hand. Bled enough to end up in the hospital. Three times."

I grab his hand, which is starting to shake, and I pull it into my lap. I want to kiss my way along his scars, I want to take away this thing that still causes him so much pain.

"You went three times?" I hate the thought that comes to me. "For that one mirror, or were there others?"

He doesn't answer, but he looks away, and that tells me all I need to know.

"Why?" I ask, hoping it's okay to ask.

"I had a twin," he says, still not looking at me.

"Your sister?" I remember the picture in his office, of the toddler.

"She died in a car accident when we were seventeen. Sh-sh-she..." He clears his throat, tightening his fingers in my grip almost painfully. "She called me for a ride home, but I told her I was busy. Which I was. Trying to work my way into some girl's pants." He pauses, remembering, regret piercing his features. "So my sister got in a car with her drunk ex-boyfriend. And neither of them made it out."

"I'm so sorry," I say, knowing the words will never be good enough, but needing him to hear them anyway. I've never understood more clearly than now why Alec doesn't use his looks and his money to bang a bunch of chicks. I have no doubt that night pushed him far, far away from that path—if he'd ever been on it to begin with. "That must've been horrible."

"I imagine it wasn't pleasant," he says; for the first time his tone comes out with a bite to it.

"I meant for you—"

"I know what you mean." He shakes his head, breathing out with a shaky gust of air. "Sorry."

I run my thumb over the back of his hand. "That's why you don't have mirrors...anywhere in your place."

It's not a question but he answers me anyway. "For a long time, I couldn't stand the sight of my reflection. Not when she never got to see hers again. We weren't identical—but we were close enough. I couldn't see me without seeing her. I couldn't see me without looking at the person I let die."

I understand him completely. Sometimes, from certain angles, Cassidy resembles her brother so strongly I can't look at her.

"It's not your fault," I say, my heart slowly deflating between my ribs, struggling to beat, like it's having trouble breathing. "You know that, right?"

"I do, because of therapy." Breath shudders through him. "My slightly bedraggled point is that I've been in therapy for the better part of a decade. Even my therapist sees a therapist—says it's good to cleanse the mind even if nothing's hurting it at the moment. That's why I still go."

"I'm sorry," I say. "To bring this to surface on a night like this one."

"Let's not apologize anymore tonight." He shrugs off my words, his eyes still far away. "It's a celebration for family. If she can't be here physically, she at least deserves a space in my mind."

My mouth twists when I try to fight the sour thought that pushes through. I look away, but he sees it first.

"Tell me," he asks. "Have I freaked you out?"

"No!" I turn toward him so fast my neck cracks. I rub it, confessing what I wish I didn't have to. "I was thinking... You want your missing family in your mind. I can't keep my mother from ruining my thoughts."

"I'm—" He starts to apologize, catches himself. "Parents have a way of haunting us whether they're here or not."

"For the longest time I wished mine would be here to haunt me," I say, my words much more casual than their definitions to me. "Now I wish they'd stop altogether."

"Your father too?"

"Nah. Too hard to listen to a voice I've literally never heard." My breath shakes out of me. "God. Kiss me again or something. Let's get this limo back on the party trail, yeah?"

So he does, and we do. And by the time we pull up to the wedding, I'm breathless with the way I need him.

Even the scene unfolding outside the windows doesn't hold a candle to my awe with him.

To call the house we're pulling up to a mansion would be to severely undersell it. It's three mansions stuffed into one and you can see it from about a million miles away, which is about how long the driveway is. It's a hotel of a house. In fact... "Is this a hotel?"

He laughs. "This is my grandfather's estate."

"Well holy shit." I throw a hand over my mouth. "I can't talk like that here, can I?"

"Kitten," he says, grabbing my hand and lowering it. "You talk however the fuck you want. You don't need to change a thing about yourself for my family. Don't be nervous."

I'm not so sure that's true; not with the way my stomach's down near my feet right now. Dread's a heavy bitch. I flash back to the way his grandfather told me to get out of his hospital room. The way his father's eyes slid over me like furniture.

That was a family emergency, though. This is a celebration. Different atmosphere. Right?

Ugh. Why do I doubt it so much?

But...

I have Alec.

And he has me.

And it's enough for that block of dread to crumble at the corners, my stomach righting itself. "I've never put much stock in people being better than me because they have money," I say. "I think I'm nervous because I..." I stutter, having to clear my throat. Why is this so hard for me? "Because of how much I care about you."

"I *know* I'm nervous now because of what I feel for you."

"Guess that makes us even then," I say.

"Even?" He laughs, his eyes dancing as he pulls me from the limo. "Not a chance, kitten. You topple me."

CHAPTER FORTY

THERE'S NO WEDDING party, Alec tells me when I ask if he's supposed to be doing something for the groom right now. "They want to be alone up there. Didn't even do a rehearsal dinner, which really pissed off my grandfather, because it was the one event he could've participated in, if he'd hosted it at his house like he wanted."

Right. Because he's on bedrest. Relief is a cool breeze against the smarmy heat in the air. His grandfather won't be at the wedding. One less person for me to worry about.

"Tell me about your brother," I say.

Alec laughs but there's not much humor in it. "Mark is three years older. A *perfect* fit for my family—which is to say he's a fucking snob—even if he went to medical school instead of following in our father's footsteps. It's literally the only way he's ever rebelled, and nobody made a big deal out of it because, you know, the prestige of having a fancy surgeon in the family has a nice feel to it."

If I didn't know him better, I'd miss the bitter undertone beneath the dryness of his words. "It's kind of romantic," is all I say, though. "Just your brother and his bride in front of all their friends and family. Like they'll be in their own world."

"It's mostly because Candace used to date his best friend. It'd be awkward to have him up there."

"But why not have you at least?"

"Mark wants the spotlight all on him. And I don't mind—not when it means I get more time with you on my arm."

I blush because he's looking at me so intensely he's impossible not to believe. He leads me along the path around the side of the house to where the music is pouring through the air, and I stop short as we turn the final corner.

The scene splayed out before me is immaculate.

Lights twinkle everywhere. Beautiful people do, too. Throngs and throngs of them. There's a trio of musicians down the way from us, playing their triplet of string instruments with tunes light enough to make a person feel like floating. Beyond that soothing sound is a chorus of laughter, a clinking of glass, the summery chirps of crickets. A mingling of aromas twists pleasantly through my nose; spiced citronella, grilled meats, and the musty vanilla scent of tobacco—the fancy kind that goes in pipes or is from cigars, miles away from the cigarette butt stench I'm used to.

The lawn before us is so immaculately manicured I'm tempted to bend down and get grass-level. I bet there's not a single strand that isn't perfectly even with the others. God. This plantation, the enormousness of the house and the land stretching out beyond it, makes it surreal that my grandparents' house is within a half an hour of here. It's like there's no way that other, less shiny world actually exists, and I start to realize why rich people seem so lost in their own lives.

My palm goes slick in Alec's hand; I don't think I can do this. I turn, and he's already watching me, amused. So I lift my chin, and I pull him forward.

A few steps in, my bravado shivers a little, and I let him take the lead. It's beautiful, this place, and it's taking every ounce of my will not to feel like an outsider. That's not how I roll. Not now, not ever.

The entire scene is draped in elegance. We head toward a huge open-roofed structure, the skeleton of a tent made for thousands of people. Hundreds of strands of twinkling lights crisscross overhead, a roof of stars that glimmer so brightly they should be blinding, but somehow aren't. Clusters of candlelit lanterns hang here and there, suspended with metal twine tied to the high sides of the structure.

TRUTH & TEMPTATION

I keep my hand tightly in Alec's. There are so many people here—hundreds—I don't want to lose him in the crowd. Tables and tables and tables line the way, surrounded by silk-swathed chairs, and centerpieces featuring lit candles of different shapes and sizes, in varying shades of ivory and cream. And crimson rose petals scattered around each arrangement.

"Is this where the ceremony will be held?" I ask.

"The ceremony's in the barn." Alec points off a ways to a red building in the distance.

"Chambers," someone calls behind us. And when Alec turns he pulls me with him until we find the voice. A startlingly handsome guy about Alec's age—surrounded by a group of other similarly gorgeous people. Alec's fraternity brothers from Harvard, it turns out, and a few from his lacrosse team. And their dates.

"We'll catch up a little later," Alec says after introductions. "I promised Teagan a tour of the property."

He tugs my hand, but I stay put. It's sweet, what he's doing. He knows I'm not comfortable, but these are his friends, his people. They're no better than me, even if I have to remind myself of it every other second. And...if he loves them, I want to know them. So I smile and I try really freaking hard to bring it all the way up to my eyes, and I say, "You can show me later. I want to hang out with your friends."

"I like her," says one girl, pulling my hand from Alec's. She smiles at me, her eyes—almost as dark as her skin—shining. "Let's get you a cocktail, yes?"

I like her right back—and follow her without a backwards glance, even if the weight of Alec's gaze is heavy against my back while I walk.

Amara is my new friend's name and she—and her other friends—love tequila.

"I can't," I say, waving away another shot. I want to stay sober tonight. For after the wedding, for the things I want to do with Alec. For the things I want him to do to me... "Liquor messes with my medication." I'm not even sure I'm lying. I should probably check on that.

"Buzzkill," one girl slurs, but Amara tells her to fuck off—a split second before I'm about to. Instead, I grin wildly at both of them.

"I was worried you would all be snobs," I confess, the words slipping smoothly from my mouth, probably an effect of the two shots I haven't waved away.

"We were worried Alec would bring Piper," another girl confesses right back.

"Not a fan?" I ask, my face suddenly feeling numb. This, however, has nothing to do with the two shots and everything to do with Piper.

The girl looks at me like there's no question about it. "Are you?"

"I've never met her." I shrug, speaking casually, as though my stomach isn't inching down toward my feet.

She's nice. She wants to meet me, I remind myself.

She'll skin you alive, Sam once said.

Why, *why*, didn't I say yes when Alec said he'd ask her to stay home?

Because I'm a fucking moron.

"Anyway," I say, turning to a girl whose name I've already forgotten. "Tell me how you all know each other."

The sun's beginning to set, though it's doing nothing to cool the air, when Amara asks me, "How do you stand it?"

"How do I stand what?" I grab a glass of water from a passing waiter, sipping it, enjoying the chill as it slides down my throat.

"Piper?"

This again? I want to snap. "He wants me," I say, instead. "That's all I care about."

"So it doesn't bother you that she's with Alec right now?"

My head turns so fast it's a damn miracle I don't lose my balance. I see them immediately. Laughing like old friends. Or lovers. He sees me almost as quickly and motions for me to join them. But I can't stop staring at Piper. She's in a dress that clings to her curves like second skin and she's...hot. Like, even *my* pulse trips over itself a little looking at her. Smoking body? Check. Long, dark hair and full lips? Check. Wide eyes that, even from here, look green, with streaks of jet black eyeliner out to there? *Check.*

I was not prepared for this. For her.

Alec signals me over again.

This time, Piper's gaze follows his gesture until her eyes meet mine. Her laugh falls away like a boulder shoved straight off the edge of a sharp cliff, and her expression darkens—right down into hatred.

The hush around me is suddenly much louder than the conversations were a moment ago, as though people are collectively holding the same breath, waiting for our inevitable confrontation.

Because *I* know their relationship was fake—*unless it's all been a lie*, but I close my mind to that annoying little doubt because I trust Alec—but everyone else here thinks it was real. Alec must realize this the same time I do because he winces. Hard.

Shit.

Double shit.

Shit times infinity.

We should've talked more about this. Like, a *lot* more.

But my feet move their direction, because I've never been one to back down from awkwardness. I've never been one to back down from anything involving a possible confrontation. I don't think I'm built that way. Like with the whole fight or flight thing, my instincts choose fight every time.

Alec leaves Piper and strides toward me, grabbing my hand, murmuring, "I'm so sorry we didn't plan this out a little better ahead of time."

"A little better?" I ask, my words loud against the echoes of his. I lower my voice. "You told me to trust you."

"I'm an idiot," he says. "I forgot to figure it out with you girls."

And then we're there.

And then she's whispering, "Play along," before saying loud enough for anyone within hearing to catch, "You *bitch*."

And then she's dragging me away. Her hand's tight on my wrist, but surprisingly not tight enough to hurt—as much as she looked like she wanted to cause me physical pain.

"Piper. Let's be adults about this." Alec's matching us stride for stride, and I'm not sure if he's playing along too or genuinely concerned about her theatrics, but I shake my head at him. I've got this. I don't need a knight in shining armor, even for a fake confrontation.

He falls off after a few more steps.

I try to pull my wrist from her grip, but she doesn't let go, pulling me along behind her.

This is growing embarrassing. People are watching, and Piper is clearly in control. Maybe it's an act, but I'm not okay coming out the loser, even in a play. My heel sinks into the grass and I stumble, yanking my arm from hers. "Hold the fuck on."

She whirls around, glaring. "Do not make me cause a bigger scene here. I will if I have to—but you'll regret it, I promise you."

Just an act. This is just an act. Just an—oh, fuck it. "How about don't make *me* cause a bigger scene?" I can't keep from adding a power-balancing, "*Bitch*." Her lips twitch, which makes it hard to keep mine steady. "I get that your feelings are hurt, and I'm sorry for it. But this is a wedding, for fuck's sake. It's not about *you*. Or me. Or even Alec."

Someone behind us laughs, covering it with a cough a moment later.

Piper starts to smile a split second before she catches herself, and giggles rise in my chest. *Whoops.* We can't lose it here, not after everything. So this time I take her wrist, this time I drag her toward the house, hissing, "Let's talk in private."

We go through an entrance a few feet beyond the string quartet and the second the door closes behind us, she whirls to face me. "That was perfect."

CHAPTER FORTY-ONE

"THIS IS A fucking meet cute if I've ever seen one," I say, trying to pretend I'm not dazzled by the foyer we walk into. All marble and a domed ceiling that must reach the clouds. One huge arched entryway leads out into a room the size of a ballroom. Hell, I crane my neck to peer in, discovering more marble flooring, multiple crystal chandeliers, bigger than my car, hanging from the ceiling, maybe that's what it used to be. Now it's furnished with gleaming gold-lined furniture and fancy rugs and the air even smells rich, like cotton and leather and something someone like me can't even bother trying to name. I'm too poor.

And this isn't even the main entrance, either. God.

"A meet cute?" Piper laughs and her entire frame shakes. "That was ridiculous. I haven't even been thinking about how we'd play this. Don't get me wrong—I've wanted to meet you, but I've had my own shit going on and... This slipped my mind. I improvised."

"And chose to go with over-the-top dramatic?" I ask. Then, panic laces through my ribs. "Alec's grandfather's in here somewhere—we need to get the hell outside." I remember how cold his eyes were when he kicked me out of his hospital room. I can't imagine how much worse it'd be to get caught in his house.

She laughs again, carelessly this time. "Oh, please. Old Man Winter's up on the fourth level playing chess with Dr. Greenwald. He acts sour because he can't come to the party, but trust me. He's loving life."

"Loving life? He had a stroke," I say, my tone dry enough to make her lips twitch.

"That old brick's got more years left in him than I probably do."

As relaxed as she is about it, my own panic loosens. "Was the scene out there really necessary?"

"Obviously." She gives me a curious stare, like she's uncertain why she has to explain any of it to me.

"Why? There are thirteen different ways we could've done this." Thirteen's a bit of an exaggeration, but... "You tried to make me look pathetic."

"I have a reputation to uphold." She twists a long curled strand of hair between her fingers, her tone bored. "Especially as *the jilted ex*, it's expected that I'll make drama. You gave it back better than I'd ever dreamed, too... Not that I'm surprised. Alec told me you were a firecracker."

I should probably be offended by that, but there's too much else to process first. "You didn't look that great yourself—isn't your entire family here?"

"They expect it more than anyone." She smoothes invisible wrinkles from the stomach of her dress and adds as an afterthought, "Shit. I forgot to check if any of them were even watching." As though she *wants* them to have been watching.

That doesn't add up for me. "Aren't you people all about class and civility?"

"There's one thing my family puts above even that." Now she studies me, long and hard enough to make a lesser girl shake. "Alec really didn't tell you, did he?"

"Tell me what—that your relationship was fake? He did." I take a few steps past her toward a table in the middle of the entryway. There's a vase full of flowers and suddenly I'd rather study them than her. But she doesn't speak until I do.

She twists her head toward me, a considering expression crossing her features. "My life would be so much easier if I could feel it for him. He's the epitome of a fucking catch."

"Guess it's a good thing you don't, as he seems to feel whatever *it* is for me." There might be some sort of weird friendship thing blooming here, but she doesn't get to assume Alec would be with her if she wanted him.

"Easy, tiger. He fell hard for you the first night he met you. I'm saying—"

"What, exactly?"

"That it'll be hard to find another beard as genuinely awesome as he is." Her mouth curves into a snide smile and she waits, waits for it to click in.

Click. The word *beard* settles into place in my mind. "Oh."

"I hear you met Kelly on the elevator?"

"Who?" I'm thrown for a moment—and then I remember. The first night I met Alec, the scene in the elevator with the girl I assumed he had history with. "The blonde asshole chick?"

Piper beams. "That's basically the best description I've ever heard of my ex."

Kelly is Piper's ex. Oh my God, *now* I get it. "You're a lesbian?"

"Let's go ahead and use the term queer, if we have to use one at all."

"Okay..." I give my mind a moment to catch up with what I'm learning. Alec never even hinted... "You like girls, and your family doesn't know?"

"I sometimes like boys too, but not as often," she corrects and then laughs, though it comes out more like a verbal representation of a sneer. "And my family definitely knows."

Click. The final piece falls into place. "They don't support you. You have to marry a man they approve of to get your inheritance."

"Bingo." She laughs again, this time more delighted than bitter. "I can't believe Alec didn't tell you."

"It's your secret, not his," I say, remembering him telling me something similar. "*I* can't believe you're telling me now."

"Oh, honey. I'd tell the world if I could—I'm not ashamed. But I want that money. And my best friend is half in love with you, which means we'll be in each other's lives. Might as well be honest."

Well who knows what to say to something like that? "Um. Sorry to fuck up your cover operation."

She shrugs. "My parents were breathing down my neck, and Alec has a savior complex where I'm concerned. It was never going to be the real thing—and there'll always be a guy somewhere out there who'll pretend to fuck me if there's a nice fat check in it for him if he gets me down the aisle." Her eyes soften. "It was nice Alec didn't care about the money. For a little while I got to be with someone who wasn't using me the way I was using him."

"That's... I mean, your family would really make you—"

"They're awful." Another shrug. "And for some reason I still love 'em. And anyway, Alec bought me time. I solidified my straightness to appease my family for at least...a year, or more. Who knows? Then I'll find someone new. Quickie wedding. Grab the cash when I'm of age. Quicker divorce. Voila."

She's so casual about it. Not even a flicker of resentment passes through her eyes. I'm...at a loss for words. "How old do you have to be to—"

"Careful, by the way," she says, gesturing toward the door. "Most of them will accuse you of wanting him for his money," she warns. But the way she looks at me tells me it's more than a warning, it's a test. And a stop sign to my questions.

"The first time I picked him up," I say, using my tone to warn her right back, "was in a seedy pool hall. I had no clue he was wealthy. Believe it or not, the fact that he's rich makes me less inclined to be with him."

"Believe it or not," she says, "I believe you. Alec's not dumb enough to fall for anyone less."

"You were there, weren't you?" I ask, suddenly realizing the truth. "When Alec... When his sister died, and he went through his difficulty with mirrors."

She blinks, and I know I've surprised her. "Not when he broke any of them, but every time after. Of course I was. Why?"

"He mentioned once that he owed you a lot. But your situation now makes it seem like you're the one who owes him." The bite of a blush stings my cheeks when I mentally replay my words. "Not that you owe him anything, I mean. Just that—"

"We're friends. Closer than siblings," she says, with an easy smile. "We don't owe each other anything. It's not about that. You're perceptive. Every minute I spend with you shows me exactly why he's falling for you."

"We should get back to the wedding," I say. "Before they send in the troops." Before she talks about Alec falling or being half in love again. Or before I drop to my knees and beg her to repeat it all, word for word.

"Nah," she says. "They're all out there pretending our little unpleasantness never even happened. They'll gossip like hungry puppies over brunch tomorrow. Old Man Winter"—I crack up at her nickname for Alec's grandfather this time—"made it clear he has a strict no-house policy that most of them are too scared to break. But you're right. Pretend you hate me for a little while out there, okay? And in a few weeks we'll *come out*," she snickers, "as the friends I can tell we'll be."

CHAPTER FORTY-TWO

ALEC APOLOGIZES AGAIN, but I brush it off. Things with Piper...well, they went pretty perfectly. We head over to the huge red barn for the ceremony. It's lit with twinkle lights like the rest of the property seems to be and it smells of hay and gardenias. It's as elegant as the rest of the setup with a more rustic tone. The center aisle is lined with burlap and lace.

We sit in the front row, and I've never been more nervous about anything. Mark is standing in front of everyone already. He looks like Alec, but in a slicker sort of way. Shorter hair. Smugger expression. Not as attractive as the one Alec usually wears. He grins at Alec and tips his head to me before his eyes slide away. Guess we're officially introduced.

The seats behind us fill quickly—and before I know it, my nerves are standing up so straight they're about to pass out, because Alec's father is ushering his mother down the aisle to take their seats. Next to ours.

Alec's father greets me with a smile, but it falls flat in his eyes. He exchanges a long, unreadable glance with Alec. Well, not that unreadable. Pretty sure under the bland surface of his expression lies a layer heavy with disappointment.

I'm going to have to fucking *shine* at work. There must be an audiobook out there on how to impress your boyfriend's father when he's also your gazillionaire boss…

Alec's mother's smile doesn't reach her eyes, either, but she offers me her hand anyway. "Nice to meet you, Teagan."

I don't know why it shocks me that she'd know my name. Of course she does. Alec told her when he announced I'd be his date tonight. And I have a feeling Mr. Chambers has been bitching about me ever since. I wrap my hand around hers, giving a small shake. "This is a beautiful wedding."

"It reminds me of my own," she says, a bit of her sour expression relaxing. "We were married here years and years ago."

"It must've been as magnificent then, if not more so," I say, proud of myself for sounding so… I don't know, able to carry on a respectful conversation, maybe? I'm also filled with a melty sort of relief that this moment is way less stressful than I'd imagined it would go. Rich people and their civility. They might loathe me, but it's barely discernible right now.

"You're sweet," she says, and before I can respond, the music changes and everyone stands.

Candace, the bride, is gorgeous in a dress that accentuates her thin frame and a sheer veil edged in lace trailing down her back and along the rose-lined aisle. Through the veil, her skin is dark and dewy, and her eyes are round and excited. She's luminous with the glow of someone in love, and it strikes something deep inside of me.

"She's stunning," I whisper.

Alec agrees. "Wait till you meet her. She's so nice it's almost painful."

"I thought you said she was the wrong girl for your brother?"

He shoots me a look, and I realize maybe I'm whispering too loudly. But everyone is craning their necks, focused on the bride—and Alec, the only one looking at me instead, cracks a smile. "She is. Mark is the one who doesn't deserve her."

My gaze darts to his father for a moment, the salt-and-peppered back of his head. I wonder if Mark's a chip off the old block when it comes to monogamy. I turn to Mark next, but his expression is so excited it's contagious. Whatever Alec's reasoning is for not thinking he deserves his bride, right at this moment, he definitely seems enamored.

The ceremony is short, and Alec's mother cries through the entire thing. Politely, of course, dabbing at her eyes with a silk handkerchief. Mr. Chambers doesn't show any emotion at all. I wonder if he's thinking of his own wedding. Or maybe he's biding his time to get back to his mistress.

Gross.

Maybe I shouldn't worry so much about impressing him. Maybe my goal should be to impress Denise enough that she wants me to work for her—regardless of whom I'm dating. Perhaps in spite of it, actually. I get the sense she'd be less than thrilled to think I'd sleep my way up the ranks of the company.

Shit.

But, I look down where Alec's fingers are twined with mine... He tightens his grip, rubbing my hand with his thumb. Oh, well. Let Denise think what she will. Let anyone think what they will.

I'm not giving this up.

That's my girl, my mother whispers. In my mind, I stab her with a kitchen knife. In real life, I slide my hand out from under Alec's. When he gives me a puzzled look, I scratch the back of my neck.

I'm not sure if I hate myself or my mother more right now. Giving a big old *fuck you* to both of us, I place my hand back on Alec's.

Because, really, fuck my conscience.

We follow the newlyweds out of the barn for dinner—surf and turf so delicious my new goal in life is to be rich enough to eat lobster every night—and then dancing. They cut a cake taller than I am and more delicious than anything I've ever tasted. Except lobster.

I don't drink much, just a glass of champagne, and Alec doesn't either. But he does kiss me after the champagne toast. He does dip his tongue into my mouth, searching for traces of the bubbly drink like he promised he'd do, making me drunk with how much I need his tongue on other spots of my body, *in* other spots of my body...

And we do dance.

We dance for what feels like hours—and also only the blink of an eye—under the twinkling lights, and though we're surrounded by miles of people and a six-piece cover band, we're in our own world.

Giddiness is its own sort of drug and I'm so high on it I don't know how I'll ever come down. I can't stop laughing, and when he asks me what it's about, all I can tell him is, "You."

A moment later, he's laughing with me.

And still, we dance, his hands on my waist, running along my spine, sliding down my arms to spin me out and back again.

Eventually I have to beg for a break to get some water. The fans placed discretely around the reception may be keeping the area cool despite the muggy summer heat, but I'm freaking parched. And starting to sweat. And I'd rather not be gross for...after.

I'd be embarrassed with how quickly I gulp down the ice water Alec brings me, but he downs his just as fast—and goes for another round without my having to ask.

"You're pretty fun," he says, pulling me in for a quick kiss. "Not that it's new information for me. But you know how to show a guy a good time."

"You think this is fun," I say, nervous my next words will make me blush. "Wait till later."

"Later?" he asks, his head tilting, a curious—and maybe hopeful—smile stretching across his mouth. "What do you have in mind?"

"Everything," I say. "I have everything in mind."

He goes still. So very still. Still enough that my own grin rises uncontrollably in the sweetness of the silence between us.

"Tell me what this is," he says, finally.

"Same answer," I say, easily, honestly. "This is everything."

"You figured it out," he says, and before I can agree, he pulls me in for another kiss. This one much better than the last. His lips are slow over mine, lingering—and simmering beneath their gentle graze with a heated passion I can't wait to tease fully out of him later.

I break it off because, well, one of us has to or we're going to end up naked in front of all these people. From the corner of my eye, I see Piper heading toward us. She notices me at the same time and winks before she glares, turning on her heel and heading the other direction. I laugh. She's good. Could be an actress.

Behind her, though, is Mr. Evans. He sees me and doesn't break stride, coming straight over. My stomach clenches at his approach. I knew he'd be here and wondered when we'd run into him. Usually,

I'd seek him out. But usually I'm not with someone he disapproves of me being with.

Still, his face is a mask of polite pleasantry as he reaches out to shake Alec's hand. "You're looking well," he says. "And Teagan, my girl, you are close to upstaging the bride."

I knock his hand out of the way when he offers it to me and hug him instead. "Where's Mrs. Evans?"

"She wasn't up to it," he says, motioning to the dance floor and surrounding area. "Crowds."

He doesn't need to explain further. I know they've come a long way in their grief since Jason's death, but Mrs. Evans still isn't much for celebrations.

"How'd the Berkeley Group meeting go?" Alec asks, smoothly steering the conversation elsewhere.

Mr. Evans' eyes light up. "Please, tonight's no time for business. But we've come up with something you'll love."

"Berkeley Group?" I ask. "Why is that name familiar?"

Alec only winks at me, though. And Mr. Evans says, "I'm hoping you'll let me steal Teagan away for a dance?"

"Like Alec has any say in the matter," I say, taking his hand. "It's time you let me see that jitterbug, Mr. Evans."

The band has other plans, though, switching to something slower. Mr. Evans shrugs, a charming little disappointment across his face, and pulls me in for a dance better suited to the music.

"I told you to call me Brad," he reminds me.

"I grew up with you as Mr. and Mrs. Evans. It's a hard habit to break."

"Use whatever you're comfortable with, but you're like family to us, honey. Seems a waste to use such formal titles."

Like family to us.

No crying tonight, I remind myself, but I have to change the topic of conversation before I lose it. "I understand if you don't approve of me being here with Alec, but—"

"He told me the truth about his...irregular relationship," he says. "I'm sorry I misjudged you. You know, I always sort of hoped you'd end up with our Jason." He pauses, his eyes going dark for a moment before his expression clears. "But it's clear you deserve someone who'll stick around. And judging by the way Philip's son's eyes follow you, he's not going anywhere."

The way he implies Jason chose not to stick around hurts me. I tense in his arms, waiting for the gale force of grief to slam into me—but it doesn't come. Instead, I'm able to relax and keep my steps in line with his. "I miss him... Jason," I add, though the clarification's unnecessary.

"Every minute of every day," he agrees, and his easy admission eases the sting of his censure toward his son. It must be hard, to have so much anger mingling with all that love. No outlet for it other than the passing of time.

I think about Jason while we dance in silence. I really think about him. About what I felt. And I think... I think it's been easy to pin my broken hopes on a boy who died almost two years ago, because I didn't have to move forward with the thing that scared me most: finding someone like Alec. Finding someone who makes me feel like I deserve everything my grandparents spent their lives showing me I didn't.

And that's... Well, that's some fucked-up shit I'll have to bring up at a future therapy session, because I'm done thinking about it for tonight. With his usual impeccable timing, Alec asks to cut in, and I swing myself easily into his arms.

"I couldn't stand watching this dress and everything in it spinning to the turn of someone else's hand," he says. And then he spirals me beneath his own like a ballerina dancing in place on a jewelry box.

"*Berkeley Group*," I say, smiling when it hits me. "They're one of the startups you want to invest in."

The corners of his lips curl up. "Mr. Evans thought it might work if we invested in one company to show my father what sort of success we could have—and then branch out to others."

"Smart. Why didn't you tell me you'd teamed up with him?"

"I was waiting till it was a done deal. I wanted to watch your face light up—though what it's doing now is better than anything I'd imagined. Now," he says, with a grin that can't possibly top my own, "no more work talk." He pulls me in close and then shoves me out, whirling me in circles.

"What was your sister's name?" I ask after, breathless from his spin, hastily adding, "If you don't mind my asking?"

I've been wondering, and I don't know why I haven't asked before. Maybe because I've never been so sure of him—of *us*—as I am in this moment. I can ask him anything.

I'll tell him whatever he wants to know.

"Elodie," he tells me. "Her name was Elodie and she was the only thing this family ever got right—until we didn't." A shadow casts its web across his eyes for the briefest of moments.

I open my mouth, but he spins me again and when he yanks me back to him, it's to crush his lips against mine, kissing me so hard I can't seem to remember to breathe. It makes me dizzy.

He makes me dizzy.

And then he spins me yet again.

"How much longer do we have to stay?" I ask when he sweeps me into his arms and sways me in an easy rhythm. I rise on my tiptoes to get closer to his ear. "Because if you like my dress, what's underneath is even fancier."

"They already cut the cake, and the limo's on standby," he says so quickly I laugh. "We can leave whenever we want. Which, for me, is right fucking now."

CHAPTER FORTY-THREE

WE MAKE IT almost all the way to the side of Alec's grandfather's mansion when his father swoops in—I swear—out of thin air to stand before us. Yeah. So I guess on top of being super rich, he's a freaking wizard, too.

"It hurt your mother to watch you walk out without saying goodbye," he says to his son, completely ignoring me. He's not even sweating like he ran to catch us. Maybe he's able to ride air like a speedboat...

Oh, man. This is not the time to giggle. I barely catch one slipping up my throat.

Maybe if I release it, some of the sudden and unwelcome fear in the pit of my stomach will leave, too.

I try to disentangle our fingers, but Alec only pulls me closer to him. "I'll see Mom tomorrow. She looked busy before."

Mr. Chambers' eyes flash, but I speak before he can. "We should've said goodbye. I'm sorry—it's my fault. My..." Oh my God, I want to lie and say my stomach's bothering me or something but I stand here gaping instead, unable to bring myself to do it. I...don't want to lie to him. What the fuck is wrong with me?

"Your...?" Mr. Chambers prompts me to go on, and I want to swallow my tongue.

"*We,*" Alec says, saving me, "will go say goodbye now."

"Why don't you go ahead," Mr. Chambers responds, holding out an arm to me. "I'll keep your *assistant* company."

My instinct is to look at Alec, to beg him with my eyes to protect me. My reality is that I've always protected myself, and I'm not going to stop here. I place my free hand on Mr. Chambers' arm, right as Alec says, "Not a fucking chance." He looks at me like I'm crazy when I step away from him to stand with his father. "What are you doing?"

"I'm..." What am I doing? I take a breath to steady myself and inhale the thick scent of cigar that lingers on Mr. Chambers. "Discussing things with your father while you're gone."

Alec studies me, and I see clearly in his expression how much he wants to stay. But I also see the moment he reminds himself that I can handle things. I see the respect that sharpens his focus—and then the irritation when he turns his gaze to his father. "We spoke about this."

Before Mr. Chambers responds, I say, "Y'all spoke about me? Well, Alec, you go on and say goodbye to your mama, and I'll let your daddy give me all the details." For some reason my sarcasm comes out in a syrupy, forced Southern accent, which is embarrassing but somehow feels fitting, too. My stomach is a twisted knot of brambles, but I refuse to let it show on my face.

Alec opens his mouth, but I jerk my head toward the sounds of the wedding around the house. After one long glance at his father, he leaves, promising, "I'll be back in less than a minute, swear to God."

I allow myself the few seconds it takes him to disappear around the corner before swallowing and readying myself to face his father.

"He's too good for you." Mr. Chambers speaks first, angling his body more toward mine, towering over me the way his son does. Though I feel absolutely nothing like what I do when I'm faced with Alec's height. Instead of tingles, there's only a fierce sense of intimidation. Not that I'll let him see it.

I drop my hand from his arm. "If you didn't believe that solely because of how rich you are, I'd agree. He is too good for me. Not because I grew up with nothing, but because he grew up with *everything*—and still managed to come out with a kind heart."

"I can't fire you," he says, steepling his fingers over his stomach. It's startling, the resemblance of his all-business tone to one I've heard his son use. Startling the way the shapes of their face match, the angles of their jaws. "But I can make sure you hate your job."

I start to slide a finger beneath the high neck of my dress—because it's suddenly itching, and I need a bit more room to breathe—but I stop myself, because, no. Fuck that. It's rare that I'm grateful for how much practice I have being a bitch, but in this moment, I've never been happier to have the spine I created.

"You sound like a villain in a movie," I say. "But you raised the boy who became the man that Alec is. So I know you're not a bad guy. You love your son. And I love my job. So good luck making me hate it."

I probably wouldn't recognize the glimmer of respect that shines in and out of his expression if I hadn't seen the identical flash on his son's face a second ago. So, I understand the game now. Direct honesty is the way to win with Alec's father. I ask, "You're worried I care for Alec because you're rich?"

"I know where you came from. Of course I am."

"Where I came from?" I want to laugh. Or maybe cry. Mostly, I don't want to understand him the way I do. But I say, "Yeah, I get it. You're right to worry. Sometimes I worry about the same thing, about whether or not there's a small part of me subconsciously attracted to Alec's wealth." This time, I've shocked him—his eyes go wide and then way narrow. And I almost smile. "But if I had to live out of a cardboard box if it meant getting to be with your son?"

He nods, barely, waiting for me to go on.

I take a moment longer to consider my answer, wanting to make sure I speak the truth. "Hell, I'd live out of a shoebox if I had to."

"Really now, Miss Walker." His expression says he doesn't believe me, but his tone is amused. "A shoebox?"

I don't miss his use of my name. It's a step up from my work title. Score.

"Yes. A shoebox. And let me tell you something else, too. Alec knows better than anyone—the first time he does something to *buy* me in any way? I'm gone. Not that he ever would, but I will never be the type of girl who wants to be kept." *I'm not my fucking mother*, I almost say. "And that is why I love my job. I want to make something of myself. Trust me, you won't have an employee who works harder. And if I need to sign something with HR to date Alec—or I don't have to work for Alec... If that makes this situation better, I'll work for someone else who needs an assistant. Or a second assistant. Or anything." Oh, God. I can't shut up. "I'm a quick learner. Well, okay, no I'm not. But I'll put in extra time and ef—"

"You should quit while you're ahead." While he doesn't chuckle when he cuts me off, I swear there's one beneath his stern tone.

And then, wait... "You think I'm ahead?"

"I think we can table this discussion for another time."

"Because it's inappropriate to discuss business like this at your son's wedding? Or because...you might be starting to like me?"

"A little of the first, nothing of the second. But I won't meddle in Alec's personal life—"

"More than you already have, you mean?" Oops. I really need to learn to shut up.

His nostrils flare. "*And* I'll have HR go over the paperwork with you if you choose to continue a relationship with him. Other than that, time will tell if you're able to impress me at the office. I'm aware you had a hand in the way he reshaped his proposal."

It's not exactly a compliment, but considering what Alec and Mr. Evans put together seems to be working, I take it as one anyway. Plus? *Time will tell.* The best phrase I've heard all night. Well, no. Alec's said some pretty fucking awesome things to me tonight, too. But this is somewhere toward the top five at least. Mr. Chambers is leaving the door open for me to be successful even if I stay with Alec.

"Thank you," I say, right as Alec rounds the corner.

He looks me over, then his father. "You're both still standing?"

I laugh. Mr. Chambers, not so much. But whatever.

"I was worried," Alec says, glancing between us a second time. "At first about you, Teagan. But the more I thought about it, the more I realized it was you, Dad, who I should be afraid for."

I want to kiss his face off. I want to jump him here, in front of his father and the stars in the sky. I want to fast-forward through time until the moment he's above me, in his bed, pushing himself inside of me for the first time.

Oh, holy hell. I cannot fucking wait for the rest of tonight. I've never been so sure of myself. Or of him.

Mr. Chambers sighs and pulls a cigar out of his jacket pocket. He steps a few feet away to light it, and doesn't say anything else. Clearly, he's still disappointed in his son. But I wonder if the disappointment's really a test, something to force Alec to prove how much he wants me. Maybe this is a game Mr. Chambers plays with everyone.

Maybe Mr. Chambers is a chess player like the rest of them…

Alec looks at me and shrugs. I shrug back. I guess we've been dismissed.

But, oddly, it kind of feels like the opposite.

CHAPTER FORTY-FOUR

"YOUR PLACE OR mine?" Alec asks, following me into the limo. "I have to tell the driver."

His question gives me pause. I hadn't considered that I have a place we can go back to now. But... "Yours."

Because that's how I've been picturing it. In his bed.

Plus, at his place we'll be alone.

And, seriously, I can't stop thinking about his bed.

"I'd ask if you're okay," he says, "But I already know you are. The second I walked away, I realized you would hold your own."

"Your dad's intimidating as hell," I say. "But we reached an agreement—well, I think we did, anyway. What..." I try to hold the question back, but I'm too curious. "What did you discuss with him about me?"

Alec rolls his eyes toward the ceiling of the car. "He told me it's inappropriate to date you because I'm your superior. I told him I'd look for a new job, now or after graduation, if it bothers him that much."

Wow. "Alec—"

He shuts me up with a kiss.

I pull away, smiling. "Okay. Point taken. No more talking about your father. There's only one thing I want to focus on the rest of tonight anyway—and you know exactly what it is."

"I do." He slides a hand over my lap, dipping his fingers between my knees. "I'm right there with you, kitten. Believe that."

The limo ride takes for-fucking-ever. Somehow, we fill it with light conversation. Did I know Alec wants to start his own firm someday? Did he know I never had a middle name? Did I know Norris Marshall's putting out a solo album while Luca James is in rehab? We spend the most time on this last one because holy shit, no, I didn't know that, and I'm fucking pumped for it.

But I'm trembling on the inside. With nerves. With anticipation. With hunger.

He offers me a drink when he gets to his place, but that hunger's roaring something fierce and I don't want to waste any more time, even on a water. I shake my head and I take his hand and I pull him up the stairs, down the hall, into his bedroom.

This, however, is where I pause, where my nerves are louder than my want. Because his bed is exactly as I've been picturing it. Like every other time I've been over here, but suddenly it feels larger. More intimidating. White, fluffy, and intimidating. A snort chokes out of me, slicing my throat with its sudden unexpectedness.

"You okay?" Alec's hand is on my shoulder, his grip tight.

I turn to him and the second our eyes meet my doubts drip away. I pull up on my toes to kiss him. "I need to splash some water on my face."

He tilts his head toward the bathroom doors. "You know the way."

That I do. What I didn't know though, is what to expect when I opened the doors.

A mirror. Huge and framed in dark wood, hanging behind the sink.

I spin around to find him watching me, amusement plastered on his face.

"But you...?" I trail off, unsure of what I'm trying to say.

He gives the most endearing shrug. "I like the way you look at me sometimes. Kinda made me want to see myself again."

I cross to him in three steps, wrapping my arms around him, sinking into his chest when he returns the hug. Even if I hadn't learned his history, I'd have known this was a big deal. Knowing what I do now? This is more than big.

It's gigantic.

"You're one of a kind, you know that, Chambers?" I glance up at him to see the amusement doubled on his features.

"Actually, I do, Walker." He lets me go and spins me toward the bathroom, slapping my ass through my dress. "Now go splash that water because I've got a craving for a taste of your sweet neck, and if you aren't back soon I'm coming in after you."

I close the doors behind me, laughing, and run the water. Not wanting to ruin what's left of my makeup, I wet a washcloth and gently dab it along my forehead and under my chin, wiping away some of the humidity still lingering there from earlier. I almost run it under my arms, too, but I can still smell my deodorant, so I leave them be.

One last glance in the mirror, where I think I'll need to take a deep breath or do something to steady my nerves...but I don't. I'm not nervous in a way that needs reassuring. All I want is to be with Alec. And so I step through the doors, and I make it happen.

He's standing pretty much where I left him, jacket off and bowtie hanging loosely around his neck. He's still in his shirt and vest and he cuts a sexy fucking picture, all swank and steam. I walk straight to him, and I kiss him, hard. He breaks away, laughing. "Feeling feisty?"

"Feeling a lot of things," I say, my hands drifting down to unbutton his vest—and then up to slide it off his shoulders. "Ready to feel even more."

He takes his bowtie the rest of the way off and I unbutton his shirt, stripping it away from him, too. He does his belt, I do his undershirt.

"Fuck." I can't keep my hands from smoothing over the ridges of his abs, the slopes of his pecs. "It's like you're carved from stone."

"Feel a little lower, and you'll know it's true." He slides his feet from his shoes and yanks at his socks, one at a time. I take his advice and unbutton his pants, my fingers grazing his erection as I slide the fabric lower.

"Yep." I nod, fighting a blush. "Your...cock certainly feels rock hard."

"You said it," he says, laughing, his eyes dancing. "Look how far we've come."

"Not far enough," I say. "But we're about to change that."

The rest of his laugh falls away and he sucks in a breath. "If you're—"

"Don't you dare ask me if I'm sure," I warn. "I wouldn't be here if I wasn't."

He's silent for a moment, long enough to make me squirm. Then he spins me around and pulls my hair away from the side of my neck, whispering against my skin, "Then it's my turn to undress you."

He licks the side of my neck, long and slow, edging his teeth along my skin in the same path—and I nearly sink to my knees at what it does to me, sparking things all the way down through my toes.

"I'm not turning the light off," he says, his tone laced with steel.

"I don't want you to," I whisper.

He stands behind me, so close the heat from his body soaks through my dress.

He unzips me, deliberately, with care.

He lowers my dress, sliding it down my arms, running his hands over my skin, guiding the material lower, lower, and he swallows when it drifts below my back, exposing the underwear I'm wearing for the occasion.

"White lace this time?" he asks in a strangled voice.

When I bought them, I figured, with a smirk, it would be appropriate. You know, white for a virgin and all? But hearing the worship in his tone, I don't care what white represents anymore. I only want to have him speaking with this reverence toward me for the rest of forever.

He drops to his knees behind me, pulling my dress with him. I step out of it and he gently wraps a hand around my ankle, pushing against me until I widen my stance. My stomach catches at what he must see—these panties don't cover much. I twist toward him. "Alec—"

But the expression on his face stops me. "Let me cherish you," he says, his voice low, steady, his hands traveling up over my calves. He closes his eyes and rests his forehead against the back of my leg. He trembles, and dips his tongue against my skin.

His hands caress the backs of my knees.

I face forward and grab the edge of his dresser. Maybe I've been feeling my own trembles—they're growing stronger now, making my legs shake.

Maybe we're trembling together.

His palms carve the shapes of my legs, the curves of my ass. He slides his fingers under my lace and another deep intake of his breath fills the air, like a sweet symphony performed only for me.

"I want to take my time," he says, and I'm not sure if it's to me or to himself. He runs gentle kisses along the tops of my legs, his hands slide around the fabric covering my hips, dipping lower, touching me. He vees his fingers through my flesh, spreading me in a way that makes me tingle so hard I nearly fall over.

My own sigh shudders out into the silence of the room.

"I need you, Alec," I find myself saying. "I need you to get up. I need you to kiss me. Because if you don't, I'm afraid I might cry, and I don't understand it—but it's there. Please. Kiss me."

He stands, smoothing his hands up my body, curving them around my waist as I spin to face him. "I'll kiss you," he says, cupping my face, "anytime you ask me."

"Then do it," I say, half a smirk climbing my mouth. He places his lips over mine before the full thing can form.

This kiss is not like our previous kisses. There's something more. Something in the pressure of our mouths against each other. Something in the promise of his tongue when it glides through my lips to dance with mine.

We walk toward his bed without breaking the kiss. But when it's there, hitting the backs of my legs, he stops, and he looks at me, a question in his eyes.

I give my answer in a simple smile. "I'm happy," I say. "Truly happy to be here with you, like this, right now."

I used to think happiness was a fragile thing. Something to be protected. But this…this is something to be displayed. To be shown. And so I slide back onto his bed, and I pull him with me.

CHAPTER FORTY-FIVE

THE FEATHERY COMFORTER covering Alec's bed swishes as we edge backwards along it.

He pauses above me, the muscles in his forearms like twisted ropes. "I need you naked, Teagan. I'm nearly in pain with wanting you."

"I need you naked," I say, lifting up on my elbows to drag a kiss across his mouth. "I need you inside of me in the worst way, Alec. Soon."

"Soon," he agrees. "But not quite yet. Let me look at you, first."

Anticipation races up and between my ribs, tightening around my heart, but I nod.

He slides the straps of my bra over my shoulders, gently tugging them down until my breasts are free from the cups. He pauses, just looking at me.

I prepare myself for the wave of embarrassment, the urge to cover myself...but it doesn't come. And I get it now, I finally understand. I wasn't ready for this before.

This time, I don't reach for the light switch when he removes my bra completely, tossing it away. This time, I'm not mentally nitpicking my body or wondering if he is. All I have room for in my mind is him. This moment.

Love.

So much it's almost painful between my ribs. So much all the breath leaks out of my lungs and is vacuumed up into my heart. Because that's where everything is at the moment.

Love.

And maybe it's a trick of the light, or the pull of my own emotion, but I swear it's reflected straight back at me on his face. In his caress.

He slips his fingers under the hips of my underwear, and I lift my body to allow him to pull them down. Over my thighs. Past my knees. Along my shins. Slowly, slowly.

All the way off.

I've never been this naked with another person.

And I don't mean without the clothing.

He rises onto his knees and pauses, a sheepish twist to his mouth. He thumbs the waist of his boxer briefs. "Yes or no?"

Conviction is an anchor in the space between us, when I say, "Yes." Then I rise onto my knees as well. "But I want to do it."

I love the way he swallows when I hook my fingers into his waistband. I love the way he shudders when I trail my wet mouth across his collarbone and down his chest.

I love the way he bucks his hips when I free him from his briefs, his erection rigid, so full from wanting me.

There's a drop of wetness at his tip, and he trembles when I run my finger over it, looks pained when I slide my finger into my mouth to lick the taste of him from my skin. Salty. Tangy. Alec.

I shove him backwards, onto the bed, so I can climb over him. So I can slide my lips over his erection, tease him with my tongue until he's groaning and grabbing my hair, weaving it into his fists.

I trail my fingers up the muscles of his thighs; I cup him and massage him. My tongue flirts, flickering around his head, and when his grip tightens in my hair, I slide him down into the back of my throat, twisting my face from side to side, never relaxing my hands, not for a moment.

He bucks his hips against my face, and I know he won't last much longer. The thought makes me giddy.

But he surprises me, letting out a strained sound that's half a roar, and sitting up. He slides out of my mouth, and I glance up at him to complain, licking my lips.

"Come here." He speaks before I can, and yanks me to him. In a maneuver the most skilled gymnast would be impressed with, he lies back and spins me until I'm positioned over his face, looking at his legs—and his tongue *plunges* straight into me.

Holy hell.

I lean forward, my hands on his chest, my head arched back, my knees inching further apart, flattening myself against his mouth, giving him access to every inch of me. And he takes it.

He licks me from front to back, leveling his tongue against me and then rounding it through me, into me. He nuzzles me with his nose and trails me with his teeth, *sucking* me, breathing on me, into me.

His hands splay across the cheeks of my ass, kneading them, spreading them, pulling me down with more force against his face. His tongue is all the way inside of me, mapping every part of me, and I bite back a scream that would bring his entire condo down.

He dances his fingers higher along my back, pressing lower, lower until I dip my head down and swirl my tongue around his erection again.

It's hard to concentrate, though, and I'm starting to pulse against his face, while his hips are jerking him further into my mouth. I rise on my knees to take him at a better angle, but he yanks my hips back, slamming me onto his mouth again, and I swear to God he's got the longest, strongest, most demanding tongue in the world. My nerves are a line of dominoes and he's brushing it against them, knocking them down in a million rippled effects.

He holds me in place, devouring me. If my stomach were to jerk any harder than it is, I might implode into absolutely nothing. Even my breathing quivers.

I add a hand along his base and stroke him while I suck.

He goes completely rigid. In my mouth. Beneath my body. He turns his face, gently biting the inside of my thigh, murmuring, "Hang on, kitten."

But I don't want to hang on. I want to bring him to the brink. I want to push him over the brink so hard he *flies*.

I suck energetically. Faster. Rougher.

He matches my speed, my pressure with his tongue and soon it's me at the brink, me about to lose control, me moaning around him.

He clamps a hand on my ankle and, in one breathtaking jerk, I find myself under him, face-to-face this time.

I'd pout but I've lost my ability to command my features. I'm too light, too full of spinning. "Alec…" I trail off when he slides a hand between us.

"Do you feel this?" he asks, pressing two fingers into me, curling them mercilessly until my chin tips up and my neck arches, and I let out a sound of pleasure I've never made before.

"That's me. *I* do this to you." His tone is intense. And smug.

"You do." My words are weak, too filled with pleasure for any real weight, and they flutter from my lips. "I never knew why I was waiting. But now I do. I was waiting for you."

His eyes narrow and his chest expands with the breath he's holding. "You have no idea what it means to hear you say that. No idea."

He flickers his fingers and I moan again, my body beginning to pulse. "Hold on," he say, easing his fingers out of me. Again, I want to pout but I'm too invested in the moment, too fully aware that everything here is leading to something bigger.

He smoothes his hand up my body again, until it rests between my breasts. "Do you feel this?" Now he taps his fingers, damp from my own wetness, against me, in the rhythm of my heart. "Do you?"

I nod and wind my legs around him, needing to feel him between them. Needing…something. More. But he holds his body away from mine, his eyes never leaving my face. "I want this," he says, *tap, tap, pause*. "I want all of it."

"Take it," I say. He can have whatever he wants from me, as long as he gives me what I need. I've never experienced this clawing sort of ache, etching itself into every inch of me. My body is quivering, begging me to beg him, but he speaks before I can.

"Don't tell me to take it," he rasps. "Tell me I have it."

"You have it. You have everything." The words tumble out so easily, so smoothly… For the first time, I realize how much of me he truly possesses. He dug his way through every wall I've ever raised and now there is only him, only Alec.

With my words, something in his expression relaxes, like a sigh cascading over his features. And finally he lowers himself between my legs, allowing his erection to slide through the wetness waiting there, and I nearly come undone with no more than the feel of his tip, nudging me open.

"Do you want me to get a—"

"No." I shake my head, wrapping my feet more securely around his waist. I don't want a condom. I only want him. Alec, unsheathed, inside of me.

And like he's reading my thoughts, he pushes himself into me. Slowly.

A tight, throbbing pressure fills me as I stretch around him, and I'm not sure if the pain or pleasure that comes with it is greater. The noise that falls from my lips is full of both. He pauses. "Am I hurting you?"

"Almost as much as you're pleasing me," I say, my teeth gritted. "Don't stop. All I want is to feel you everywhere."

He pulls away, and I gasp at the lack of contact but before the sound is finished leaving my mouth he's back. Inside of me. His entire head, pushing through me, *into me*.

And then he pushes harder, further in. I gasp again, this time...a little more pain. But I tighten my ankles around him before he can pull out. "Don't stop," I repeat. "I knew there would be pain. That doesn't keep this from being the most meaningful moment of my entire life."

His eyes soften; he wants to stop. I can tell by the tense set of his shoulders, by the worry in the muscle ticking in his jaw, that hurting me destroys him. Piper's words flash through my mind, the ones about him being half in love with me. I believe it now more than ever.

"I won't stop." He shifts his hips forward another inch. And another.

The more he gives me, the more I want. The more the pleasure pulls ahead of the pain. I grab his ass and I pull him toward me, but he locks his stance without budging.

"I need you, Alec," I say. "All the way inside of me."

"Teagan..." He stares at me, into me, and he crushes his mouth against mine, breathing heavy, and when I open my mouth to accept his tongue, he pierces me, pushing all the way inside.

I moan, and I hold him, digging my nails into his back. My body yawns around him, spreading to allow him a full fit.

It's uncomfortable—but it's also amazing. There's not a single nerve in my body that wants him to stop.

"Teagan," he says again, his whisper right at my ear. He kisses my neck, he says my name. I turn my face to capture his mouth with mine, needing him to kiss away the discomfort. He uses his mouth, his tongue, his teeth. He runs his hands along my body, lightly, forcefully, everything in between, and my back arches, and I ache for more.

Yet, the inside of me is tender and tense.

But I breathe deeply and discover undercurrents of pleasure running beneath the surface. The more I focus on them, the stronger they grow, whirling, flooding, *rushing*. And because of the way the sensations surge through me, I notice how still Alec is against them.

He is still. So, so still.

When I open my eyes again, he's watching me with a sort of tenderness I never knew existed before this exact moment. Part of me dissolves under his gaze, a brick I'd stacked against emotion deep in my soul that I will never, ever get back. But, in this moment, I don't want it anymore anyway.

I'm not sure which of us is more surprised when a tear slips down my cheek.

"It's okay," I say when he starts to speak, concern etched into his brows. "It's because I'm *happy*." The last word quivers as I speak it, and another tear escapes, slipping sideways down my other cheek. I keep my gaze steady on his, but soon my vision is too blurred to see clearly.

He's done this to me. He's found the center of who I am, and he's set it spinning.

Me.

I am spinning.

In love.

Alec kisses me again, feathering his lips over mine and whispering sweet nothings against my mouth and across my cheek and into my ear, and he slowly, slowly rocks his hips back.

Then forth.

Back.

Then forth.

And small blossoms of pleasure unfurl, growing and growing until my mind is unable to focus on anything else.

My hips start to rock too, and soon the way I dig my fingers into his back is a sort of mindless pleasure rather than to ward off the pain of moments ago.

We move together fluidly, his stomach and chest easing over my body as he thrusts. Soon, I'm bucking my hips to meet his force, because it feels *good*. Better than good, with every moment, every motion that passes. He pauses here and there to combine our mouths in sweeping kisses, but our bodies never slow for long.

Except for once.

Except for when he goes still again, pressing his forehead to mine and closing his eyes. I roll my hips, needing to continue the beautiful friction, but he shakes his head against me and whispers, "hold on," so strangled, I'm oddly tempted to giggle. Oddly tempted to press on and make him lose control. But I don't want the moment to end, so I hold my body motionless the best I can.

A moment later, he loses a bit of the tension from the way he holds himself, and when he opens his eyes there's a wicked gleam in them.

He pushes up on his knees and, before I'm expecting it, he pushes all the way into me—at a different angle.

An angle that has him ridging deeper into me, knocking every nerve down along the way.

An angle that has him hitting a new spot at the depth of his drive, one that makes me shiver uncontrollably underneath him.

And then he reaches between us, rolling me in his fingers, pressing me in circles until I'm begging him not to stop, never to stop... He slams into me again and again and again and a wildness builds in me, my hips rolling, rolling, needing to reach a peak I never thought I'd find tonight. Not my first time.

But Alec is determined. And there's sweat on his brow.

I want to lap it up with my tongue.

I settle for his mouth though, pulling his face to mine, slipping my tongue through his lips, clawing my hands through his hair, down his back, to grab his ass and pull him harder into me.

And harder.

He responds in kind, slamming so hard into me my head slides halfway off the bed. Instead of stopping, he thrusts again and lowers his head to pull a nipple into his mouth. He doesn't hold back, sucking as hard as he's fucking, as hard as he's tucking me between his fingers, and I can't bite back a cry. It rips out of my lungs and fills the room, and I wrap my arms around him, holding on, holding on and somehow starting to fall without actually falling.

He's grunting, and I'm spiraling down around him in the no-longer-steady room. Flashes of heat span out from between my ribs and twist lower, lower in the both familiar and also achingly new sense of a looming orgasm. I tighten, tighten, tighten around him with so much force he loses himself too, and we're thrashing and moving and swimming in each other.

I don't know who finishes first. All I'm aware of are the echoes of pleasure writhing through every single part of me. They're so intense I lose track of all else and when I come back down, Alec is panting over me, his dark hair tangled and sweaty against his forehead.

My heart is slamming in my chest, and I am tingling from head to toe. Trembling, too. And when Alec collapses on me, I discover I'm not the only one.

"*Fuck*, kitten." His voice is hoarse, and he slips out of me—and the loss of him there makes me whimper. His shoulders shake when he laughs, burying his face in my neck.

I love you, I want to say, but don't.

"Come here." He tucks an arm under me and rolls us to the side, folding me into his chest. I let him hold me, because I've never felt so cherished, so *safe*.

For a while, a long while, there's nothing but the sounds of our breathing and the racing of our hearts. I hear the way his pounds in his chest as clearly as I feel my own.

Another set of tears well in my eyes, though these I'm able to blink away. Mostly.

I thought... I thought it would be real, raw even, with nothing separating us. But it turns out the lack of a condom has nothing to do with why the moment is so raw between us. This goes so much deeper than that.

"You know me for exactly who I am," I say, leaning away to study his face, tugging my fingers through his damp hair, treading them down his back. "And I love that you do. I've never..." I clear my throat. "I've never felt this way."

He kisses me, slowly and smoothly, before he says, "Neither have I."

CHAPTER FORTY-SIX

I'M NOT SURE when we fall asleep. Sometime after we discuss pancakes for the morning, and sometime before I tell him I love him. Because I chicken out repeatedly on that front.

When I open my eyes, the first things I see are his hands, wrapped around my own. One of his arms is thrown over me, the other under my neck. Spooning. I've never done it.

I never want to stop.

His chest is hot against my back.

He's got morning wood between my legs.

It makes me grin.

It makes me want to do wicked, wicked things.

Until my mom's whispers twist through my mind. *That's right, sweetie, that's how to keep him hooked. Spread your legs, and he'll do the same with his wallet.*

I've never scrambled out of bed so fast in my entire life. Alec cracks an eye, stretching—totally uninhibited by his nakedness, by the thickness of his arousal. "Get back here," he grumbles, reaching out for me. "I can't stand one moment without you in my bed."

"Gotta pee." *Gotta pee?* What the hell is wrong with me?

But I dart into the bathroom and do it anyway, hanging my head in my hands. Really, what is wrong with me? How do I get my mother out of my head? How do I keep her from ruining this?

I love him. That love has *nothing* to do with his money...right? So why the hell is my stupid make-believe mother still taking over my thoughts?

I wonder if Straight Talk No Jacket does emergency Saturday sessions.

Then I think of my last session. Self-determination and self-knowledge. Maybe those things don't only have to apply to my career. Maybe they can help me here, too.

Alec raps on one of the doors. "I'll start breakfast."

And I love him more now than I did a second ago. He wanted me back in his bed, but he knows I need some time. He's not pressing me.

Still, it's another few minutes before I can let myself out of the bathroom. I smile when I notice the undershirt he's left on his bed for me.

I slip it on, and then, after a moment of silence to make sure my mother has nothing left to say, I head downstairs.

Alec's mixing batter in nothing but boxer briefs, and he looks fucking delicious.

"What's going on in that head of yours?" he asks, a knowing look across his face.

God. He can read me like a book.

Better than I can read an actual book...

Ha.

I'm so punny.

I take a deep breath, surprised to be more nervous about this than I was about sleeping with him last night. Self-determination, I remind myself. And self-knowledge. I know what scares me, and I know I want to be honest with Alec. Because that's our thing.

And I don't want to lose him.

I open my mouth—right as my gaze falls on a familiar folded piece of clothing. Cassidy's blazer. "I forgot I left this. Why do you still have it?"

"At first, I didn't know how to find you to return it." He levels me with a look that'd pass as stern if he wasn't smiling so wide with the memory. "Then...it was my safety measure. If all else failed, I had a reason to talk to you one last time."

He shrugs like it's no big deal. But it is. It's a really big freaking deal, and it makes me melty all over, knowing he didn't want to give up on us from the start.

"Score, there's fifteen dollars in the pocket, I think. Coffee money!" I smile when he laughs. "What happens when you go to Harvard in the fall?" I ask. It's not the thing I wanted to say, but it's one of the things I've been afraid to bring up. So I guess it counts.

He looks surprised—and then aware. "You think this is a summer thing?"

"I don't know what to think." I know what I *want* to think...

"This is more than a summer thing," he says, serious and tender. "I've got one more year there. I'll come back all the time. And you can fly out on the weekends. If you want, I mean."

"I'm not sure I have the budget for that," I say, quietly. But I offer him a smile, anyway, because he clearly hadn't even thought about the end of the summer, like the possibility of us being over hadn't entered his mind. And I love him for it.

"I'll fly you out," he says, like it's so simple. Like it doesn't make my stomach sour.

"I don't want you to fly me out. I mean, I do. But... I'm nervous that part of me likes you because you're rich." There. It's out in the open now.

"Because of who your mom is?"

Because she's in my head. "For one thing. But also. You're rich. I'm poor. Isn't that how these things work?"

There's a long pause before he responds. "Is that really what you think? Really how you define me?" His jaw clenches. I've hurt him.

"Wait—hear me out, okay? I don't *feel* like what I feel for you has anything to do with your bank account." I reach halfway to him, but he moves away. Understandably. Heartbreakingly. "But I have my mother's genes. And she chases bank accounts like dogs chase balls. With zero discretion. And you're rich. And you're pretty. And it makes me nervous."

He doesn't say anything and the silence between us is a balloon full of tension growing closer, closer to popping.

"You know what—can we go back to a few minutes ago and start over? Forget I said anything?" Because...because what if this has nothing to do with his money and *everything* to do with my mind finding a way to hold on to my mother's voice, since it's the only interaction I'll ever have with her? How did I never pick up on this before? Instead I, what? Have been using her as an excuse to keep myself from being happy with Alec?

No. Not an excuse, a valid reason. What I said to him is true—I do have her genes.

But, still. Maybe there's more to it.

This...is something I might need more time to digest.

And later—because right now Alec's expression is so grim, my stomach clenches. I want to fill him in on my epiphany, but I don't know how to put it into words that don't make me want to punch myself in the face. Then he asks, "You think I'm pretty?"

And the balloon of tension I thought was between us bursts into laughter.

"You know you're pretty," I say, thrilled that I've somehow found my way to this guy who's so easygoing, who lets me be a little neurotic—and then let's it all go. "I..." *love you.* Why can't I say it? "I... I'm starving. Hurry up with those pancakes."

But when he turns from me, toward the stove, I have an idea.

I'm going to set something up for us. Something special. So when I tell him, there'll be no doubt it's true. So when I say the words he won't wonder if they're a part of the euphoria that comes with how perfect last night was.

"You've got a nice ass," I say, admiring the way his briefs shape it. "God, even yours has more shape than mine, all flat." I sigh, all dramatically.

He leaves the batter on the counter, striding toward me, a devilish grin across his pretty mouth. "You do not have a flat ass, you beautiful idiot. You have a gorgeous ass. I could kiss every inch of it. In fact, get that sweet ass over here so I can do it right now."

And when I shriek, attempting to run away, he captures me with the grace of a lion springing on its prey. And he makes good on his word for the rest of the morning.

We never do get around to those pancakes.

CHAPTER FORTY-SEVEN

I TELL ALEC I want to take him somewhere next weekend. He asks for details, I refuse to give them. So he thinks it's a surprise—which I guess it will be—which puts extra pressure on me to figure out where the hell I want to take him. It needs to be special.

Clearwater Heights comes to mind. But to get reservations there before next year I'd need to be...well, Alec. And that place is so far out of my budget it's about as available to me as Mars is, which is to say I'd pretty much need to sell a spaceship to afford it.

I almost ask Vera if she has any ideas. But... I'm not ready for her gooey-eyed response when I say the L word.

I almost ask Sam for an idea at work. But... I kinda want this to come from me. And Sam's busy trying to decide if he's going to forgive Ty—who's begging for another chance—while also stressing out about leaving for his freshman year at Brown in a month.

A month.

That's how long I have with Alec. Should I be panicking?

Because I'm not.

Maybe this is how love works. Maybe love gives us faith that things will work out. And even if they don't, my life is better for having him in it.

Holy shit I'm a sappy motherfucker these days.

For obvious reasons, it's difficult to avoid Alec at work. And not like I really want to avoid him, but I'm so tempted to blurt out my feelings every time I see him, I find myself cleaning the break room a lot. And I take over the supply room for Sam to keep me away from my desk. It really does help me to pass a shit ton of time, considering I have to read labels for specific things, like types of pens and printer paper and a bunch of crap people leave wherever they please. Things people without a learning disability could sort in ten minutes or less. It's annoying, but I know I have options to make it easier. I'm choosing in this instance not to use them because the entire point is to keep me out of Alec's line of vision for a little while longer.

Because when he looks at me, even if I'm not facing him, I swear to God I can feel it.

On Wednesday, he calls me into his office.

"You," he says, leaning against his desk, all forced casual and still sexy as fuck, "have been avoiding me. Should I be worried? Is it the HR stuff?"

"No," I say, my eyes widening. I'm such an idiot, giving off mixed signals. I take a few steps toward him, then I stop when the words try to bubble their way up my throat. I am not going to tell him I love him at the fucking office. "I'll sign the papers whenever they send them."

"Then talk to me. What is it?"

Oh God, he's going to trap me with this annoying habit I've developed of being honest with him.

But there is one truth that might get the job done without my having to tell him *everything*. "This job's important to me. Being around you makes it hard to be competent because all I want to do is jump you when I see you."

"I get it. I can't look at you without wondering what you're wearing under your clothing. You've ruined me," he says, with a smile.

Warmth. Straight between my legs. Flutters, too. I cross one ankle and lean against the door, hoping he can't see right through me. "*See.* This is what I'm talking about! How am I supposed to stay professional when you say things like that... When you make me *feel* things like this?" *Also? I love you.* I want to shout it so bad I literally bite the tip of my tongue.

"So you're saying you want to keep it professional on business days?"

"No—but also yes." I hope my expression shows my chagrin. Because, "Believe me, Alec. Even right now I'm having trouble"—*not telling you I fucking love you*—"not begging you to bend me over your desk. But this is the sort of thing HR will definitely not approve of, regardless of what we sign."

Plus, honestly, I feel the weight of necessity to do a fucking awesome job here. Nobody knows better than I do that I'll be under Mr. Chambers' scrutiny for the foreseeable future. I don't want a reputation as the office flirt or to be seen as a girl who screws her way into keeping her job... Not to mention the fact that, while Zoloft seems to be helping, I'm well aware how quickly a person can slide back into depression—and losing my job, or my reputation? Yeah, I've got firsthand experience with those triggers.

"Screw HR." Alec wets his lips and shoves off his desk, taking one deliciously menacing step toward me. His nostrils puff out in a small flare when he takes a breath, and his face is so full of desire, my mouth goes wet. Aaaaand there go any thoughts about the possibility of depression. Damn, he's fucking hot.

"Alec," I say, pleading—though whether for him to let up or keep going, I'm not sure.

"Fine. I'll behave," he says, "But on the weekends you belong to me. With me."

Four more weekends, I estimate, before he goes to school, and my stomach tenses. "Starting with this weekend," I say. "Friday night. Don't forget."

He gives me a blandly amused look. "I'll be thinking of it every hour at least, and yet somehow I'll remain professional." His expression sharpens into something much less bland and a lot more dangerous and he takes another step toward me. And then another. "Unless you stand here for one second longer."

I want to take him up on it. I want to bounce myself off this door and straight onto him. He glances at my mouth, and I run my tongue over my lips, and...

"I—" I cover my mouth with my hands before *love you* can follow. And I hightail it out of his office.

Time passes excruciatingly slow. I'm aware of Alec every second of every minute, like this whole being professional thing actually makes me want him more even if I'm the one who set the parameters.

At one point he's just standing there, down the aisle in front of my desk, at someone else's desk, and he's drinking a bottle of water. I watch him tip the bottle to his mouth. I watch the liquid travel down his throat.

My own mouth goes so wet I wonder if it's possible to be overhydrated.

And, because I swear he came complete with Teagan-mind reading capabilities, his eyes slide over to mine, and they freaking twinkle because there's no doubt he knows what I'm feeling.

I spend a lot of time cleaning the break room.

I catch him looking at me too, sometimes, with this speculative expression, like he's...nervous. I try to keep my hopes from pole-vaulting, but they leap right out of my reach—because maybe he wants to tell me he loves me too.

On Thursday, I figure out what I want to do.

Nothing fancy. I can't afford it—and it's not me anyway. And I want the moment I tell him to come straight from who I am.

Which means peanut butter and jelly sandwiches, hard ciders, and chips. Lake Imperial and my picnic basket, the one I made in middle school. Maybe the blanket I made, too, to spread on the grass. We can skip the picnic tables. I'll take him to a spot I know doesn't get much traction. We'll be alone.

It might not be much, but it won't matter to Alec. We'll have the lake and the setting sun. We'll have the fireflies and the chirping crickets and birds overhead. We'll have each other and I'll tell him I love him.

Oh my God. This is too much. I'm so...ugh. What has happened to me? I turn to Sam, typing away at his desk. "Hey."

"What?" He doesn't bother looking over. I envy his multitasking abilities.

"Say something annoying."

This gives him pause. He looks at me, his expression unsteady. "Uh, why?"

"Because I haven't been irritated in a while and I need to make sure I still can be. You're usually good at it—so give me your best shot."

His mouth twists in that cocky teenaged smug sort of way we all lose the ability to master once we hit twenty. "You had VPLs yesterday."

"I had what?"

"Visible panty lines."

Yep. Turns out I can *definitely* still get pissed off. "You're such a little shit. Why didn't you say anything? Why did you even look?"

"Sorry. They were noticeable." He at least has the decency to blush, even if his mouth stays in the smug twist from before. "Also sometimes you talk out loud while you type. It's annoying."

"*You* are annoying." I throw a pen at him and the nib leaves a black mark on the chest of his shirt. He looks from it to me and the expression on his face is so bewildered, I burst into laughter. "Guess it's your turn to walk around with something embarrassing for people to stare at all day."

It doesn't occur to me to apologize until later. But the fact that it registers at all...well, I'll call that progress. Even more so when I actually do it.

Another thing that doesn't occur to me until later is that in order to have the picnic I want, I have to get my things from my grandparents' house.

Fuck.

CHAPTER FORTY-EIGHT

I TAKE FRIDAY off of work, texting Alec that I'm fine but I have to deal with some personal stuff. I swear, I have to stop calling out. Alec may be cool with it—but he won't be my boss for much longer and I need a better track record. Especially with Mr. Chambers probably looking for reasons to get rid of me. Plus, I only get fourteen days off *a year*.

But today... Today I'd be a waste of space at work. Today I need to focus on dealing with my grandparents.

Ugh. It's too early to think about them. I'm going back to bed.

Alec calls me a few minutes later, and my voice is still groggy when I answer. "The sun is barely up. I was so close to falling back asleep."

"I'm taking off today too, to be with you," he announces. He doesn't sound groggy at all. He sounds awake, alive. Even wired, maybe. "Let's do your personal stuff together."

I sit up, rubbing sleep from my eyes. Yum. An entire extra day with Alec? I'm tempted. My entire body's tempted, if the tightening in my nipples is any indication. The warmth in my belly. The wet between my thighs...

But I say, "Go to work, boss. I need to do this on my own."

"Sounds serious."

I shrug, laughing silently at myself when I remember he can't see it. God, I need coffee. "I'll tell you about it tonight. I'll text you where to meet me."

He's hesitant before responding. "Are you sure?"

I'm touched when we hang up, because I think he was able to read the nervousness in my voice.

I *am* nervous. I have to face the people who raised me with as much care as they might have given a fucking slug. I need to get my basket and my blanket—and, hell, most of my other stuff while I'm at it. But this might be the last time I ever see them, and there are some things I need to get off my chest.

Just...not first thing in the morning.

Brunch in an hour? I text Cassidy. *My treat.*

How about breakfast now? she responds. *We're leaving in a couple hours for North Carolina.*

Kelsey's Diner, I say. *And you can bring Gage if you have to.*

She brings Gage.

I want to be annoyed, but he makes her happy.

And he's a nice person.

And... I'm not sure why I want to be annoyed anymore.

They walk toward the table, Cassidy all blonde and curves, Gage all sharp-featured and disheveled. Even in a sallow old diner, they shine. Ugh.

She hugs me. He hugs me. And, add the fact that he smells awesome to the list from before. Not as good as Alec, but close enough.

Cassidy drops into a seat, but Gage stays standing. "I've got some lyrics to work through. Thought I'd give you girls some alone time, cool?"

A grateful smile widens my lips. "Gig tonight?"

"Yeah. Then some much needed beach time." He leans down for a quick kiss from Cassidy. "With the sexiest bikini chick in the Outer Banks."

Cassidy rolls her eyes, but her cheeks are prettily pink and there's a smile in her tone. "You haven't met Quinn yet."

"Doesn't matter." He tweaks her shoulder, nods to me, and then heads off to his own table. A moment later he's lost in his notebook, scribbling away.

After a waitress takes our order, Cassidy levels me with a stare. "What gives?"

"What do you mean?" I aim for an innocent tone, but my pitch is way off.

"I haven't heard from you this early in the morning since we were in high school and you were texting me not to pick you up because you were ditching."

"Those were the days." My words feel almost as crooked as the smile I'm trying to come up with. "Are you excited to see Quinn?"

I don't quite understand why Cassidy cares enough about her roommate to visit her. The few times I've been down to North Carolina to see them during their school year, Quinn's been...distant, to say the least. She hides in her room and barely responds when Cassidy tries to make conversation. I wondered if she was shy, but Cassidy said no, that she'd drastically changed this past year, growing secretive and kind of moody.

I would never be friends with someone like that, but...then again, I can't be surprised Cassidy would be. She's friends with *me*, after all...

Maybe it's her calling, collecting all of us rejects.

"Teag. Out with whatever you're holding back." Her expression softens. "Is it Gran? Is she still bothering you?"

"No. Yes—she's part of it. But..." I find my shrug comes easily. "I'm going over there after this to get my stuff, and then I'll be done with her—with both of them—for good."

I expect Cassidy to ask if I'm sure that's what I want, the eternal optimist that she's always been, but all she says is, "Good. You're better without them."

Relief shudders through me in a laugh. "Anything is better without them."

"Do you want me to go with you?"

"No," I say, meaning it. "I need to do this on my own."

"You're really okay about it?" She studies my face, and I nod. I can tell the moment she believes that I'm telling the truth because her own stance relaxes. "You get to turn a whole new page. Ugh—and you get to do it living with Vera. I'm so tempted to move back in—how much fun would that be?"

"Awesome," I say, imagining it. "Though then she couldn't sneak around with that Gold Rush Standard roadie from last summer."

"The one she made out with last year?" Her mouth parts and her eyes go wide and—oops—I guess she didn't know.

"They're doing quite a bit more than making out if the noises in her bedroom a few nights ago were any indication." Guilt shoots little arrows my way for sharing Vera's business, but it's not like Cassidy wouldn't find out eventually anyway. "Have you heard from Luca?"

"Nope." Cassidy's jaw tightens. "I told him to burn my phone number last time he called."

"No such thing as forgiving and forgetting, huh?"

Her eyes burn with anger. "He wrote a song as his apology. I forgave him long before that. But how can anyone fucking forget when that song's played like every five minutes?"

I glance at Gage, erasing something in his notebook. "Does it bother him?"

"Not anymore." Some of the tension drains from her expression. "At first it did, but...he says he's confident enough in how much I love him not to let a stupid song bring us back down. And he says he'll write me millions of songs, so who cares about one fading pop artist." She shakes her head, laughing.

I'm a little swoony myself. "He's halfway decent."

"I sometimes feel like I don't deserve him." She twists to look at him, and like he senses her movement, he catches her eyes, grinning a lopsided smile. She's wearing the same one when she turns around. "But all I have to do is look at him and I'm better. Better than better."

The waitress drops off our food. I use the interruption as an excuse to ask what I really want to know about.

Okay.

I open my mouth to ask about the first time she told Gage she loves him, but something else comes out instead. "I slept with Alec."

She blinks at the change of pace, and then her features twist into something pleased, something greedy, and she rubs her hands together. "I want the details—was it amazing? I can't believe you waited this long."

"Believe it," I snap. "And not just with Alec either."

"Not just with Alec?" She tilts her head, considering my words—and then her eyes light up. "Holy shit—did you have a three-way?"

"God—*no*. What is wrong with you?"

"What's wrong with you?" she snaps back this time. "It's not like you've never said you wanted one." She shovels eggs into her mouth, chewing angrily.

"I was a *virgin*," I say, angrier even than the motions of her jaw. "I'd never had sex. And you can wipe that shocked expression off your fucking face because if you were any kind of friend you'd already know this."

"But you always... I mean..." She slowly lowers her fork to the plate in front of her, eggs forgotten. "Why would you always say—"

"Because it was fun. It was easy." It was making myself the thing my grandmother always said I'd be—but defiantly, like *in her face* defiantly. Like her words never hurt me, never bothered me. "And you never even questioned it. Never even stopped to wonder why I was spreading my legs for everyone I came in contact with." My voice is sharp enough to slice someone—it's like I *am* my grandmother right now. God. Antidepressants have definitely helped to stem some of my mood swings, but I still have so far to go along the self-improvement path. I fucking hate lashing out like this. *Hate.*

"First of all," Cassidy bites out the words, "even if you had been sleeping with the guys you said you were—why would I judge you for it? You want to be ashamed of your imaginary sex life—go ahead. But don't put that on me."

"I..." Damn. I can't believe I'm fighting a smile. "You grew some claws this year, huh?"

"Kinda have to with you as my best friend." She's not ready to smile yet. Which makes me lose the battle with my own—it forces my lips to curve, and even wider when she glares at me.

"I'm sorry I lied," I say.

"I'm sorry you ever felt the need to."

I push my pancakes around. "It was never about you, or not trusting you. It was... I don't know how to explain it. My mind's a fucked-up place sometimes."

"Tell me something I don't know," she says, her words drier than the Sahara.

"You should be careful what you ask for," I say. "But it's too late to take it back now."

And I tell her everything else, too.

And we talk for hours.

And she's late leaving for the Outer Banks. But this, I don't apologize for. Because we needed these hours.

"How did I not know you had feelings for Jason? I was so blind," she says, squeezing me into a huge hug.

"It was kind of a whirlwind. It happened so fast, somehow we noticed each other at the same time, and there were a few weeks of flirting. He... He didn't want me to say anything until we knew what it was, so we spent that weekend together—but I didn't hear from him again after, so I thought he'd changed his mind. And then he was...gone." I wrap my arms around her, ducking my face into the hug so I don't have to see the tears that shimmer in her eyes. "I'm sorry."

"Don't be. Please. I'm sorry there was no closure after your weekend together, but I'm glad it happened," she says. "I'm glad he had that weekend with you. That he knew happiness with you. Before he died."

Before he died. Before he died. These are such horrible words, and my heart splinters all over again. I don't care whether or not we would've ended up together; nothing changes the fact that Jason should still be here today.

He died too young. And over something so stupid.

There's a question Cassidy's too nervous to ask—I feel it in her stance, and I answer anyway. "I never saw him using drugs. I never knew."

I want to tell her I'm nervous he was using around me and that I didn't pick up on it. I want to tell her I've spent more nights than I can count sleepless over wondering how I missed the signs, or if I could've prevented his death. But I don't. I let it rest. Because my fears aren't facts, and transferring them to her won't do any good. And because I feel closer to her than I have in ages. The distance has been all my fault, but it's starting to close and that's what matters most.

Well, that and getting my shit from Gran.

Double fuck.

CHAPTER FORTY-NINE

THERE'S A SHINY black truck with new tags parked in front of my grandparents' place. I pull up in my ancient clunker and sputter to a stop right beside it. The sight makes my stomach twist, but I'm not sure why.

Actually, maybe I do. If Gramps has a new truck...is that where my payments have gone? Rather than to water bills, he stashed them away for the down payment?

Irritation starts to simmer in my gut, but I smother it. Why should I care about cold showers when I'll never have to take them here again? I'm letting go of this place today. Of them. Of everything from my past.

I ignore the truck and I take the few steps up to the front porch. And my fucking house key doesn't work when I try to open the door.

They changed the locks.

Well, fuck this.

I bang on the door until my hand feels tender. I kick it a couple times, too. I'm about to break through one of the screened windows when Gran finally opens the door. "Oh. You."

"You changed the locks?" I don't meant to sound so hurt, but my voice is smaller than usual and, instead of anger, a confusing sort of sadness fills me.

"You left."

"You told me to."

"Eh. You're old enough to look after yourself now." She glances over my shoulder.

"Expecting someone?" I *almost* manage to laugh—my grandparents literally never have company—but the mangled sound makes it as high as the base of my throat before it fades. I brush past her. "Don't worry. I'll be gone in a few. I need my things, and then I guess this is over."

I wrinkle my nose against the ashtray stench that assaults it. The stink seems worse now, but maybe that's because I was used to it for too long. I take the stairs, skipping the broken ones and avoiding the splinters of the handrail, and there's a certain sort of elation that begins to fill me when I remember this is the last time I'll ever do it.

Because if something goes wrong with rooming with Vera, I'll live in my car before I come back here. I'll sleep under my desk. I don't care. Anything is better than this.

I stuff most of my clothing in a duffel bag. I grab the basket, pulling out my baby blanket and holding it against my chest. Only for a moment. It's a bit more worn than I thought it was, but maybe that'll add to tonight's charm.

Gran's still watching outside when I return, bag and basket in tow. "Where's Gramps?" I ask.

"Trading in my car." She's sucking on a cigarette and…for the one moment while her cheeks are hollowed, I notice how the years have aged her. She's bitter, always has been, but maybe that's the life she was dealt.

Her answer makes a bit more sense about the truck—maybe they traded in both their old cars for it. I glance at it out the front door. "Guess I won't get to tell him goodbye."

Her snort puts a horse's to shame. "Guess not."

Considering the last time I saw him he hit me—unintentionally doesn't make it that much better—I can't say I'm too upset about it.

"Do you blame me?" I ask quietly, my stomach tighter than a dead man's noose.

"For what?" Her words are more warning than question, and still she watches out the front screen. Hot summer air pulses through the grating, sticky on my skin. Her shirt is damp under the armpits and beneath her breasts.

"For my mother leaving." My clarification is quieter than the question was.

The answer's always been implied, but I've never had the guts to ask.

Now she swivels her head my direction, and if looks could kill...

I wave my hand in front of her monstrous expression. "I know, I know, mentioning mommy dearest goes against rule number one. But... I don't care." What I do care about, however, is the way my voice cracks. It doesn't stop me though. "I want an answer."

Still, she doesn't respond.

"What is it?" I pause, waiting for my throat to stop constricting. It takes longer than I'd prefer. "Do you have some... I don't know...some long lost fear? You can't let yourselves love me because you're afraid I'll leave you like she did?"

For a moment, I can't read her expression. The type of tension that's actually hope runs its way along my ribcage, like mallets over a xylophone, lightly at first and then, after the reality of the moment sinks in, hard enough to snap. Because this is it. This is the moment I've always feared, always craved.

In the deepest, most hidden parts of my mind, the rest of the conversation goes like this: *Love you?* she'd ask. *Of course we love you. But your mother broke our hearts, and it's too hard to show love after that. You look so much like her it's sometimes painful.*

In reality, she begins to laugh, which is interrupted by series of hacking coughs. "When did you get this needy?"

I press harder. "Is that it? You raised me to be hardened against needing things, or people, because she left you and you didn't want me to ever go through what you did?"

She drags on her cigarette and the soured twist to her face takes regular contempt and makes it a little bitch. "What the hell sort of sissy shit are you talking about?"

A part of me wishes I wanted to tear at my hair.

A part of me wishes I wanted to scream.

A part of me wishes I wanted to do anything other than offer the quiet smile that I do.

Because that would mean I hadn't given up, that there was still some sort of hope for a semblance of a relationship with the only relatives I know. But it's over. Has been for a long time. From the very beginning, honestly.

"Thank you," I say. "I needed to hear that."

Tires crunch over gravel and a new truck—delivery, this time—pulls up to the house. And I watch, stunned, when a man uses a dolly to haul two boxes from the back. A new washer and dryer.

There is a thought slamming its fist at the door of my mind, and I am doing everything I can to keep it out. Double lock. Triple lock.

But this thought... It cuts through those locks with a chainsaw and comes through anyway.

"Why did Gramps trade your car in?" I ask, a hot, tingling sort of pain dancing along my skin.

"To make room for the new one," she says, her tone slow and steady, like I'm an idiot for asking.

"For the new truck out there?" Please, please be for the truck.

"No." She smiles a brittle smile. "That's his. Mine's a station wagon."

"A...new station wagon?" Oh God. Oh God. "Where did you get the money?"

Her smile goes from brittle to gloating in no time at all. "A friend of yours, actually. You seem surprised."

My heart.

My heart.

There is a piece of barbed wire circling my heart, and my stupid fucking heart is twisting back and forth, like the wire is a Hula-Hoop. And it's *shredding* me.

"Alec," I say. "He gave you these things?"

Where is my breath? I clutch my stomach and bend at the waist. I'm so close to falling to my knees I almost give in and do it. But I don't think I'd get up after. And I have to be able to leave. That was my entire reason for coming.

But I wasn't expecting this.

"Why?" I ask, the word dropping like an anchor, pulling me down, down, down with it.

"Guess you'll have to ask him." And after a few beats of silence, mine full of shock, hers full of gloat, "Told you you'd end up like

your mama," Gran says, her cigarette breath making me gag. "Least when you spread *your* legs, we reap the rewards rather than just the consequences."
Just the consequence. That's what I am to her. To both of them. I'm not their grandchild. I'm not their blood. I'm the mistake my mother made and didn't want to face. They were stuck with me.
They never loved me.
Never bothered trying to.
This is actually what I came for. To learn the thing that will give me no regrets about never seeing them again.
And now I have it.
And now I can leave.
I do it without a backwards glance.
And with a heart dead in my chest.

CHAPTER FIFTY

PERCHED ON A picnic table with the orange setting sun rolling over the water before me, I slap at a mosquito after it's had a few seconds of ankle blood. It's probably the tenth in the past five minutes. Guess I forgot citronella candles. Or bug spray.
    Guess I forgot pretty much everything.
    Guess I don't really care.
    My anger's only ever been a scorching thing. So this coolness coursing through me is difficult to understand. Difficult to feel. Or maybe it's so cold it's made me numb.
    The headlights of Miles' town car come into view, and in the back of my mind I wonder if I should be nervous. Shouldn't my stomach jump?
    Shouldn't I feel something?
    Anything other than empty?
    Because if that's the case, I'm failing.
    Even Alec's familiar stride through the park toward me only brings the smallest twinge.
    He's smiling.
    He's smiling, even when he knows what he's done.
    Huh.

Guess I can feel pain after all. It hits in the weirdest spots. Beneath my belly button. Along my collarbone. At the base of my throat.

I'm not sure what he sees in my expression, my face alone is still too numb for me to understand, but whatever it is, he falters as he gets closer, his smile vanishing.

"Aren't you going to ask me what's wrong?" I ask when he doesn't.

"Let me explain—"

"Did you know I wanted tonight to be special?" I say. My voice comes out like a song, teasing with a bitter edge.

"If you let—"

"It needed to be," I say, talking over him. "Because I wanted to tell you I loved you."

Surprise washes the edges from his expression.

Pleasure follows, and he steps toward me.

But uncertainty comes next, and he goes still.

"Yeah, it's confusing, isn't it?" I laugh. It twists humorlessly through the air. "Thinking you know something and then realizing you don't."

"You spoke with your grandparents." He's not surprised, just clarifying to fill the silence.

"I've had all day to think about it—and, maybe it's because I'm slow," I pause, swallowing past the lump of torn pride in my throat, "but I can't figure it out. Were you trying to make peace with them for me?"

"N-no, I—"

"Because that is never, ever going to happen. I went there today to get my things and to cut them completely free from my life. To cut *myself* free from them." I study the water for a moment, steeling myself. My insides seem to be swaying with the gentle ripples. Soon, too much time passes and I have to look at him again. It nearly kills me. "I didn't realize I'd have to do the same with you."

"Don't say that." His eyes dart between mine, like he's searching for a way to replace the meaning of my words with something else, something less set in stone. Panic loosens his features, tightens his stance.

But anger is a zipper trying to close my ribcage, making me choke. It hurts. Every part of this hurts. "I am so fucking stupid. I thought...when you called me this morning you seemed nervous—I thought it was because of me. I thought you were reading the anxiety in my tone. But you weren't. You were nervous for yourself, because you knew I'd find out what you'd done."

"You were always going to find out," he says. "I would never keep that from you."

"When did you go to them?"

He doesn't say anything, guilt wringing the truth from his expression.

"When?"

"Tuesday."

I stare at the setting sun until my tears clear. "You did keep it from me then. All week."

"Because I knew you wouldn't agree to it."

"Oh, right." I scoff at him and grip the picnic table so hard a splinter slides into my palm. Guess I was always going to get a splinter today, no matter how hard I try to avoid them. "Because you know better than me. I'm just a little woman and you're the big man who gets to march around beating his chest and making decisions over my head when I'm too dumb to know any better."

"You know that's not me." His tone is level but there's an entire ocean of anxiety beneath it.

"The Alec I *thought* I knew would never, under any circumstance, go behind my back and to the people who literally never showed me any love in my entire life and reward them with shiny, new, expensive toys."

"Hear me out," he says.

"Oh, I'm going to," I say. "You get to say your piece—that's the only reason I didn't cancel tonight. And then I get to say mine. And then we get to go our separate ways."

He winces and the pain in the shadows etched across his face makes my heart shred itself all over again. "You told me you didn't believe what you'd been told about your father."

My soul goes still as stone. "I told you I had childish hopes that maybe he wasn't a total monster."

"I wanted to give you the truth," he says.

Not just my soul now—everything is still. The lake. The crickets. The air. "And?"

"They were lying. The moment your grandmother asked how willing I was to make it worth her while to tell the truth, I knew they'd lied to you about him." He steps toward me, thinking I'll need him to hold me or shatter with the news, but I've reached my full shock capacity for the day and this... This is so big it will take me a lifetime to understand.

Still, a question rises from my gut, from a place I can't keep it back. "He's not a monster?"

"I can't speak for the kind of man he is," Alec says. "I wanted you to be able to choose whether or not to look into him, or contact him. But I can give you the number where he can be reached. And I can tell you...he never knew your mother was pregnant."

My father never knew he was my father.

My father...

I start to laugh. Just a few whispers of a humorless sound, really. And when Alec's expression drops to absolute sympathy-laden concern, I laugh harder.

And then I go quiet.

I feel it happen.

I feel my mind open to his words. I feel my mind sweep them inside and guide them into a very faraway corner, one I rarely access. I feel my mind lock them away to keep them safe until I can process them.

I wonder if this is what going crazy feels like.

Because all I feel is an icy calm.

No.

Wait.

Rage.

Rage I'm unused to, because there's no heat in it.

My rage is an ice storm, and Alec's caught out in the cold.

"How dare you?" My tone is dry ice, my words, raspy, scraping my throat. "Am I supposed to be *grateful?*"

"No, I n-never intended—"

"You can't just throw money at things to fix them. You can't—"

"Yes, I can," he says, finally snapping, and I've never wanted to punch someone more than I want to punch him right now. He shakes his head at what he sees on my face. "Not the important things, Teagan. I know the things that matter most can't be purchased. But them? They don't matter. You matter. And you deserve to know who your own father is."

"Stop." I throw my hand up like it'll do anything to block the word *father* from my ears. "You don't get to talk to me about my father. Don't you understand?"

"You know what I understand?" he asks, his voice suddenly so quiet I have to strain to hear him. "I understand that I love you. That I started falling the moment I met you. That it's real, it's there, and it's not going away. *That* is what I know more than anything I've ever known. I never intended to hurt you."

All week, this is what I've been dying to hear. I've hoped beyond my wildest anything that he would return the words I was so giddy to offer him.

Now they're the last things I want to come from his lips.

"You know nothing," I say, bitter with the truth of it.

Heartbroken.

Heart-kicked-out-of-my-chest.

Heartless.

"You don't love me. If you did—you would know I value my ability to act on my own behalf. You would know I can't *stand* when people go behind my back. For anything, but especially when it comes to my family life. I almost kicked Sam's ass the other week when he took my cellphone without my permission. And this? What you did? I don't give a shit about your intentions. Your *intentions* are the very reason I'd never be able to trust you again."

"Teagan—"

"Piper was right." I almost laugh again with this realization. How did I miss this before? "You have a savior complex." My world starts to crumble, finally, with the weight of my anger and my sadness, and I stand from where I'm perched before I crumble with it.

"Piper?" he asks. "What are you—"

"You're trying to save me. You've *been* trying to save me." I can't breathe. I am trying to pull air into my lungs but they've been crushed by my sudden understanding. "Audiobooks. Making sure I have health insurance. This thing with my grandparents. I can't *breathe* without feeling you somewhere in my life."

Oh my God.

I've been like my mom all along, letting him make my life better.

And with this, my world is no longer tilting.

It's disintegrating. I have no footing because it's no longer there beneath me.

Dust. All I'm left with is dust.

My face crumples a split second before tears run razors across my eyes. "You turned me into my mother," I manage to gasp out before I sob.

"You're nothing like her." He strides toward me, all furrow-browed and concerned, and sweeps me into his arms and holds me against his chest and... I let him.

I let him because I want to remember the feel of him, the scent of him.

I let him because I can't stem my tears, and I'd rather press my face against him than let him see them.

I let him because I need to walk away, but I'm too weak.

"Tell me how to fix it," he says, his voice a jagged mess.

"You don't get it." Finding the will to step back is like looking for an unburned sliver of wood after an all-consuming bonfire. But I dig, and I dig, and I find it. Even if it still burns me. "You took the one thing I based my entire life on and crushed it."

"Teagan." Panic makes a knife's edge out of his voice. He drops to his knees, gripping my calves, looking up at me, the destruction of the entire world in his eyes. "D-don't do this."

"I'm not doing it. You did." I swallow, my throat so swollen with a fresh batch of tears I almost choke. "You can't fix this. There's nothing to fix. It doesn't even exist anymore."

And it turns out I'm not too weak to walk away after all.

CHAPTER FIFTY-ONE

I LOOK BACK, because of course I do. Numb or not, I can't leave without turning.

Alec's no longer on his knees, but he's still facing the water, his hands fisted at his sides, his shoulders rigid. He's all shades of black and white, a silhouette against the last few moments of sun, and a hairline fracture splits beneath my sternum and races out like a crack in ice, spreading in rivulets through my chest, across my ribs, down my spine.

I have to get to my car before I fall to pieces.
I have to make it home.
Miles is smoking a cigarette, leaning against his hood.
He smiles.
Then he frowns.
He asks a question.
I give an answer.
I make it to my car.
I make it to Vera's.
And then I don't remember much.

CHAPTER FIFTY-TWO

PANIC IS A red-hot branding iron shoved straight into my stomach. I sit up in bed, gasping, sweating, trembling.

The burn of my reality scorches until I double over in pain.

Besides me, Vera snores, softly, almost prettily. Did she come to bed with me? I have a vague memory of stumbling into my room and her hands cool on my hot, tear-streaked face.

Did she help me change into my new pajama set? I honestly can't remember.

I slip quietly out of bed, knowing sleep is done for the night, but less than a minute later Vera's joining me in the living room, rubbing her eyes. "What time is it?"

"Three thirty."

"Want me to make you some tea?" she asks through a yawn. "Making some for myself."

I don't like tea, but I nod. Maybe it's time to start liking tea. Maybe tea will make me calmer. Maybe tea will keep Gran's careless, laughing expression from swiveling on repeat through my mind.

Vera makes us tea.

It's fucking gross.

It's so gross I spit mine back into my cup. The moment the last of the liquid passes my lips, though, I keep them open and I tell her everything.

My tone is dead, the way I'm trying to keep my insides.

"Wow," she says, and her eyes glint, wet with tears. "I couldn't really understand what you were saying when you got home. I'm so sorry, Teagan."

"Please don't be emotional," I say. "I don't want your pity."

"There's a difference between pitying someone and hurting along with them because you care for them," she says, but the rebuke is gentle.

"I have trouble feeling the difference," I say, calmly. "So I'd prefer neither."

She sips her tea, also calmly. If she's struggling to compose herself, I can't tell. And I'm grateful for it.

I'm grateful for her. I don't have many friends, but the ones I have are worth more than millions.

"I texted Cassidy," she says. "She's coming back in the morning. I figured you could use both of us right now."

Oh. Great. Now I'm going to end up the emotional one. I take another sip of my tea. Spit it out again. "Gross."

"If I was going to look at this like a journalist—detached and professional," she says, looking at me expectantly until I nod. "I'd divide this into four parts and tackle each one separately."

"Four parts?" I ask.

She counts off on her fingers. "One. Your grandparents are horrible people. You always secretly longed to discover a shred of decency in them and you've had that longing smashed to smithereens. That might take some time to process, but ultimately, it's not surprising. Two. You have a father out there who doesn't know you're alive."

"Stop." I stand. I pace. I clutch my stomach. "I'm going to throw up."

"Breathe," she says, rising to stand with me. "Deep breaths. You're not going to throw up. That's the hard one. I had to say it to get it out of the way. The rest will be easier."

"I can't think about..." I pause, panting like I'm out of breath. I *am* out of breath. "I'm not ready to deal with that one."

"Fine," she says, her tone stern rather than placating. It helps ease a bit of air into my lungs. "Three. Alec took your trust and twisted it. He—"

"Twisted it?" I tilt my head, wondering where her faulty logic comes from. "He demolished it. He—"

"Is in *love* with you." She sips her tea again. "He wanted to give you something that matched the depth of what he feels for you. He did it the wrong way."

"You're wrong," I say, but my words are weak.

"As dumb as his actions were," she says, "he did them for the right reasons."

Instead of snarking at her, I rub my eyes, furiously, willing the threat of tears into submission. "Who needs therapy when you're around?"

She cracks a tentative smile, and I can't match it, but I don't bite at her for it, so she pulls me back to the couch and sits closer to me this time. Just an inch. Just close enough to place a hand on my knee. "And here's the fourth part: You love him, too. You love him and he loves you, and nobody in the world can ease your hurt better than he can right now."

"I have you," I remind her stubbornly. "I have Cassidy, coming all the way back from the beach."

"You have us," she agrees. "But he's the first person you trusted enough to tell these things to. He's the one you want by your side. He's the one who can make right the wrongs he's done. If you want to let him. And we both know you do."

I want to push back harder, but I don't. Because she's speaking the truth, my truth, a feeling in my gut I haven't been able to name.

"Or," she says, her tone suddenly aces and spades lighter than before. "There are a dozen eggs in the fridge. We can take 'em and throw 'em at your grandparents' fancy new cars. I'm always happy to go that route with you, too."

Finally, finally, I laugh. It's a small thing, this laugh. Short and without much energy, but it's there. I didn't force it.

And beneath it is a steadiness that wasn't there before.

"I love him," I say. "But he hurt me, in the worst way he could."

She opens her mouth, but looks away, and it's closed when she faces me again.

"Don't you have something to say to that?" I ask.

"Don't you?"

"You sure you don't want to switch your major to shrink-hood?"

She lifts one meticulously groomed brow. It's her only response.

"Fine. Whatever. Clearly, journalism suits you." I sigh, and then I give in. "I should forgive him. Because I love him." The more I say it out loud, the clearer my answer becomes. "And because he didn't *mean* to hurt me. And sometimes intent matters." I pick up my own tea, sipping. And, of course, it's still disgusting. I put it down. "I don't want to talk about my father, but I will when I've had time to process it. And I wouldn't have that option if Alec hadn't done what he did. I might even be grateful when that time comes."

Oh my God. Relief is a splash of cold water shocking my system. It's like being reborn, right this instant, from someone who's always quick to rise in fury—into someone who's also now quick to forgive, quick to understand that sometimes things aren't black and white. *Even* while my feelings are still so bruised. So raw.

I'm usually the best grudge-holder I know. This moment, this realization that I don't have to be… It's jarring. In the *best* way.

"What else?" Vera asks, her eyes all wide and happy. The entire atmosphere is changing, no longer as heavy with my pain—it's tightening with anticipation.

"He makes me happy when he's not being a fucking idiot." A honey-like smoothness melts slowly through my chest, down my arms and legs. I've wondered if my mother's voice is in my mind because I can't help clinging to any interaction with her, even imaginary. But Alec gave me the means to have an *actual* interaction with my father. "I need Alec. I don't want to be without him. I'm going to go get him."

"In the morning?" she asks, covering a yawn. "Because I'm happy to snuggle the rest of the night with you."

But I'm wired. I couldn't sleep right now if I superglued my eyes shut. "I'll text you later."

She yawns again, this one stretching out over her grin. "Go get him."

I'm going to. I'm not even changing out of my pajamas first. I grab my bag, and I open the door to go to Alec.

He's already here.

CHAPTER FIFTY-THREE

ALEC IS SITTING in the landing of the concrete stairwell of Vera's apartment. His head's resting against the wall, and his feet are on the ground, his knees pulled up. His eyes open a second after I open the door.

It'd be nice if my emotions didn't tend to get completely snarled together so I could tell what exactly I feel right now. Excitement, I think—but maybe it's dread. I think maybe I'm happy, too, but my entire system's been under so much strain the past few hours, everything has a hollow tinge to it.

"How long have you been out here?" I ask, and turn to see if Vera's witnessing the same thing I am.

She seems in complete control of her emotions, grinning wide enough to break her face in half.

"I wanted to give you this," Alec says, his voice hoarse, and when I look at him again, he's standing, stepping toward me. He hands me a folded piece of paper. "I brought you your father's information, if you want it."

My breath catches in the steel trap of the word *father*. Just because I've come around to the idea of possibly interacting with him doesn't mean I'm ready to address it yet. "You could've texted me."

"I wanted to hand you something solid."

"You wanted a reason to come here." I almost smile. It's like Cassidy's blazer. But this is so much bigger than that.

"I would've been here even if I'd texted you."

"Why?"

"To tell you I'm sorry." He grabs my hand, covering it with his. I try not to sigh at the contact, at the way it steadies me in such an unsteady situation. Vera was right. I need him.

"I should've told you everything from the beginning," he says. "I thought if I surprised you... But I know you better than that. I wasn't thinking things through. I'm sorry I hurt you. I'm more sorry than you'll ever know." He lets go of my hand. It drops to my side, the folded slip of paper still between my fingers. "But you deserve to decide whether you know your history. I had the means to get it for you. I won't apologize for that."

"I..." I glance back for the comfort of Vera's support, but she's gone, the door to her room closed. I can do this. It's not *weak* to give in, even if my pride still manages to protest. But I know now, there's a strength in the ability to let go of anger. So I say, "I won't ask you to apologize for it."

Shock makes a fresh playing field of his face, erasing some of the divots left from our earlier fight. A fresh determination rises along the sidelines, too. "I won't lie to you, even to make things right. I learn from my mistakes."

"Good," I say, relief making my voice softer. It's the best thing he could've said. "Do you want to come in? Because there are some things I need to tell you."

"Yes. Because I have a few things of my own to say. And this time you're going to listen to them."

Still, he waits for me to motion him inside. When he crosses in front of me, though, he stops and takes my face in his hands and he kisses me. Without permission.

But he didn't really need it anyway.

I cling to him.

He yanks me tighter, lifting me off of my feet.

His mouth is hard, merciless.

So is mine.

One of us relents, I'm not sure which, but after a few moments, the kiss changes. Stretches. Expands.

Softens.

A tremble begins in the center of my chest and ripples out. Down my arms and up my neck.

I pull away before I begin to cry.

"I'm not going to apologize for that either," he says, placing me gently on the floor.

My laugh is watery at best. "I'd use my knee to hurt you if you did."

He sees it now, that I'm leaving the possibility for *us* open, and his entire body loosens, one vertebrae at a time. He follows me into my bedroom.

I close the door behind us, while he takes in the room.

"It feels weird that this is my first time here," he says.

"I haven't been here that long." I still have my father's information in my hand. I'm still not entirely ready for it. I might not be for a while. I slip it into a dresser drawer.

I'm...comforted to know it's there.

Alec paces my room, checking out Vera's various decorative touches and knickknacks on the bookshelf. "So this is where you sleep without me." Now he faces me, though we're both far from the bed in the center of the room. "Every night we haven't spent together the past week has been a mistake."

"I'm not sure I agree," I say, hating the words. Hating the truth.

"If we'd been together this week, maybe I would've seen how stupid I was—"

"Not because of that," I say. "I mean, yes, that too. But..." I stop, gathering my thoughts, taking a few deep breaths. "I'm depressed, Alec. Not just right now because I'm sad—but clinically. And I have a lot of work to do, righting myself and dealing with the shit I've avoided dealing with. I've only taken baby steps so far, and I don't know what the future holds in that regard."

"You're treating it," he says. "That's what matters. Depression isn't something to be ashamed of—and it isn't something that should keep you from having the future you want."

He's right. I know he is. "Even so... The other issue is that I also don't know how to be with you without becoming like my mother. All she's ever wanted was a man with a pretty face and huge bank account. I hear her, goading me on toward your wealth. She's in my thoughts. Which means those are my thoughts."

Maybe I'm not one hundred percent convinced that's why she's in my mind, but the fact is, the direction of her voice when she speaks to me is always about his money. And that will always bother me.

"Those aren't your *thoughts*. They're your fears," he says, his face relaxing, like it's no big deal. "That's a different thing."

His words shine a beam of relief through me. He's right again. *My fears are not facts.* But...still. I can't keep from saying, "Even if I'm not actively with you because you're rich... You have more than I do, Alec. This will never be equal."

The change in him, the shock across his expression, then the furious understanding, is startling. Suddenly he's the angry one, and I have to fight the urge to drop my gaze when he comes toward me. He drags a hand across his face, his eyes bright and livid. "Of all the stupid—"

"Watch it," I warn. "I'm the only one who gets to use that word about myself." Which I'm trying not to do anymore.

"Of course *you're* not stupid. But, Jesus, Teagan. *Think*. What about what I get from you?" He shouts the question, his raised voice shocking me all the way through my core. "Did you ever consider that? Did you? So from me, you get fancy meals and restaurants. A few flights out to Boston. Big fucking deal. I could shower you in money and it still wouldn't tip the balance in my favor. You inspire me. Do you have any idea what that's like? I refused to cave to my *father*—for the first time ever. The one place in my life I've never felt comfortable taking charge, and you pushed me to do it anyway with the proposal. I didn't give up because of you. And because of it—and for so many other reasons—I won't give up on us, on this. You make my life better."

I don't know what to say to that. I hadn't considered that I might bring anything to the table. I hadn't considered I might not need money to make things between us equal. And he stood up to his father about *me*, too.

"Listen to me." He grips my shoulders, not too rough, but not too gentle either. His voice is broken though, his expression worse. "I am so much better than the person I was before I met you."

Actually, I discover, I know exactly what to say. "Alec, I—"

"Think of every obstacle we blew to bits before us. Your fake name. My position above you at work. My fake engagement. Teagan, we can get past this. I will spend every day for the rest of time making it up to you. I will never go behind your back again. And if you can't believe it right now, I won't blame you, but give me a chance. Let me show you." His voice breaks right down the middle. "Let me love you."

I grab his chin, not too rough, but not too gentle either. My voice is strong, steady. "You done?"

"Depends on your answer." His face is purposefully blank, and I finally realize it's what he uses to hide fear. He's afraid of what I'm going to say. Which makes me speak so fast, I almost trip over the words.

"Well, *before* you spoke over me, what I was going to say is this..." Deep breath. Look in his eyes. Memorize what they do next. "Alec, I love you."

Glassy. That's what happens next in his eyes, they go a little glassy. Or at least I think they do. I don't have more than a split second to study them before he's kissing me. Gently. Smoothly. His hands are pressed against my lower back, pulling me toward him. I slide my palms up his face, along the scruff of his jaw, into the mess of his hair. It's almost as soft in my fingertips as his lips are against mine.

This kiss is a languid thing, almost lazy, though one of us is shaking against the other.

I'm surprised to discover it's him—his arms are shaking around me.

"What's wrong?" I ask, breaking the kiss. "You're trembling."

"To keep myself from crushing you," he says, holding himself very, very still. "Hearing you say that stirs things in me that would frighten you."

"Bet you're wrong." I step away from him, smiling as suggestively as I'm able. "Try me."

"I will." His eyes fall to the bed, then back to me, and my breath begins to stretch for the marathon that it senses is coming.

I take another step away. "Why are you still standing there?"

"Because I need to get this right first."

I lift a brow, not as easily as Vera does it, but somewhere close. And I fight a smile because I know him. And I know what he's about to say.

He doesn't disappoint. "I love you, Teagan."

"Oh, that?" I affect as bored a tone as I can. "That's old news."

His grin is quick, sharp and infectious. He closes the distance to me. "Your turn."

"For what?" I blink up at him, all innocence.

"Say it again," he demands.

"You're bossy." I fight a smile as wide as a yawn.

"Say it again." His voice is lower, and there's a muscle twitching in his jaw. He tightens his grip.

I squirm in his arms, purposefully rubbing myself against his body. "You can't tell me what to do outside the office."

"Let's play make believe." He walks me backward toward the bed. "This is my office." When we get to the bed, he yanks me around and pushes me forward onto my hands. And nerves start to synchronize in my belly. The hottest flash of longing zapping them all in a row. "And this," he says, his hands at my waist, holding me in place, "is my desk. And if you don't tell me what I want to hear, I'm going to keep you bent over it and tease the words out of you."

I snort, and though unladylike, it releases an entire flock of giddy relief. We're *in love*. We're about to have sex, and he wants me to tell him I love him again first. "Now you're tempting me not to say it."

He leans over me, his scruffy chin rubbing against my shoulder, and he nips at my earlobe. "What if I promise to tease you anyway. Will you tell me before I do?"

I push us up from the bed and twist around in his arms, because I want to face him when I say the words. It takes about a year and a half for my mouth to release its grin to let them out. "I love you, Alec Chambers. And I'll say it whenever you want me to, forever."

His expression darkens in this delicious sort of way, and he kisses me, biting my lower lip before he pulls away. "Again."

"I love you." I jolt when he draws my camisole down, his thumb grazing my nipple, his pupils going wide in his dark, dark eyes.

"Again." He pushes me back until I catch myself on the bed, and he pushes himself between my legs.

"I love you."

He bunches the fabric of my tank top in his hands and *rips it*. The sound tears through the room, and my shirt splits right down the middle. Now he drops his gaze, and I do too, to my stomach. It quivers, and my breasts rise and fall with the quickening of each breath I take.

"That was *new*," I say.

"Again." He drops before me, taking his time, dragging his hands down my body, roughly, perfectly. He bites my stomach. He growls against my skin. He pauses at my pajama shorts, looking up, with a steady, commanding gaze. "I said, again."

"I love you." Somehow I get the words out even without any breath left in my lungs. He pulls my shorts down. Underwear with them. And once he's dragged the fabric down to the floor, he slides his hands up the insides of my legs, pushing against them until I widen my stance and I think I'm going to fucking die.

"Again." His gaze holds mine so intensely my entire body starts to spark, and his fingers are touching me, tickling me, pulling my skin apart. "Tell me."

"I love you." This comes out barely a whisper, and before I've finished speaking, he licks me. Long. Slow. His tongue rolling over me in a way that forces a moan from deep in my chest. He doesn't drop eye contact, and the slow swivel of his face against me nearly makes me collapse. With one hand, I twist the comforter between my fingers, and I grab his hair with my other, gripping his head while his tongue slips, slips, slips through me.

He pauses, purposefully breathing hot air over the sensitive flesh spread before him, and I yank his hair so hard it shocks him. His mouth twists in a wicked grin.

"I want you inside of me," I say, panting. "I need you."

"Say it."

"I love you." I match his grin. "Now please fuck me."

His quick intake of breath makes me laugh—and then he levels me with a look so intense, I forget to breathe.

"I love you so fucking much." He says it like a threat, like a promise. He says it like it's everything. And he's rising now, trailing his tongue along my skin. The room is filled with the sounds of my breathing, finally remembered, and with the clanking of his belt buckle coming undone, with the rustling of his jeans as he shoves them down his legs. He pauses for the shortest moment to rip his shirt off.

"I love you," he says, kissing me, lifting me and tossing me on the bed and easing himself over me. "I love you."

"Listen here," I say, grabbing his face and returning the lip bite from earlier. "I'm all for your manhandling tendencies in the bedroom, but let's establish some ground rules. *I* get to be in charge sometimes."

In a move I'm quite proud of, I wrap my leg around his and roll us until I'm on top of him. And, okay, he probably helps it along, but a girl can enjoy her moments regardless. He glances between our bodies, his wicked grin widening. "You want to ride me, kitten, believe me, you'll get no complaints."

A lesser girl might flee at the size of his erection, but the thing is…I've never been one to back away from a good challenge. And this? It's the absolute fucking best.

"Kitten?" I ask, dryly—though it thrills me to my core that he still calls me this. "Let's see which of us is the first to purr."

I wrap one hand around him—and lick my lips when he jerks against my palm. I lift on my knees, and I lower myself over him, *onto* him.

He moans, and when I begin to rock my hips, falls silent, the look on his face one so full of pleasured intensity my entire body shivers to have it directed at me.

Or…

Maybe I shiver at the way he feels inside of me. Hard and slick and huge. He *fills* me.

When he thrusts himself harder into me—faster, too—I grab the ridges of his ab muscles to steady myself, and I slam my hips over him, back and forth and side to side and *holy motherfucking hell* I've never felt so good in my entire life.

And then he reaches out to grab my breasts, flickering his thumbs over my nipples in the rhythm I ride him with until they're so tight against his caresses I bite my tongue to keep from begging him to pinch them harder, to help ease some of the way he's made them ache. He does it anyway.

"I love you," he says.

And he says it again, fiercer this time, as he slides his hands down my body, down, down, all the way down, to use his fingers against me.

With me.
Against me.
With me.
In circles.
With varying pressure.
Until that pressure sinks through to the core of me, expanding in my belly, hot and fierce and spinning.
Until my head falls back, and I grip his thighs and discover how much deeper he can go from this angle.
Until I'm crying-whimpering-moaning his name, which maybe makes me the first to purr.
But it's not long till he's the first to roar, so I'm pretty sure I'm the winner.
If these things need keeping track of.
Pretty sure they don't.
But it doesn't keep a smug smile from my face anyway.
Until he kisses it off of me, and we start all over again.

CHAPTER FIFTY-FOUR

WE SLEEP MOST of the day away. And when we wake again, he slips into me with a sigh that twists into a moan that twists into another roar.

And then again.

And then I tell him I have to take a break for at least twenty-four hours. "I'm still getting used to this," I say, sinking my teeth into his shoulder. "I'd like to be able to walk tomorrow."

His laugh is loud and rich, and he pulls me against him, and we doze some more.

When he next opens his eyes, I'm sitting on the edge of the bed, fresh from a shower. The sheet of paper containing my father's contact information is in my hand, still folded.

"You want to talk about it?" he asks, rising to wrap his arms around me.

"No." But in his arms, I instantly relax, and I speak about it anyway. "What if...what if he's a convict. Or worse? What if the number's wrong? What if he doesn't want to hear from me?"

"But what if he does?" Alec asks.

And that one question changes everything.

I stand and I slip the paper back into the drawer, closing it.

"You aren't going to call him?"

I shake my head. "Maybe tomorrow. Or maybe in a week. Or a month." I turn toward him. "I need a little bit more time to adjust to the fact that he's out there and to the possibility that he might want to know about me. As long as you'll hold my hand when I do."

"I'll hold your hand anytime you ask." He rises, crossing to me and kissing me. "And plenty of times when you don't."

"Go shower," I murmur against his mouth, glowing. I start to step away, but he holds me at an arm's length.

"Listen," he says, his expression serious enough to twist my stomach. "Last week, you brought up me returning to school, like you thought this could end when that happens."

"But you reassured me," I say. "I don't think that anymore. I get it. I was—"

"I need to know you *really* get it," he say, running his thumbs over my collarbones, making me start to tremble—again. "This—you and me?—this is it for me, kitten. One year of school between us and then I'm home for good. Or we can go wherever you want—wherever *your* career takes you. Us, I mean. Because it's you and it's me and it's final. Do you understand what I'm saying?"

"That you love me," I say, the corners of my lips rising so high they feel like they're halfway up my cheeks. "That you want to love me forever."

His eyes soften, they dance, they blink...and when they look into mine again, they're full of pleasure. "I *will* love you forever."

When I close my eyes, I can envision the outline of our future. The details are blurry, but his shape and mine—they're together through it all. I don't know how I got so lucky. I don't know how *we* got so lucky.

But it happened.

I kiss him. I kiss him hard. I kiss him sweet and soft. I kiss him and kiss him and kiss him until there's no way he'll ever doubt my response. "Same goes, Alec."

"Good," he says, biting my lower lip. "Just so we're clear."

"Crystal."

After one more lingering kiss, he slips into the shower, and, when the grumbles of my stomach grow louder than the leftover euphoria in my mind, I head out of the room to fix us something to eat.

I walk straight into a room of my friends. Cassidy, Vera, Gage...

They're all looking at me with expectant, shit-eating smiles.

"What?" I ask, ignoring the matching smile that's tugging so hard at my own mouth.

"We weren't sure if you were ever coming out," Gage says, sipping a beer.

"We also weren't sure exactly what sorts of sports you had going on in there," Cassidy adds, wrapping me in a hug. "Sounded intense. Did you score?"

I open my mouth to make a ballsy sort of statement—and then I shut it again and head to the fridge for a hard cider. There's an array of Mexican food on the table, and I dig in, ignoring their protests and demands for information. I offer a plate to Alec when he steps out a few minutes later, shirtless, with wet hair. He looks as shocked as I felt when I realized we had a bit of an audience waiting for us.

I think it's the first time I've ever seen him embarrassed.

And, because of it, I can't stop giggling. All the way through introducing him to Gage, and re-introducing my best friends.

Later, when an unfortunately *shirted* Alec is bouncing quarters in cups of beer with Gage, Cassidy nudges me. "Okay. Now you have to tell me. How was it?"

"Sorry I made you ditch your beach weekend," I say.

She waves my words away. "I think Quinn was relieved for us to go, honestly. She had some of her own stuff going on. Now. Stop stalling. I want details, Teag. Come on." Her words are teasing, playful. Then she pauses, considering. "God. Sorry. It's none of my business. Old habits and all..."

I tell her I don't mind her question and she doesn't need to apologize—who could blame her for being curious? Especially with all the tall tales I've spent the past few years telling. "But you know... I'll keep it to myself all the same." I glance at Alec, pressing my lips together to suppress a smile. Because what we do in the bedroom? Hell, what we do anywhere...

It's all ours.

And there's something really fucking special about that.

He catches me the next time my eyes wander his way, and he mouths, "I love you."

I mouth it right back.

I've never known such happiness.

ACKNOWLEDGEMENTS

There are not enough thank yous in the world to send everyone who helped to make this book what it is, especially:

Katy Upperman, Alison Miller, Elodie Nowodazkij, Elizabeth Briggs, and Tracey Neithercott. You girls are brilliant writers, and I'm blessed—*beyond* blessed—to have you in my corner. That you made the time to read this so quickly and so thoroughly during your busy lives means so, so much to me. And your feedback was (as always) invaluable. (And Liz—*thank you* for the title!) And thank you, Cindy Thomas, for your unwavering encouragement.

My spreadsheet girls. As always, thank you for keeping me on track!

My hideaway girls. You guys are the fucking best.

All the readers and bloggers who've been so wonderful along my author journey. Especially Silvana Reyes from Hopeless Book Lovers & NA Source—and everyone in Riley & Crew. You guys give me such huge heart eyes.

Stephanie Parent. Copyeditor extraordinaire. Thank you!

Cait Greer. For all your paperback formatting—you're the best, and someday I'm totally going to hug you.

Sarah Hansen of Okay Creations. For yet *another* lovely cover.

Nelson. For talking about equity firms with me, and for helping me find the time to write.

Sweet girl. For just being your sweet, sassy, hilarious self. I love you.

ABOUT THE AUTHOR

RILEY lives in Northern Virginia and spends most of her time with her characters, playing with her toddler and husband, and pretending she knows how to be an adult. Former dancer. Current writer. Lifelong lover of accessories, books, and the beach. And cats. Can't forget the kitties, of which she has two.

Visit RileyEdgewood.com to contact Riley!
She loves hearing from her readers!

@Rileyedgewood
Facebook.com/rileyedgewoodauthor

Made in the USA
Lexington, KY
19 March 2016